"BOYS OF ENGLAND" EDITION.

No. 2 Gratis with No. 1.]   [One Penny.

FRED FROLIC

HIS LIFE AND ADVENTURES.

LONDON: EDWIN J. BRETT, 173, FLEET STREET, E.C.

FRED FROLIC:

k

HIS LIFE AND ADVENTURES.

BY THE AUTHOR OF "GILES EVERGREEN."

BEAUTIFULLY ILLUSTRATED.

EDWIN J. BRETT, 173, FLEET STREET, LONDON, E. C.

MDCCCLXXII.

"THERE'S SOMETHING BY WAY OF ARREST, MASTER FOGHARTY," SAID LANTY SHAN.

FRED FROLIC;

HIS LIFE AND ADVENTURES.

FRED FROLIC'S TRIUMPH.

FRED FROLIC:

HIS LIFE AND ADVENTURES.

By the Author of "Giles Evergreen."

---◆---

CHAPTER I.

THE WELCOME HOME.

"HOORAY! hooray! the Frolics for ever, and down with their inimies! Ah, good luck to your handsome face, Master Fred, and may all your wrinkles be at the back o' your head. Open your wind-pipes and shout hooray, ye spalpeens. Ah, that's the darlings; bedad a drop of the crayther will do them no harm, your honour."

This was uttered by a tall young Irishman, who stood in the front of about some forty or fifty men, women and children, in the court-yard of the mansion belonging to Fred Frolic, himself a fine handsome young fellow, with an eye in which gleamed fun, frolic, and merriment. He was dressed in the half-military frock of the day, white pantaloons, and top boots, worn well up to the knee ; and the costume showed greatly to advantage the fine, well-proportioned figure of the wearer.

Such was Fred Frolic, who had just returned after a three years' ramble on the Continent—returned home to find his father no more, his house, like his fortune, a wreck.

By his side stood a person who commanded some little attention, from the peculiarity of his appearance.

He was short in person, and seemed all legs; the upper part of his body was broad and massively built, his back was round and hunched, his face was wrinkled, although he was but a year older than his young master, by whose side he stood, and the hair that thinly covered his head was here and there strewn with streaks of grey; his eyes were dark and brilliant, and looked up glowingly and brightly at the handsome youth by his side, while the rough, bony hand stole into that of the "masther's" with the grip of devotion that could only be unclasped with death.

The master and the man, the handsome, chivalrous-looking being, and the poor misshapen semblance of humanity had one tie that, through all the changes and mischances of life, would *never be broken.*

They were *foster brothers.*

From the same breast they had drawn the fount of life, and that holy link was one never to be broken.

"Another hurroo, Pat Fagan; ye blackguards, one would think your voices had gone birds' nesting. Shout, ye divils, long life to the Frolics."

Then came the shouts of delight; hats minus crowns, and, in many cases brimless, went flying in the air; and shillelaghs waved and clashed together with the bright "ten thousand welcomes."

"I'm glad to see you all, my boys," said the clear, manly voice of Fred, slightly tinged with the brogue so dear to an Irishman's heart. "Ah! there ye are, Tim Doolan, as wild and rollicking as ever."

"The heavens be praised, I'll never change, your honour," was the reply; "hurroo!"

"Where's Mike Murphy, the tailor?"

"Here I am to the fore, yer honour, that he should think of such a——"

"Ninth part of a man," roared Tim Doolan.

"Hear to that, an' you'll get a blessing from the ninth part of a man that will make you snuffle for a month," and with that Mike Murphy aimed a blow at Tim's nose with the sleeve-board, that would have prevented him taking snuff for a time, had he not warded it neatly off with his shillelagh.

"Be quiet, boys; kape all the fight in you until fair time. Where's Biddy Connor?"

"Here I am," screamed out an old woman, rapping the heads of some half dozen ragged gossoons in the front of her with a thick stick. "Here I am, yer honour. Oh, mushra! it's me heart that will break wid joy to see that face again. Oh, the saints be praised!"

And the old woman raised her palsied, wrinkled hands up as if to call down blessings on his head.

"Here, Lanty," and he turned to the man who stood by him, "take my purse and give them a trate. Myself will wait your coming back here."

"Sure I'll make one at that, Master Fred," and, looking at the purse with a sly grin, "it won't take *long* to do that same thing."

Then, taking a jump off the step, he was in the midst of the crowd, while they shouted,

"Lanty Shan! Lanty Shan for ever!"

"Lave go of me, ye spalpeens, and let's have fair play."

"Fair play for ever!" shouted Tim Doolan, whirling his shillelagh round his head, without a thought that Mike Murphy's pate was near, and the next instant Mike lay flat on the grass.

"Now, then, lads," shouted Lanty, the first that catches me gets an extra noggin. Give the word, Master Fred."

"One—two—pase, ye divils!" shouted Fred.

Away went Lanty Shan, whose long legs seemed like the wings of a windmill, and away went the merry crowd after him. Over a low fence went Lanty, and cleared well the lot of pigs that were quietly sleeping on the other side; the noise of the crowd woke these gentle animals up, and they were still further disturbed when they saw the long legs of Lanty flying over them.

Tom Doolan was the next, and he cleared the elderly male porcine cleverly; but, little Mike the tailor, whose head was still ringing with the visitation of Tim's shillelagh to it, went flying into the lot of grunters, followed by half a dozen more, much to the anger of the "father of the family," who at once charged Mike in the rear like a troop of cavalry.

"Bad luck to ye, kape off, or I'll score your hide whid the slave-board, till ye fancy its roasted ye are!" he shouted.

But the pig bored in upon Mike, until he was glad to turn tail, followed by the brood, with or without tails.

The race for the extra noggin was all very well for the young and active, but to the old ones, it was out of all question, especially to Biddy O'Connor, who stood by the fence looking at them.

"Hurroo! more power to yer!" she shouted to the pig. "At him! he's only a tailor! Sew him up! Ah! bad luck to ye, Mike, to run away from a palthry pig. If ye'll do that, what would ye do if the bailiffs—bad scran to them—were after yer? At him!" she shouted to the pig, "at him again! Hurroo!" and so kept on until all the parties were out of sight.

We left Fred Frolic standing on the steps of his home, laughing, and dancing at the fun.

When they had disappeared, he placed his hands in his pockets, and giving a look up at the house, whistled loudly; and then walking to the place where the gates might have been, he sat down and looked up earnestly at the place. For a moment a shade of sorrow passed over his face, which quickly changed to his old smile and laugh.

"Well," he murmured, "the least said the soonest mended; and by the powers that's what the glass there wants. Humph! six left out of fifty."

Here he looked round at the shadow that was passing along the wall.

"Hilloa, Lanty, back again, old boy; sit down on the other stone, and let us fa-los-o-fise a bit."

"Fa-los-o-fise, bedad, it's what I've been doing for many a day," was the reply of Lanty, taking out his pipe.

"Ah, it's a grand thing when you can bring your mind to it, Lanty."

"There's little doubt of that, Master Fred. I wanted that same fa-los-o-fy to bring back a great many things to my remimbrance."

"Ha, ha, ha, what were those, Lanty? let me have it."

"Why, in the first place I wanted falos-o-fy to bring back the pair of wooden gates that were made as strong as iron."

"What became of the gates, Lanty?"

"Well, you see, Master Fred, the hinges, like everything in the course of natur', got rusted, and the nails fell out, and the divil a nail was in the house, 'cept an ould screw-driver, and two broken gimlets."

"Ha, ha! well, and you made them do?"

"Bedad! I did, and a clever piece of work I made of it; but they fell out, for the next morning I found them quite gone, and the wind had been blowing, and there lay the gates on the broad of their backs, like spread aigles."

"But why didn't you——"

"Whist! I know what you'd say. Now what I'm going to say, ye'll not take unkindly, but——"

"No, no, out with it. I can guess.'"

"No yer can't. Yer can't guess that when the squire (rest his soul) died, there wasn't a thirteen in the house."

"My poor father!" said Fred, and sank his head between his hands.

"Don't go on in that out-of-the-way way; there was a matter o' ten pounds in the house. May they burn their fingers for staling it.

"Stolen, eh, Lanty?"

"Little doubt of that; and may they lay upon a porcupine feather-bed, with the rheumatiz for it, say I. So being short of coals, although slates were plentiful, we made iligant fires of them same gates."

"But what did the people say?"

"Why, masther, I said, that as the old house was a comin' down——"

"Many a true word spoken in jest. It's very shaky, Lanty."

"And that an iligant mansion was to crop up in its place. Why when that came, the new gates would be there to the fore."

"Well, the one is as likely as the other, Lanty."

"It will be all right. Horroo!" he said, springing up. "We'll snap our fingers at the world and the McDonnells into the bargain."

"And what have you got to say about the McDonnells?" said a voice, and the next moment a thick-set man, about thirty years of age, walked into the yard, but without seeing Fred.

"By the powers, what I've always said, that listeners generally hear what they don't like," and Lanty grinned in his face.

"Indeed; but pray how was it my name was mentioned?" and he spoke with a proud, haughty air, "eh, fellow?"

"Fellow, bedad. I am no fellow of yours."

"Humph! Nothing. Not heard of the heir to this *splendid* property, I suppose?"

And pointing to the house, he laughed loudly.

"The heir," and Lanty scratched his head. "I suppose as you mane Mr. Fred Frolic, Esquire, eh, Mr. McDonnell?"

"Yes. When he returns, I'll pay him a debt I owe him," and the fellow scowled.

"Well, perhaps you'll pay it now, for I'm rayther short of money."

And Frolic tapped the gentleman on the shoulder.

McDonnell sprang back as though he had been stung by a serpent.

At last, recovering himself he said, coolly,

"You are aware that it is not a *debt* of money that is due to you?"

"Oh, yes. I took good care it should never come to that. Let me see. What was it? Why, it can't be because I beat you in the steeple-chase. Was it in the boat-race, where I took half an hour's nap before you came in *second?*"

McDonnell ground his teeth with rage.

"This banter and assumed loss of memory is a mere subterfuge," said McDonnell.

"Don't use hard words, McDonnell, or else I'll——"was Frolic's fierce reply.

"You'll what?"

"Make you swallow them, as I did *once*, before. I suppose you have not forgotten that?"

"Oh, no, nor shan't very easily."

"It's inconvenient at times to remember the drubbing you got in taking an advantage of an unprotected orphan girl. I say it's not pleasant to remember those interesting occurences in one's life, is it?"

"No," roared the fellow, who was boiling over with rage, "they can only be forgotten when repaid." And suddenly drawing a short stick, with a murderous leaden top on it, he rushed on Fred, aiming a terrific blow at his temple.

Frolic, springing lightly aside, caught McDonnell by the throat with one hand, and with the other seized the deadly weapon.

"You won't pay the debt this time nor in *this* fashion, you cowardly ruffian," and with almost supernatural strength, he hurled him to the ground, at the same time holding the weapon up.

At that moment the party returned from the "Pig and Bagpipes," bringing with them several jugs of whisky.

They all stopped with amazement on seeing McDonnell on the ground.

"Hurrah," said Tim Doolan, "by my soul it's the only place you're fit for, the dirthy kennel. What's he been a doing, masther?"

"Attempting my life with this dastardly weapon; but let him go," and Fred turned towards the house.

"Under favour no, masther; there's a mighty dale of love between the Frolics and the McDonnells. We've been fighting about that strip of land for the last fifty years, and the divil a fut are we nearer to it. Mike kape guard on one side, and Phalim O'Fog, you stand on the other."

"I'll have no violence upon an unarmed man," said Frolic.

"The divil a bit of violence, your honour, armed or unarmed," was the answer, with a sly grin; "he's come up purlitely to drink your health and happiness on your return home. Ain't you. *Mister* McDonnell?"

"Oh, if that's it," and Fred entered heartily into the frolic, "I can have no objection to it."

"Of course not, your honour. Fill up the horn of the crayther that shall make his eyes glisten like stars, and his tongue wag like a mimber of parlyment," said Tim Doolan handing him a horn of whisky.

"Hark ye, darling," whispered Tim Doolan, "do you remimber how you aarved Pandeen O'Rafferty. Drink that whisky, and with it the health of the masther and his happy return, or we'll tar and feather you from the top of your head to the sole of your fut, so that your own beautiful mother would not recognise her darlint son."

McDonnell stirred not a muscle.

"Mike, avick, have you the bag of goose feathers ready?"

"It's ready and willing," was the reply.

"And the tar?"

"In beautiful condition."

"We'll trouble you to walk with us, my friend."

McDonnell saw that the party were not only in earnest, but that they had drank so freely of whisky as to render them totally regardless of anything they might do.

"I'll do it," he said, sullenly.

"I thought you'd come to your senses darling," said Tim, as he handed the horn of whisky to him. Here's health and long life to Squire Fred Frolic. Fill up, boys."

McDonnell repeated the toast slowly, muttering between every word something that could not be heard.

Then the Frolics made the air ring again with their wild shouts.

"I have drank one toast against my inclinations; may I drink another of my own free will, without personal injury? Do you promise that?" he said, sternly looking at Frolic.

"Yes, I pledge my word, you shall not be harmed," was the prompt reply.

They handed him another horn of liquor.

"I swear by this to pursue with eternal hatred, as my forefathers have done before, the house of Frolic and its adherents, and may a curse fall upon me and mine if I fail to keep my vow."

With these words, he dashed the horn to the ground, and walked from among them, amid the groans and hisses of all around, who would not have left a sound bone in all his body had not Fred stood between.

"My *word*, boys, my *word*," he said, and all the uplifted menacing shillelaghs descended gradually towards the ground.

CHAPTER II.

THE FAIR, THE FACTION, AND THE FIGHT.

THE next morning Fred was seated at breakfast in a sitting-room in a little better condition than any of the others, and opposite sat Lanty, with a steaming basin of buttermilk and "praties" before him, while from the village close by Lanty had procured another kind of breakfast for his master.

"Your honour," he said, "from travelling in foreign parts, has lost all stumack for honest food, and, instead of good buttermilk and praty, you drink a pison called tay, which, they tell me, is a close relation to a birch broom, although they pretends it comes from the Inges. Praises be to it that I don't know that same place."

"It's a matter of taste, Lanty," replied his master, relapsing again into deep thought.

"Well, it may be," was the reply, "and there is no accounting for that," and Lanty plied his spoon vigorously; then, looking up, saw that his master had pushed aside his breakfast almost untasted.

The affectionate creature had the next instant laid aside his half-finished meal, and slowly walked up to him.

"Bad luck to that Mother Rafferty, but she's sold me something else than tay. Och, murder! p'raps senna tay, given in convulsions when the teeth and the gums fall out. I say, masther."

"Well, Lanty, what is it?"

"Is it tay or anything else you've been a takin'?" he asked, anxiously.

"Well, it's hard to say what it is, Lanty."

"There, listen to that now. Och, murder! Missus O'Rafferty, I'll make your hide smoke for this. May I jist take a small taste, your honour?"

"Yes, but you won't like it;" and Fred poured him some in a cup.

"I'll take my oath I won't; but I've heard say what is good for the goose—" here Lanty took a gulp, which, going the wrong way, caused him to splutter, and brought tears, too, in his eyes.

"Och, murder! it's choking I am; it's pison. Oh! what'll I do?"

Here Fred burst into a hearty laugh at the comical twistings of poor Lanty's face.

"Oh, don't larf, master, don't larf."

"I can't help it, Lanty. What makes you think it is wrong?"

"What makes me think it's wrong, because old Mother O'Rafferty is as deaf as a broom-stick, and makes killing mistakes; how do you think she served Mike the tailor?"

"How?" laughed Fred.

"Why, he takes snuff by the bushel, and so, having been powerful busy, he and his wife fancied some coffee for tay. Well, he asked for two ounces, and Mother O'Rafferty, put him up *two ounces* and with that and a cruel salt sojer. Mike and his wife determined to injoy themselves; and they boiled the whole two ounces.

"'This is quare coffee, Biddy,' said Mike, after the first cup.

"'It's meself that thinks the same. What did you ax for, Mike?'

"'Two ounces of the best,' replied Mike.

"'Best what, avick?'

"'Why, the best; two ounces of the best.'

"'But the best what, Mike?'

"'Thunder and ouns! what are you driving at?' roared Mike.

"'That, ye divil,' said she, catching up a three-legged stool that the younger Mike was sitting on, and giving him a small taste on the head fit to split a crowbar, which made Mike dance as if he had been sitting by mistake on his hot goose.

"Well, after the fight was over, they became the best of friends, and went to Mother O'Rafferty.

"'What did you sell Mike this morning, mother?' said Biddy.

"'Eh—oh—two ounces of the best.'

"'Best what, mother agrah?'

"'Oh—ah—yes; why it was ah—yes —two ounces of the best rappee.'

"'Oh, murder! and he asked for two ounces of the best coffee.'

"Then there was such a scrimmage; smash went windows and———"

Here a knock at the door stopped Lanty.

"Come in—who's there?" bawled he.

"It's meself," said Tim Doolan, looking in.

"Well, Tim, what is it, my boy? Give Tim a thimbleful of whisky; the morning's rather raw."

"You may say that, your honour, and the fog (which is going off) gets in your throat, and spoils the nateral notes of the voice," and with that Tim let a good drop of the cratur slip down his throat like so much cold water.

"It's mate and drink when a man's cold, sir."

"Well, what can I do for you?"

"A great deal, and that in a small compass, if you'll only say the word."

"What word, eh, Tim?"

"Well, sir, it's a mighty asy one," and he winked his eye at Lanty, who returned it. "It's as asy as pase."

"Well, out with it. What is it?"

"Well, you see, the fair's held this afternoon, and a beautiful sight it will be for any Christian to look at; especially the booth where there's a lot of shillelaghs that would bring the tears to an Irishman's eyes."

"No doubt," laughed Fred. "Well——"

"Well, then, your honour, we want to see you there, because you never missed afore you went to foreign parts, and bad luck to them say I, if they've taken all the *homely* feeling out of ye."

"So say I, Tim; no fear of that. I've seen a great deal, but there's no land like my own; no mountains so majestic; no lakes so clear; no hearts so warm; no eye so mild and lovely; no grasp of the hand so true as that of the sons and daughters of my dear, dear country. Glorious Erin-go-bragh!"

And Fred sprang up.

"Hurrah! Erin-go-bragh! Another for the rose and one for the thistle, and may the man who tries to separate them get stung to the bone."

Off started Lanty with his long legs into an Irish jig, and Tim, tucking up the tails of his long frieze coat, keeping one hand carefully up the back of it, was not a moment behind Lanty; while Fred Frolic by name, and frolic by nature, dashed into it with all the fire of youth and patriotism.

The jig ended, Fred grasped the hands of both.

"I'm with ye, my boys; ye have warmed my heart, and sent the blue devils to the right-about. What time does the fair open, Tim?"

"It opens for *divarsion* at two; by that time the pigs, and the poultry, and the rest of the animals are disposed of, and we begin to enjoy ourselves like rashional creatures," said Tim.

"On the Green, as usual?" asked Fred.

"Why, where on arth would you have it, your honour? Ain't it on the Green that the fun will begin about the strip of land that we mane to have from the McDonnells by hook or by crook?"

"Ah, I see what it will end in. Why, the land is not worth a thirteen, and I'd give it up."

"Give it up—and not worth a thirteen—it's not the worth, it's the honour and the lark. Give it up to the dirty McDonnells! Oh, that I should live to hear the son of your father and mother say that. Look ye here,"—and from the back of his coat he pulled forth two formidable shillelaghs—"that's for your honour"—putting one on the table—"and this is my own, that has laid thirteen McDonnells as flat as pan-cakes; and, plase the pigs, it will go in for the score this blessed day."

And he twirled the shillelagh round his head like a toy.

"You'll be there, your honour; a pretty crow that McDonnell will have if you are not."

"I shall be there, Tim," was the reply.

"Then I'll just go and get the boys together. You'll not bring those," he said, pointing to a pair of small pistols lying on the table.

"Why not?" asked Fred.

"Because you'll never want those so long as you can hold this."

And away went the shillelagh round again. Then, trailing the long tail of his coat on the ground, he said,

"Will any dacent man just tread on that! Whoo! Horroo! Up wid the Frolics, and down wid the McDonnells!"

And cocking his crownless hat on one side of his head, and tucking his shillelagh under the left arm, he whistled a favourite air, and made the best of his way to the boys.

"I suppose, Lanty, you'll take care of the house?" said Fred, with a merry smile.

"May I have blame on my shoulders

all my life, but the house may take care of itself. It's the only *quiet* divarsion I have in the whole year," and going to a cupboard, he brought out a shillelagh. "He's been lying up in lavender twelve months, and, plase the pigs, it's a beautiful airing he'll get to-day. Tim Donovan said he would take the shine out of you. We shall see."

During this, Fred had left the room to write some letters.

"Give it up," muttered Lanty. "Och! Murder! It's a pervarsion of taste, and all comes of going to foreign parts. Stop at home!—whoo!"

And Master Lanty left the room to get ready for his day's "quiet divarsion."

The village near which the ancient mansion of the Frolics stood might be said to contain some five hundred inhabitants; it had a main street—and "mane" enough it was—at the end of which stood two long rows of cabins facing each other; at the end of this row of buildings was a ditch composed of some excellent mud and offal, which afforded great recreation to a colony of pigs in the daytime.

Through two portions of this ditch there ran a path leading on to the "famous Green;" in the centre of that was a circular plot of ground covered with grass, and this had been for time immemorial, the great "bone of contention," (for which many bones had been broken) between the families of the Frolics and McDonnells.

Up each side of the Green the "divarsion" fair was held every year.

The tents for the sale of the "rale stuff" were most of them fixed up by poles and clothesprops, thick hedgestakes, and anything else that came "handy-like," and these were roofed in with blankets; and sometimes, when the wind took it into its head to waken from a sleep and get up, it was mighty "divarting" to see how they rocked to and fro, and tore away the old blankets, to the dismay of the owners.

On the one side of this imposing array of tents, hung up a tawdrily painted sign, explaining to the uninitiated that it represented the McDonnell arms, and on the opposite side an equally artistic affair floated in the wind as the armorial bearings of the large family of the "Frolics."

Into this place, long before the hour of two, came the people from the country and little places, some on cars that seemed breaking down under their weight, the miserable horse having broken down long before; then the weary animal, with a pillion strapped on his razor back, bearing some little farmer and his "bitther" half.

There were grand amusements in wax-work, and more than one tent with only half a blanket as its canopy (the other having paid a visit to another part of the Green) had a board upon which was painted, "The Royal Pavilion for taching the Nobel Arte of Silf-Difince, by Mike Dunagain." Swings and roundabouts were there, with a hundred other classical entertainments.

The Green was getting full, and the fun and noise becoming very exciting, when, headed by their several pipers, the two factions came marching on at opposite ends; the McDonnells were headed by McDonnell himself, who had been taking "potations bottle deep."

The Frolics were headed by Tim Doolan; but scarcely had they gained their quarters, when loud shouts rent the air as the handsome, manly Fred Frolic came sauntering down the Green, Lanty Shan following close behind him.

At the same time Norah O'Shea came tripping along the side of the McDonnells.

No sooner did McDonnell see the girl than he sprang to her side, and, throwing his arm round her waist, attempted to kiss her; but, if Norah was pretty, she was likewise prudent, and she gave McDonnell a blow from her fist that made his face tingle again; but still the fellow, maddened by drink, kept his arm round her.

"For that blow, my darling," said McDonnell, "I'll have a dozen; all's fair at fair-time."

An observation received with shouting and laughing by his followers.

"Take yer hand off me," said the girl.

"Not till yer paid yer futting," was the savage reply.

"Will no one help an unprotected gal?" she called—the tears streaming from her indignant eyes—"and you, Squire Frolic, to stand by and see this outrage committed."

This appeal was sufficient for the Frolics.

"Let her go, McDonnell," shouted Fred.

"Eh, who are you, to crow in this way? If yer want her, *come and fetch her.*"

In an instant the invitation was accepted, and the two had a firm grip of each other, the girl falling unconscious on the ground.

The struggle was not a long one, for the best wrestler of his day in that part of the Emerald Isle was Fred Frolic.

In strength, perhaps, they were nearly equal.

In a few moments Fred had got the crook, and McDonnell was hurled on the ground by a fair back fall, fit to take the breath out of a windmill.

To snatch the girl from the ground, and throw her over his left arm, was the work of a moment, and then he walked coolly back.

Seeing this, one of the McDonnellites, rendered furious by the disgrace inflicted upon them, rushed forward, and throwing his coat on the ground before him, asked Tim Doolan to put his fut on it.

"Hurrah for the Frolics!" shouted Tim Doolan. "Come on, ye thaives, and we'll whip yer like dogs!"

And there stood Fred Frolic, with the girl on his left arm, while in the right he waved aloft the shillelagh.

At his back were his followers, standing "like greyhounds i' the slips," ready for the word, while, on the opposite side, the McDonnellites were busy attending to their leader.

By this time he had got over the shaking.

Seizing a shillelagh from the hands of a man, he stood glaring at the triumphant Frolics.

"You've got the luck on your side for the present," he said.

"Yes, and we mane to kape it," shouted Tim.

"We shall see about that. Follow me, my boys!" shouted McDonnell, and with that they rushed towards the strip of land in the centre, and took possession of it.

But the next moment the Frolics, with waving shillelaghs and loud shouts, were in full chase.

CHAPTER III.

THE END OF THE SCRIMMAGE.

It was a glorious sight to see the two parties, the chased and the chasers, scampering off; but the McDonnellites were not flying from the Frolics in anything like fear or cowardice, but to get possession of the "strip of land" which had been so long the bone of contention between the two factions.

Norah Shea had soon recovered from the alarm she had been thrown into by the outrage of McDonnell, and which left Fred at liberty to be with his adherents in the coming struggle.

Grasping his shillelagh, for his hot Irish blood was well up, Fred started after his men, and in a few minutes was racing at their heels.

Upon the "strip of land" the McDonnellites were dancing and shouting like wild Indians, while their shillelaghs, waving above their "caubeens," looked like a small forest of trees.

They kept sending forth invitations to the Frolics, who had reached the mound of earth, "to come on, and have a small taste, for it was quite hot, and ready to be served up."

"You have no right on that land, so come down, McDonnell," called out Fred.

"Hark to that, now," replied McDonnell. "P'raps you'll tell me the name of the school where they *tried* to tache you your letters?"

"It was the school where they took in *only gentlemen*, so, as a matter of course, you were not there," was the ready answer.

"Put that in your mother's tay just by way of a sweetener," roared out Tim Doolan.

And with that he made a spring upon the mound, and down went the leading man of the McDonnells with a broken head.

The next minute the whole of them were engaged in the deadly conflict.

The air rang with the shouts, "the Frolics for ever," and "bravo, McDonnells," and for a time the victory hung in suspense; but nothing could withstand the impetuosity and fierce courage of the Frolics.

Fred was everywhere in the thickest of the fight, calling out for McDonnell; but that worthy was deaf to the call, for, although naturally brave, he had no particular desire to come within length of the shillelagh that Fred was wielding, to the great dismay and broken crowns of the McDonnells.

At length the McDonnells could contend against them no longer; inch by inch they fought, and inch by inch they were beaten off the "strip of land," and retreated towards the tents.

The next moment, Fred was hoisted upon the shoulders of Tim Doolan and Mike O'Leary, as the victor, amid the shouts of the Frolics, and the waving of their shillelaghs.

Then, setting him down, they started after the retreating foe.

Here another phase of the fight occurred.

The owners of the tents on the side of the vanquished McDonnells prepared to stand by their friends, and in an instant up went the poles and stakes, and down came the coverings upon the luckless individuals who were indulging in the comforts of a quiet dhudeen and a measure.

The partisans of the Frolics were not a whit behind their enemies.

Up went the supporters of their tents *outside*, and down went the supporters *inside*; and there they were twisting about in the folds of the "iligant" blankets like so many serpents, and half smothered into the bargain.

"Molly Flanagan, not a sound bone in your body will you find when we get out," shouted some of them under the blanket.

"Tim Durfey, your own mother won't know you again when we get a hold o' ye," roared others.

Then the market people took sides, and, upon the whole, the fight that *was* impending looked more than usually serious.

Here Fred Frolic, seeing how affairs stood, waved his hand as if to address them.

"We've gained the 'strip of land,'" he said, "fairly and honourably, and the fight is over."

"Is it," shouted a voice, "that's a divil of a mistake; it's just a going to begin."

"McDonnell," he said, "there's my hand."

"Put your hand in your pocket and hould tight the money that *arn't* there."

And here they set up a laugh and a shout.

"Come here, McDonnell," shouted Lanty, "and I'll lend you as much, and that's more than your dirthy family ever had."

"Barring the timpenny piece the pawnbroker lent them on the gridiron that never had a taste of mate on it," roared out Doolan.

"I'll pay you for that, Tim Doolan," shouted McDonnell.

"You'd better *pay* the Widder Mahoney for the last week's washing," replied Tim.

The McDonnells, at this, grasped their shillelaghs and prepared for the onslaught; but both sides stopped at hearing the shouts from the far end of the Green, and seeing the people run as if for their lives.

"Run, ye divils," shouted a voice. "The Kerry bulls have broken loose, and are down upon us; the born divils are ramping mad."

It was no false alarm.

A large herd of those animals had been brought down for sale, and had been safely penned up, and left in charge of two Kerry drovers. But when the *fun* began in the fair, they ran off to see that, and after a time the Kerry bulls thought a little enjoyment would diversify their lives a bit as well as their masters; so, by constantly butting against the pen, at the very instant the second fight was about to begin, they got loose.

A few cars and carts that stood in the way went flying into the air, and then they made for the Green.

"Master," shouted Lanty, "the divil a bit do I mate the bull; come on wid you home."

"Have with you, Lanty; I am sick of this."

And the next moment Lanty's legs were seen stretching across the Green; but, with all their length, Fred kept up with him, much to the delight of Lanty Shan.

"For fighting and running, for breaking the heads of the boys, the hearts of the girls, and the backs of the horses, there ain't a couple can bate us anyhow," he shouted.

"Home first, at any rate, eh, Lanty?" as Fred dashed into the courtyard.

A Kerry bull at the best of times is not the most agreeable tempered animal, and upon this occasion they had an opportunity of showing their amiable qualities, heightened, as it had been, by there being kept without water the best part of the day.

Here there were about twenty of them.

The scene was one of great peril, yet attended by so many ludicrous circumstances. Biddy Malowney, who vended sausages, and wore a red cloak, went flying into the air, though she did not let go her hold of the pan.

As luck would have it, there was a dunghill near, and Biddy fell aisy on it on the broad of her back, and lay there shouting out that the breath in her was clane knocked out, and she was kilt for a month.

Mike Murphy, the little tailor, had indulged in more than one noggin of whisky; his nose had received a polthough from a shillelagh in the fist of a McDonnellite that had spoiled its proportions for the rest of his life; his coat had been torn up the back and was only kept on by the collar, thus exposing his flaming red waistcoat back and front.

The remains of his hat hung round his neck by way of ornament; and thus filled with glory and the craythur, Mike was indulging himself in all the delights of an Irish jig when the Kerry bulls rushed upon the Green.

One of them, seeing Mike dancing and twirling the shillelagh about, made direct for him.

Mike stirred not an inch, but kept up the dance with more spirit, snapping his fingers and twirling his shillelagh.

"Kape the step," he shouted. "Bad luck to ye, kape the step. Pat Mulligan, it's myself that owes you a summat, so take it," and with that, he made a blow at what he thought was Pat, and an instant after found himself shooting up in the air and then falling on a large stack of hay.

He sat there for a time looking round him and wondering.

"It's draming I am," he said, "and the best way to settle the question is to slape it off. Good-night, Biddy. Pat Mulligan, it's one I owe you," and Mike fell fast asleep, and was only awakened by his rolling off on to the ground; and Biddy, who had come in search of him, rousing him up by repeated applications of the sleeve-board.

The Kerry bulls had completely cleared the fair and the Green, their last act being the tossing up the blankets over their own heads, which blinding them, so enraged them with each other, that they fought madly and desperately among themselves.

In the midst of this, the shadows of the night fell upon a scene where nothing but wreck and ruin lay around; and the last to leave the place was Mike, dragged along by the powerful arm of Biddy, who, at every whack of the sleeve-board, cried out, " kape the step, darling, kape the step."

Upon the arrival of Fred at home, he found a car driver waiting for him, the man who had brought his luggage from the post town, and, likewise some letters.

" I think you'll find everything intirely correct, your honour; it's been rather a heavy load, but the bone and the blood of the baste brought us through in a triumphant manner, seeing that the mud and slush covered the wheels intirely; it's rather dry work. The last time I was here, your honour's father, rest his sowl, gave me a drop of whisky, the likes I never tasted afore. Oh, he was a great man, for when he ordered the whisky, 'Tague,' says he.———"

"Lanty, take this good man, and give him something to eat and drink, and then come to me," said Fred, and he made the best of his way to the room he had occupied in the morning.

"Ate and drink, Tague," said Lanty, "What would you like?"

"Anything that's quite convanient," said Tague, with a quiet leer.

"Ah, you're a boy after my own heart, as far as ateing goes. What a pity it is you did not come yesterday."

" Why? Lanty—why?"

" Why listen, Tague. We'd an iligant fowl and pork. Do you like the taste of pig?"

"It's meself would give thanks for a pound or so off the line," and Tague smacked his lips.

" I'll go bail there is some in the panthry left. I suppose yer not particular about fat?"

"The divil a bit; fat or no fat, let's have a taste, Lanty. I've been fasting ever since the blessed sun rose."

"Bedad, it's meself that's sorry for it. I'll be back in a pig's whisper."

"Lanty ain't a bad sort; fond of larking, but none the worse for that."

At that moment Lanty returned, with a cake in one hand, and a tin can.

"It's meself that's sorry to tell you that there isn't a bit of the pig—the *line*

FRED FROLIC;

HIS LIFE AND ADVENTURES.

THE APPARITION OF THE BANSHEE,

is clane gone—but there is a cake that meself put by for supper."

Tague took the cake with a very sheepish look, and turned it over.

"What are you turning the cake over in that fashion for, eh? Do ye think it's a teetotalum, that you want to set it spinning? Bite away, man, if you're hungry."

Tague put it between his teeth, but not a bit could he get out of it.

"It's mighty hard, Lanty."

"It's harder where there's none, my darling. At it again."

"I'll not have a tooth left in my blessed jaws if I try any more. Haven't you got a taste of whisky?"

"A taste of what?" said Lanty, elevating his eyebrows. "Lots—here take this," and Lanty forced the cup into his hand; "do you see that pump?"

"I do."

"Well, then, you'll find lashins of whisky there."

"What, at the pump?"

"Yes; if you'll only pump *long enough.*"

"By my soul, Lanty, then if you poke fun at me, when I'm ready to drop for the want of the bite and the sup, I'll——"

"Ah, bathershin, don't be a fool, Tague, here's the money the master told me to give you, and a trifle over, to go to the 'Pig and Bagpipes' and drink his health."

"It's meself will do that same thing," said Tague, his face brightening up; may trouble always be a long way off the Frolics; hurroo! Lanty, you're a jewel of a man."

"I'm just as I am, Tague. Well, the next time you come this way, mayhap the *line* of pig will be handy; good day, agra. It's a *line* I am remarkably fond of. The horse you've got there has got an iligant back to *shave with,* Tague."

And then Lanty went into the house, muttering,

"I mustn't tell him a word about Old Phil, it will distress him, and by my troth he'll have enough of that shortly. Bedad, if something ain't done, there will be an ind of the Frolics, and when that comes the world will be at an ind."

And Lanty looked in at the door.

"Did you call, master? Not here—where's he got to now, I wonder? Oh, murder, not found Old Phil; I'll just crawl up the stairs gently," and so he did, and, looking round for an instant, he saw the gleam of a light underneath the large doors that led into the drawing-room.

"The Heavens be gracious to us, a pretty wreck he'll see there,"

And he opened the door gently; but the noise roused Fred, who was standing in the centre of the room holding up a candle which shed but a faint light upon the scene before them.

It was a large and handsome apartment, and had been the scene of many a frolic and carouse.

But the furniture had fallen into decay; the paintings, most of them portraits of the "Frolics," were covered with a thick coat of dust and cobwebs.

Against the walls hung the heads of foxes and a decent sprinkling of brushes, showing that the owner was an ardent sportsman; while at the end of the room there was a large stained glass window looking into the gardens.

Fred threw himself into a seat.

"We have had some fun in this room, eh, Lanty? lots of frolics."

"Lots of Frolics. Ha! ha! ha! you may say that; and wait till you get married to some great heiress, that when she opens her mouth let's fall diamonds by the bushel, and plase the pigs, you'll have lots of Frolics agin. I've dreamt all that *twice,* and, mayhaps, I may be in luck's way and drame it *three* times, who knows?"

"Ha, ha, who knows; we must put our wits to work, Lanty."

"Wits; by the powers, if *wits* would put good ateing and drinking in the way, why, the cellar and the panthry would be full to bustin. Wits; if wits would find wittles, Lanty Shan would keep a family as large as Pat Leary's; there was two-and twenty on 'em sat down to an—empty table every day."

"That's very sad, Lanty."

"Sad; why it would break the heart of anyone else but an Irishman—who never loses heart. Why, look at your father, where'll you find his aqual, 'cept yourself?"

"Ah, I wanted to ask some questions about my father's death, Lanty."

"Not to-night—not to-night. You say I don't like talking about death;" and Lanty looked round in a state of great alarm.

At that moment, there was a rush as of cold air through the apartment, and they were in total darkness.

"Holy mother! what was that?" and poor Lanty's knees shook, and his hair stood on end. "Let's get down below, in the name of all that's——"

"Ha, ha! Why, Lanty, I never knew you was such a coward in the dark !"

" I'm not a coward in the dark, although I prefer the light. She'll be here this blessed night."

"She! Who do you mean?"

"Who should I mane by *she* but the banshee? Wasn't it she that come the very night afore the master went to glory —and now — oh, master ! — oh, master !——"

"What now, Lanty?"

" As I am a living man—although it's nearly kilt I am with the shock—ye'll hear a pritty *piece* of music, that will——"

Here a wail rose upon the air, so touching and so plaintive as to transfix them to the spot.

Fred had never heard it before, but poor Lanty had, and he knew that it boded trouble and death to the house they were in, and so the two stood, wrapped in awe and wonder, poor Lanty feeling as if he was sinking through the floor.

Again the boding sound rose upon the air, and then a sudden flash of light shot across the window.

Then came something which appeared like circling wreaths of mist.

This gradually formed itself into a palpable shape, and the figure of a young ethereal being appeared; the face beautiful, but so sad that no eye could look upon it without tears.

Then her hands and arms were raised, and again the cry wailed forth, and then—

All was darkness and silent gloom.

"It's gone, master," whispered Lanty, "and there'll be one less in this house in less than twenty-four hours; and I know the man."

"You do?"

" I do, more sorrow to it; but come down stairs, if we can find the door."

At that moment, Lanty banged his head against it.

"Much obliged to you, my friend? I'll not forget that. Come along, master, and I'll tell you all about it."

They gained the apartment that Fred had occupied in the morning, and there Lanty told the young master that old Phil Neal, the whipper-in, was dying.

CHAPTER IV.

IN AT THE DEATH.

THE news afflicted Fred so keenly that he would at once have gone to the room and cheered up the old huntsman, had not Lanty restrained him.

"You'll do no good, sir," said he, his teeth still chattering from the fear of the banshee's wild wail of sorrow. " He is fast aslape, and it would be a thousand pities to disturb him; for when he wakes he wants, poor old soul, to go down and see the hounds, that have gone to the dogs——I beg your pardon, master."

" Pshaw, Lanty! do what you like, and say what you like; I'll go and see Old Phil,"

" Well, I don't know if it ain't best, after all. He does nothing but ask after you, and——"

"What room is he in?" said Fred, jumping up.

"Why, it was the room where the master kept the guns and whips, like, and——"

"I know; come along. He hasn't wanted for anything, has he?" and he looked searchingly at Lanty.

"The divil a ha'porth. He's had every mortal thing that he asked for, except turtle soup; and I could make that iligant, barring the principal ingradient— the turtle. He'll not be angry at his being put in that room, bekase it was the only one up there where the ceiling was safe."

By this time Fred had made the best of his way up-stairs, followed by Lanty, who kept looking behind him, and muttering,

"It's himself that won't get over the night. Phil, you're booked."

Fred paused more than once to gaze upon the walls where many of the old paintings and decorations were fast tumbling to decay and ruin.

" Perhaps, some fine day, we'll put you all to-rights," he thought to himself as they went on.

"I'll be bound for fifty thousand pounds, and it's a small sum considering *I* make the bet, that we do it—nothing asier, we'll——Whist, astore," and he placed his hand upon Fred's arm. "Do you hear that?'"

"Hear what? yes, yes, I hear it."

It was the old huntsman crooning over a verse of one of his old songs. Then he paused suddenly, as if the memory of other days was too much for him.

"That's what the craythur is always a doing, singing about the horses and the hounds, and the fox upon the grounds," said Lanty.

The sounds ceased, and Fred opened the door quietly and looked in.

The old man lay in a doze, his pale face uplifted to Heaven.

Upon the wall over his bed head hung his old worn-out top-boots, clean as print; by the side of them his spurs, and close by them the well-used saddle.

The hunting cap was on the old man's head and the whip, with its silver top, was in his hand, the fingers nervously clasping it.

A slanting moonbeam played upon the wall over his head like the light of a coming glory, or a ray of the happy past.

"Phil, my dear old boy," said Fred, through his tears.

Oh, the smile in the old man's eye when he looked up.

"Ah, Masther Fred, it will do my poor ould withered heart a power of joy to hear that voice again, and to know that the last hours of the dying ould huntsman are cheered by the boy whom he tached to go over any mortal thing, if it was as tall as the monyment—which I never saw, and never shall, small blame to it; but I'll never do it again, ochone, Master Fred."

"Don't be downhearted, Phil, I never knew you were ill until Lanty here told me," and Fred kindly pressed the withered hand of the faithful huntsman.

"I am not *downhearted*, Masther. Do you think I fear being *in at the death*? No, no!" And the dying man's eyes lighted up with all their old fire and vigour, as though he heard the view-halloo and saw the first burst of the chase. "God bless you, Masther. You've got the *rale* Irish heart in ye; and the Irish heart is never hard to open; a few kind words always does that."

"I've sent for the doctor for you, Phil."

"Sent for the docther, have ye?" and the old man started up. "The divil fly away wid him and his pills. Do you want to kill me before my natural time, Masther Fred?"

"No. What makes you think so?"

"Thin bad luck to it, what did you sind for the docther for? Och, I'm murdered afore my time. You'll not see *that* done, Lanty Shan?"

"It's meself will pison him first with the end of a shillelagh," said Lanty.

"Masther, for the love of Heaven, don't let the docther come near me. I'll faint if I hear his voice."

"Well, then, he shan't Phil," was the reply; "but I did all for the best."

"And who says you didn't? But this arn't a collar-bone job, or a smashed rib; but it's the journey we'll all go; and at eighty you can't ride up to the hounds. Sorra the one is there left, and when you can't do that the sooner your fut is up to the buttercups the better."

"You've lived all your life on the estate. Is there anything I can do for you? When you go, Phil, it seems as if the last link of the family was leaving me."

And the bright drops of sorrow came into Fred's eyes.

"You'll have Lanty left," was said in a soft tone.

But the dying man's ears caught it.

"Of course he will. Your own foster-brother he is, and he'll never desert you. I'll have a word about that with you, Lanty, by-and-bye. Ah, ye don't remember what I once was. I had a bright eye and a mighty gay heart, and I gave the light of the one and the pulse of the other to all the world, and sorra a bit the better was I for it, until I fell in love wid one that I think I see afore me now. Ah! master, if yer had seen her, you would have seen perfection. She had the brightest eye, and the smile that came from it was like a hot coal dropping on a fellow's heart; and then her voice, och! murder! no music was ever like it; but niver mind, it's getting mighty could. Oh! what would I give for a small drop of the rale craythur?"

Lanty shot out of the room like a rocket, and the old man seemed to fall into a doze; but he kept muttering all the time,

"He's come back! he's come back! and we'll have the hounds agin, plase the pigs, and—it's getting mighty could."

At that moment Lanty entered the room, with a large stone bottle, and a couple of glasses, and looking mighty knowing.

The noise he made caused Old Phil to look round.

"I'll never drink all that," he said.

"You'll drink *all* that's in it, a cushla ;" and he poured out a glass with great difficulty. "It's the *only* one left," and whispering to Fred, "I thought I'd bring up the bottle, just to *kape* up *apparances*."

At any other time Fred would have laughed at this. He was now too sorrowful to smile.

"There, Phil, my darlint, down with it, and if it don't rouse up the cockles of your heart, the muscles of your body are lumps of ice. There's lashins more—the Lord save us from onthruths."

"It's a beautiful drop," said the old huntsman, dropping the glass on the blanket, "and so it should be."

"Why?" asked Fred.

"Bekase it's the *last*. I'll not throuble you long, my boys," he said.

"Trouble, Phil, you know better than that."

"Of course I do, and I didn't mane to offind. You don't mind my asking a favour of yer, master?"

"No; anything in the world shall be willingly granted."

"That's kind; well, then, you see, master—and may the heavens be your bed—when I die, I'll lave no one beyant me, 'cept a great granchil, that Lanty knows of——"

"I know that same," said Lanty.

"A grandchild!" ejaculated Fred. "I never——"

"Of coorse yer never heard of him, and I wish I never had, for he added sorra upon sorra, like coals of fire, upon the head of the ould man. May my cur——"

"Phil, this is not the time to curse."

The eyes of the dying man at this sank into their usual dullness.

"Ah, yer right, yer right. Lanty, ye tell the tale to the masther, some other time; there's an uncommon queer faling in my throat.

"Have you anything more to say, Phil? I promise to you I will take care of the child as if he were my own."

"I knew you would—I knew you would, Lanty. You'll look after the master when I'm gone, and,"—here he paused for a moment—"I'm glad you polished off the McDonnell so nately at the fair to-day. I heard all about it. I'd a given a trifle to have been there, and have given them a whack or two, just for the honour and glory of the Frolics. Plase the pigs, we'll mate by-and-bye ;" and then he relapsed again into silence, Fred and Lanty watching him. Suddenly, he started up.

"The coat! the coat!" he cried out; and with that he tried, with a convulsive grasp, to get something under his pillow, but, failing to do so, fell forward, and would have fallen to the floor, but that Lanty and Fred held him up. "Underneath the pillow—look—look! Haste, or I'll go without saying my say."

Fred thrust his hand beneath the bed, and brought out an old faded huntsman's coat.

"Prop me up wid your iligant back, Lanty Shan, there's a dear bhoy," said Phil.

Lanty did as he was asked.

The old man extended his feeble hands, and taking the coat, that had been in many a good day's run with him, gazed at it with a dull, heavy look, while the tears ran down his poor, withered cheeks, and then he raised it slowly to his lips, and reverently kissed it.

"It's all over now, and I'll niver put you on again; and if I could, you'd be of no use, for the hounds are gone—the master's gone—but you've been trusty through life, and now, like the oldest of friends, we must part. Put your hand in the breast-pocket, master."

Fred did so, and pulled out a large canvas bag, tied and sealed up.

"They're all goulden guineas I saved up in the sarvice, and when the trouble came I offered them to the master, and bedad! he threatened to horsewhip me wid my own whip for my impudence, and so I put them by for you when the dark day came, and now, Master Fred, you'll——"

"But, Phil, my good fellow——"

"Whist, don't say a word plase; I ain't any time to argefy, and you'll kape the coat. It was the one I wore—a bran new one given by the master (rest his soul in glory, maybe I'll see him soon) the day you had the first mount on the pony, Firefly, a thorough-bred."

Here the old huntsman seemed to have new life instilled into him.

"Ah! that was a run? Forward, niver mind the river; yoicks! thunder and turf! did ye ever see a boy ride like that same? Ha, ha! and I tached him! Murder! he's cleared the stone wall as if it had been only a wheel-barrow; and, now see—see—we were the only—only—two—two—in at the—the de-de-death, and—and——"

He waved his hand convulsively in the air; then his head fell back.

The old huntsman was dead.

The oldest link in the family chain had snapped asunder, and sunk down into the dark, unfathomable ocean of eternity.

Phil, the old huntsman was gone, and over the death-bed of the faithful follower of his family, the last heir and his foster brother gazed with sorrow-stricken hearts and saddened faces, and then the low, plaintive wail of the banshee was heard again crying in the distance.

"He's gone, and pase be with him, Master Fred. Rest your sowl, Ould Phil; ye did your duty on arth, and you'll meet your reward," said Lanty, reverently covering up the old man's face.

"He shall be buried well, Lanty, and lie at the feet of his old master. God bless and rest you, Old Phil, you kept side by side with the Frolics in all their 'ups and downs,' and you shan't be divided from them when the breath is out of your body."

"Lave it all to me, master. He shall be put under the turf like a gintleman, as if he was the King of Prusher, or Emperor of Chanay, or any other cliver man. You'll take care of the coat, sir."

"I shall hold the money in trust for the grandchild, which you will find, and bring here."

"I will, sir; but there is one thing, now Ould Phil's gone to his long *slape*, must be done."

"What's that, Lanty?"

"*Wake* him, master," was the reply.

"And so saying, Fred, taking up the old hunting coat, left the room, followed by Lanty, muttering,

"Plase the pigs, we'll give you a screeching fine wake, old boy!"

CHAPTER V.

A FROLICSOME RENT-DAY.

LANTY SHAN kept his word respecting the wake of the old huntsman, which was held in the stables where Phil had so many times led out his horse for a day's diversion with the hounds.

"Well," said Lanty, looking over the coffin of Phil, "it was time he went, when everything in the shape of sport had gone. All the horses, 'cept one, went to the dogs afore their time, but that can't be helped; and if we don't get the plasterer and the bricklayer to look after the roofs, some fine morning they'll be a rowling in, and burying us all when we are in our beds in the house far away. Well, plase the pigs, we'll wake you up to-night, ould Phil, and we'll give you a screeching view-halloa, just by way of a parting blessing."

At night the scene was of a very exciting nature, for the old huntsman was well and truly respected by all parties, both near and far.

Of course, all the "Fighting Frolics"

were there, headed by Tim Doolan, and Mike Murphy, the tailor, and Biddy, and all the young and the old, the lame and the blind, of the place, coming to take a last look at Ould Phil, who had often made the hills and the valleys ring again.

Then came a lot of the McDonnells, to pay their last respects to the ould boy in a *paceable* manner, each man carrying his shillelagh up the back of his coat, in case of accidents, for they did not know what might take place, plase the pigs, at a *pinch*.

Over the coffin of the departed all the deep animosity of faction seemed to slumber for awhile, and the fists that had been shaken at each other in deadly hatred, were now locked in the close grasp of friendship.

Close by the body were plates of tobacco and snuff, and around it lighted candles and lashins of drink.

"I'll take care," said Lanty, in answer to what Fred had said to him, that nothing was to be spared to show respect to the "old link of the chain," "I'll take care, masther, that the honour and dignity of the Frolics is kept up at Phil's wake, and you'll do me a favour by granting me another."

"And what's that, Lanty?" said Fred.

Lanty rubbed up the crop of hair upon his head, which looked mighty like the back of a fox's when hard run, and looked down upon the ground.

At this Fred could not help laughing.

"Well, Lanty, you simpleton, what's the favour?" and Fred smiled.

"Well, you see, it's a mighty big un, more than you'll be able to grant."

"That you don't know anything about?" was the reply.

"Well, p'raps not, but I *guesses* it; well, you see, there'll be a little matter that Phil spoke about—about—the——"

Here Lanty stopped short, as though a small pratie had stuck in his gullet.

"What the devil are you driving at, eh, Lanty?"

"Sure I'm not driving either a coach and six or a tinpenny nail, but a standing still; but it's about the——"

"Oh, about the money that he left in the ould huntsman's coat. Oh, that's all right."

"May sorrow be my portion if I said a word about the dirthy money; but it's money I want to spake about, and that's the favour."

"Well, out with it. Here, take that note; it's for fifty pounds. Lay it out, every farthing of it, so that the old fellow has proper respect paid him. Have you sent for the grandchild? Have you——"

"Stop, stop, yer honour, till I get the wind agin into my bellus!"

And Lanty approached the table with his eyes glistening, his fingers moving about like wires, and his lips tightly compressed.

"May I touch it, your honour?" at last he said, in a whisper.

"Touch what? Ha, ha, ha! Do you mean the note? Yes. It won't bite you."

"And is that bit of paper fifty pounds? Oh, my darlin! Many's the time I've had a swate drame of you, and I've laid on my back and seen goulden bhoys dancing about; and now who's convarted them into that?"

And Lanty put his fingers upon it as though it were a baby's cheek.

"It's a note, Lanty. Take great care of it. I haven't many of them."

"I dare say not. They don't grow much in *these parts*, except where the leprechaun, that little cunning varmint of a cobbler, sits a mending his shoes, and there, underneath the sole of his fut, there's always a great pot of gould; but I'll take care of this, masther."

And, so saying, Lanty, venturing a kiss upon the note, took out of a secret pocket in his waistcoat a seal-skin pouch, and placed the paper reverently in it.

"Rist there, my darling," he said, "until I whisper ye to come out. And didn't ye ask about the granchil?"

"Yes; where is it?"

"Och! it will be here in a pig's whisper; but I've got a little bit of a sacret to tell you about him. He's a fairy's child, and hasn't got the sinse of a Christian."

"Half-witted, Lanty?"

"Half, bedad; he's got more wit in his little finger thin many of my frinds have in their whole carcass; but still he is soft like. Yer see his father was a sodger, and having fnst deserted the army, he then deserted his wife, bad luck to him. Well, then' the little Phil was borned in a great dale of trouble; but the 'good people' took care on him; yet all that trouble and bother worked upon poor Ould Phil, and he sent the youg *gossoon* out to nurse."

Here the door of the room opened, and a woman entered, leading by the hand a boy about nine years of age.

"God save ye all," she said, "and may the heavens look after the rest. Is that the masther?" and she pointed to Fred.

"Well, if you guess agin, Molly, you'll guess wrong," said Lanty.

"Well, agra, I've brought the boy home," and she curtsied.

"Come here, my little man," said Fred; and he held out his hand.

The little man had the remains of a great coat, at least two sizes too big for him, fastened to his throat by a bit of string; a pair of thread-bare corduroy trousers reached up to his knees, and a pair of men's stockings, cut off at the ankles, finished the rest of his toilette.

His feet were bare; the features of the little "gossoon" were regular and handsome, and the eyes of a wonderful brilliancy and light.

He looked up fearlessly at Fred when addressed.

"He's got a touch of Ould Phil's face," whispered Lanty to Fred.

"He's a fine-looking fellow, and shall be taken care of," replied Fred.

"Taken care of—ha, ha, ha—I'm always in good hands; don't trouble yourself about me. But I like you, and that's a plain fact," and the little fellow placed his hand in that of Fred's.

"Did ye ever see the likes of that before?" said Lanty, rubbing his hands.

"What is your name, my boy?" said Fred.

"Name! hurroo! You may call me any name. By some I am called Phil the soft one, by others the Little Man, and what would you call me, eh?"

"I'll call you Little Phil. Do you remember your grandfather?"

"What, the old huntsman, as they called him? Oh, yes, I saw him once; where is he?" and the boy looked around the room.

"He is dead," said Fred sorrowfully, and then he whispered to Lanty.

"I'll do that same thing," he replied. "Come along wid me, my little man," and, so saying, he took him by the hand, and led him from the room.

The sun was just sinking behind the hills when Fred entered the stables where the body of the old huntsman lay. He led the boy by the hand, and as he took the little fellow up to the coffin, the people who had assembled rose to greet him in silence and respect. Leading the boy up to the coffin, he held him up to take a last view of him, and then he silently withdrew.

The moment he had left, the tongues were let loose, as well as the whisky, which went round with great liberality under the direction of Lanty.

Then the keener began to call the many good qualities of the dead, and so far into the hours of the night went the wake of the old sportsman, and by daylight all that remained of him was duly placed in the vault of the Frolics, in the chapel at Ballyran.

Fred, leading Little Phil by the hand, paid the last tribute of respect to the old servant of his family, and then left, taking the boy with him.

But with the rest (and there wasn't a soul that lived for miles round but what was there) the road home was diversified by more than one fight, for no sooner had the priest left than the old ill-blood broke out, and the "Fighting Frolics" and the McDonnellites showed their love for each other by repeated visitations at each other's heads; and, in a twinkling, the little churchyard was converted into a battle field, which might have been serious to more than one of them, as in the heat of the conflict, Mike Murphy, the little fighting tailor, was knocked clean into a muddy grave that had been left open, but was rescued, and afterwards whacked dry, by Biddy.

"You'll hould your rint-day as usual, in the grand drawing-room?" said Lanty to his master, a few days after the funeral of Old Phil.

"My what?" said Fred, laughing.

"The rint-day. It's not such a large one as you ought to have had, but yer can't help that. Foggerty, the lawyer, has got the best of the day, at prisint, but, mayhap, we'll get the best of him yet."

"I don't see how, Lanty. He holds the lands of the Frolics pretty tight in his fist, and I don't think he'll let them go very easily."

"Bad luck to him, if he won't let them go out of his fist, we'll rap his knuckles, and make him drop them. But the rint-day you've got to hould is among the little people——"

"The what?"

"The little people in the town, you know."

"I know! I know nothing about them."

"Och, murder, here's a man don't know where his rint is! How do you intind living, master?"

"Well, that's the very thing that is puzzling me, Lanty; and there'll be another person living here in a few days."

"Another person! Will there be any harm in asking who that same person may be?"

And Lanty's great eyes were opened to their fullest extent.

"A friend of mine from England."

"Och, from England — that's a long way off—a friend of yours——"

"Yes, Lanty, and a good friend, too."

"Ah, I'm glad he's a *good* friend."

"Why, Lanty, why?"

"Bekase a *good* friend, I've heard, is a scarce commodity — what I've heard Father Phalim call a rara avis, and what that manes is rayther a puzzle to Lanty Shan."

"Ha, ha, ha! And not only a puzzle to you, but to a great many others; but we must get the place a little in order, Lanty."

"Order, you said, masther; by my sowl the order is beautiful; and I'll go bail for many a day that there's no one can bate us for that same thing; but you'll step up stairs and look at the draw-ing-room; the roof of that don't let in the rain, and that's a blessin' any how."

"Well, it's rather unpleasant."

"Unpleasant! Now, look ye, masther; we have been doing our best in getting things in order, as you call it. In the fust place, the library, that's where the books are. Oh, the lashins of larning there is there; and the best of the mat-ter is, they kape it all to themselves, for the divil a sowl have I seen anybody handle them for years. But whist at present on that matther. Ye'll get into the drawing-room, for I see some of the tinants coming, and we must meet them in *order*—I think that's what you said."

To humour this devoted " follower of his family," Fred made the best of his way to the drawing-room; and, to do Lanty justice, he had put things a little in order.

"Ye, see, masther," he said, " the car-pet is a little the worse for the wear and the tear, and where there was a hole, I put a chair over it; it's as well to hide all imperfections that we can. And where there's a leg twisted off a chair (bekase when there was a scrimmage—many's the one I've seen after dinner here—and there was no shillelagh, the leg of a chair came in mighty handy) I've clapped that same agin the wall; and so the person who sits down upon it must do it tinderly, or he'll be down in the world like many others."

"Ha, ha! well done, Lanty. But what made you hang my ancestor, the general, upside down?"

"Bekase I couldn't hang him up any other way; you see he's a mighty heavy man that same gineral, and one day he came down by the run; the rings gave way, and the wood was like tinder, so Tim Doolan and I clapped the rings in at the *other ind*, and hung him up again, clane and dacent."

Here there was a loud scuffling of feet heard outside.

"Whist! here are the tinants; take your chair dacently. I'll be your clerk, plase the pigs; there's only one pen, but we'll take it by turns; the praist tould me how to write my name by making a cross. I found a little ink, as thick as mud and as black as the divil, so I filled it up with whisky, and if it don't write by itself, Lanty Shan is no judge."

Fred laughed heartily at the shifts his foster brother had recourse to, and took his seat at the head of the table, with Lanty at his elbow.

"Come in, ye sowls, and don't be wearing the floor out by scraping your feet upon it—come in."

Upon that the door was flung open and a motley group presented themselves.

There was Tim Doolan, leading by a string a pig which seemed, by his uneasy movement and gruntings, to be quite out of his element in the drawing-room of the Frolics.

Mike Murphy had brought an elegant piece of red cloth under his arm, while Biddy, his wife, had in her hand a basket of eggs that looked as if they had been smoked up the chimney. Old Mother Rafferty had a small parcel, and Phelim Dogherty, the village Crispin, had only his strap in his hand.

A number of women and children of course attended, and many years had elapsed since the grand drawing-room in Frolic House, Ballinafad, had been honoured by such a mixed assemblage.

It was quite out of the nature of a Frolic to resist having a hearty laugh at this, and Fred indulged in it to his heart's content.

"By my sowl, it's a trate to hear that laugh, your honour. It goes a long way to make up our shortcomings. Glory to you!" said Tim Doolan. "Hoorah! shout, ye divils! niver mind the sail-ing."

And then came an Irish hurrah, that almost turned the picture of the general into its proper position.

The hurrah was in a great measure as-sisted by the loud barking of a number of stray curs, that had followed the peo-ple as a matter of course into the room, and the loud grunting of the pig.

"I am happy to see you all, my friends," said Fred, " and hope shortly to give you a better reception. The Frolics always knew how to give a rale Irish welcome to their neighbours, I believe."

"Always—always—your honour; may

the divil fly away with them that say otherwise."

"Tim Doolan," said Lanty, "before we commence the bisness of the day, if ye turn your eyes, with the illigant black round 'em, to the sideboard, you'll see a beautiful jug of whisky. Sarve out the famale ladies first."

"I'll do that same thing. Hould the pig, Mike, and don't pull him back, or he'll bolt like a divil for'ard."

Mike did as he was bid, and Tim served out the whisky, at times not forgetting himself,

This libation to the honour of the master having been done justice to,

"Mistress O'Rafferty, I call on you first," said Lanty.

"Well," said the old woman, "had yer called on me *last* it wouldn't have made much difference. Times are hard, and there's no money, and what's owing can't be got in, as some people know."

Here she glanced at Biddy Murphy, who returned, with a look of grim defiance,

"Manners, Mother Rafferty!"

"Manners yourself, and see how you like it to sweeten your tay! So you see, yer honour, I've brought you——"

"The rint," said Lanty.

"No, that ain't possible, Lanty Shan," said the old woman.

"Then what have you brought, a cushla?" said Lanty.

"An illigant pound of tay!"

"Och, murder! to the divil I pitch——"

"Stop, Lanty," said Fred. "You know you are fond of tea, and so you shall have that, and welcome. What rent do you pay, Mrs. Rafferty?"

"Well, yer honour, it's so long since I paid *any*, that I've clane forgotten *how much*."

"Ha, ha, ha!" laughed Fred. "That will do, Mrs. Rafferty. Well, Mrs. Murphy, where is your rent?"

"Well, yer honour——" said Mike.

But the fist of Biddy, like a large, red pratie, clapped on Mike's mouth, effectually stopped what Mike would have said.

"Where the divil is your manners, Mike? The masther spoke to me. I think yer said *rint*, yer honour? I put by a trifle towards that same. It wasn't much, but it showed the principle, if it's ever so little."

"Where is it, Biddy? You are an honest woman," said Lanty.

"There's little doubt of that, Lanty Shan; but if you want the rint, you had better go to the 'Pig and Bagpipes,' where Mike left it."

"If ever I——"

Here Biddy's fist went upon Mike's teeth a trifle harder than the first time.

"Mike, you swallowed the rint, and you know it all went down your dirthy throat, bad luck to it. But if yer can't have the mate, you must put up with the malt. So I've brought yer some eggs instead of the rint, Master Frolic. I have been saving them up for a year or more, and you'll find them *new*-laid; and I will say, honest woman that I am, that——"

What Biddy Murphy would have said, was cut short by an untoward event.

Tim Doolan had during this kept in the background, and paid, unseen by anyone, hasty visits to the sideboard, not forgetting the jug.

"Hould the string, Barney," he said, to a wild, ragged gossoon, "and kape off that dog of yours, Tim Flaherty, while I look at that beautiful picture hanging over the sideboard, I think they call it."

"I'll do that same thing iligant," said Barney winking his eye at Tim. "By my soul, Tim, we'll have an iligant cock fight with the pig and the dog; what say you, agra?"

"Say," said Tim Flaherty; "why, you ought to get a medal for inventions, ye divil. When the dog gets tight hould of the pig's ear, let go the string, and then I think the fun will be iligant."

"You'll kape the sacret?"

"Kape the sacret; what do you mane?"

"Ye'll promise me not to say a word about the dog?" and Tim Flaherty gave a knowing wink.

"And not a word about the pig."

"I'd blister my tongue first," was the reply.

Now between the two animals there existed a deadly feud; the pig belonged to the Frolic faction, and the dog was a thorough-bred McDonnellite.

No sooner was the latter let loose than, with all the hatred of faction, he fastened upon his enemy with a growl, as much as to say, "lind me the loan of yer ear;" and the next moment he was biting it fiercely.

Barney made a feint to hold the string tight, and then shouting out, "The baste is too strong for me," let go, rolling over on the floor, at the moment the pig and dog closed in mortal conflict, and Biddy Murphy was holding up the eggs.

Rush went the pig and his enemy between Biddy's legs, and over rolled Biddy, bringing down Mother O'Rafferty and Mike.

"The divil burn ye! what do you mane by that?" said Mother O'Rafferty, dealing Biddy a whack with her fist, which was the next moment returned with interest.

In the fall the eggs were banged into Mike's face and ran down it in streams, sending a most powerful odour through the room. The other dogs that had paid a visit to Frolic House thought they would have some fun, and by universal consent fastened upon the unfortunate porker. Over went chairs, and a table or two.

The blood of the Frolics was up, and so was Fred, on a chair, shouting and laughing. Tim Doolan, who had finished the whisky—which had mounted to his head—was trying to catch Barney and Tim, but, in the chase, the "crayther" having rendered his legs a trifle unsteady, he went rolling over Mike, who, in the confusion, not knowing who his adversary was, fell to with his fists upon him.

The rest of the people had crowded round the door, laughing and screaming.

Lanty was shouting out—

"I'ts a smart whacking I'll give you for this, Mr. Tim Doolan."

"You spalpeen, it's not me; it's the pig," was the reply. "Catch him; catch him!"

The pig made a rush at the door, and, that being close to the stairs, down went the lot—pig, dogs, and a girl with a basket of praties—out rushed Tim Doolan, followed by Mike, streaming with *egg sauce*, and Biddy shouting, with Mother Rafferty's cap and bonnet in one hand, and the wig and curls in the other; while the old woman, with her bald pate, sent a three-legged chair flying after her, which catching Tim Doolan and Mike, sent them rolling downstairs with the rest.

"Stop the pig," roared Doolan.

"Give him fair play, and a clear run," shouted Fred. "Lanty, ma bouchal, I'd give a hundred for another rent-day like this. Ha, ha, ha! the pig's got clear off. Stop him who can."

Then the shouting, the fighting, and the chasing crowd went plunging through the yard, over the fields, and finished by the grunter bringing up at the "Pig and Bagpipes."

CHAPTER VI.

THE BALLINAFAD STEEPLE CHASE.

ALL Ballinafad was out, for it was the day of the great steeple chase, open to all comers and goers. Both parties—Fighting Frolics and the McDonnells—were not only to try their own mettle but likewise the mettle of their steeds.

The steeple chase was in points like the fair, faction spirits running very high. On this occasion it rose to fever heat, when it was known that Fred Frolic, the young squireen, as he was called, was about to contend for the prize—a silver cup, and the head of the McDonnells had sworn to carry it off.

There were several other parties about contending for it, and as it was announced for *all* comers, a strange medley of persons were about contending for it.

At the starting post a great crowd had assembled.

Every species of conveyance that could be found was pressed into the service, because the odds ran high that Fred Frolic had no mount. Lanty and his master had kept their counsel. The celebrated hunter, belonging to the old Frolic, had been brought from a distant place, and taken in the dead of the night, when the Ballinafadonians were wrapped in the arms of Morpheus, to the stables; but beyond Lanty and Fred, not a soul knew a word about it.

"What's that you say, thief of the world, that the head of the Frolics won't be up to the fore to-day? I'll bet you a bating that he's not only here, but he'll be the first in," and Tim Doolan swung his shillelagh round his head, in token that *his* part of the bet was ready.

"Will you have the bating *now*, or wait till I wish it," replied the McDonnellite.

"VILLAIN!" CRIED FRED, AS HIS BLOWS RAINED HEAVILY UPON HIS FOE.

"Batherslim O'Reilly will win in a canter, and I'll bet you two batings to one on the matter."

"Why there's only one horse, and that's in the house widout a leg to stand on. To be sure they can always mend a *clothes* horse," and at this the McDonnellites laughed heartily.

"Of course they can, man; and if they run short of wood they can get a crop from the skull that calls you owner," replied Tim.

A loud shout from the Frolics.

A louder one from the McDonnells in return, as the head of them rode up, mounted on a fine horse.

"You'll have it all your own way to-day, master," they shouted; "good luck will be on you and the McDonnells."

McDonnell was so elated at this that he threw a handful of small coin among the crowd, the greater part dropping in the mud.

"It's dirthy money you've sent us, McDonnell, but we'll spend it in clane liquor, and drink good luck to you, contrary wise," said Tim.

And now as the time was drawing near for the steeple chase, and no Fred Frolic appeared, his partisans began to get nervous.

There were a dozen or more competitors ready at the post, but no young squire.

But all at once there rose a deafening cheer, for, coming across the fields might be seen Fred, mounted on the gallant grey that had so often brought the old squire in at the death, along with poor Phil Leary.

The McDonnells could scarcely refrain from cheering at the handsome appearance of both, for so well was Fred's seat kept that the horse and rider seemed one.

With the courtesy of a true gentleman, Fred raised his cap to all, and more especially to McDonnell; but it only seemed to raise all the bad passions in the latter's breast, smarting as it was from the defeat he and his party had met with at the fair, and the wresting of the "strip of land" from him.

Off they are like the wind at the given signal. Lanty, who had of course accompanied his master to the post, kept alongside of him, his long legs serving him upon the occasion most admirably.

Mike, the tailor, had borrowed for the steeple chase, a donkey belonging to a friend of his; he was a fine one to look at, and a good one, too, when you could get him to start.

"Lave him to me," said Mike, to his friend; "I'll get him to start. I'll use what I often use to Biddy when she's a trifle obstinate and cantankerous, which is nothing uncommon in a woman, the Lord save us. I think they call it by a quare name—Stratty Jem. I wonder who he is."

"I niver heard of the man afore," said his friend, Black Dan, the tinker, as they called him; "but mind, when *once* he starts, ould Nick himself can't pull him in."

"Lave him to me; he may go like thunder and lightning, and the faster he goes the better I'll like it. But don't whisper a word to Biddy; she thinks I'm on the way to measure old Chime, the *bell-ringer*, for a waistcoat; and by the powers, this is a *steeple* chase of another colour."

There were horses and animals of all and every description, followed by cars and carts, and a flying squadron of the Frolics and McDonnells.

The first leap of consequence was a wall, but not of a very great height.

McDonnell was determined to be over first at all and any hazard; he was a bold rider, but lacked coolness.

Head to head came both the gallant steeds; boldly they charged the wall, and, like an arrow, over went the pride of the Frolics safely, amid loud cheers. This so enraged McDonnell that, giving his horse a stroke of the whip when it was not required, the animal swerved, and over went the rider on to his *head*, while close after him came Mike and his donkey, with a bag at the end of a shillelagh, with the magic word "corn" upon it.

It was a complete failure for McDonnell, but remounting, he set off after Fred at a terrific gallop, amid the shouts and laughter of those who stood by.

CHAPTER VII.

AN OLD ACQUAINTANCE IN A NEW CHARACTER.

ALL parties had some ugly jumps to take before they could reach the winning-post.

A tolerably wide and deep ditch was the next difficulty, and Fred on the grey cleared it splendidly; but the man who came next (for McDonnell had been thrown out of the second place) was mounted on a powerful horse, who dashed at it wildly.

The animal rose too soon; he cleared the ditch, but fell with his chest against the opposite bank, his rider under him, and his chance was out.

McDonnell came next, urging his horse on at his topmost speed, and the noble animal cleared it well; but, whether from the fall, or some other cause, appeared to be lame; of the others, some pulled up short, shaking their heads, and, turning round those of their horses, went back.

Black Dan was quite right when he told his friend Mike that once the donkey had a good and powerful start, there was no pulling him in.

The spirited little creature had taken it into his head not to be the last in the chase; and, as he came flying along, Mike was obliged to let go the gentle persuader that hung over his head, in order to have both hands at liberty; the speed of the flying donkey was still further accelerated by the shouts and hurrahs which resounded on all sides.

"Hurroo! hurroo!" they shouted. "Mike wins! Mike wins! Oh, what'll Biddy say to the cup? Stick to him, Mike! stick to him! Hurroo! What are you pulling the baste in for, agra?"

Mike was pulling double, for he knew the ditch was before him.

"It's smothered I'll be," he muttered, "and Biddy will be fatherless, and the childer widders. Will yer stop, you limb of the ould 'un? Ye shall have the corn jist the same as if you'd won; on the honour of a tailor you shall have——"

It was too late.

Right into the middle of the ditch went the donkey, while Mike, turning a somersault over his head, went flying into the mud, and there he stuck up to his armpits, shouting out "murder."

Fred, finding that he was a long way ahead of the others, was about easing his horse, when, turning his head for a moment to see his position, he was wonderstruck to see a young lady on horseback tearing after him.

Her hat was dangling loosely behind her, while her magnificent glossy curls were toying with the faint breeze.

Her riding-habit was the real emerald green, and the horse she rode a fine noble chestnut.

As she flashed past Fred, she waved her hand, and sent forth such a stirring view-halloa that the hunter he was mounted upon sprang forward with renewed vigour.

Side by side, though some distance apart, the pair went over the next field at a rattling pace.

Before them, at some distance, was the winning flag, and there a great multitude had assembled; here was the last leap over a stiff hedge.

At it they went so evenly that a handkerchief might have covered them, and into the winning-field they sprang together, amid the shouts of the hundreds assembled, Fred gaining the winning-post by a neck.

Here stood the owner of the castle, and a numerous body of guests who were on a visit to him.

The sight was at that moment a very exciting one; there, on her panting horse, sat the lovely girl, her cheeks crimsoned and flushed with the exercise she had been taking, while close to her was Fred Frolic, his handsome, laughing face, beaming with happiness and triumph.

"Bell Stanley," said a voice from the carriage, "you will meet with some accident in one of these madcap frolics of yours."

"My dear father," said the girl, riding up to the carriage, and placing one arm round the neck of the person who had addressed her, "don't prognosticate evil."

"Bell Stanley!" uttered Fred aloud. "Surely it can never be?"

"And pray why not, Fred Frolic? You see I know you although you have forgotten me. But, come let me introduce you."

And, with an air of mock gallantry, she took the rein and led him up to the carriage.

"Ladies and gentlemen—hem! allow me, to introduce Fred Frolic, of Frolic House, Ballinafad, an Irish gentleman, just returned from his travels, now on a visit to his old home. He has been renowned all his life for being of a steady disposition, totally belieing his name."

The brow of the gentleman whom Bell had addressed as father, darkened at the mention of the name. This, however, neither Bell nor Fred took any notice of.

By this time the rest of the riders made their way up to the winning-flag, among others McDonnell.

"What, Miss Stanley, have I that pleasure?" and McDonnell, taking off his hat, extended his hand to the lady.

But the cool, indignant look he was greeted with, made him draw it back as though some person had clapped a hot coal in it.

"The *pleasure* is all on your *own* side, *Mr.* McDonnell," she replied, without turning.

"Well, the steeple-chase being over, we'll get home, *Miss* Stanley," said her father, very pointedly. "It looks as if a storm were coming on. You will ride with us in the carriage?"

"On the contrary, I shall walk Rocket slowly home; and Fred—you see I have not forgotten *earlier* days—you can ride with me as far as the cross-roads; it's an age since we met."

"But, Miss Stanley, I must——"

"No, you must not, storm or no storm." Here she looked her father smilingly in the face. "I am going to have a quiet chat, and so now, Mr. Frolic, I am your humble servant."

She saluted the company, kissed her hand to her father, who sank back in his seat with a dark cloud of dissatisfaction on his face, while Fred and Bell started off, and were soon engaged in a very earnest conversation.

All this was gall and wormwood to more than one of the parties. As to McDonnell, he could have shot Fred on the instant had he dared. Mr. Stanley relapsed into a gloomy silence, while upon the faces of more than one of the guests surprise and vexation were depicted.

The carriage drove off, the mob gradually separated, and McDonnell stood alone; he had, in the struggle for the prize, and the reckless manner in which he rode, lamed his horse, and, therefore, would be compelled to leave it at the inn, near where the winning-flag still waved.

Taking the bridle under his arm, he walked slowly towards the place.

"Is that infernal fellow to thwart me in every possible shape and way? I must concert some plan by which he may be got rid of. Should he once gain a footing there, down will fall the other fabric that I thought I was rearing so safely and so strongly."

"So, you're not the winner *again* to-day, eh, McDonnell?" said a sharp voice abruptly at his elbow.

He turned sharply round.

"Hulloa, Murtough, is that you? No, I lost; you see, the horse fell lame, and——"

"A lame excuse is better than none," and the man uttered a loud coarse laugh. "That young fellow has come back at an awkward time for you. You seem to get the worst of it in every possible shape; you lost at the fight and the 'strip of land' is theirs, and to-day—— Och, murder, but *yours* is luck of a sort."

At that moment they gained the inn.

"Will you step in, Murtough, and have a glass? An hour's rest and a good rub down will put the horse to-rights. We might *talk over* matters a bit during that time."

"I am one wid you for a glass and a talk," replied the man.

McDonnell, giving his horse to the landlord, with some directions as to his food, and so forth, walked into the house, followed by the man Murtough, and, sitting down, they soon began indulging in their glasses, and their *talk over matters*.

Here, for the present, we leave them, and return to the point where Mike and his high-mettled racer fell in the centre of the ditch.

Neither the one nor the other could move; the more they tried to extricate themselves the worse they made of it.

"Well, this is a pleasant sort of place for the father of a family to be placed in. What'll I do?" and Mike groaned.

At that moment a troup of men and

boys came rushing across another part of the field, headed by Tim Doolan and Lanty, having a steeple-chase to themselves.

"Here—hurroo, Tim, for the love of Heaven! and Lanty, here, avick, here I am, Mike Murphy, stuck in the mud. Good luck to you, don't lave me, an ould friend, and a Frolic."

The party stopped at this appeal, and came running to the edge of the ditch.

"Who are yer?" said Lanty, pretending not to know him.

"By my sowl, I'm Mike Murphy," was the reply.

"How did yer get there, Mike, and how will yer get out?"

"That's what meself would like to know."

"Here, Tim, run off to Biddy, and tell her that Mike is stuck in the mud along wid Black Dan's donkey," cried Lanty.

"Och, murder! stop, my jewel; if you do that, I'll never have a whole bone in my body but what'll be broken."

"And the poor animal, too," said Tim; "the pride of Ballyran. Black Dan will be the death of you. How did you get there, Mike?"

"No matter how I *got* here, bad luck to yer; try and get me out of the scrape," was the reply.

"Scrape! By my sowl, it will take a good long scrape to get ye clane and dacent," said Lanty; "and it's mighty soft."

"Soft! If I had you here, Lanty, you'd soon see how soft it is. I'll not forget this the next time you want a nice fit for your carcass."

At this moment a boy came running back with a man with a long rope.

"Now, then, Mike, when I throw the rope, tie it round the neck of the *smaller* donkey of the *two* first."

"To the ould 'un I pitch you and the donkey. Self-preservation is the first law of nature."

"Is it? Why, you thafe of the world, would you lave the dumb animal to starve? You'll do that, or, by my sowl, I'll send for Biddy and the slave-board."

"Say no more, but throw the rope."

It was thrown with all the skill of an experienced lasso hunter, and Mike proceeded to tie it round the neck of the donkey.

But the patient animal did not seem inclined to move, although Lanty, Tim, and half-a-dozen others pulled well at the rope.

Stir he would not, or could not.

"Get behind," shouted Lanty, "and push him well."

"How'll I get behind? The divil a fut can I stir; the mud's drying like plasther of Paris, an' I'll niver get out; I'll stick here the rest of my life, and the day after."

"You great omadhaun, not the laste stir will you make to save yourself; pull away. Oh, glory to ould Ireland! he begins to move. Lay hould of his tail, Mike, and we'll pull both of you nately to land;" and Lanty winked his eye to the rest.

As the animal was pretty well in front of Mike, he had no great difficulty in doing as Lanty wished, and accordingly he laid hold of the tail.

But the beast did not seem to understand this double purchase—stem and stern at the same time. The affair so enraged him, that suddenly, with great exertion, he released his hind legs, and sent them with all his force into the pit of Mike's stomach, and down went the unfortunate tailor out of sight, amid the roars of all, by the edge of the ditch.

Up he was, and, mad with rage, he began to pelt them with mud.

The donkey had made great exertions, and got safe out, and, Mike following in his wake, the pair looked such outrageous figures, that the boys began to roar and dance like mad.

"I'll never forget this, Lanty Shan," spluttered Mike, trying to get the mud out of his eyes.

"Not a word; we don't require any thanks," replied Lanty, "do we, boys? Murder! murder! make haste, avick, and get the mud out of your eyes, and see your way clear for an iligant run. Here's Biddy with the slave-board, and Black Dan with a whacking shillelagh."

Lanty was right, for across the field, running like mad, came Biddy and the tinker.

"Round by that hedge, Mike," said Lanty. "Your sowl to glory, run, run!" and Mike, having got the mud pretty well out of his eyes, started off at a rattling pace.

"Come here, you thafe of the world, and take the bating I'll give you," shouted Biddy, waving the sleeve-board, and dashing after him, while the rear was brought up by the rest, roaring and shouting; while the donkey, wishing to make the best of his way home, set off at a gallop after them, followed by Black Dan, vowing vengeance against his friend.

CHAPTER VIII.

THE LIGHT OF OTHER DAYS.

FRED FROLIC and Bell Stanley rode along for some little distance in silence, both of them somewhat surprised at the novel circumstances that had once more brought them together.

"And, so you did not remember your old playmate, eh, Mr. Frolic?" said the lady.

"Well, I confess that at first I did not, Miss Stanley," Fred answered. "But, now, really, how was I to think that the sweet, merry, romping little girl——"

"Sir, those foolish things should be forgotten," said Bell, with affected indignation.

"No, they are the very things that ofttimes shed a charm over life when its romance has nearly faded out; the happy days of youth will then come sometimes as a gleam of hope and sunshine over many a broken charm, and bring a momentary light amid the gloom. It is so now."

"Indeed!" There was a slight quiver in the voice of Bell Stanley, and the fair and graceful head was bowed down. "Is it possible that Fred Frolic is growing sentimental?"

"It is only momentary, and has vanished. What a glorious horsewoman you are, Bell—I mean Miss Stanley," and Fred's eyes beamed with admiration.

"Leave the *Miss* out, and call me *Bell*," was the reply. "I don't wonder at that when you are the master that taught me, you and poor old Phil, that is dead. I tried hard to follow him to his last earth, but couldn't, poor old fellow!"

What would Fred have given to have brushed away the diamond drops that stood trembling and twinkling in those beautiful eyes? They looked so like dew-drops in the starlight.

"You remember him, then?" said Fred, in a voice full of emotion.

"Remember him!" and her lustrous eyes flashed upon him as she drew herself up erect. "Is it likely I'd forget the man that saved my life? Not that it's worth much, but still, gratitude is a glorious feeling, and I should be sorry to be without it. You have had a great loss, Fred."

"Yes, they are all gone, Bell. Father, mother—there is only one Frolic left besides myself, and where he is would puzzle any one to tell."

"Only *one* Frolic left! Ha, ha, ha! Well, I like that. Shall we have the pleasure of seeing you at the castle, because here are the cross-roads, and I must ride hard to dress for dinner?"

"So soon? Why, I did not think we were *half* way there."

"Ha, ha, ha! well done; the last of the Frolics," and her laugh rang out merrily.

"Not the last by a good many, I hope, my lady," said the voice of a man, standing against the old, worn-out finger-post that still stood, although all the names of the roads had long been obliterated by the all-effacing hand of time.

The head of the man could not for one moment be mistaken.

"What, Lanty, my dear old friend, is it you? Give me a grip of your honest hand."

And Bell held out hers, which was grasped with such an Irish welcome that brought a tear in Bell's eyes.

"A cushla machree, it's ten thousand welcomes to you and yours, and, hurroo! the day's our own—the day's our own!"

And the long legs of Lanty flew from the ground in sundry jerks and jumps, while his fingers kept cracking about like castanets."

"Still the same light heart, Lanty?" said Bell.

"And why not? Plase the pigs, I'll get through this throublesome world all the better for it; and it makes my heart all the lighter, and my eyes the brighter, when I see the likes of you—I may say both of you."

"Ha, ha, ha! well, now, after that I must really go. I am coming to pay you a visit some fine day, Lanty Shan. I suppose now you've come home you'll be sending out cards to all the gentry round, to a grand Frolic ball; don't forget to ask *me*."

And again the merry, ringing laugh was heard, as both horse and rider started off at a smart pace down a road leading to the castle.

"Still the same daring madcap," muttered Fred, quite loud enough for Lanty to hear.

"Daring madcap!" said Lanty; "I'd give a thousand a year to have the light of her eyes shining upon me every day for thirteen months out of the twelve all the year round." Then, looking up, he found that Fred had slowly ridden towards home. "Ah! so would you, or I don't know buttermilk from split pase."

And lanty, putting his long legs in motion, was soon alongside of his master.

He placed his caubeen on one side of his head, the shillelagh under his left arm, his hands in his pockets, first lighting the dhudeen, and walked alongside of the horse in a deep study.

Fred rode silently and slowly along, and both parties showed that for a time they wished to have a little private conversation to themselves.

"So much talk is mighty tiresome at times," said Lanty, at last, taking the dhudeen out of his mouth, "and it's a pleasure to be wrapped up in your own thoughts. I have heard that at times when two persons are in company it's mighty oncivil for all dat——"

Fred laughed heartily.

"Ah, that's better," said Lanty, brightening up. "And so you've won the cup, you gramachree, have you?" and he fondly stroked the head of the horse, which showed by his delight that he was once more noticed by Lanty.

"Ah, that we did, Lanty, and in gallant style. We went over everything we came across, while, on the contrary, McDonnell went *down* at everything. I was sorry for him, and——"

"Sorry!" roared Lanty, "sorry! To Ould Nick I pitch such sorrow; not that I owe him anything like animosity, but I'll bate him swately the fust time Lanty Shan gets the chance. That's for sorrow,

whoo!" and the shillelagh went twirling round his head.

"But, Lanty, a little generous feeling is only——"

"Ginerous failing! listen to that. I tell you, Master Fred, those foreign parts have complately spoilt you. Whoo! mighty ginerous he was to your poor ould father, Heaven rest him, when he and the dirthy attorney, Mr. Fitzpatrick Phalim O'Fogharty (the divil fog 'em), got a bond, I think they call it, for a hundred pounds in their hands, and they were going to sind the bailiffs in, only they knew that if they once got *in* they'd have very quickly gone *out* through the winder and not broken any glass anyhow. Ginerosity!— as much as would go on the top of this," and he put his finger on the knob of the shillelagh.

"And how was it all got over, Lanty?" said Fred, deeply interested.

"Got over! Faith, thin, we got over it in a week. In the first place, we barrowcaded the place; that is, we fastened it up so that the divil himself couldn't get in or out. I walked round the front of the house wid the double-barrelled gun—and a beauty it was, by rason that one barrel always went off by itself, without as much as calling out pase —and Mike, the tailor, we put in the stables, bekase the horse was there, and they warn't agoing to have him; and thin I called out all the Fighting Frolics, and every one of them came up to the house, every man armed with a pistol that never missed fire."

And he gave the shillelagh a twist.

"And the bailiffs, Lanty, the bailiffs!"

"The divil a bailiff came within speakin' distance; only one fine morning Mr. O'Fogharty came riding up, and when the bhoys saw him, they raised a shout ye might have heard in Dublin, if it had been near enough; and the animal that he rode turned round, like a sinsible baste as it was, and galloped back. Well, I pinted the gun at him, *only* to frighten him, when the barrel went off *by itself*; and thin O'Fogharty cried out, and clapped his hand behind him, as if he was hit *somewhere*, and that was the last we saw of O'Fogharty.

"Then the money never was paid?" said Fred.

"Niver. It warn't likely or raysonable that we could pay a hundred pounds when we hadn't fifty pince to pay it with.

P'raps as you've been in furren parts, you could tell me how that could be done. Can they pay in that way in those parts? bekase if they do, I'd like to live there,"

"I must go to Dublin and see Mr. Righton, our old solicitor, Lanty, or I shall be dunned to death."

"And pray who the divil is going to dun you?" was the reply. "It would be well for them to try that game on; and as for Mr. Righton, that's the man I would see; but you may spare your legs that journey, for I sent Tim Doolan for him when the squire went to peace, and he came; and a right one he is; he did it all nate and complate. He took away all the papers, and sealed up the cupboard in the squire's room that had the rest, and said he'd be back in a month; that was to give you time to get home, and home we are."

They both at this moment reached Frolic House, where they found Tim Doolan.

"Give me the horse, Master Fred," said Lanty.

"The baste must be rubbed down, and fed, and put to bed like any other Christian."

"Well, we'll all go together, and look after him, and find him a snug corner to sleep in after his day's work. Has he got anything to eat?" and Fred looked earnestly at Lanty.

"Ha, ha, ha! I like that; you are poking fun at us, masther. Ain't he, Tim?"

"I don't think you are far out, Lanty," was the reply.

"Lave Tim and I alone for managing matters," and, so saying, Lanty threw open the stable door.

"Yer see, Masther Fred, the door was no door afore, bekase it was off; now it's on, and over the roof —that is, where the roof ought to be—we've put all the old sacks we could find, and an iligant skylight it makes, only it's as dark as pitch. Now, then, Tim, out with a light that's great," as Tim struck a light. "We'll make haste, masther, bekase the bit of candle is no great thing; and now, Tim, take that wisp of straw, and we'll make his coat shine like the mahogany table."

At it they went, and soon dry and well polished was the horse's coat, while Fred stood smiling on.

"Now, avick, the sack wid the corn; fill the manger, and jump up and cram the hay in there over his head in the rack.

Now then, ma bouchal, you can't have been better trated if you had been the Emperor of Chany's. What do you think now of that, masther?"

"Why, that you have both astonished me," said Fred; and I have little doubt the horse will feel the same."

"Come along, Tim, and faicks, you'll see how I'll astonish him still more. You'll plase follow me, sir; we've taken care of the horse, and, plase the pigs, the rider won't be forgotten. Tim, ye divil, we've won the cup, and it's a stiff brewing we'll have in that same before long."

Lanty now led the way into a small room that had once been the favourite retreat of Fred's mother from the noisy Frolics.

The room itself was in excellent order; the furniture clean and nicely arranged, and on the walls hung three portraits; a cheerful fire was burning, and the arm chair (alas, now vacant), that he had often seen his dear mother in, and where he had stood by her knee and said his simple lessons, was wheeled up to the fire; a snow-white cloth was on the table, and, to Fred's still further astonishment, a small quantity of plate, the old *family* plate, and a full decanter.

"Are you hungry, sir?"

Fred, overcome by a host of recollections and emotions, sank back in the chair, unable for the moment to answer.

"Och! by the powers, you are faint;" and in an instant Lanty had filled a glass with port wine."

"Take hould of that, Master Fred, and drink; it will do you a power of good. Don't be afraid; it's your own, and paid for. Oh! the wonders of the creation; that's right, *cushla ma chree*, and now for the dinner. Tim, yer *gonnoch*, don't stand staring there like Phalim's pig when it was stuck, but make yourself handy."

And Lanty ran quickly out of the room, followed by Tim.

They were back in a few moments, and, to Fred's surprise, each carried a small tray containing some dishes covered over.

"Off with the covers," said Lanty.

It was done, and so was the fowl—to a turn. A delicate piece of pork, and vegetables as fresh as the day, also stood upon the table.

"It's been a grand day for more than one reason, masther, and it's the best we could get, and——"

"But, Lanty, tell me how, in the name of——"

"There, niver mind," cried Lanty Shan, "ate your dinner, and, mayhap, after that we'll have a bit of talk. We've got an iligant bit of that same pork down stairs, with lashins of praties, and not forgetting the craythur. I hope I'll not see a bit of that left when I come back."

The next moment Fred was left in the quiet enjoyment of his dinner, which having done ample justice to, he resigned himself to a train of thought upon the events that had taken place within the last few hours.

He knew nothing of the position of his affairs; they were bad enough, no doubt. The estates, originally large and good, had been heavily encumbered by his grandfather; and his father, a good, easy, high-spirited, yet indolent man, finding that he could not rescue them from impending disaster, plunged the property still deeper in the gulf.

He saw nothing before him but ruin.

In the midst of this the face of Bell Stanley rose upon the gloom and darkness like the sun rising over the void and gloom of night.

"Dear Bell Stanley," he murmured. "Dear little playmate of my boyish hours. How all the youthful love I felt then returns now with double force! Stuff, nonsense!" he said; "the heiress of a proud, hateful man; the loved and admired by all; *she* think of me! she was only laughing at me; but, if I thought she loved anybody else, I'd——"

"Wake up, masther, wake up. Och! murder! it's the pork that's done it."

"What the deuce is the matter, Lanty?" asked Fred, starting up.

"The matter! why, you've been slaping for hours, and murdering no end of people in your slape."

"Give me a light, Lanty. I'll go to bed," said Fred, completely bewildered.

"The best place for a man to go," said Lanty, "when he is murdering everybody in his slape."

The whole of the next day was passed by Fred and Lanty going over the house and seeing how it could be put into decent repair.

That done, Fred, taking up his hunting whip, and telling Lanty that he should stroll across the fields near the common, walked out.

"By the sowl of my father you don't

go alone; there's plenty of those murthering McDonnells about, and they'll think no more of cracking yer shull than they would an egg-shell."

With that, Lanty put on his caubeen, and seizing his shillelagh, sallied forth after Fred.

Over two fields Lanty ran like a greyhound; he thought he heard voices of persons in angry altercation; he saw his master leap the low bridge that separated the wild heath from the fields.

The next moment, Lanty was after him.

There stood Fred, laying his double-thonged whip with all his strength upon a man, Bell Stanley standing with flashing eyes near him, and Murtough and a ruffianly-looking fellow who were just about to rush upon Fred.

Down went Murtough, however, with a crushing blow from Lanty, who placing his foot upon him, kept the other fellow at bay.

"Villain! coward McDonnell!" shouted Fred, as the blows rained heavily upon his adversary; "you little thought I was so *near* to you."

"Whack it into him, masther, whack it into him!" shouted Lanty; "the thafe of the world, to be milesting young ladies when they are taking their walks abroad; and, oh, Billy O'Rooke, there's a nate one for yourself," he added, aiming a blow at him with the shillelagh.

The well-intended blow only partially hit Billy, who, thinking that "discretion was the better part of valour," turned hastily round, and took to his heels in the direction of the mountains.

Fred, having given McDonnell a pretty sound chastisement, flung him from him, and, rushing up to Bell, took her hand tenderly in his own.

"Let me lead you from this place, dearest Bell," he said, warmly; "I don't think either of those fellows will molest females again for some time. You are not faint?"

"Oh, no; I was at first somewhat alarmed at being stopped by McDonnell and seeing the other two ruffians so near; but I feel re-assured now," said the young girl, smiling.

And, placing her arm within his, she walked with him in the direction of her home.

McDonnell had sprung to his feet, and was searching in his bosom for something, when Lanty sprang before him.

"Look ye, Mr. McDonnell; if you don't put down the iligant pistol that you are trying to find, I'll not lave a whole bone in your ugly carcass;" and he twirled the shillelagh before his eyes.

"Curses on it! it has dropped out of my pocket somewhere," McDonnell said, his lips white with the passion that was raging in his breast, and stamping upon the ground in all the frenzy of disappointed revenge. "No matter, my revenge shall fall upon him yet, and in an hour when he fancies himself most secure; and be assured I'll not forget you, my friend." And he shook his fist in Lanty's face.

"Don't do that, don't do that," said Lanty. "or I'll forget that yer unarmed, and give you a taste of this; I owe you a small account in that business of Fogharty's. That's for yer threats, and when Black Murtough recovers tell him the same," and, snapping his fingers at them in derision, he set off in a run after his master.

The blow that Lanty had bestowed upon Black Murtough had for a time stunned him, but, with the application of brandy and a good shaking, he partially recovered, and sat up gazing around him.

"Have I been slaping or draming?" he muttered, looking about him; "there is a powerful dale of singing going on just now in my head."

"I should think there would be," said McDonnell, assisting him on his legs, "after the smart rap that ruffian Lanty Shan gave it."

"Lanty Shan!" and he looked at him incredulously; "Lan—och, murder! I remember all about it now;" and he snatched up the shillelagh that had fallen from his hand. "I'll after him, and see if that same thing will occur again."

McDonnell placed his hand upon his breast, and stayed his further progress.

"Not now, Murtough, not now," he said. "I was rash and foolish enough to address that girl, and cause all this. We'll go to work another way. To-morrow I expect Lawyer Fogharty to call! he's got enough in his hands to drive the fellow again either from home or into a gaol. I have sworn his ruin, and no power on earth shall stop me from carrying it out."

"Right!—right! I owe him and his family a grudge, and they shall be paid. I've sworn it on the holy book, and Black Murtough isn't the man to go from it.

That will break the spirit of Lanty Shan first, and I'll break his head afterwards."

"Good! On the second day from this, I'll stroll down, accidentally, of course, to the Devil's Grip. You'll get all the men out of the way, because it won't do for me to be seen by them. Have you been working well, Murtough?" And he looked cautiously round to see if he was seen by anybody, or that no eavesdropper was nigh.

"Indade we have. They have been rare times lately. Bedad, I think the guager and the milentary have been fast aslape."

And then he looked round suspiciously, and, although there was not a soul upon that wild heath but themselves, he whispered to him,

"We've enough to fill the boat, and plinty to sind other ways."

"That's good news, Murtough, and we'll soon set about it. Here we'll part; and on the second day from this I'll be at the Devil's Grip," and he walked away.

"Ah, yes," said Murtough, looking after him, "I've no doubt you will, now the place is full, and you run no risk;" and taking his hat he felt the side of his head. "There's a mighty large lump coming on the side of my head, as big as a turnip. I'll pay you for that lump, Lanty. I'll go down to the place agin, and give it a good rubbin' wid some craythur, and at the same time, a little taken inside, by way of medicine, won't hurt."

And so saying, Black Murtough made the best of his way to the shebeen shop, vowing vengeance against Lanty Shan, as he went.

For some little distance Fred Frolic and Bell Stanley walked on in silence.

The agitation she had experienced at the sight of McDonnell and his two followers, however, speedily subsided.

"What in the name of fortune brought you so opportunely to the place, eh, Fred?" she asked.

"Well, I suppose my usual good luck; but, in truth, I was coming up to the castle to ask after your health," he replied.

"Well, then, I'm very glad you did not," and Bell looked rather embarrassed, "for you would not have been welcome," she said.

"Well, that is candid, at all events."

"It's the truth, Mr. Frolic, although it ought not at all times to be spoken."

"But why not welcome, Miss Stanley?"

"Ah, that's a secret I can't tell you."

"A secret! Upon my word, I do not understand you. What is the secret, eh?"

"Ah, there you puzzle me. All I know is that you are no favourite with the grand Bashaw, my father."

"I suppose he has forgotten me," said Frolic.

"No; on the contrary, he seems to *remember* you very well. What have you done to offend him?" and Bell glanced slyly at him.

"I offend your father? Why, I never saw him but once before in all my life, and then I was but a boy. What mystery is this?"

"One I cannot fathom. He was in a mighty rage with everybody when he got home, and was as sulky as Blue Beard with me; but I never take any notice of those fits and starts, and so he ate his dinner, and then took himself off to his study, and sent for Wilson the butler. I got it all from him."

"You did? and pray what was it?" asked Fred, very anxiously.

"Why, it was this—that if Mr. Frolic called at the castle, there was to be nobody *at home* to him."

"You amaze me, Miss Stanley!"

"I daresay I do. But here is the lodge-gate, and I must say adieu; I suppose we shall meet *some day* or the other? Many thanks for saving me from that fellow, McDonnell. You made the whip sound finely on his shoulders;" and then, whispering in his ear, "Try and find out how you offended the great man up yonder," with a merry laugh she ran through the gate that led into the park, leaving poor Fred staring after her in wonder and amazement.

Rousing himself, however, he set off towards home, followed by Lanty, who, with his shillelagh ready for action, kept at a respectable distance; every now and then looking about him in case any of the opposite faction was near, that he might accommodate him with a small taste of the *wood*.

Walking into the house, and gaining his room, Fred flung himself into a chair, and gave way to a train of thoughts upon what Bell Stanley had told him.

Lanty who was busy laying the cloth for dinner, kept glancing every now and then at his master.

"Lanty," said Fred, abruptly, "you know Sir Edward Stanley?"

"What, up at the castle? Bedad! I don't know much about him. He's been an absentee for a long time, and the less you know about those men the better, say I."

"Did my father ever say anything about him to you?"

"Not a word. He wasn't the sort of man your father (rest his sowl) would care much about; bekase as I said afore he was an an absentee. He married the great heiress that belonged to the castle, and half the town of Ballinafad, and went off into furrin parts to spend the money, and I wish all that do that same thing all sorts of luck except one—that's the good. What noise is that? As I live it's a car driving into the court-yard. Who the divil's that? P'raps O'Fogharty."

"Well, show him up if it is," said Fred.

"Show him *up!* faiks, I'll show him *out*," muttered Lanty, running from the room.

He was not long absent.

"By my sowl, there's a couple of visitors—Captain—Captain——"

"Frank Hardy!" said Fred, jumping up, "my dear friend, from England."

"Yes; but there are *two* dear friends and——"

"Well, show them up, Lanty."

"Bedad, there ain't no occasion to do that, for they are showing themselves up."

The door being open, the two gentlemen entered, wrapped up in the heavy cloaks of the day,

"My dear Frank, I am glad to see you," said Fred, shaking the taller of the two by the hand, "and your friend, too."

"Thanks, Fred! thanks, old boy! A very dear friend of mine—rather diffident—hasn't seen much of the world—completely knocked up with the capital travelling over your bone-dislocating and break-neck roads." And he sent forth a hearty laugh.

"I wish the roads had been turned the other way before you'd have found your way here," muttered Lanty.

"Well, I must confess the travelling is rather rough," replied Fred, with a smile.

"Rough!" said Lanty. "By my sowl I can't make that out, seeing that they are up to your knees in mud."

"Here, Lanty, show the gentlemen to *my* room," said Fred; "they can take

"THE MAN WHO HAD ENTERED WAS BLACK MURTOUGH, THE SMUGGLER."

half-an-hour's rest before dinner. You must put up with a makeshift dinner, Frank. Eh, Lanty?"

"Make shift!" echoed Lanty. "The gentlemen have only to *say* what they'd like, and—" with a wink of his eye, and a sly grin on his countenance—"it will be sarved up at the earliest possible convanience."

"Oh, anything—anything," said Hardy. "Now, lead the way, I'll go with you. I want to say a word or two to my friend —shan't be long, Fred."

And Lanty led the way out of the room, followed by the captain and his friend; and before Fred had time to recover from his surprise, Lanty was back.

"Well, I think we are in luck's way, anyhow now," said Lanty.

"How, Lanty, how?" asked Fred.

"How? Why, you take it as coolly as though it was raining snowballs. Och, murder! there's *three* come to dinner, and there ain't more than a smell for *one*."

"Lanty, old fellow, you must do the best you can. I'll give you some money, and——"

"May the divil fly away wid the dirty money — it's not that. I've plenty. There's the fifty—but there ain't nothing to be bought; and——"

"But is there nothing in the house?"

"Well, yes; there's plenty of that same thing—nothing; but yer can't make a dinner off that. Asy, there's the remains of the fowl, and the pork, and there's an iligant bit of bacon hanging up; and—ha! by the powers—has your friend been in furrin parts?" and Lanty looked eagerly at his master.

"Yes. Why?"

"Why, then, it's asy enough!" and Lanty gave a jump, snapping his fingers. "We'll get over the matter asy enough now; we'll give 'em *lashins of tay!*"

Fred burst into a loud laugh.

"Not so bad, Lanty, not so bad."

At that moment Captain Hardy returned, and Fred whispered to Lanty,

"For the honour of the Frolics, Lanty."

Lanty rushed from the room like a rocket.

"Now, my dear fellow, sit down," said Frank; "I want to have a few words with you before your friend Lanty returns."

Fred seated himself.

"I have come down unexpectedly upon you, haven't I?" said Frank.

"Well, I didn't expect you for a week, I must confess. You see, the death of my father has rather put me about."

"Ha, I am sorry for your loss," replied Hardy, abstractedly.

"Well, you see, I was just going to have the house put in order; but now——"

"Ah, yes. Ah, wait a moment."

So saying, Hardy rushed from the room.

Fred, amazed at this sudden flight, looked after him. He saw him lift his portmanteau upon his shoulders, and, rushing upstairs, deposit it in the room where he had left his friend; then back he came again, and seated himself as before.

"I hope your friend is not going through the needless ceremony of dressing for dinner?" said Fred.

"Eh—oh, yes; it will be necessary for her—I mean him, to dress."

"At present I don't know whether there will be any dinner at all," said Fred.

"Ah, just so—suit my friend, because he thinks of going to bed."

"Going to bed!" said Fred, astonished.

"Yes—knocked up—not a strong constitution, and we have been travelling for the last week, and, you see, she——"

"Ha, ha, ha! What are you driving at there, Frank? You sit, knocking the poker and the grate all to pieces, and talking about——"

"I know—all right. It's very comical, is it not?"

"What's very comical?"

"Why, *that*, you know."

"Know! I don't know. Hang me if I don't think our iligant roads have jolted all the senses out of you. What's the matter, Frank?"

"Nothing—a great deal—put my foot in it."

"Have you? Not the first time by some dozens of times. Bailiffs, I suppose?"

"No, not this time; worse than that— had a run for it. No joke all the way from Gretna Green to Ballinafad."

"Will you speak intelligibly, and tell me what you really mean?"

"Yes; I mean to say that the man upstairs is not a man. Now you have it."

"Not a man? Well, then, it's a woman. Joke away, old boy," and Fred laughed heartily.

"A logical conclusion," said Frank, joining him.

"And pray, what is the *man* upstairs?" asked Fred.

"My wife!"

And Frank looked him full in the face.

"Your what?" said Fred, throwing himself back in his chair.

"My wife; ran away with her from London to Gretna Green. Got married; threw them all off the scent."

"A runaway match!" said Fred. "Just like you, Frank."

"Yes, all right in the long *run*, I hope.

Harkye, Fred, I have run away with a ward in chancery."

Here Lanty opened the door, and looked in.

"And the *officers are after me.*"

"The Lord save us!" whispered Lanty.

"And if they get me *it will be for life,* perhaps; they'll show no mercy."

"You'll excuse me, sir," said Lanty, touching him on the shoulder, "but don't you think that you and the t'other chap had better cut and run?"

At this the friends burst into a loud laugh at poor Lanty's countenance, so full of wonder mixed with fright.

CHAPTER IX.

THE DEVIL'S GRIP.

FRANK HARDY was quite right; the Lord Chancellor's officers, backed by others, were after him for a contempt of that high official.

In those "good old times," the punishment for such an offence was very severe, and, in the case of Frank Hardy, he had, in defiance of notices and a prohibition from the Chancellor himself, run away with a rich heiress and a ward, and the rage of his lordship (not at the best of times the sweetest temper in the world) was so great, that if Frank Hardy fell into the iron grasp of the law, it was likely to go very hard with him.

All these circumstances were detailed to Fred over a dinner which Lanty, for the "honour of the Frolics," had hastily got up with the aid of the old woman in the kitchen, and who had likewise the charge of Little Phil; though the remark respecting the "officers" had rather upset his nerves.

"What has he done, I wonder?" said Lanty to himself. "Murder! the Lord save us! P'raps a trifle of forgery; that's a neck or nothing job. If it's only the bailiffs, that for them," and he snapped his fingers. "We'll asily get rid of the likes of them."

Then Lanty was still further astonished when he saw the captain take a small portion of dinner up to the room where the other "gentleman" was, and, after staying there some time, return, locking the door after him.

"What the divil does he lock the door for? I'd like to get at the bottom of this. Save us! if the officers should come and take up masther along with them." and then, Lanty, going to the corner where his trusty shillelagh was standing, grasped it. "I think, my friend," he said, "there would be *more* than two words to that bargain."

Then tea was ordered, and that was taken into the room upstairs, Lanty watching from the bottom, and then entered the room in which his master was seated.

"If the gentleman is sick I'll wait upon him with the tenderest care, masther; or maybe I'd better fetch the doctor before it is too late."

"No, no, Lanty, it is not so serious as that," said his master, laughing. "But I'll tell you what you can fetch us."

"What yer honour?"

"The materials for making some punch. The ride has been long and wearisome, and I don't know anything better to cheer the hearts of travellers, eh, Lanty?"

"Ah! bedad, you're right, and I'll do that same thing; it bates all the doctor's stuff to smithereens; and if you give the sick man upstairs a good stiff jorum of it, he'll be a different craythur in the morning."

And away ran Lanty amid roars of laughter from both Fred and Frank.

"I don't see anything uncommon to laugh at in that," said Lanty.

In a few minutes after the materials for the punch were placed on the table.

"Now, Lanty," said Fred, "we've done with yon for the evening; go and enjoy yourself."

"I'll not niglict that same thing," was the reply.

"Here, stop, Lanty," said Frank Hardy, who had completed the brewing; "down with that," and he handed him a glass full of the smoking mixture. "Here's your health, my good fellow; I've often heard your master speak of you."

"That I'll be bound you have, and nothing to my discredit either anyway, I'll be bound; and here's your's, sir, not forgetting the sick gentleman upstairs," and, finishing the contents of his glass, he smacked his lips. "By the powers you've got a nate fist for a good mixing; and I wish you a good-night."

"Oh, by the bye, Lanty," said his master, "let us have a good breakfast; everything nice, you know."

"As if I didn't know what an iligant breakfast was. I'll go bail that the butter-milk and praties shan't disgrace the house."

"And don't forget the tay, Lanty."

"It will spoil the breakfast intirely; but there's no accounting for taste anyhow," and so saying, with an expressive shrug of the shoulders, he left the room, leaving the two friends to remain up to a late hour in anxious conversation as to what course should, under the circumstances, be taken.

The next morning Fred and Lanty were up early, and by their joint exertions the table for breakfast was well and capitally laid out.

Biddy Murphy's stock of the newest-laid eggs had been procured, and, in short, the shops in Ballinafad had been ransacked for anything that could contribute to the comfort of Fred Frolic and his newly-arrived friends, and things that had not visited Frolic House for many months were again there.

"Now, Lanty, we're all complete except one thing," said Fred, rubbing his hands.

"And what's that, sir?" asked Lanty, staring at him.

"Some nice thin toast fit for a——"

"A queen or a duchess; you'll have that. I'm up to that. I made it for your father (may the Heavens be his bed). Is it for the sick gentleman, sir?"

"Well, yes, it's the only thing he can fancy."

"Ah, fancy goes a long way in this world; it 'ud be a long time before I'd fancy burnt bread with hot water and broom clippings for my breakfast; but taste goes a long way, like fancy, and by that, I suppose, they were brought up together."

And, so saying, Lanty departed to make the toast.

He had not been absent many minutes, when there descended to the room Captain Frank Hardy, having on his arm a young lady, who, with many smiles and blushes, was introduced to Fred Frolic as Mrs. Hardy.

She was very young, and, without being transcendently beautiful, was sufficiently pretty and interesting to pass through the world.

Her figure was well-proportioned, and, without affectation, she had all the bearing of a lady about her.

"Welcome to Frolic Hall, my dear madam," said Fred, warmly shaking her by the hand. "I hope in a few days to make it a little more comfortable for you."

"Travellers and runaways must do the best they can. We have a kind and generous welcome, and the rest will soon follow," replied the lady.

At that moment the door opened, and Lanty entered with a plate of toast.

"Here it is, masther, hot as——"

And, as he looked up, the plate fell from his fingers on to the floor.

"The Lord save us! here's a ghowst!"

And he was rushing from the room, shouting murder, but was held firmly in the grasp of Fred.

"Be quiet, Lanty, and don't be a fool; this is——"

"Och, murder! I see it all; it's the sick man transmogriated into as purty a woman as ever I clapped my eyes upon."

"Come, come, Mr. Lanty, be easy," said the lady; "I've heard of the blarney stone before."

And she extended her hand to him.

"It's not for the likes of me to dirty that purty white hand wid this ugly fist, but I'll kiss the tips of the fingers, if I die for it."

And, with a gallantry that would have shamed many a better educated man, Lanty put his lips to them.

"Well done, Lanty," said the captain,

slapping him on the back; "and now then for breakfast."

During the meal Fred informed Lanty of all particulars, and especially impressed upon his mind the necessity of not saying a word to a living soul about it; the captain and his wife were to remain in strict seclusion in case they were tracked and the officers came, and then every ruse was to be tried to baffle them.

"I don't know what you mane by a ruse, but if it's misleading them, by the hokey they're come to the right place, whoo! plase the pigs they'll see some fun! lave it all to me, lave it all to me," and Lanty's eyes twinkled like stars at the notion. "That's what you meant by the officers."

Frank and his wife laughed heartily at Lanty.

"But there must be no violence, Lanty," said Fred.

"The divil a haperth, as if meself would do violence to an officer; lave me alone for hurting his failings without hurting his back. Whin do you expect 'em, sir?"

"Well, not at all, Lanty! but they might follow us up," replied Frank, "if once they get the scent."

"Scent! Bad luck to them officers, they have got noses like a foxhound; but if there's any sent here you'll see how soon they'll be sent back, and with something in their ears that ain't polite to mintion in a lady's presence. Have you done with me, masther?"

"Yes, you may go, Lanty," replied Fred.

"Thank ye, sir; don't be afraid, marm, about officers. We've got the 'fighting Frolics,' long life to them, that know how to manage them."

"But, Lanty," said Fred, "I——"

"All right; I know what I am about;" and away went Lanty down the stairs, muttering—

"In the first place, I'll load all the guns, not that I mane mischief, but you don't know how soon it may come; then I'll send round for Tim and we'll hold a cabinet council in the stables, and then—whisht, Lanty, the old woman's there—she's as deaf as a mile-stone, and 'll hear every word."

Later in the day, Fred telling Lanty to be very careful, took up his double-barrelled gun and prepared to go out.

"Where are you going, masther?" said Lanty, anxiously.

"I think there is some game in the valley of the Devil's Grip, and I'll go and try my luck," was the answer.

"Don't go far beyond that, sir! there's an iligant storm brewing," shouted Lanty.

The Devil's Grip was a large mountain, bounded by the sea shore on one side, and by a gloomy valley on the other.

There were a great many legends connected with the place, most of them relative to the dark deeds of smuggling, and crimes belonging to that nefarious trade.

There was a cave in connection with it, which had long been the resort of all the reckless and desperate characters in the neighbourhood.

It was situated about four miles from Frolic House, so that it did not take Fred long to reach it, in the hopes that he might be able to make some little addition to the dinner table.

The wind that had been howling and whistling all the morning began now to increase in violence, while large rain drops began to fall; the thunder began to boom in the distance, and to send its echoes through the gloomy valley, and then came sharp short streaks of lightning.

"If this continues, I must find a shelter in the cave; at present this overhanging bank will serve my purpose;" and he crouched down under the place.

"I wonder when I shall see Bell Stanley again," he murmured. "I have been trying to think, ever since I saw her last, what can have occasioned the animosity of her father towards me? Can't fathom it—can't divine it—can't——how fearfully the storm is beginnging to rage, and——"

Here Fred crouched nearer to the bank, and shielded his eyes for a moment, for a blinding flash of lightning darted through the valley, lighting up every object in it; then followed a peal of thunder so loud and so fearful that the young man involuntarily shuddered.

Suddenly a scream was heard so sharp as to make him rush out into the pitiless storm, and gaze down the valley to see from whence it proceeded.

He was not long left in doubt, for a horse came tearing madly up the road.

Another flash, and the horse reared up as though shot, and he could just see the rider spring off as the animal rolled on the ground.

The next instant came another peal of thunder, and with a loud cry the horse bounded to its feet, and, dashing wildly past him, was lost to sight.

Fred Frolic rushed to the spot, and there, standing erect and unharmed, stood Bell Stanley.

"Gracious heaven! you here, Bell! Quick—quick! let us gain the cave! Are you hurt?"

"No, Fred; but fearfully frightened."

For the moment sinking on his shoulder, the next she had regained her usual firmness, and ran quickly by his side round the hill, on to the sands, to gain the entrance to the cave.

To Fred's surprise, in one part of it there was burning a capital fire.

"What means this?" he said, in astonishment.

A powerful effluvia also ran round the place.

"There is a private still here, and there may be some of the desperadoes now within—rather brave the storm, Bell, than them."

They were rushing back again to the entrance; when, suddenly, they heard the voice of a man.

"Quick, Bell!—this way!"

And Fred rushed back again into the Devil's Grip.

Nearly opposite the fire there was a large fissure in the place, into which Fred hurried the girl, and standing before her with his gun prepared to defend her.

The next instant a man entered, and, as he seated himself close by the fire, the red flame playing strongly on his face, showed that it was Black Murtough, the smuggler!

CHAPTER X.

A NARROW ESCAPE.

THE situation of Fred Frolic and Bell Stanley was one of extreme peril, and although he did not for one moment feel the slightest alarm, yet, as he felt the arm of the tender and heroic girl clinging to his, his heart beat with a quicker pulsation.

His only fear was that he should be discovered and surrounded by numbers with whom he would be unable to cope.

"Into what fearful peril have I drawn you, Fred?" whispered Bell into his ear; and he felt her press his arm almost convulsively.

"Be silent for your dear life's sake," he murmured in reply; and with the deadly weapon levelled and ready for action, he stood watching the movements of the smuggler, Black Murtough.

The storm still raged, and the rain fell heavily.

"Not a soul will be here this day," said Murtough, looking round, "so, in an hour's time I'll wake up the boys, an' we'll go on wid the brewing. This pelting rain has chilled all the blood in my body, and it would not be at all amiss if I got a drop of something to warm it."

And so saying, he rose up, and made his way into another part of the cave, returning almost in a minute with a good-sized stone bottle, with which he again resumed his seat.

"If this don't warm up the heart, why, then, it's a wonder," and, lifting up the bottle to his mouth, he took a good draught, and then, smacking his lips, he placed it down again by his side. "That's an iligant drop as ever crossed the lips of an honest man. Och, murther! it's me own head that's splitting with the taste of Lanty Shan's shillelagh. I'm not a living man if I don't pay him and his thafe of a masther out for it. I'll be one wid you, Mr. Frolic, in some shape or the other, by day or by night, for that same thing and others, and that I swear, or may the drop I'm about to swallow stick in my throat."

He was in the act of raising the bottle again to his lips, when a whistle was heard from without, and so sudden and shrill was it, that he started up, nearly falling, bottle and all.

"What's that? Jan, by all the powers! it's his whistle," and making his way to the entrance, he answered the whistle by another as loud.

A few minutes elapsed, when the entrance of the place was darkened, and a man strode into the cave of the Devil's Grip.

He wore a heavy, round, hairy cap on his head, and a heavy coat reaching down to his knees, partly covering the high boots that reached half way up the thigh; his beard and whiskers were of great length and thickness, so much so as to hide a great portion of his face.

"Ha, ha! What, mine goot friend, Black Murtough, here? ha, ha! Sapperment, you are always at your post; shake hands, my friend," and he held out a great, brawny hand.

"By the powers, you're the very man that me own eyes wanted to rest upon. Sit down, and lay hould; this storm is enough to wash you away. I am glad to see you, I am. Come, thin, we'll be comfortable," and rolling out an old empty cask, he seated himself upon it. "Drink heartily, Jan; there's more where that came from, praise be to it. Pull hard, now!"

It did not appear as if Jan, as he was called, wanted any particular pressing upon the point, for he lifted up the bottle as though it had been a feather, and, in an instant, it appeared glued to his lips.

"Yaw, dat is goot," and he smacked his lips so heartily that the report rang through the cave. "Here, mine friend. Ha, ha! donder and blitzen, I shall drink your goot held."

And he took another pull, and then handed it to Murtough.

"You shall drink mine goot held, sapperment," and he snapped his fingers.

"By the powers, there ain't a man in de whole world whose health—— Ah, bathershin! Good luck to you."

"In their deep drinking lies out safety," whispered Fred.

"Well, my friend, what is de news?" asked Jan, putting a cigar in his mouth, and handing another to Murtough, "how is de trade? Have you got a goot cargo for me, eh?"

"Bad luck to me if ever you had a better," was the answer.

"Dat is goot—vera goot. I shall leave the cutter in the old place, where dey'll never find it."

"Bedad, you're the man to outwit all the world and hoodwink the rest. But, listen, avick, if ever you kept your eyes open, you'll have to do it now,"

"Yaw, why? It will not be well for anybody to stand in mine path. I have a goot friend that knows how to deal with them," and he pulled a brace of heavy pistols from under his coat, and held them before Murtough. "Sapperment, they have done that thing before. Yaw——"

"No one doubts that same. But, put the muzzles t'other way, good luck to you, Jan," and Murtough held up the bottle before him.

"Ha, ha, what shall you be frightened at, eh?" Do you think I would hit you, mine goot friend?" and, laughing, he levelled one at him.

"Put it down, Jan, put it down. Yer see, it might go off by accident, and it's meself that don't want to go that same way. Whist, my darling, and listen to what I say. Bedad, my throat's like a lime-burner's wig."

He took another draught, and then handed it to Jan.

"I am all over in my throat like de wig myself, yaw."

"We have got an inimy come here to live among us, Jan; bad scran to him."

"Yaw, yaw, mine friend, I say so."

And he began to sway backwards and forwards on his seat.

"What is the matter with the seat, sapperment! it is running away from me."

And so it appeared, for it slipped from under him, letting him roll easily on to the ground.

"Yaw! dat is goot. Well, who is de enemy, aye, my friend, Murtough?"

"Why the man that has come to live at the castle, Sir Edward Stanley; he will hunt us down; he has said so."

"Yaw! has he? I shall not care that for him. If he shallinge me, I shall make one littell hole in his body, my goot friend. Yaw! I am all over sleep, so I shall take the goot old forty winks, and when the rain is over, I shall—ah, donder!—I shall —yaw!"

He gave a yawn, and, throwing himself down full length by the fire, was soon in a heavy sleep.

"Ah!" cried Black Murtough, "there's nothing that sticks to a man so constant and thrue as you, my friend; there's no decate about you." And he lifted, with some difficulty, the bottle to his lips. "By the powers! that slapy fellow knows how to drink; he's—he's been most alarming —loving—to—to you, my craythur. Bedad! I mustn't let the fire down; I'll just make it up, and take 'de goot old forty winks' myself," and he tried to rise. "By the powers! it's tired my legs are; the wet has got in and given me the cramp; there's plenty of ould fire-wood over there."

And he pointed to the place where Fred and Bell were concealed.

Fred felt the fingers of Bell clutch him as though they would render his arm powerless.

"Leave my arm free, Bell; he is a dead man, if he approaches many steps nearer," he whispered.

During this, Murtough was making ineffectual endeavours to get on his legs, and it was fortunate for him that he could not.

At last, by a great effort, he got up, but the next moment he went rolling over the cask that his companion, Jan, had been seated upon.

The weight of his body broke up the old staves, and there he lay in the midst of them.

At any other time Fred would have laughed heartily at this, but he mentally thanked heaven for it, because it had prevented him shedding the blood of a fellow creature, brutal and bad as he might be.

"What's been and got into the legs that calls you owner?" he hiccuped; "but, however, you'll do."

And he picked up one or two of the staves, and went crawling on his hands and knees towards the fire, upon which he threw them.

"There, burn away, bad luck to ye; I'll have another—another drop—of—of —the——"

But the potent stuff had done its work, and in the endeavour to reach the bottle, he fell down on his back right across the path that Fred and Bell would have to pass in order to escape.

Fred put down the gun an instant to wipe off the damp that had gathered in large drops on his forehead, while poor Bell, spite of her high courage, seemed as though she would faint.

Spite of all he had taken, the ruffian kept muttering in his sleep.

"There's one for you, Lanty Shan," and he threw out his fist as though the shillelagh was in it; "and there's a taste for you, Mr. Frolic. Whoo! hurroo, Murtough!"

But at last the strength of the potheen overpowered him, and he seemed to drop into a sound sleep.

Not a moment was to be lost.

"Step lightly over the fellow, Bell, and Heaven look down upon him if he but stirs a finger."

With that Fred, followed by the excited girl, left the place of their confinement; Fred standing with the gun pointed to the temple of Black Murtough, while Bell passed over his inanimate body.

As she was stepping lightly over him, he threw out his hand, and nearly caught her dress.

"Lanty Shan, I'll bate you to a mummy," he muttered.

Had he clutched her dress Lanty would have been saved from all chances of a beating; but, as it was, Bell was in safety, and Fred, having passed over him also, they were soon out of the Devil's Grip.

The rain was still pouring down.

It was only noon yet, but the clouds hung gloomy and lowering upon the earth as though it was the dark hour of night.

Scarcely had Fred and Bell reached the valley, when, overcome by the perils and dangers she had escaped during the day, she fell senseless to the earth before Fred could move a hand to save her.

To raise her up in his arms and rush with her into the high road, was but the work of a moment, and never did a burden feel so light and so precious.

Scarcely had he reached the road, when he was alarmed at seeing at some distance before him, and fast approaching, a strong glare of light.

Still, in spite of any danger that might occur, and never stopping to think whether they were friends or foes that were approaching through the drenching rain, he hurried on with the insensible girl in his arms.

Suddenly turning the bend of the road, he came upon a body of men congregated around an open carriage, in which was standing a tall gentleman, whom he recognised as Sir Edward Stanley.

At the same moment loud shouts were heard, and a dozen or more men rushed upon the scene; they were the "Fighting Frolics," headed by Lanty Shan, Tim Doolan, and Mike, the "fighting tailor," who, in his haste in leaving home (and Biddy having hid the shillelagh), had caught up the never-failing sleeve-board.

"Here's the master, thank the saints!" cried Lanty. "Hurroo, my boys! hurroo!" and they sent forth a shout that nearly set the horses off that were in the carriage.

By this time Sir Edward Stanley had descended from the carriage, and rudely snatching Bell from the arms of the man who had so nobly and lovingly protected her, had placed her in the vehicle and had sprang in after her.

Standing up, with his long grey hair streaming in the wind, he bent upon Fred a stern look of hate and defiance.

"It is to you I am indebted for this, which, perhaps, may result in the death of my child; I shall take a fitting opportunity of acknowledging the obligation."

Then he turned to his coachman,

"Home!" he thundered out, in loud tones, "with all the speed you can!"

And before Fred could explain, the carriage had wheeled round and was rapidly making its way to the castle.

The act was so sudden, that for a moment it deprived Fred of all speech and motion, and he stood staring after the retreating carriage as though he was in a dream.

Lanty, during this, passed his hand lightly over Fred's shoulders, and then gave a spring high up in the air with his long legs.

"Hurroo! hurroo! the saints be praised, there's not a bone broken—sound wind and limbs!" and he shook Fred heartily by the hand.

He whispered a few words to Lanty, who, starting off at the top of his speed, soon returned, bearing Fred's gun with him.

"It was the masther's, and many a blessed bird and other wild animal have I seen him bring down, when they've been out of sight in the clouds; oh, it's a mighty gun, is that same."

Absorbed in his own reflections, and thoroughly drenched through, Fred now made the best of his way home.

The "boys" kept pace with him, remaining, however, a little in the rear.

"I'd walk to the ind of the arth, Tim," muttered Lanty, to his companion, "and a trifle over, to see that sight agin; and the old 'omadhaun' to talk in that way; we'll see it yet, Tim, we'll see it yet."

"By the powers, we may; let's hope for the best," was the reply.

"You'll not forget the night, Tim?"

"Not I, by my sowl!" said Tim.

"What's in the wind, now, to-night?" muttered Mike, to himself, overhearing them. "I'm in that, anyhow. What's the secret, I wonder?"

At that moment they reached the house, and Fred made the best of his way to his room, while the "Frolics" wandered away into the kitchen to see what was going on "wid regard to the bit and the sup."

CHAPTER XI.

LANTY SHAN'S CABINET COUNCIL.

CAPTAIN FRANK HARDY and his bride soon made themselves at home in the house of the "Frolics."

It was quite a new era in their lives, and they determined to enjoy it; and it was with the greatest pleasure that Lanty saw them wondering and delighted at all they saw in the place.

During the absence of Fred upon his shooting excursion, Lanty had asked permission to have a word with the worthy couple.

Of course the request was readily granted.

"Well, Lanty, my friend, what is it?" said Frank.

"Well, sir, you'll pardon my bouldness, and you, too, marm, *ma collen oge*, bekase you see I am rather puzzled with regard to some matters," and Lanty stroked down his hair.

"Well, what are they, Lanty?" said the captain.

"Why, you see, you have come down upon us like a thunder-bomb, and are taking us quite onawares like; but that doesn't matter much, only it's of consequence, that now we've got you here, we should take oncommon care of you, and not let you be kilt or done away with for the matter of that."

"What does he mean, Frank?" said

the lady, clinging to her husband in fear and trembling.

"Oh, nothing at all; don't alarm yourself, dearest," was the reply. "What do you mean, Lanty?"

"Ah, that's the thing I want to find out the maning of it. When do you expect them same officers?" and Lanty looked round. "Don't spake loud, for ne'er a sowl can hear yer."

"Ha, ha, ha! well done, Lanty; but I tell you we don't expect them."

"Then why did you say they were after you? What sort of men are they like?"

"I can't say. I have never seen them, and don't want to, Lanty," said the captain.

"No more do I. For the matter of that, I only asked the question, bekase if they should come I'd like to give them a *warm reciption*," and Lanty's eyes lighted up with a merry twinkle, "a reciption worthy of the Frolics; you understand."

"I think I do," was the reply.

"That's why I wanted to know, bekase, yer see, it would be onkimmon awkward to make a mistake, and intertain the *wrong persons*. Do they know *you*, your honour?"

"I am not certain about that; they might have seen me."

"And the lady, bless her eyes?"

"Very likely."

"Och, murther! that's onpleasant. But we'll get over that; we'll come what the masther called a—a *ruse* over them. Bedad, we'll do that same thing; we'll trate them to a little bit of a disguise," and Lanty rubbed his hands with great satisfaction."

"A disguise? I am at a loss to understand you, Lanty."

"I daresay. Lave an Irishman alone for inventions or circumventions. There's some iligant dresses upstairs that belonged to the masther's mother—rest her sowl in glory—that will be just the thing; not a whisper about it."

Here a terrific peal of thunder broke over the house.

"Och, murther, that's a rattler, and the masther out on the mountains."

And poor Lanty, whose honest, true, and faithful heart beat only for his master, and foster brother, looked anxiously out of the window.

"Oh, it will soon pass over," said Frank.

"Yes, when twenty and four hours have passed over. Ah, you don't know a storm in these parts. How should you? Many a game it's had wid the roof you're under. It's a grand sight then to see the iligant waterfall that comes pouring through it, makin' it's way down the stairs, and going out at the door wid all the purliteness in the world."

This grand treat seemed likely to be seen by the guests, for the rain began to descend in torrents, and the clouds to form in large dark masses; then the awful rolling of the thunder over the neighbouring mountains and the flashing of the lightning caused the lady to cling to her husband in terror.

"Don't be alarmed, marm," said Lanty. "The old house has had many a worse bout than this. Don't be alarmed, bekase if the ould roof should come in, it won't hurt this part; it's tried it on before, and gave it up as a bad job."

"But, Lanty, the house ain't so bad as all that?" said Hardy, anxiously.

"Bad? The house bad? Och, murder, what do you mane? You may travel a hundred miles and more, and never see another like it. You'll excuse me, but I'll just see what the weather is like *outside*."

And Lanty hurried from the room, and jumped, rather than ran, down into the kitchen. It was there he found Tim Doolan and others, who had taken shelter from the storm, busily engaged round a large turf fire, smoking their "dhudeens."

"It's well for the likes of you to be smoking your 'bacca in the house, when, perhaps, the masther of it may be in danger."

At this the start up of every man to his feet was something electrical.

"What do you say, Lanty Shan?" shouted Tim Doolan. "Where is he, avick?"

"By the Devil's Grip," replied Lanty, seizing and grasping his shillelagh, "and perhaps some of the murthering McDonnells there, too," and he rushed out into the open air and the wild storm.

There was a fierce shout, and the rest were after him with the fleetness of hounds.

Scarcely had they crossed the field that branched off to the lands and the castle of Sir Edward Stanley, when they were struck with wonder and amazement at the flashing of torches, and then came sweeping up the road a body of men, followed by the carriage with a few horsemen, the guests at the castle.

On they went, at as rapid a pace as the road and storm would allow them.

As they ran swiftly along, Lanty gathered from one of the men that Bell Stanley had ridden out to relieve some poor cottagers, and that the horse she had ridden had come galloping home bathed in foam, and that scarcely had it reached the stables when it gave a shrill cry and dropped dead, and the "misses—God be wid her—had been killed intirely—strick dead, p'raps, wid the lightning."

Lanty gave a heavy groan when he heard that, for he thought perhaps the same fate had fallen upon his master.

"Och, murder, why did I let him go? I'll be in sackcloth and ashes all my life," he said.

Here they were joined by Mike, the "fighting tailor," who having heard the McDonnells were upon them, had caught up the first thing at hand. At any other time his appearance would have excited shouts of laughter, for he had jumped off the board, and with only the red waistcoat and corduroys on, had started off with only his stocking feet. Nevertheless he kept good pace with Lanty, shouting and waving the sleeve-board instead of the never-failing shillelagh which Biddy had hid in the thatch, but which Mike threatened to make her *acquainted* with the next time he laid finger and thumb on it.

The joy and rapture of the "boys" at again finding their own "Frolic" with all his bones whole, we have already described, and during the evening, while the "bit and sup" were going round, loud were the expressions of happiness at the fact that the young master was in safety.

He had soon shifted his wet garments, and shaken off all the ill effects likely to occur from them. But the singular manner with which Sir Edward Stanley had treated him he could not forget.

To his guests he related his adventure, suppressing that portion of it. The evening passed cheerfully, and with many a hearty laugh at Lanty Shan's "intended ruse."

In the kitchen the "boys" dropped off by ones and twos as the night came on, leaving Lanty, Tim and Mike seated round the hearth.

"What on arth did that 'shoneen' mane

by threat'ning the master in that way, Lanty?" asked Tim.

"If you wish me to kape my sinses, don't puzzle me," was the reply; "it will all come right in the long run, as the first horse said to the last when the race was over; mortal man can't stop what is to be. Ain't you going to be jogging, Mike, ma bouchal; not that I'd hurry the mother's son of yer. Biddy will be uncommonly anxious about you, Mike," and he winked his eye at Tim.

"She'll be thinking you've been at another steeple-chase, Mike," said Tim.

"Mike would have won that same thing if it hadn't a been for the ditch," said Lanty.

"To the ould one I pitch Biddy, the ditch, and the lot of yer. What's your hurry, ma bouchal?"

"Oh, no hurry; stop as long as you're welcome," said Lanty. "I'd be sorry to be the first to say go."

"There's a nice bit of fire left yet, and it ud be a pity to let it be all by itself; it's warm and comfortable, and the one side's dry and comfortable."

"Well, then, turn round, and dry the other."

"Then sure," replied Mike, with a grin, "I'll do that same thing, that is with your permission."

"Well, *bannath lath*,* Mike," said Tim Doolan going out.

"And *bannath lath* to you, and many of them; and now I'll finish the drying meself," and with that Mike threw himself at full length before the fire to get thoroughly dry outside.

"That's mighty clever, Mike; and you'll get a good dry and a slape, and go home to Biddy right and comfortable," and Lanty took down a lantern, and lighted the candle; "and, then, *ma bouchal*,† yer can pull the door after yer."

And, so saying, Lanty left the kitchen, pulling the door after him.

Whether the fire had any effect upon him or not, Mike lay perfectly still for full five minutes; he then lifted up his head and looked about him.

"So, you're coming your kimmeens‡ over me, are yer? What the divil's all this, I wonder? Surely they ain't private stilling? If they are it's a burning shame, bekase I know a drop of the stuff with here and there one. I'll find out this

---

* Good-night.   † My boy.   ‡ Sly tricks.

MIKE HUNG SUSPENDED LIKE MAHOMET'S COFFIN.

mighty sacret, or Mike don't know a shil-lelagh from a slave-board."

And, with that, he took up that very useful instrument of his trade, and was making for the door, when the fire fell in, and left the room almost in darkness.

"What made that go in, I wonder?" said Mike. "I'll niver get to the door, plase the saints. It was there, or there-abouts, I know," and, with that, he made for it in the direction he thought it was in.

Mike was right so far, but forgot that a heavy chair stood in the way, and, of course, over that rolled Mike, sleeve-board and all.

"Powerful bad luck to yer! I've broken my shin over yer great, ugly car-cass, and it's me nose that's a bleeding strongly; it's all owing to you, Mr. Lanty Shan, and——"

Here his head came in desperate con-tact with the door.

"I'll not be sorry when I get out of this," and, with that, he flung the door open.

He looked round, and through the chinks of the stable saw the glimmer of a light.

"The thaves of the world are in there," he said, "consarting high trayson, or some other light affair," and, with that, he walked cautiously along to the stables.

"I'll find it all out, or my name ain't Mike. Well, well, we are clever, any-how," and he walked round and round, trying to find out a convenient place where he could hear all and yet not be seen.

Tim and Lanty were inside, seated round a barrel turned upside down, and upon which Lanty had placed a bottle containing a trifling drop of the craythur.

Lanty had locked the door, and the place was entirely free from intruders.

"I think this place, ma bouchal, is snug and comfortable for our 'cabinet council;' take a drop, Tim, before I begin."

"Wid all my heart; it's fine stuff to cement a friendship," and Tim took a very fair pull at the bottle, and handed it over to Lanty.

"*Cead mille failthe** to you, agra," re-plied Lanty," and he followed Tim's ex-ample, and held the bottle in his hand. "I think you can kape a secret, Tim?"

"If it was yourself being under the hands of the *skibbeah*† no one would be the wiser," said Tim.

"It's about the masther I am about spaking. You know I am his foster-bro-ther, and how intirely my heart is wid him and all that concarns him, and if grief came to him it would also come to me?"

"I know all dat; it's the truth," said Tim. "You'll hould as tight to him as the fist of yours houlds on to the bottle."

Lanty put the bottle down.

"I am afraid the masther's got into trouble."

"Well, then, we must get him out, Lanty. What's that?"

And Tim looked frightened.

"What's what? What's come over you? Your face looks as if it had been washed in the blood of a turnip. What ails yer, Tim?"

"Nothing; it's only my fancy. Do you see or hear anything?"

"Nothing, sure."

And Lanty held up the lantern.

"Take a drop; that will drive away your fancy."

Tim acted upon the advice in an in-stant.

"Now, then, I was just saying——"

"That's a mighty quare noise," said Tim. "It's like a scratching."

"Hould your whist. I've locked the door, and not a soul can get in."

At that moment a quantity of decayed thatch came falling into the stable; then a head and shoulders followed, and then a body came rolling through; but, in fall-ing, a large hook that had been used to hang a lantern upon, caught the intruder by the waistband of his smalls, and there he hung suspended like Mahomet's coffin.

"Bad luck to yer, Mike, what did yer come in that way for?" shouted Lanty.

"And, bad luck to you, what did you lock the door for?" was the reply, as the sleeve-board came flying among them.

"Arrah Lanty and Tim, you thaves of the world, don't let me be hanging up here like an iligant kite. Help me down, I say," shouted Mike, "or I'll be breaking the neck of me!"

"Wid all my heart. What do yer mane by breaking the masther's roof in that fashion for, eh?" said Lanty.

"Laving out the fright yer gave me, Masther Mike," joined in Tim.

"Well, good-night, Mike, and pleasant drames to yer. I'll send word to Biddy, and say that you are snug and comfort-able.

---

* A hundred thousand welcomes.   † The hangman.

And Lanty, taking up the light, winked his eye at Tim and went towards the door.

"Lanty Shan and Tim agrah, yer don't mane to say that yer going to lave me here to slape the whole night. Get me down, and, on the word of a jontleman, I'll stand a noggin apiece, and——"

Here the further offer, whatever it might have been, was cut short by an accident.

Mike had been struggling and whirling about the whole time, for the point of the hook by which he was suspended at times tickled him a little, and added still further to the unpleasantness of his situation.

He hung, too, by a slender piece of his waist-band, and it was just as he was about adding a "triffle" of something to the two noggins, that the slender material gave way, and, with a loud shout, Mike came tumbling down into a heap of straw and hay, which pretty nigh smothered him.

"Och, murther! I am clane kilt and dead! Ochone! Oh, Biddy, Biddy, acushla machree! Where are yer?"

The next moment, by the aid of Lanty and Tim, he was placed upon his legs.

"It's to be hoped that you'll think twice before you'll act once, and disturb two jontlemen, who want to talk over matters of deep importance, Mike Murphy!" said Lanty.

But Mike was busy applying the bottle containing a small drop of the craythur to his mouth.

"Why, you great big *omadhaun*, what do you mane by drinking up the craythur in that unsamely fashion, eh?" said Lanty, snatching the bottle from him.

"Ah! Hark to that, now. Why there wasn't enough to drown a fly let alone satisfy an honest man's thirst," replied Mike, laughing.

"Fill the bottle, and then let's to business. Will you promise, Mike, not to say a word about the matter to a living sowl? Can we trust him, Tim?"

And the pair whispered together.

"Whispering and colloging together ain't very purlite, anyhow," said Mike; "but I'll promise on the 'Book,' if yer like, that I'll not say a word o' the matther to a living sowl or a *dead* un either, for the matter o' that."

"Well, then, we'll 'journ the 'Cabinet Council,' to the fireside, and all three con-

coct the measures for the safety of the house."

And so saying, Lanty led the way from the stables, and in a few minutes they were all again round a good turf fire and the "dhudeens" lighted.

"Mike," said Lanty, after a pause, "I'm hurt in my mind to say the masther—long life to his him!—is in trouble."

"The saints preserve us," said Mike. "What is it?"

"Officers," replied Lanty.

"Are they coming here?" asked Mike.

"That's onknown; maybe or maybe not, but we won't let him or any of his *friends* be taken, will we?"

"Taken!" said Mike, crushing a bit of lighted turf into the bowl of his pipe; "taken where to?"

"The 'Stone Jug,' mayhap," was the answer.

"Not a bit on it. We'll first try the effect of the slave-board or anything that is handy on their heads, and then, if breaking them don't answer, why, then we'll smash the 'Jug' itself. Hurroo! long life to the 'Frolics,'" and the lively little tailor sprang up and began dancing a jig.

"Your sowl to rest, what do you mane? Give him one and make him quiet, Tim," shouted Lanty; "he'll alarm all the neighbourhood."

Tim Doolan made a snatch at Mike, and, failing to catch him, went rolling on the floor; but Lanty, more rapid in his movements, laid hold of Mike by the legs, which had the effect of bringing him on the broad of his back.

"Whist, ye skein of thread! Will ye be aisy, and not wake up the masther and——" here Lanty stopped. "By Jabez," he said, to himself, "I was near letting the cat out of the bag."

"I'll be as aisy as an ould coat," said Mike, "for the back of my head is as soft as butther," and Mike rose and quietly seated himself on the floor. "The next time I fall, I'll fall aisier, plase the pigs."

"Now, then, avick, listen. We must get the best men of the Frolics togedder and stop up the roads. There's yourself and Tim will do for two, Black Dan and Pandeen Flyn will stop up the others: and, as there are no more, the ould un may take the rest. I'll be gettin' an iligant tub of tar and feathers. There's an ould feather bed upstairs of no use bekase it's empty; and if any one on 'em should get into the house, he shall go out all feathers, like the giniral I once saw, and sure he was a *Cock* of the Walk. Yer understand, boys?"

"Sure we do," was the reply.

"Will, thin, ye'll niver desart the Frolics?"

"Sure, I'd desart Biddy, my own wife, fust, and the little gossoons—thirteen on 'em calling me father. I'll take the elder, Mike wid me—he's clever, by rason that he whacked his brother, Pat, the oder day nately wid a shillelagh, that it did one's eyes good to see."

"You'll not mintion a word, Tim?"

"The divil a bit—not even in any shape, by rayson that I'll kape wide awake," said Mike, with a knowing shake of the head.

"Well, then, to-morrow we'll commence, and it will go hard if any of those blaggards get near the house."

"I'll be standin' on my post by daylight," said Tim, "and not a sparrow shall pass me widout I know the rayson."

"Right you are, Tim; you're an honuor to the Frolics. And Mike?"

"Oh, lave Mike alone; I'll take the road that lades in a straight line round the corner to de castle, and bedad I'll go at ons't; there's a snug bit of grass in that same field, and I'll just lie down wid me eyes wide open, and pop upon the officers if they should come before they can say pase; I'll take the slave-board wid me. Have yer got any 'bacca, Lanty?"

"Sure, an' I have," pulling out hi box, "and yer ontirely welcome."

"It's mighty convanient when you have no time for breakfast, and sarves to wile away the time when you're thinking of nothing at all. So, good night, Lanty and Tim; yer may depind upon me."

"I know I may, *ma bouchal*, and the saints be wid us. We'll never see the Frolics fall. Good night." And, so saying, Lanty flung open the door.

"The Lord save us!" he said, starting back. "It's the blessed morning already."

"So much the better," said Tim; "it's come handy for the work."

And, placing his trusty shillelagh under his arm, Tim made for the place appointed for him.

Mike made the best of his way to the door, with the sleeve-board under his arm, and, for a time, every now and then a loud "Hurroo! Mike and the Frolics for ever!" might have been heard for some distance.

"Well," said Lanty, as he proceeded to make up the fire, "the 'cabinet council' will save the Frolics."

CHAPTER XII.

A DARK MEETING.

SIR EDWARD STANLEY had, when a young man, married a rich Irish heiress; her death bestowed upon him the splendid castle that had been named after him, in addition to the baronies and towns of Ballyran, Ballinafad, and Ballyduffin. A small portion of the town of Ballyran was the property of the Frolics, and the long range of land outside the park walls extending down to the sea shore was held by them, but was heavily mortgaged. This system of ruin was commenced by the grandfather of Fred; and Fred's sire, finding his position, as he thought, irretrievable, had plunged still deeper into the mire.

At the time that Edward Stanley married the rich heiress that conferred upon him so much wealth, Fred's father was travelling upon the Continent, leaving his estates in the towns we have mentioned, besides valuable property in Dublin, in the hands of trustees, and what has been generally known as putting "the sick child out to nurse."

A few months after the marriage, Sir Edward Stanley and his bride left for England; the castle was shut up, and only inhabited by a few domestics.

The estates were placed in the charge of an agent, who, with a rapacity not sanctioned by the owner, exacted heavy rents, despite bad crops and other natural causes; and so things went on, and the landlord's name was only mentioned in terms of execration and hate.

Then came the news that the Squire Frolic had married and was returning come to his native country, bringing his bride with him.

Old men and women shook their heads in doubt, and, with incredulous shrugs of the shoulders, asked when the skies would fall so that birds would be cheap in the market.

But the Frolics did return home, and great were the rejoicings. Bonfires were lighted, and all around the place for miles the greatest joy and merriment was shown, for the Frolics were well known and esteemed from one side of the Green Isle to the other.

The Frolic money went out much faster than it came in. A pack of hounds, and the expenses attending them, swelled up the balance on the wrong side; and when a young Frolic opened his sweet eyes upon the world, there was as much rejoicing as if a prince was born.

Born to good luck is all very well, if the luck will only last; and the silver spoon in the mouth is very neat and proper so long as the spoon is kept in the family plate chest; but when once it leaves, it is an age, perhaps, before it returns.

The health of Fred's mother was of such a delicate and fragile nature, that the heir of the Frolics was given to the care of Biddy Shan, and so, "Lanty with the long legs," the son of a turf cutter, drew the stem of life from the same fount as the heir to the turf himself.

They grew up together, and the young squire and his foster-brother became the most daring and adventurous boys for miles round. No sport came amiss to them, and in wrestling, leaping, hunting, shooting, and running, Fred and Lanty stood at the head of the list.

Then suddenly the great lady of the Castle arrived there with her only child, a girl, with the real type of Irish beauty, like her mother.

Lady Stanley came unattended by her husband, to seek health from the air of her own native mountains; and so in the course of time the two children became inseparable companions in their walks and rides, and on their ponies took the most daring leaps in the chase, to the great delight of Old Phil, the huntsman.

But a sunshine so glorious as this was not fated to last long.

First Fred lost his mother, and the whole place was plunged into gloom and despair.

This event drove the bereaved husband into still greater excesses and trouble, and the motherless boy could only find relief in the society of Bell Stanley and her mother, with whom Fred was an especial favourite; and so, in the midst of his dark gloom at home, there was always a gleam of joy for him at the Castle.

But that slight glimpse of happiness was soon fated to be dispelled.

The illness of Lady Stanley became of so serious a nature that she was ordered to seek some more genial climate, and the south of France having been selected by her medical advisers, Fred and Bell were doomed to part, and not to meet again until the day when Fred won the cup at the Ballinafad steeple-chase.

The sudden and unexpected meeting, and the subsequent events, awoke in Fred's breast the long-slumbering passion that had so long lain dormant; and when his guests had retired to their rest on the evening of that day that had witnessed Bell's eventful escape from the Devil's Grip, Fred sat alone in his mother's room to think and ponder over the past, and to conjure up and draw pictures of smiling hope for the future.

"I wish Righton would come over, and let me go into these fearful accounts, so that I might know the worst at once. At present I am in the dark, and without helm or compass to steer by, The little I have by me now can't last for ever, and if I did justice, and put the old house in order, it would be swallowed up entirely."

And then he sank into a reverie, and that not of the most pleasing nature.

"It's preposterous to think of it," he said, starting up. "Ha, ha, ha! Marry a girl, and bring her home to a place with the roof half off. Why, the most desperate, despicable fortune-hunter would hardly do that, and, hang me, if Fred Frolic shall have that character tacked to his name! No, no! Fred, my boy, the world is a large cake, and industry and perseverance must get a slice of it, if they try for it; so I'll see Bell to-morrow, tell her my mad passion, make the best of my way to that land of gold and glory, the Indies, and see what luck an Irishman will tumble into. And then again, her father. What ails him? If any other man had done what he did, in snatching that girl from me, by the powers, I'd have seen how much earth the length of his body would have covered."

Here he flung himself upon the sofa, and burst into a loud laugh.

"I suppose it's all owing to my being the owner of this *illigant* mansion, and—well, never mind, my boy, you never did a dirty action yet, and——"

Here the coy goddess shut up the senses of Fred Frolic for a time, and Queen Mab took possession of him, and blessed him with those happy, happy moments of bliss—golden dreams.

At the first break of day, Fred awoke from his blissful slumber, and sprang up.

It was a glorious morning, and Fred, feeling thoroughly refreshed, with his short but happy sleep, threw up the window to inhale those fresh breezes so conducive to health, and felt new life as the warm sunbeams fell upon him.

The first person he saw was Lanty, walking up and down in the front of the house, the dhudeen sending out wreaths of smoke, his long frieze coat buttoned up to his throat, and his *caubeen** stuck jauntily on the side of his head.

"Why, Lanty, ma bouchal, what are you doing there?" asked Fred.

"Ah, *mavourneen*†, and is it yourself? The top of the morning to you, masther," was the reply, as he doffed the caubeen. "What am I doing? I am looking for *them*."

And he gave Fred a sly wink of the eye.

"Looking for them! What do you mean?"

"What do I mane! Whist! Yer knows well what I mane; but we don't want all the world to know it. You know what I mane."

And Lanty gave a searching look all round him.

Fred gave a loud laugh, for he remembered all about the officers now.

"What, have you been watching all night?"

"Sorra the bit. We had mightier business to transact. The Cabinet Council did not break up till daylight."

"The what! What on earth do you mean?"

"My maning is as clear as the Hill of Howth—and that's no swearing—in a fog. Lanty Shan won't give half a chance away, so don't bother me, masther."

"Stop until I come down, Lanty," said Fred.

"Oh, faiks! I'm not going to budge an inch, that you may swear to."

And again Lanty resumed his march, keeping a sharp look-out on every side of him.

"Ne'er an officer gets in here wid a whole skin," he muttered.

"What have you been up to, eh, Lanty?" asked Fred, who had joined him.

"I'll make bould to answer one question by axing another. What have you been up to up there?"

And Lanty pointed his thumb over his shoulder in the direction of the Castle.

"What do you mean, sir?" said Fred, sternly.

"Oh, murther! don't frighten a man out of his sinses; it's meself would give all he's got in the wide world—and for that rayson it ain't much—to know what you've been doing to the *shanduine** up there."

"What, Sir Edward?"

"Guess agin, and you'll be wrong. He looked in a powerful rage when he took the girl out of your arms. There's many a man would have kissed the earth for that same thing—whoo!" and round went the shillelagh.

"I am as much astonished at it as you are yourself, Lanty; but I mean to-day to seek an explanation."

"That's only proper and just; and I suppose you'll be going up to the Castle for that same purpose?"

"Yes, and that as soon as I have had breakfast. You'll say nothing of this to my friends, Lanty?"

"Not a whisper. Bedad, I think they have got enough on their own hands. The ould woman and Little Phil are getting the breakfast ready. Masther, dear, yer'll just answer me a trifling question?" and with that Lanty crept closer to him. "Is it a murder he's been doing?"

"No, Lanty," replied Fred, with a laugh. "He's run away with a rich heiress—a ward in chancery."

Lanty looked earnestly at his master for a moment.

"I'll be glad to know the maning of that, sir. Is it a new name for shape stealing? Can they hang him for it?"

"No," and Fred laughed. "Not so bad as that."

"Well, then, if it's not a hanging matter, why need he care? More power to his elbow! If he's run away wid a pretty girl wid plenty of shiners in de stocking, it's meself would make one in dat party."

"Well, who knows, you may have luck some day. Lanty, do you ever remember my father saying anything about the Stanley family?"

"Sorra a bit; your father was not a man that talked much; he was as proud as the div—manners, Lanty—no, sir, ne'er a word did I ever hear him say for or against them."

"Very well; while I am away you will attend to my friends, and see they want for nothing. You'll want some money, Lanty?"

"Ne'er a haporth. Whoo, money! we've lashins of it! I've got lots of things—a kitchen full. I am laying in in case of a sage."

"A what?"

"A sage. Who knows but there may be *two* sets of officers?"

"Two sets of officers! What do you mean?"

"Mane! Faiks, there may be *one* set come for him, and anoder for somebody else that shall be nameless. I haven't forgotten Mr. Phalim Fitzpatrick Fogharty, bad luck to him."

"Well done, Lanty; you are determined not to be taken by surprise. Ha, ha, ha! I'll leave all to you," and Fred went towards the house.

"You can't do better, sir; they'll find I'm up to a ruse, I think you call it, as well as most folks; altho' I havn't been to furrin parts, it's aisy to learn them sort of things in this country."

"I believe you, Lanty, and in none better."

And, so saying, Fred entered the house.

"By the powers, I think I've got my hands full; as Biddy said when she carried Mike home on her back, 'There's more licker than love here,' says she. What'll I do? First there's the masther to look after, bekase them McDonnells will be makin' it all right wid the great man up there. Bedad, it takes a man all his time to settle other people's business. I'll send for Biddy Murphy; she's worth half-a-dozen men when her blood's up. I'll send Little Phil on that same errand. It's a lucky thought, Lanty Shan."

"It's meself that's glad to see you,

Lanty Shan, this fine morning," said a voice.

Lanty started back at the sound of it.

"Talk of the——It's meself glad to see the likes of you, Mrs. Biddy Murphy," was the reply.

"Have you seen Mike, Lanty?" and her right hand seemed to be grasping something tightly under her cloak.

"Yes, mavourneen; Mike has been helping me Biddy."

"Helping you! Come none of your *kimmeens*, Lanty Shan, over a poor woman."

"Upon the word of a man, Biddy. Whisht, darling, whisper; we're in trouble."

"In trouble! Have they killed Mike?"

"No. Mike is safe and sound. It's the masther—but, you'll not tell?"

"Ne're a word shall pass my tongue."

"You're a jewel of a woman if you can kape a *still* tongue. But, what have you got under your cloak?"

"Only Mike's shillelagh," she said, with a sly grin. "I thought *he might want it*," and she gave it a twist.

"Oh, you're an iligant woman. Come this way, Biddy, come this way. Oh, you're a darling! A dish of buttermilk and praties will do you good after your walk, mavourneen."

And, so saying, Lanty lead her round the house and from thence into the kitchen.

After Fred had breakfasted and written a letter to Mr. Righton, he dressed, and started off to seek Sir Edward Stanley, to ask an explanation of his extraordinary conduct towards him

Fred walked along without meeting anyone, except now and then a peasant, who gave his usual friendly greeting of "God save you and be wid you, sir," which kindly salutation was heartily returned by Fred; but as he neared the gate leading to the plantation, a man whom he knew to be a McDonnellite scowled at him, and refused to respond to the kind wish and greeting Fred gave him.

This was so common an occurrence that Fred smiled at it and passed on.

After walking some distance, he turned off into a broad, gravelled path, and could see in the distance the noble mansion and the lake, upon whose peaceful surface he and Bell had passed many a happy hour together.

For a moment he stood gazing upon it, and, with a sigh, turned from it, and was passing through another part of the plantation deep in thoughts of the past, when suddenly a voice called upon him to stop.

He looked up, and there before him stood Sir Edward Stanley, the man he had come to meet.

It was a dark and gloomy spot, with old, mournful, waving trees around it; and at the back, four large trees had so grown up together, that they seemed as one.

"May I ask, sir, by what right you intrude yourself upon my property?" was the haughty salutation of the baronet. "Perhaps I am wrong in asking it?"

"You are perfectly right in asking it, and I will frankly answer the question, Sir Edward. I came to seek you."

"Indeed! and for what purpose?"

"Frankly to ask an explanation of you."

"A what, sir! an explanation!"

"Yes. It is the usual course pursued, I believe, between gentlemen."

"Ha, ha, ha! gentlemen!" and the contemptuous tone with which he spoke brought the hot blood with a rush into Fred's face. "When I am asked for any explanation of my conduct by a gentleman, I shall certainly give it," and folding his arms, the baronet looked at him with the greatest scorn and contempt.

"Is this meant as an insult, Sir Edward?" asked Fred, warmly.

"Just as you please—yes," replied Sir Edward; "leave the place."

And raising his arm with his clenched fist, he seemed as though he would fell Fred to the ground.

Had either of them glanced round at that moment, and looked narrowly where the trees stood, they would have perceived a girl, pale and trembling, looking with a deep and fearful anxiety upon the two men, who, standing face to face, seemed as though they were on the point of engaging in a mortal conflict.

"Leave this place, sir, and that on the instant, or I shall proceed to very harsh measures," said Sir Edward.

"And I shall be prepared to resist them," was the cool, determined reply. "How dare you treat me with this contumely?" and Fred stood firmly. "You insulted, grossly insulted me yesterday, although I was the humble means of restoring to your arms your only child."

"And which child, I suppose, you came to ask as a reward for your super-human courage. How well and how craftily those plans have been laid! Thanks to a friendly communication, I have been well prepared for it."

"He is a base and cowardly calumniator who has so informed you. I demand his name."

"You'll not have it."

"Then if you refuse it, you will not feel offended if I doubt the friendly communication."

"Well, for a penniless adventurer, the son of a bankrupt spendthrift, you are the finest specimen of the class I have ever seen. Return home to that ruin that, bad as it is, shall not shelter you for long. Now, will that explanation satisfy you?"

The mental suffering that Fred underwent during all this time was something fearful, but the thought of Bell came like a guardian angel to him, and he speedily rallied his energies, and in an instant his hands became unclenched, and his face resumed its usual expression of frankness and good humour.

"I shall take another opportunity, and that in public, to ask you to repeat the degrading terms you have heaped on me and on the memory of one who is no more; in the face of assembled hundreds you shall retract the shameful and insulting terms you have this day applied to me; until then——"

"Enough, enough, sir! You will take this home with you; if you have the faintest idea of any union between yourself and my daughter, banish it. There is a gulf between you that never can be passed over; and now, sir, as quickly as you can, leave this spot never to enter it again, and take with you the explanation, which, as you sought it, I sincerely hope will delight you."

And with that, Sir Edward, with a haughty curl of his lip, turned his back upon Fred, and, striking into another path, was lost to sight.

Transfixed to the earth at what he had heard, Fred Frolic felt as though life had departed from him; his every sense felt numbed and dead, his hands fell listless by his side, and he would have fallen had he not tottered to the trees and leaned against them.

Then it was that he felt the warm pressure of a hand grasping his, and a whispering voice.

"Courage, Fred. Has he gone?" said the voice.

"You here, Bell? Have you listened to this?" said Fred, faintly,

"Yes," and the next moment Bell Stanley was by his side.

"Know you any cause for his vituperation of me, Bell?"

"None," she replied, energetically. "Although he is my father, I do not believe there is the shadow of a foundation in truth for what he has been saying. Treat them as the idle wind."

"But, I cannot live under this foul aspersion. What have I to live for?" he said, desponding.

"Much; to be happy, and to confer happiness upon others," she replied, gaily.

"Ah, Bell, my hopes were bright as a summer's sun when I rose this morning."

"Well, and why cannot they be as bright when the *evening star* brings on the night, and with its light bids us hope for a brilliant morrow. Call yourself a man and an Irishman! After this I shall have very serious thoughts of McDonnell."

"By Heaven, I'd murder him first," said Fred, the old blood running free again through his veins.

"Ah, just like you men, either all ice or all fire. Why should you murder the man?"

"I'd shoot any man who would dare aspire to your hand, Bell."

"You have allotted yourself a difficult task, Mr. Frolic; but I can't see what reason you have for wasting so much powder and shot. Whom am I to have? I suppose I may have *somebody?*"

"Oh, Bell, until now I had hopes——"

"Well, and who has driven hope away? I am sure I have not."

"Bell!"

And Fred seized her hand.

"There, that will do. I have Irish blood in my veins, and am not easily daunted."

She took a small ring off her finger, having in the centre a single emerald.

"Take that, Fred. The stone is the emblem of our glorious country. Read well the motto engraven inside, and whatever may betide us, let it be the pass-word between us—'Courage and hope!'"

He felt a slight pressure of the hand, and she was gone.

There was the motto in the ring.

"Courage and Hope!" he read, and kissing it fervently, left the spot.

He did not perceive that, as he passed, he was dogged by the man who had scowled at him as he entered the park.

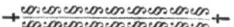

CHAPTER XIII.

A TIMELY RESCUE, AND FOGHARTY'S VISIT.

FRED FROLIC walked slowly through the plantation, and gaining the gate that led to the high road, stood leaning upon it for a moment.

He kissed the ring with fervour, and gazed upon it until the tears rose in his eyes.

"Courage and hope," he murmured. "Aye, by Heaven, I will have both, dear, dear Bell; for you I will win fame and fortune; for what man confiding in courage and hope ever failed yet? but for all that I must get at the mystery that seems to be connected with the baronet and my poor father; perhaps Righton can clear it up, and in a day or so he will be here."

He walked on rapidly, and gained the cross-roads.

At that moment he heard a loud shout, and, starting back at the sound, saw to his amazement a man standing at each road, armed with a formidable shillelagh.

They were ferocious-looking villains, and the worst belonging to the McDonnell faction.

He thrust his hand into his breast pocket, in the hope that his pistols were there, but found, to his great vexation, they had been left at home.

But not for one moment did his courage sink.

Placing his back against the old finger-post he calmly surveyed them.

"By the sowl of your father," said one of them, by name Jack McGrath, "it's meself that's glad to see the likes of you."

And the others set up a laugh of derision, pointing their fingers at him, and flourishing their shillelaghs.

"Well," said Fred, coolly, "*now* you *do* see me, what's your business, eh?"

"You'll soon know that," replied Mc-Grath, "and when you *know* the bisness it will be best for you to arrange it dacently," and the villain leered at the others.

"Indeed. And supposing I don't choose to settle it to your liking, what then?" replied Fred.

"What then? Why, then, it's a bating you'll get until you do."

"Well, that's pleasant," said Fred, with a smile of contempt, "and only *four* to one. But, I may as well hear what the business is. So begin."

"You take it mighty cool," said the ruffian.

"It's my habit to do so; but, I think this is about as *cool* a piece of business as I have seen for some time. Go on, ruffians."

"Civil words, bad luck to yer; you're not out of the wood yet. You've had the best of it for some time."

"Indeed. Well, what of that? I don't intend to give up my good luck. Go on."

Leaning against the post, so that they could not get behind him, Fred crossed his legs, and, folding his arms, surveyed the group with the greatest nonchalance.

"By my sowl, he don't seem a bit frightened," said McGrath to the others.

"Frightened! Ha, ha, ha! that is a good idea. Frightened!" laughed Fred.

"Yes, frightened, bad luck to yer."

"What, at four *cowardly* fellows waylaying an unarmed man! Why, you're a disgrace to the wildest savages that ever lived. You can't be Irishmen."

"Ain't we; you'll soon find that out. Look yer, at the last fair you got that strip of land by foul play, and——"

"You lie, you ruffian! it was won by our having stouter hearts and arms, and having right, too, on our side; and now we *have* won it we mean to keep it."

"You'll have to give it up," said Mc-Grath.

"When, ma bouchal?"

"Now take out your pocket-book; I daresay a gentleman like you carries one —and write, 'That now and for ever and a day, you'll give it back to the McDonnells.'"

"Would you like it for a *longer* time?" replied Fred, with a sneer.

"If you don't, we have sworn upon the Book to bate it out of you."

"Have you? Then you'll perjure yourselves, you villains!" was the undaunted answer.

While this was going on, Fred had been casting his eyes around, and saw close to him on his right hand a tolerably thick hedge stake.

With a sudden bound he sprang upon it, and, by a desperate effort, tore it from the ground; it was rather heavy, but, in the present desperate emergency, it would serve to defend him.

This staggered the fellows a little, and they looked upon him with something like wonder.

"We don't want to hurt you?" said McGrath.

"I'll take good care you don't. Mind I don't do that same thing for you, you cowardly spalpeens."

This was too much for one of the villains.

He sprang forward, aiming a desperate blow at Fred's head, which, had it taken effect, would have settled the question of the "strip of land" for ever.

But the brave young fellow jumped lightly aside, and the blow intended for him fell harmless. The next moment a crashing blow from the stake descended upon the face of his assailant, and, with a scream of agony, he sprang up a foot or two from the ground, and fell, covered with blood, upon it.

"That's *one*," said Fred. "Now who is the next?"

"I am," shouted the infuriated Mc-Grath, rushing at him.

"By my sowl, yer right," shouted Lanty, springing over the hedge, his long legs flying in the air, and down went McGrath as though he had been shot.

Over came the fighting tailor, Mike, with the sleeve-board, and after him a man with an old caubeen and a long frieze coat on.

"To the ould un I pitch yer! Whoo!" shouted Mike, dealing the man a whack with the sleeve-board, which sent his shillelagh flying in a hundred pieces.

Then the two discomfited ruffians took to their legs over the field, pursued by Mike, flourishing the emblem of his calling.

"Sure, masther, dear, now you'll be putting me in a passion. What makes yer go out widout something to defend yourself wid? You'll come home some day kilt, and say you were sorry for it."

"Lanty is perfectly right, Fred," said the man in the old hat and long coat.

"And pray who are you, sir," said Fred, haughtily, "that interferes, eh?"

"Ha, ha! Capital!" laughed the person addressed. "This is what Lanty calls a 'ruse,'" and taking off the *caubeen*, disclosed the laughing, handsome features of Frank Hardy.

The two friends shook hands warmly with each other, while Lanty was busy inspecting the faces of the men who lay upon the ground, senseless.

"More power to you, Lanty Shan, my friend," he said; "and so it's you, Jack McGrath, anyhow. I think yer got a rap that will kape you studying the Multiplication Table for a week, at laste. Why don't yer wake up, yer blackguard!" and he gave him a gentle reminder with his shillelagh. "And who are you?" he said, turning over the one whom Fred had levelled on to his back. "Tim Mullins, by all that's holy! Oh, the thafe of the world! By the powers, the good woman that owns you won't know that iligant phisog again! Get up, you baste!" and Lanty treated him to the same dose that he had given McGrath. "Here, avick! Come here, and help me drag these bastes to that iligant pond. We'll throw them in, and the could wather will bring 'em to."

Lanty and Mike pulled them to the edge of the pond, and then dipping their *caubeens* in, plentifully smothered them with the dirty pond water.

"Now, masther, and you, sir, you'll just be making your way home. The vagabonds that have escaped will bring down more McDonnells than will be pleasant."

"But you won't leave the men to die there, will you?" said Frank.

"Die! whoo! They know a trick worth two of that. We'll lave them *to dry.* Die, what of?"

"Why, both blows are very severe."

"Severe; they've had many worse, and they're used to it. They're no Irishmen if they can't take a bigger bating than that widout dying. Come along, Mike; I think they're pretty well served up, ma bouchal."

"I'm wid you," was the reply, "for my throat is as dry as tinder."

"No doubt," said Lanty; "it's the driest throat I ever knew in my life. Come along, man; the masther and his friend are a long way off," and Lanty put his long legs in motion.

"But who is the friend, Lanty, avick?" said Mike, running alongside of him.

"Don't ax questions, Mike, or I'll not believe that your troat is quite so dry as you say."

"This will be a purty day's work; by taking you away from the place, bedad, p'raps the officers are down upon us."

"What will we do, then?" asked Mike.

"Return the compliment, and be down upon them," said Lanty, giving the shillelagh a flourish. "There is no harm in that, and the sooner we get home the better," and they started off at an increased speed.

Fred and his friend had struck off into another route, in order to converse more freely together.

Lanty and Mike, therefore, made the best of their way home by themselves.

As they turned into the open road, leading up to the house, they heard the shrill tones of a woman's voice.

"That's Biddy's voice, Mike," said Lanty.

"Tell me news, if you plase," muttered Mike. "What brings her here?" and he took a firmer grasp of the formidable sleeve-board. "There's a something going wrong, or she wouldn't be here to the fore."

"Whisht! kape dark now, and we'll know what it is."

And Lanty moved forward, and peeped round the corner of the wall where the gates formerly stood.

"Och, murder!" he said. "It's Fogharty and two of his men, bad luck to them! Oh, what'll I do?"

"Do! be down upon em," said Mike, with a twirl of the sleeve-board.

"Be aisy, and let's hear fust," and the two stood listening.

"I tell yer, Lawyer Fogharty, there's ne'er a sowl at home."

"Well, then, let me in," said the lawyer, "and I'll wait."

"It's clane against orders, or I would. It ain't likely I'd kape a jontleman—and a kind-hearted one, the Lord save us!—a standin' out there. I know manners better."

"I mean no harm," woman, said Fogharty.

"LEAVE THIS PLACE, SIR," SAID SIR EDWARD.

"And who said you did? Harm!" she said, in her shrillest tones, "who ever knew the likes of you do harm? Haven't you more than once taken away the bits of sticks to save us the expinse of moving them ourselves? Harm! Ould Nick may have the man that——"

"Well, then, let me in, woman, or I'll break in," and the lawyer kicked against the door.

"Don't do that, Mr. Fogharty, bekase I'd be unwilling to harm you. But I'm only a lone woman by myself in the house, and I don't know what your intentions may be, and I'm bound to defind myself. I've got the natest double-barrelled gun here, and three brace of pistols, and if any one on 'em should go off incidentally on purpose, you'll not blame me; if you don't belave me, they say seeing is belaving."

And at that moment the barrel of the gun came peeping out of one of the places where the window might have been.

"The Lord save us!" roared the little lawyer, making a hasty retreat. "Would you commit murder, woman?"

"I'd be sorry to do that, but in case one of them went off permiscous like, it can't be laid at my door. I know the law; it's no murder, it's accidental homicide."

"Let's get round by the back way, Mr. Fogharty," said one of the men.

"There is only one way you'll go, and it's that," said Lanty springing at him, and, seizing him by the collar, he swung him with such force, that, reeling against the poor weak pony that Fogharty rode, away he sent Fogharty, man and beast into the mud.

Meanwhile Mike rushed at the other with the sleeve-board, and the man, not used to these matters, uttered a cry of terror, and started off at his utmost speed across the fields.

"I beg a thousand pardins, Mr. Fogharty," said Lanty, helping him up with much politeness.

While he was doing so, a strip of parchment fell out of the lawyer's pocket, which Lanty secured unobserved.

During this confusion, Biddy kept up a continual cry of,

"Shall I fire, Lanty, darling?"

"Not yet, my cushla; Mike's in the way."

"Batherashin! then here goes. Is Mr. Fogharty in the way? I'd be sorry to hurt him."

At this moment Fred and Frank entered the court-yard.

"What is all this disturbance about," asked the former. "Eh, Lanty?"

"There's no disturbance, anyhow, only Mr. Fogharty has been a-trying to break into the house, and, as I had put Biddy there as a century, if I hadn't come up Fogharty would have gone to glory or elsewhere."

"That's all, masther," chimed in Mike.

"Happy to see you at last, Mr. Frolic," said the lawyer, his keen grey eyes resting upon Frank for the moment. "But this is no place to discuss matters in; we will walk inside, and talk over the——"

"We shall do no such thing, Mr. Fogharty," replied Fred, firmly. "In all matters of business I refer you to Mr. Righton, my attorney."

"Ha—oh, indeed; but, in the meantime, I've just stepped over to serve you with this little bit of——"

Here the little pettifogger thrust his hand into one of his pockets, and drew it out hastily as though something had stung him; then he tried another, with equally the same result.

"Bless my soul, why, where the——oh, ah, there it is," and he picked up his pocket-book out of the mud. "Ah, here it is all right," and he untied the dirty piece of red tape by which it was fastened, and eagerly looked over its contents. "Where the deuce has it got to?" and his face had such a perplexed and dismayed look as set Mike and Lanty on the broad grin.

"Have you lost anything, Mr. Fogharty?" asked Lanty.

"Lost!" roared the discomfited lawyer; "yes, curse it; the very thing I came to serve. I've been robbed."

"Of what?" asked Fred.

"What of? A paper of importance, which I wanted you to read."

"A writ, I suppose," said Fred; "and so you have really lost it? Well, then, in that case I can only wish you——"

"What, sir, what, sir?" he said, in a blustering tone.

"A very pleasant ride back," and raising his hat with a hearty laugh, Fred walked into the house, followed by Frank. Biddy having opened the door, which she immediately closed again.

While this was going on, Mike had slyly busied himself in getting the pony outside of the place, and started it off at a gallop across the fields.

"Well, I am sorry for you Mr. Fogharty," said Lanty, "although I don't suppose you belave it," and he grinned at him full in the face.

"Believe it, you vagabond, no; but this I do believe, that you robbed me of the paper, and——"

Here his speech was cut short by Lanty inserting his left hand between the learned gentleman's throat and his neckerchief, and Mike, following the example, did the same to the bailiff, who stood shaking and shivering behind him.

"And so you mane by calling me a robber that I am a thafe, do you, you black keerogue* you!"

And Lanty shook him like a reed in the wind.

"And you are another," said Mike to the follower, giving him a shaking, with the addition of a whack from the sleeve-board.

"Let me go," said Fogharty, alarmed out of his life, for at this moment Tim Doolan, Billy Doyle, and others came in.

"Oh! I'll let you go, you ould scoundrel; and when I do, get out of this part of the country as fast as your dirty legs can carry you, or I wouldn't give a rap for your life, my bhoy, and let me whisper this to you; don't go into the town, for there is a body of women lying in wait for you, mothers from whom you have taken the very rags that they and their families slept on. Take the advice of Lanty Shan, go five miles round rather than face them," and Lanty sent him spinning from him.

Fogharty wanted no second warning, but rushed out of the place vowing vengeance, followed by his man, amid the contemptuous laughter and jeers of the "Fighting Frolics."

CHAPTER XIV.

THE STILL AT THE DEVIL'S GRIP—UNEXPECTED VISITORS.

OVER the gloomy valley, and the lofty hills in the far distance, the moon is shining with an unclouded brilliancy.

The scene was a lovely one for its peaceful stillness and its majestic beauty.

The only sound that broke in upon the quietude was the sullen dash of the waters upon the beach that opened into the mouth of the Devil's Grip. Close by the recess, which had so providentially sheltered Fred and Bell, sat three men in deep and earnest converse; between them burnt a turf fire, which gave them sufficient warmth, without sending forth any very strong reflection that might betray them.

The men seated there were McDonnell, Jan, and Black Murtough.

"The news is black enough," said McDonnell; "black as the heart of the absentee aristocrat who has caused all this stir, and who won't spare us. How did you gain the information?"

"Red-haired Pandeen, the Fox, brought us the news that the man up at the Castle was determined, with the aid of the government, to put a stop to our trade, and——"

"Sapperment! if he tries that game, I'll put a stop to him," growled Jan, and he drew a pistol from his belt; "and Jan never misses his man—blitzen!"

"That must only be done as a last resource. He is a great man with the lord lientenant, and an injury inflicted upon him will be severely punished. There are a thousand ways of punishing him besides taking his life."

"You're right, McDonnell, you are right," said Black Murtough. "Friend Jan, you are too fast."

"Well, I shall not care about that; I am all ready when the time comes for anything. I shall leave all to you; but you shall not forget that I have von large stake—sapperment, it is too large—in this business."

He rose from his seat.

"I shall go into the inner place and see how the thing shall work there. All I can say is that I am ready for this," and he placed his hand heavily on his pistol, "or anything else—blitzen!"

He staggered to the opposite side of

---

* Black beetle.

the cave to where they were sitting, and throwing open a door, revealed another cave.

A strong light flashed from it, and by it might be seen a dozen men, hard at work in illicit distillation.

A dense fume came rolling into the cave, but the next moment Murtough had sprung to his feet, and closing the door, securely fastened it.

"He won't disturb us any more this night," he said, "so we can finish our chat, for I must be among them, or everything will go wrong. What do you think of my plan, eh, McDonnell?"

"What, against that fellow, Frolic? I like it. Everything goes right for us there. The man that has bestowed so many *favours* upon me, shall not go unrewarded," and he smiled grimly, as he placed his finger on a scar upon his forehead. "He did that when we were but boys. That I have never forgotten, and it is not likely it will ever be forgiven. Anything to ruin him, and bring him to 'Gallows Green.'"

"Well, he's done the like favour for meself, and what his father did for mine won,t be aisily driven from me. It caused the old man's death, far from the place of his birth, and I swore that him and his should be paid for it. So there's my hand upon it, and he must be clever to bate the pair of us."

And he took a deep draught of spirits, and he handed the bottle to McDonnell.

"Besides," said the smuggler, Murtough, "he has got a bitter enemy in the Man at the Castle."

"Ah, how know you that?" McDonnell cried.

"Why, Jack McGrath overheard it all; and I tell you that we've got a friend up there as against him that's sartain, and, if we work the thing well, we'll make matters blacker than ever between them."

"We'll do that, Murty, we'll do that," said McDonnell rubbing his hands. "Leave me alone for keeping that fire burning; you'll see to what we have been talking with regard to the plan. Spread it well about. Who is the man that is living up there with Frolic? It's a new face."

"I don't know him. What's he like— a man?"

"Yes, a stranger in these parts."

"Indade. I'll soon find that out. I'll

put Mickey Doyle upon the watch; he is a ferret that can find out any rat. Lave it to me. Have you seen Fogharty lately?"

"No; he's to meet me two days from this in the county town," was the reply.

"He must come down with more money," said Murtough sullenly. "He holds too much of ours in his hands."

"That's true; but we can't well quarrel with him. We must be easy with him; if we angered him, he could sell us," was the reply.

"Could do what?" said Murtough. "*How long* would he live after that, eh? Or anybody that was colloging with him. It would be a black death for them," and he looked McDonnell fiercely in the face.

"And sarve them right," said the other. "Do you suspect anybody of doing that, because you had better let me know, that we may stop it."

"I may have my suspicions; and I am inclined to think that O'Fogharty plays fast and loose with us; he has not settled for the last cargo that went over, and——"

"Oh, that will be all right," and McDonnell rose. "Fogharty is long-winded but he's safe; but when I see him I'll bring him to a reckoning. You can depend upon me, Murty."

"Well, yes; you have that part of the bisness in your hands, and if the rascal Fogharty played us false, you would suffer as well as the rest."

"Of course I should. Well, goodnight; you'll carry out your plan about that accursed Frolic. He'll turn out a bitter thorn in our side if he's not stopped."

At the entrance of the cave they separated, McDonnell going along the beach, and keeping well under the rocks in the shade, until he came to a winding path that took him into the road.

Black Murtough stood with folded arms, with the moonbeams shining faintly upon him, until McDonnell had disappeared.

"He could sell us, could he?" he muttered. "Yes, but he wouldn't do it alone; there would be another hand in that dirty transaction. Whom do I suspect? Ah, well, you can depend upon me, Murty; oh, yes, by the devil's hoofs, as far as I can see you."

He walked back into the cave muttering, and then disappeared in the inner one, well fastening and securing it from the inside.

*   *   *   *   *   *

"Courage and hope" were the last words that Fred whispered when he sank to rest, and the first that passed his lips when he hailed the rising sun in the firmament; and he descended to the court-yard, to find Lanty there as usual, as sentry.

"Why, Lanty, ma bouchal, do you ever take any rest?" said Fred, kindly to him.

"Rest. Why, thin, I have more than I want. I slape as soundly on the flure by the turf fire as a prince in a feather bed, and what more can a man want? You are looking well this morning, masther," and poor Lanty's eyes appeared as if they were filling with water. "God save you, Fred Frolic, and may my eyes be closed in death before they see you look ill, or yours rendered dim by misfortune."

"Thank you, Lanty, my own faithful foster brother," said Fred, placing his arm on Lanty's shoulder. "Whenever misfortune comes, ma bouchal, it will only bind our fidelity to each other the more enduring."

Poor Lanty put his hand to his throat.

"Don't spake in that fashion, masther; don't, or I shall choke."

"Ne're a bit, Lanty; come rouse up."

"I am better now. I am plased you have come down, bekase I wanted to spake to you when no one can listen," and Lanty looked round, and having satisfied himself that no one was nigh, approached Fred. "Whisper," he said, "and come close."

Fred did so, laughing.

"Ye have heard, no doubt, in your time that there is a sartin bird that get's up so airly in the mornin' that he picks up the worm that must have been out all night. I say, you have heard all that?"

"Yes, Lanty; go on."

"Well, the bird has been out airly this blessed morning, and picked up the worm, and by rayson there is the blessed token."

And with a great deal of mystery, Lanty, diving his hand into his pocket, brought out a small note, which he handed to Fred.

In a moment it was torn open, and there he read the heart-inspiring words,

"Courage and Hope!"

He pressed the letter to his lips, while Lanty took several wild jumps in the air.

"Whoo! Whoo! Hurroo! Hurroo! The day's our own!"

And the never-failing shillelagh twirled about in the air.

Then off went his coat, and down it went on the ground.

"Put the end of your toe on that, ye dirty spalpeens! Not a mother's son of yer dare do it!"

And then the long legs danced a jig round it, the shillelagh keeping time to it.

"Lanty, are you mad?" cried Fred.

"Ne're a bit, but I'm clane out o' my sinses."

"Listen. I'll tell you good news."

"Out with it, masther. May it always be side by side wid us."

"I am going to put the house in order," replied Fred.

"Hurroo!—and the stables?"

"Yes."

"I knew it. Hurroo! whoo! Ireland for ever! Dance, me jewil, dance," and away went Lanty footing it again. "And whin will it commence, masther?" he said, stopping suddenly.

"Directly after I have seen Mr. Righton, and then, I think, we'll get rid of Mr. Fogharty."

"If you don't, I'll take that job off your hands. It was a lucky fall for us when he went on the ground, and that bit of parchment fell out of the blaggard's pocket. You see I was right about the two sets of officers; the next will be after the two young craythurs indoors."

"Well, we must do the best we can with them, Lanty; we won't give them up easily."

And Fred walked into the house, reading again the magic words that set Lanty into such a transport of joy and excitement.

"Give them up," muttered he, looking after Fred, and putting on his coat. "I don't think that's at all likely. The Fighting Frolics never give anything *up*; they are more in the habit of putting things *down*. And so everything is to be put to-rights, and the masther will get married, and——Whisht! now what are you about? We are going to have a hard day's work, to clean out the stables, and not a day before they want it. Ah, I see, there goes Tim and Mike to get the bit and the sup before they go to work.

Oh, Lanty, that ever you'd live to see the *old* house made into a *new* one."

And so, Lanty, with his honest heart full of the rising glories of the family he loved so much, went into the kitchen to try the excellence of the praties and the butter.

On the second day after these occurrences, the little barony of Ballyran was thrown into a state of commotion by the arrival of a small body of soldiers from the nearest barrack town, commanded by an officer.

They halted, and the officer, having inquired the nearest route to Frolic House, said that he should take a rest before marching for that place.

In less than a minute after that the "Fighting Tailor" was rattling over the fields, taking everything just as they came in the way.

Rushing into the house, he shouted out,

"Your sowls alive, the red coats are down upon us."

The consternation was extreme.

But all was prepared.

In less than a quarter of an hour, Frank, dressed as an Irish peasant, and his wife attired in a dress of the old woman's were seated round the turf fire in the kitchen, and, in less time than was anticipated, the officer and his men marched into the court-yard, followed by the whole population of Ballyran.

"Is the master of the house within?" asked the officer of Lanty.

"He is, sir, and will be glad to see you."

The officer, smiling, followed Lanty, four soldiers bringing up the rear, to the room where Fred was waiting for him.

"May I be favoured by knowing the object of your visit?" said Fred.

The officer politely handed him a paper.

Fred, taking it from the officer's hand, saw, with some surprise, a search-warrant.

"A search-warrant," said he, indignantly starting up. "What for?"

"Take it aisy, masther," whispered Lanty.

"My instructions are to search the mansion and premises attached to it. Of course you will offer no opposition."

"Opposition. It is not likely. But what have you come to search for?" said Fred, warmly. "Who is the person who has been the cause of this outrage upon me? I demand his name!"

"Your tone, Mr. Frolic," replied the officer, "is somewhat haughty, but, under the circumstances, excusable. I am not aware of the person's name who gave the information."

Here they were interrupted by loud cries from the court-yard, for there Tim Doolan and Mike were heading the rest of the "Fighting Frolics."

They had been informed that the red coats had come to take away the master.

"Down with 'em!" shouted the mob.

"Never mind their pop-guns!" shouted Mike.

"I'll stand fire from half-a-dozen of 'em, and not get my hair singed!" roared out Tim.

The women and children added to the wild scene, by the shrill cries and vociferations they made.

The officer told his men to stand by their arms, an order which, being promptly carried out, caused a clattering of the muskets, which was heard outside.

At this the cries were redoubled.

"There'll be blood spilt as sure as pase are not parsnips," said Lanty, to his master, "unless you spake to them."

"You are right, Lanty," and Fred advanced to the window.

At the sight of him, the "caubeens" went flying up in the air, and the shillelaghs twirled and clashed against each other, while the women took off their old shoes, and sent them up to join the "caubeens."

"The masther, the masther, good luck to him," was the cry. "We'll stand by you, wid the blessing of St. Patrick, hurroo! hurroo!"

"Very well," replied Fred, "if you will stand by me, as you say you will, and as I know you will, I ask you to do me one favour."

"A thousand! a thousand!" was the reply.

"That's enough. Then respect the laws of your country, and the men who are here to see them carried out; the first act of violence, and I am no longer your friend."

"All right, your honour, there shall be no violence, but if they want to come any *kimmeens* over you, we won't put up wid that," said Mike, appealing to the rest.

"No, no, Mike's right; the tailor's got the right thread of the argyment," they said.

"Lave Mike alone for that," was the

answer, with a knowing wink; "he can count up beans wid any of you."

"You'll mind what I say," said Fred, leaving the window.

"Sure we will, your honour," said Tim; "but, at the same time, we'll kape a tight hand on the corporal," and he took a tighter hold of his shillelagh.

"Sir, you are a gentleman," said the officer, "and I honour you; but my duty must be performed."

"Perform it, sir," was Fred's good-humoured reply. "Where will you begin?"

"In the stables," was the reply.

"The murder's out," said Lanty.

"What do you mean?" said the officer.

"Bedad! nothing at all."

"Will you lead the way, sir?"

Fred bowed.

"Attention, men!"

Then Fred and the officer went out through the wondering crowd towards the stables, the men and women following, while in the rear came Lanty, Tim, and Mike, dancing and flourishing their shillelaghs, and telling the others to stand firm.

CHAPTER XV.

THE PLOT DEFEATED—THE OATH OF VENGEANCE.

IT was rather an exciting sight to see the party proceeding to the stables.

Fred led the way, followed by the officer, the military bringing up the rear, flanked on each side by the men of the Frolic faction, who eyed the soldiers with anything but smiles of welcome.

The low muttered whisperings that broke from them occasionally, plainly showed that it required a very small spark indeed to cause an explosion.

The stables gained, Lanty threw the door wide open, and, taking off his caubeen, said, with a low bow, and a quiet grin,

"Perhaps your honour would like to walk in first, and examine the place, although if yer find anything beyant nothing at all, ye'll be mighty cliver."

And Lanty stood on one side, with Tim and Mike, while Fred and the officer, with half-a-dozen of the men, passed into the place.

It had been the intention of Lanty, in conjunction with Tim and Mike, to have completely set the stables in order, but shortly after they had commenced, a circumstance occurred that caused them to abandon the attempt.

The officer at once proceeded to the empty stall at the further end of the stable.

"Move away all that rubbish from underneath that manger," he said to the men.

The men went actively to work, and in a short space of time removed a vast quantity of loose, rotten straw and hay, until they came to the firm, hard earth, without discovering what they had made up their minds was concealed there.

The officer looked at a paper that he took from his breast pocket, and then slowly counted the empty stalls in the stable.

"The sixth from the door," he muttered, "perhaps they made a mistake," and so directing his men to renew their exertions, they minutely searched every part of the stable, but without success.

By this time the impatience of the "boys" outside had risen to such a pitch that it required all the exertions of Lanty to keep them from crowding into the place.

"What is it they're searching for, eh, Lanty Shan?" said Biddy Murphy, who stood at the head of the females. "Is it gunpowder, avick?"

"It is myself can't tell," replied Lanty; "p'raps for a pot of guineas."

At last every part of the stable having been carefully examined, the officer desired the men to give over. He then approached Fred, who, with folded arms, was standing near the door.

"I believe, Mr. Frolic," he said, "the authorities have in this instance been made dupes, and I am sorry that you have been subjected to so much annoyance."

"And pray, sir, what has caused all this annoyance, as you call it?" was Fred's reply.

"I am at liberty now to inform you

that the authorities have had information that you have been for a long time carrying on a secret trade in illicit spirits and——"

Here the rest was cut short by the loud and derisive laugh that broke forth from the crowd.

"Why, bad luck to yer, do you mane to say that my masther, the head of the Frolics, is a dirty smuggler? Do you hear that, my boys!" shouted Lanty.

They did, and responded by a loud groan.

"And pray who was the scoundrel who informed in this case, sir?" asked Fred.

"Aye, aye, the name of the dirthy craythur," roared the mob.

"Was it McDonnell, *bad scran** to him?" and shrill yells rose upon the air.

"The likes of you to come searching honest men's houses," screamed Biddy, "with your red coats and your guns, and your bagnets; and all for nothing at all, at all. By my sowl, if the men were of my mind, you'd take back more than you brought with yer."

And the virago clapping her hands violently set up a screech, which example was followed by all the rest.

"Be quiet all of you," said Fred, sternly; "this gentleman has done his unpleasant duty firmly but without offence. I suppose, sir, you'll wish to search the house?"

A groan of indignation burst from the mob.

"No, sir; my instructions do not extend so far, and I feel perfectly certain that you have been made the victim of some unprincipled scoundrel, whom I wish we could discover.'"

"It would be well for his bones to be amongst us now," was the cry.

The officer held out his hand, which Fred grasped warmly.

"You will enter the house with me," said the latter, "and partake of some refreshment. Lanty, do you attend to those brave men."

"I must beg to decline it," replied the officer; "we must proceed on our route to Stanley Castle, where we expect to be quartered for some time; I hope that my report will prevent your being troubled again with a visit of this sort."

"Wid all my heart," muttered Lanty to Tim and Mike.

"Fall in, men. We shall meet again I trust, sir," said the officer; then, raising his hat courteously to Fred and the rest, he placed himself at the head of his men, and marched out of the court-yard, followed by the shouts of the mob.

Then Fred, re-entering the house, re-assured his two friends, who were still seated at the fire, that there was no danger, at which they enjoyed a hearty laugh at the sudden surprise, and the oddity of their disguises.

Having doffed them, and put them carefully away in case of another surprise, they sat down to some refreshment, waited upon by Lanty.

"It must have been McDonnell who has served me this dirty trick," said Fred, "and it shall go hard if I am not even with him for it."

"That he may make up his mind to," replied Lanty. "He's at the bottom of it all, and with him a dirthy lot. We're surrounded with gunpowther, masther, and we must mind we are not all blown up."

"Good heavens! my dear Frank," said the lady, alarmed. "What is to be done?"

"Done, my lady; we must kape our eyes open, and the fist tight hold on the shillelagh."

"Now, Lanty, what do you know of this?" said Fred.

"What do I know of what?" and Lanty's eyes twinkled with fun.

"About the spirits."

"What sort of spirits? there are so many."

"Come, come, Lanty, we can keep the secret."

"And for the matter of that so can I, but as it belongs to one equally as much as the other, you shall have it in a pig's whisper. When Tim and I and Mike went a few days ago to clear out the stables for the horses that may be expected home some *day* or the *other*, we began at the wrong end—I mane the long end of the stable jist where the jontleman with the appleats and the long sword searched. Mike went to work wid the pitchfork—only its been widout a fork this many a day—whin he struck something mighty hard,"

"'What's that?' says he, 'What's what?' says I, while Tim began to pull the hay and straw aside.

---

* Bad food.

"'Murder!' says all three of us, 'who the divil put six barrels there?'" says we.

"And did you find six barrels of——"

"Don't break the thrid of my discourse plase. At first we thought they were gun-powther, and so we put away the pipes—for I remember the fate of Jack Ryan who once put a light to a barrel, and whiz! it went up and so did Jack, so high, that he's niver been down yet, and that's some years ago. Well, we found an old gimlet wid a screw as big as your fist, and it warn't long afore we found out it was the craythur by the smell, and by the time we had taken a quarter of a cask, we were convinced by the taste that it was the rale poteen."

"And what did you do—destroy it?" said Fred, hastily.

"Not for Lanty, thank ye, masther; we saw through the divilry at onst, and in a short time five of the iligant craters were lying cheek by jowl at the bottom of the well, bekase we felt pretty certain that no one with brains would think of looking for *whisky* in a *well*."

"I'll have it all destroyed, Lanty," said Fred, warmly.

"Whisht, masther, it won't take long to do that! It's slow work but sure. There's only three of them waiting for destruction, and och! murder, three days will do that, and thin it will be off my mind intirely. But it was placed there by McDonnell for your destruction."

"The villain!" said Fred. "We must be on the look-out, Lanty; it won't end here."

"Lave Lanty alone for that. It will be a fox's slape wid us. I am going to call all the Frolics out, and we shall see what we shall see. You'll do me a favour and not stir out to-day, and not be seen at the windys, sir, and marm."

"Why not, Lanty?" asked his master.

"Why not? Bekase Biddy Murphy says that Biddy Maguire told her that three suspicious men—strangers—are in the town, and that they were seen in close conversation wid the amiable Fog-harty."

"If I find that fellow interfering with me, I'll break his bones!" said Fred, warmly.

"To stop him intirely you must break the bone that belongs to the neck of the varmint. But lave him to me; I'll give a good pcount of him."

And Lanty, giving a sly grin, left the room.

Fred Frolic and Lanty were both right when they said McDonnell was the person who carried out the plot, which, had it succeeded, would have ruined Fred Frolic beyond all hopes of redemption.

The laws against illicit distillation of spirits and their possession were so severe and stringent that nothing could have saved Fred Frolic from a very heavy fine and imprisonment; the fine would have been beyond his means of paying, the imprisonment have broken his health and spirits; and, in fact, from the position which Fred held, it might have been set forth by his enemies that he ought to have set a better example, and his sentence might, therefore, have been one of a harsher description.

The mere accident of Lanty, Tim and Mike, finding the illicit spirits which they did, and the promptitude with which they stowed it away, beyond all chance of its being found, counteracted the dark villany of McDonnell and his associates, and saved Fred.

The placing of the spirits in the stable had been carried out by Black Murtough and some of his desperadoes in the dead of the night.

The information of its being there, and the exact spot where it would be found, was conveyed to the magistrate in the barrack town of Tramore, and in a very short space of time the military were on their march, with what result we have seen.

On the same night there was a great meeting of all the desperadoes connected with the illicit trade in the cave of the Devil's Grip,

Men whose very look and bearing proclaimed the lawless calling they followed, came stealthily into the cave as soon as the dark shades of night fell upon the earth and the waters.

In the outer cave, as before, stood Black Murtough, looking anxiously out along the rocks, upon whom the giant waves were rushing with maddened fury.

"He can't come *that* road until the tide turns, and it won't be safe for him to come by the roads, and so I must have patience."

And, seating himself on an old tub by the entrance of the cave, he lighted his pipe, at the same time keeping a wary.

keen look out both upon the rocks and the ocean that was roaring around him.

"Mickey Doyle won't do anything until all is safe and sure around him," he muttered; "he's a lad we *can* trust. Bedad! there's no spy or informer like him in the land! By this time that lively blade Frolic and his house is safe in the hands of the sojers—ha, ha, ha! Mighty good luck go wid him. Ah! what's that dark speck upon the face of the waters? That divil Jan, I suppose. I must give him the signal."

He went into the cave, and returning with a lighted lantern, swung it three times.

At the third there came a report across the waters, as though from a pistol.

"That's the fellow, true enough."

And, placing down the lantern, he re-seated himself.

At times a dark figure would enter the cave, and move cautiously in.

A wave of the hand was all that passed between Murtough and his visitors as they glided into the inner cave.

"By my sowl! we'll have a pretty muster this night, I'm thinking, and it should be so, for there's business to be settled, and——"

At that moment the boat grated on the sands, and the next Jan had sprung out upon them.

Then he gave some order to the men, who sheered round and rowed out again to sea, until they neared the rocks, where they lay waiting for further orders.

"Well, Jan, ma bouchal, you're to your time," said Murtough, handing a bottle to him.

The rough smuggler seized it, and, applying it to his lips, took a hearty draught.

"Sapperment, dat is good, and warms the heart, after the cold sea breeze has been blowing through your very marrow. Ha, ha, ha!" he said, looking round. "Where are the others, eh?"

"Waiting in the inner cave, ma bouchal. We'll soon have them out when they are wanted."

"Ah, well! I shall not wait long. I shall not like leaving the cutter. I am so full of the low spirits that I know there is something that shall happen. Besides," he growled, "I shall not like the weather."

And he cast an uneasy glance out seaward.

"Bathershin, man alive, the weather is right enough. Take another pull. The cold has made you shake like a child."

Jan again applied the bottle to his lips.

"Donder! I shall feel all the better after that," and he handed it back. "Now, then, let's to the work."

"Wid all my heart. The boys are idle to-night, because of the meeting. There are ugly rumours about, Jan. What the devil keeps Mickey so long?" he muttered. "Well, we must get on without him."

Rising, he went and threw open the door of the inner cave.

"Cead mille failthe to every mother's son of you! Come out with you, and try the drop."

And then came slowly out, the men who had been all that day gradually assembling.

They all wore long frieze coats, which, in many instances, were patched with pieces of cloth of all the colours of the rainbow.

Many of them had a loose handkerchief dangling round the neck, but most of them had dispensed with that article, the absence of which showed off the strong muscles of the neck, and as the shirt collar was, in most instances, flung open, there might be seen the stalwart chest, bronzed by a continual exposure to the weather.

There was not a man of them but what was armed with a shillelagh or bludgeon of some sort or the other.

Black Murtough stood at the head of a cask, upon which was a can filled with the strongest potheen that could be brewed; by his side stood the burly Jan, with his large fur cap on, while the thick coat being flung on one side, showed that he was well and powerfully armed.

A quantity of tin horns or cups stood by the can; these Black Murtough filled up with spirit.

As they stood, each man with his hand uplifted, with the cup in it, and the light shining upon them from the cave, they presented a wild and unearthly picture of savage grandeur.

"A long knife and a sure shot for all our enemies, ma bouchals," said Murtough, draining off the spirit.

And the same was drank in low, earnest tones, that showed that the men who uttered it were in earnest.

The rays of the moon that had shone fully into the cave were for the moment darkened by the figure of a man standing at its entrance.

Murtough, whose back was towards the water, did not perceive him, but the movement of those before him—the sudden grasping of their weapons—made him turn round.

"Ha! Mickey Doyle; thunder and ouns, where have you been stopping, *ma bouchal?* Come in, you're welcome."

The man thus addressed, entered the cave with a limping gait, as though one limb was shorter than the other; he was rather bowed about the back, as though slightly humped; his eyes were black and piercing, and the foxy colour of his hair, cropped as close as it could be, gave a peculiar wildness and cunning to his eyes whenever suddenly addressed.

"I know *I am* welcome, although I know the news I bring will be on the contrary side," was the reply.

He lifted a horn of spirits to his lips.

"I've had a throuble to get here, I have."

"Ha, ha! my boy, no doubt. Well, now you are here, what's the news?" said Murtough, eagerly.

"Bad!" was the emphatic reply. "The scheme against the Frolic has entirely broken down."

"Thousand divils! how was that, eh? Spake, spake, ye limping son of the old one! How did it fail, you spawn of——"

And Black Murtough's face grew dark as a thunder-cloud.

"Be aisy, Murtough; ye'll get nothing out of me wid hard words, that you know," said the spy, coolly.

"Then I will wid blows," was the reply.

And he made a rush at him, but was the next moment held firmly in the grip of Jan.

"Sapperment and the tyfel, what are you about, eh? Let the man speak his say, and you shall see. Go on, Mickey."

"The whisky has got into your head, Murtough," said Mickey, "or you'd know better. You struck me *once* before, *you know*, and you nearly had this through your heart," and he showed a long, glittering knife. "Listen, you omadhaun, I fear you not. When the soldiers went to the stables according to the directions given, and searched the very spot where it was placed, it had vanished. Ne'er a keg or drop of whisky was there. You

have been bowled out nicely," and he grinned; "you have lost the game and the whisky as well. You are clever, *ma bouchal.*"

Murtough looked aghast at the news.

"I say, Mickey, no joking; is it thrue?"

"True? ha, ha! well, do you think I have *gone a shaughan** in my mind? It's as true as the holy book; and it's worse than that. The sogers have gone to the Castle, and more, are coming to hunt up the hills and the smuggling; so not a bit of tay or baccy, or a drop o' the rale poteen will you get for love or money. It's small comfort I bring you, but it's the truth."

"Indade!" and the word came slowly out between his firmly set teeth; "but they'll find we are not boys. Will you one and all stand by Black Murtough?"

"All, all," was the deep, stern reply.

"Well, then, we'll swear to give no rest or peace, by night or by day, to those who are our enemies; they shall perish by shot or steel, and that we swear by all our hopes."

"We do, we do," was the reply.

"A cup to it," he said, and again the horns was replenished. "May the blood of the man turn to poison who turns a traitor or breaks the pledge he has taken this night."

"Amen!" was the deep reply, as the burning liquor was drained to the last drop.

"To-morrow night we'll meet at the Widow Mullany's shealing in the mountains, and draw lots who shall be the first of our enemies who shall fall, and the man who shall do the deed."

A low murmur of assent ran through the ranks of the men who stood in that cave.

Again the right hand was uplifted, the oath renewed, and the hands that would soon be red with blood, were grasped in each other.

"Remember," said Black Murtough.

"We will," was the reply.

"And now, *bannath lath* to all."

"*Bannath lath,*" was the answer, and in a short time a deep silence reigned in the cave of the Devil's Grip, broken only by the murmuring dash of the waters without.

---

* Gone astray.

"A SURE SHOT TO OUR ENEMIES," CRIED BLACK MURTOUGH.

CHAPTER XVI.

THE CASTLE AND ITS MASTER.

THE arrival of the military at Stanley caused great surprise and excitement to the domestics, but to Sir Edward it was a matter of great joy.

He had very clearly foreseen that there was a great deal of discontent seething up with all the people in the serveral baronies, and being a man of a bold, brave disposition, he made up his mind to crush the affair in the bud.

It was, therefore, particularly grateful to him, when he saw the military crossing the park, and he hastened out with Bell, and one or two of his guests, to give them a hearty welcome.

The military were drawn up in line in front of the house, and Captain Brabazon, having saluted Sir Edward, advanced towards him with a letter.

"Ah! from my old friend, Sir Lawrence," said Sir Edward, after reading it. "You will find plenty of employment here, sir. The trade for making and running illicit spirits has become somewhat alarming in this district, and must be put down. We shall do the best we can to assist you in suppressing it."

"I expected no less from Sir Edward Stanley," replied Captain Brabazon.

The men were dismissed, and taken into the large and ample kitchen, and every preparation made for their comfort, while the captain, apologising for his travel-stained appearance, sat down to luncheon with Sir Edward and Bell.

"I have already commenced a portion of my duty this morning," he said, in reply to a question from Sir Edward.

"Indeed!—and successfully?" said the baronet.

"On the contrary, a dead failure—false information—and I am not at all sorry for it."

"Sorry, why, where was this?"

"Oh, at a near neighbour of yours, Sir Edward," was the reply.

Bell looked anxiously at him.

"Yes, and a handsome fellow he is, too; he gave me a hearty welcome, though at one time I thought it would have been rather a rough one."

"Are you talking of Fred Frolic?" said Bell.

"The same person," said the captain, bowing.

"How in the name of common sense could they connect Fred Frolic and smuggling together?" said Bell.

"I think it very likely," was the sharp reply of her father.

"And I think there is nothing more unlikely."

"What on earth can you know about those things, my dear?" said Sir Edward, sharply.

"I know everything about them. You forget the best part of my existence was passed in this spot, and that I have had frequent opportunities of seeing all about him. Who in the name of wonder sent you on such a wild goose chase, Captain Brabazon?"

"I have no opportunity of knowing that, because I have only to act upon instructions given. The name of the informer is always kept in the dark."

"It must have been some secret enemy of Fred's," said Bell, looking for the instant at Sir Edward. "I should so like to have seen you at work, because Fred——"

"Be silent, Miss Stanley. The fact is that the young man, Frolic, and Miss Stanley, by an unfortunate oversite of Lady Stanley, were, as children, suffered to do as they liked, and that will account for the familiar terms in which Miss Stanley speaks of him; but I do not visit or recognise him," and the baronet drew himself up proudly.

"Yes, but I do, Sir Edward, and I shall not fail to do so. Why should the poor young fellow be condemned because his father was a harum-scarum man? The only legacy he left his son was a mountain of debt; but a finer, more open, free-hearted Irishman it is not easy to find in these parts. Pray how do you like the look of the mansion, captain?"

At this the captain laughed outright.

"And so you found nothing in the

shape of contraband goods on the place?" asked Bell.

"No, not anything."

"And yet the information was given on oath, and must be correct?" said Sir Edward.

"Why my, dear father, I should have as soon thought you had turned smuggler *yourself*, as Fred Frolic. What's so easy to be done by any enemy of his as to place the articles on the spot, and then swear they are there?"

"I agree with you there, Miss Stanley; and, as regards Mr. Frolic, I shall be happy to renew my acquaintance with him."

"Yes, but not with a posse of soldiers at your back." And Bell rose. "I am going out for my usual gallop, Sir Edward. Adieu, Captain Brabazon; we shall meet again at dinner."

And so saying she quitted the room.

"A wayward girl, Captain Brabazon," said Sir Edward; "left only under the care of her mother, and allowed almost to run wild among these poeple, it is not to be wondered at."

"She has a charming frankness about her, Sir Edward, which is very delightful," replied Brabazon.

"Yes, but not at all times proper in one in her station, or for the rank that she will ultimately attain," said Sir Edward, proudly. "We will now, if you please, go and look after the accommodation for the men. I am one of those who think that too much cannot be done for the brave spirits who defend us by sea and land."

If the people at Ballyran had been astonished when the red coats under the command of Captain Brabazon marched in, that astonishment was greatly increased by the arrival of another body of them, who, much to the terror of the inhabitants, were to be, it was understood, permanently quartered there.

"We'll have terrible doings here now!" was the thought of all.

"I am shure we are highly honoured Biddy Maguire, by having the milintary sogers here to look after us, anyhow!" shouted Biddy Murphy. "What have they come to look after, mavourneen?"

"Well, it's not sartin sure; but Pat Maguire let out the sacret to me this morning," was the reply.

"Then sure you'll tell it to me, Biddy, ma cushla?"

"Well, you see, I promised my lad that I'd kape it all intirely to myself."

"That's bad, Biddy, and onkind, bekase whenever I have had a *sacret* confided to me I always let you into it; but I know what you want."

"Bedad, I want a power of things."

"But what would do you good this cowld morning, eh, Biddy Maguire?"

"Get out wid your blarney; it's coaxing me you are; but I'll not deny that a dhrop of the craythur this morning would——"

"By the powers, I thought you wanted bribery and corruption; come here, ye sowl, I have got an iligant drop I hid away from Mike the other night, and sure yer welcome; come away, avick."

And Biddy Maguire, at the invitation of Biddy Murphy, crossed the road, and entered the mud cabin of Mike Murphy, the fighting tailor.

With a great deal of caution Biddy closed the door upon her friend—not a very difficult job, seeing that it hung by one hinge—and then taking the three-legged stool that Tim, a "gossoon" was sitting upon, and sending him sprawling into the mud of the floor, she got on it, and putting her hand in the thatch, pulled out a bottle, containing about a pint; then she found an old tin mug, and with great care pulled the cork out of the bottle.

"You'll say it's the finest drop your lips ever came across," she said, as she poured some out. "I played the *commether** over Mike nicely last night. Here, my sowl, drink."

"Well, here's to yer health," said the other Biddy; "it's a pleasure to find we live so neighbourly, Mrs. Murphy, and I hope it will continue," and down her throat went the liquid.

"What should prevint?" said the other.

The next minute the contents of the glass was ejected on to the floor.

"That's quare stuff," said Mrs. Maguire.

"What's quare stuff, yer fool?" was the reply.

"That. To make sartin I'll try another."

"Why, yer born divil, what do you mane?"

As she poured it out this time, Biddy Maguire put it first to her nose, then she

* The fool.

applied it to her lips, then flung the contents of it in Mrs. Murphy's eyes, then she ducked her head as the bottle went whizzing past, and the next moment, their large brawny hands had clenched each other's hair.

"I'll tache you to come the *commether* over me," then came a blow.

"And I'll tache you to spile my eyesight by throwing in that what was meant for the troat."

And then the fight commenced amid a din and uproar seldom heard.

The poultry that Mrs. Murphy owned, and which roosted just over the bed, sent forth their loudest cries, and went flying about in wild confusion.

The lean and hungry cur called a dog, joined in the fray by seizing the pig by the ears, which, in return, sent forth powerful notes of lamentation, and the *gossoons*, determined to have their share of the fun, fell to pummelling each other, amid shouts and cries.

In the middle of this the door flew off its frail hinges, and in rushed Mike.

"Hurroo! what's all this?" he cried, as he threw himself among them; but here Mike had made a slight miscalculation; as he separated them for the moment and stood between them, they paused to take breath, and then, with increased fury, flew upon him.

This was too much for the poor tailor, for the blows rained thick and heavy upon him.

"What are ye about, ye born tigers? Would you kill me out and out?" he shouted, as he struggled hard and desperately with them.

"Take that, ye thing of a tailor!" said Biddy Maguire, giving Mike a whack with her fist.

"I can give you one of the same sort!" roared out Mike.

At that moment Tim Maguire rushed in.

"Is it killing the mother of my childer ye are, ye villain?" shouted Tim, and the next moment he was in the thick of the melee.

Then loud hurrahs broke upon them from the outside, which caused them to rush to the door.

The whole population were out and shouting, for, riding up the street upon her beautiful bay, was Bell Stanley, and walking by her side Fred Frolic.

"Hurroo! hurroo!" shouted the whole mass. "The Frolics and the Stanleys for ever! Hurroo!"

* * *

CHAPTER XVII.

THE RIOT.

THE whole population of Ballyran had turned out to welcome the heiress of Stanley Castle, and the sight of Bell's handsome face was rendered doubly more dear to them when they saw the manly Fred Frolic walking by her side.

Then again, the people remembered Bell's mother, whose hand was always open to assist them in their poverty and distress, and they knew that the "darlin' *mavourneen*, her child, was as like her as two pase."

"May the Heavens be your bed!" shouted the hundred voices.

"*Cead mille failthe* to you!"

And away, high up in the air, went flying the *caubeens*, and a hundred other things, and shillelaghs waved and twirled about in honour of the "darlin'," who had paid them a first visit.

"The Frolics for ever!" shouted Mike, waving the sleeve-board, while the blood was running from his nose, the effect of the visitations of Biddy Maguire's fist. "I'll down wid de fust man that says black is the white of my eye upon that. Hurroo! They are the handsomest couple in all the world."

Bell stooped down and whispered to Fred, and then placing her hand in the pocket of her dress, she drew forth a quantity of silver, and gracefully threw it among the crowd.

At this, the scrambling, the pushing, the fighting, and yelling, was something indescribable, and in the midst of this Bell drew her horse away from the mob, and, with Fred, was moving off on the road towards home, when suddenly, and at a rapid pace, Sir Edward Stanley and Captain Brabazon dashed into the street.

Sir Edward's eyes flashed fire when he

beheld Fred, especially as he had hold of the bridle-rein, guiding the high-spirited horse through the mob, whose shouts and cries had somewhat alarmed the animal.

But, at his appearance, the feelings of the people seemed suddenly to have changed.

Instead of the cordial welcome they had given the daughter, hisses and yells, and muttered exclamations, proceeded from them, which plainly told the captain that his host was no favourite with them.

Irritated at this, and the sight of Fred Frolic with his daughter, he spurred his horse forward.

"Take your hand off the rein, sir !" he shouted to Fred. "Cannot my daughter ride out without being pestered by beggars ?"

At this a loud yell arose.

"Who does he call beggars ?" shouted Mike. "Do you hear that *ma bouchals ?*"

And again a yell of execration rose in the air.

"I did not mean you. I meant that man there !"

And he pointed with his whip to Fred, who, calm and collected, still stood by the side of Bell.

At this moment, Lanty and Tim, with a body of the Frolic faction, came hurrying up, and the captain, thinking that things looked rather serious, gave a sign to the soldiers, who stood wondering at this strange scene, and they at once formed in line behind him.

"I can bear much from you, Sir Edward, but beware how you step over the line."

"Do you threaten me, sir ?" was the reply.

"No, I only warn you; you have before applied such language to me, that, if it were not for the respect I have for this lady and her deceased mother, I should not have allowed the insult to pass over. I met Miss Stanley accidentally."

"Indeed !" and he cast an incredulous look at them both; "but for the future I'll take care there shall be no meetings, either accidentally or otherwise,"

"Listen to that," shouted the Frolics; "he is as good as you are, bad luck to you."

"You will do nothing of the sort, Sir Edward," said Bell, firmly; "you are wronging Mr. Frolic by vile assertions and names which you have no right to use to him. You forget that more than once I have owed my life to Mr. Frolic, and if

you have not any gratitude in you, I have," and she held out her hand to Fred, which he respectfully kissed.

"Listen to that, you old *omadhaun !*" shouted Mike; "you'd better give in, and let things take a nateral coorse; what do you say, ma bouchal ?"

"As for you I'll drive you out of this place, and teach you the difference between a landlord and his tenants. To-morrow Mr. Fogharty, my agent, shall receive my instructions, and clear the place."

At this a yell of deep execration came ringing through the air, and then a heavy stone in an old stocking went whizzing past Sir Edward's head.

"Bell, for Heaven's sake, make for home," said Fred.

"What, and leave my father, Fred. How came you to think so meanly of me, eh ?"

"No, no," he hastily replied, "I was only fearful for your safety; forgive me."

During this Captain Brabazon whispered to the baronet.

"What, sir," said the baronet, "fly from such *scum* as this? never," and he looked defiantly at the mass of wild, haggard faces that were lowering upon him.

"He calls us scum," shouted Tim, "scum; and will we put up with that ?"

"No, no," and they grasped their shillelaghs.

"Be aisy, now," shouted Lanty, springing before them, for Fred kept close to Bell, determined to protect her at all hazards; "be aisy, I say. I suppose, Sir Edward Stanley, you're callin' these honest poor people *scum*, bekase they are poor and in rags, and you can see through their jaws like a lantern, bekase starvation, I've heard say, never brightened the eyes, or fattened the cheek, and it ain't possible that rags will ever add to the adornment of the parson; is that what you mane ?"

"I come not here to argue with you, fellow," said Sir Edward.

"P'raps not, and it's meself that don't want to argue with you; but, by the blessing of all that's holy you shall hear a bit of good, honest Irish truth, scum or no scum,"

"Hurroo, Lanty, hurroo; give it him; more power to your elbow !" shouted the mob.

"Lave it to me, lave it to me," he replied. "I am not your tenant, the Lord be praised, and so not any of your scum;

but if you'd do your duty, and be amongst them, and not lave them in the hands of that petty Fogharty, you'd find them a different race of beings; but no you tack the last thirteen out of their fists, here, and you spend it abroad, and so long as you get the rint, the divil may take the scum; am I right, ma bouchals?"

A loud and wild hurrah followed this, and a threatening movement among the crowd made Captain Brabazon fear that a serious riot was about to take place, and he called to his men to fix bayonets.

At this command the men rushed forward to the front, and, throwing off their coats, held their shillelaghs as though they were about to spring on Sir Edward.

The women had filled their stockings with heavy stones, and stood ready to hurl them with a fatal accuracy, while the *gossoons* had armed themselves with old rusty knives, and gathered a heap of stones ready for the assault.

Bell, at this fearful sight, sprang forward, and the next moment was by the side of Sir Edward.

"Bad scran to you! What do you mane by scum?" shouted the women Biddy. "If it warn't for the *gilli ma chree** at your side, we'd tache you a lesson," and the deadly weapons were raised as though they were about to be showered amongst them. But at that moment Fred sprang before Sir Edward and his daughter.

"What are you about doing?" he called out, in his clear bright tones. "Are you going to commit murder? Some of you were cowardly enough to hurl a stone just now, an act dastardly and disgraceful, whoever it was," and he glanced at Mike Murphy, the tailor.

"Bad luck to me if it was me," shouted Mike. "I niver throw stones while I've got this in me fist."

And he waved the sleeve-board round his head.

"It was wrong, whoever it was. Whatever intemperate words Sir Edward Stanley used were at least uttered in the excitement of the moment, and are, no doubt, by this time repented of."

"But he called *you* a *beggar*," they shouted.

* Brightness of my heart.

"That's my business. That rent in the coat is easily mended, my boys. I wish the rents in the roof could be done as quickly."

"We'll put a new one on, your honour," shouted a voice.

"Arrah, is that you, Pat Hoolagain? I'll take you at your word, only let the slates be stronger than brown paper, because it's not pleasant to have a shower-bath in your feather bed."

"Ha, ha, ha!" roared the mob. "By my sowl, he's got you there, Pat; you're the finest slater in the world for a ventilating roof."

"You can see the blessed stars winking at each other through it," said Lanty.

The tact and firmness used by Fred had its effect, and the wild turbulent feelings of the mob had been lulled by it.

Captain Brabazon, with the true spirit of an English gentleman, saw through it all, and quietly ordered the soldiers to unfix bayonets.

At this the "boys" cheered, and when Fred grasped the captain by the hand, the "boys" rushed over, and gave the *cead mille failthe* to the men, nearly shaking their hands from their sockets.

"It was then Sir Edward, drawing himself erect in the saddle, prepared to ride home.

The crowd drew aside in silence to let him pass, the soldiers saluting him.

But, as he rode slowly through the line formed by the men, women and children, not a finger was raised to the head; they all looked stern and defiant at him as he passed from them attended by the captain.

Not so when Bell followed with Fred walking by her side; then the wild scene of joy was again enacted, the caubeens and shillelaghs flew up in the air, and, amid the blessings of all, she rode from them, with her eyes gleaming with joy, although tears stood trembling in them.

"Leave me now," dear Fred," she whispered; "it will be for the best, and remember——"

"Courage and hope," he whispered; "the talisman to a bright and glorious future."

Their hands clasped each other's, and the next instant she gave the rein to her barb, and had joined her father and the captain on their road to the castle.

CHAPTER XVIII.

LANTY AND THE BOW-STREET RUNNERS.

"Lanty," said Fred, abruptly starting; "come, let us go home."

"Under favour, I must decline the honour of your society," replied Lanty, drawing close to him. "There's a particular bit of bisness going on in Ballyrun, which, if not looked after, will turn out to be Ballyriot."

And Lanty, in his usual expressive manner, placed his finger by the side of his nose.

"What is the matter now?" asked Fred.

"Nothing at all—at all. It's only in the bud of the matter; but you'll tell the good people in the house to kape quiet; you'll understand what I mane by that?"

"Perfectly. But how do you know this, eh?"

"Oh, bathershin, I know what I know; and what I know I'll kape to myself. It ain't the longest tongue always that is a sign of wisdom. You're particularly quiet yourself, sir."

"Come, Lanty, no blarney."

"Ne're a haporth; but over in the house yonder, the 'Frolic Arms,' there's ould Fogharty and four men they call runners—scarlet runners, I s'pose, bekase of their red waistcoats, and they've come after the—whisht! there's that Mickey Doyle, creeping about like a sarpent as he is. Here, Tim, avick, borrow the loan of a shillelagh for the masther."

"I'll do that same," said Tim. "I'd be proud to lind him mine, only what would I do myself?"

And off started Tim, returning almost on the instant with a most formidable-looking one.

"But I don't want one. I am tired of them, and want to see peace and quietness," said Fred.

At this Lanty and Tim looked at each other as though they saw the clouds falling down.

"Well, what's the matter?" said Fred.

"Well, bedad," replied Lanty, smoothing his fox crop, "it's meself that don't know, but the man can't be an Irishman who says he is tired of a shillelagh; and

then again, wanting pace and quietness here! I'd be glad to see an impossibility made into a fact. You'll take that in your fist, sir," and he handed it to him, "widout you'd see me an absentee and go to foreign parts abroad."

Fred took it somewhat reluctantly.

"Ain't you going home all alone by yourself, and ain't the McDonnells out? do you remimber the day by the Cross Roads? will you be kilt and then be sorry that you broke the heart of Lanty Shan——"

"I see, Lanty," he said, grasping his hand. "I'll take your advice," and he hurried off.

"And the shillelagh; good luck to you, yer a broth of a boy. If any one mislests you, give a good count on 'em. Tim, avick, follow the masther at a rispectful distance. Kape out of sight round by the hedges, God save us, if you can find one; and when he is safe, run back as though somebody was behind you, and it warn't convenient to stop; away wid you, Tim," and away went Tim, while Lanty made for Mike Murphy's cabin.

There was a tolerably hot discussion going on at the same time, for now the excitement of the visit of the Stanleys had passed away, and the town of Ballyran had relapsed into its usual quiet.

There were a few fights more or less; in other places, the song and dance was being kept up with great spirit.

When Lanty opened the door, it fell in by itself, as if to avoid giving him any further trouble, and there discovered the Murphys and Maguires seated round a turf fire in the middle of the floor.

"Well, of all the men in the world it's meself that's glad to see the shadow of you cross the threshold. Come and sit down by the side of an honest woman," said Biddy.

"There's a dacent seat between us on a nice bit of dry turf, Lanty Shan," said the other Biddy, and Lanty sat down; "and now your between two honest women."

"It's highly flattered I am," said

Lanty, "and it's not every day a man gets such a trate, that it isn't. Who has been blacking your eye, Biddy?"

"I'm given to walking in my slape, and I must have knocked it against the bed—I mane the bed-post, Lanty."

"Ah, sure the post of a bed on the *flure* must be mighty difficult to put up. By my sowl, Biddy Murphy has been walking in her slape, too, for her eye is the same iligant colour."

"It would do your eyes good to see a *bed* or a post, except Mike, for the latther. How did you manage to fill the bottle wid water, Mike, avick?"

"What, did you mane the bottle you hid in the thatch? Biddy, my jewel, didn't you play the *commether* over me, then, mavourneen. Lave Mike alone for slaping wid one eye open and the other wide awake,"

"You're clever, Mike," replied his wife.

"I've sarved a long apprenticeship, I think they call it, to you, darling. Oh, it's a great lesson for a man to get married! I saw you hide the bottle in the thatch, and, by my sowl, a nater drop of whisky I niver tasted."

"The divil doubt you!"

"And how did you like the wather, eh, Biddy Maguire?" asked Mike, with a grin.

"About as much as you like that, my darling!" and away went Mrs. Maguire's fist into the pit of Mike's stomach.

Up jumped Mike, and an "iligant scrimmage" would have taken place but for Lanty.

"Here, Mike, follow me. I have a sacret for you."

And with that, Lanty bounded out of the place, followed by Mike.

"We're after you, my lads!" shouted the two Biddies; and they kept their words, for, no sooner had the men disappeared from the door, than the women were out after them.

It was just getting dark, and Lanty and Mike led at a rattling pace on to the green where the fair was held; there were no two runners in all Ballyran, or any other of the Baronies, that could at all compete with Lanty and Mike, but the two women held on at an excellent rate.

Mike and Lanty cleared the sharp corner of the street, and were racing across the green like deer-hounds, but just as the Biddies were turning it, rather winded,

Black Dan, the tinker, was coming round it with his donkey.

Before he could pull up, or they could stop, they were all four in the mud at Ballyran, which, unlike its votes at the election, was greatly admired for its consistency.

The race was over, so far as the Biddies were concerned, for they clung so tightly to Black Dan, and the unfortunate animal, that they ran some chance of being suffocated, until the donkey, getting his hind legs free, gave Biddy Murphy such a vigorous kick as to cause her to spring up as if a galvanic battery had charged her.

Then, seizing Mrs. Maguire, she pulled her on to her legs, and Black Dan also arose.

From their appearance it was almost impossible to say which was the tinker, so black were they all from their roll in the mud.

An angry and violent altercation followed, in which Dan got the worst of it, and had it come to force, his chance would have been hopeless; and so the unoffending tinker admitted that he was wrong in being in the way, and settled the matter over sundry noggins of poteen.

Lanty and Mike doubled round by the green, and in a very short time were again in the town, and coming out by the back of the "Frolic Arms," stopped under a tree which kept them effectually concealed.

"Mike," said Lanty, "how is your wind?"

"Well, by my sowl, it's right, but it will be better for a drop of the craythur."

"Well, then, your sowl, you shall have it; go in, avick, and tell Pat Donovan, the landlord, I want to spake wid him."

"I'll do that same," said Mike, moving off.

"And do it aisy and nate; you understand?"

"Sure, then, I'll do it nate," said Mike, as he moved off to do Lanty's bidding.

"I'll fix Mr. Fogharty, or else my name ain't Lanty Shan. The blaggard, he's got the runners, has he? We'll see if we don't make them runners in right down arnest."

At that moment Pat Donovan came out.

"You've got a fine houseful, Pat," said Lanty, "and it's meself that's glad to hear it; and you have got the sojers

...e illigant Mr. Fogharty and the ...ers."

"I have, bad luck to them," was the answer.

"It's meself that wants to be in the same room wid 'em; but it must be in disguise."

"How's that to be?" asked Pat scratching his head.

"Well, I've been thinking, and it's as aisy as an old boot. Can't ye borrow me a sojer's great coat?"

"I'll be taken up for robbing the milentery."

"Don't be a fool; it's only borrowing the loan of a great coat and the cap."

"You'll bear me harmless if I am taken up?"

"Sure, then, I will. I'll pretend to slape, and overhear all they have to say, and so circumvent the blaggards."

"Anything to sarve out Fogharty," said Pat, as he went into the house.

In a few moments out came Pat, carrying under his apron the soldier's great coat, and heavy cap.

"Make haste, yer sowl! they'll be coming down stairs, bekase there's too many sojers up, and they can't talk—quick! into it. It's an iligant officer you'd make," added Pat, as Lanty slipped into the coat, and clapped the hat upon his head, which nearly smothered him.

"Now, then, into the room wid yer; follow me, you sowl."

Lanty, following Pat, found himself in a small room, with three or four chairs, and a table and a bench placed close against the wall.

Upon the bench Lanty threw himself, and covered himself well up with the great coat, not forgetting to grasp the trusty shillelagh under it with one hand, and scarcely had he done so when the voice of Fogharty was heard descending the stairs.

"I thought I told you I wouldn't have any one in the room—that my business was private," said Fogharty, as he saw Lanty.

"It's one of the sojers top-heavy," replied Pat.

"Top-heavy or not, out with him," said Fogharty, in a passion.

"P'raps you'll try that on yourself. I have been trying it on for an hour or more, and the divil a bit will he stir," was the reply. "Besides, he promised to do me a *favour* if I disturbed him again.

Them English are the owld un's own, I belave!"

"Rouse him, or we'll do it."

"Then if you plase, you do it; only look out."

"Look out—for what?"

"For the favour he intended for me."

"The favour? What was that?"

"Why, he's got his bagnet under his coat, and he promised to whip it into the first dirty blaggard that tried to disturb him. P'raps you'll try the could steel first, lawyer."

"The Lord save us—not I! What's to be done?"

"Sit ye down, and make your life clane and comfortable. Why, the baste snores like the Seven Sleepers. You'll not be disturbed by him, I'll go bail!"

"Well, I suppose it must be so. Bring in the punch I ordered, and don't let a soul disturb us."

"I'll take care of that, Mr. Fogharty; and, as for the punch, it's the finest brewing in the wide world, for I tried it over and over again until I got it right.

And, with a sly chuckle, Pat left the room.

Mr. Fogharty and his four guests now sat down, the lawyer placing himself opposite the window that overlooked the place at the back, and very shortly after Pat entered, bearing a bowl of whisky-punch.

It was not the usual handsome china bowl, but a wooden one, that had seen a good deal of service in the washing of the Donovans, great and small, and a small crack having been made in it, owing to a whack the elder gossoon had given the younger one, it had been very neatly covered over with a piece of tin, which did not entirely prevent the leakage.

With all due ceremony, this was placed upon the table before Fogharty and the men, who stared at one another in surprise at this, which was still further heightened by the sight of four glasses, without any stems, but fastened by some wonderful mechanical contrivance into four flat pieces of wood.

A couple of tallow candles, stuck into the necks of two empty wine bottles, completed the arrangements of the table.

To the lawyer, who was used to these sort of things, it was not at all surprising, but in the men it created a profound disgust.

"Is this the best inn in the place, sir?"

said one of them, just as Pat was leaving the room.

"The best!" said Pat. "What the divil more do you want than *iligance* and *comfort?*"

And he pulled the door indignantly after him.

"Keep your hats on, gentlemen," said the lawyer, helping them to the steaming liquid. "You'll find the punch good."

The men tasted.

"It's thundering strong," said one of them.

"That's one of its many vartues," replied Fogharty.

"It tastes very soapy, Jem," said another.

"It's the flavour of the whisky," replied the lawyer. "The more you drink the better you'll like it."

The faces of the men did not seem to agree with the lawyer's expression.

"And, so you have come down to apprehend a man who has run away with a ward in chancery, eh?" said the lawyer.

Lanty's ears opened wide at this.

"Yes, you see there's a strong suspicion that he's got over here, because, when his lodgings were searched, a letter was found, asking him to Frolic House, Ballyran, and signed Fred Frolic."

"Ah, ah! no doubt, no doubt," said Fogharty, rubbing his hands together. "What's his name?"

"Captain Frank Hardy."

"A tall, good-looking man?"

"Yes."

"He's there disguised. I'll swear it's the man I saw dressed as a countryman, and Mickey Doyle saw the woman standing at the window one day."

"Well, there is a reward of five hundred pounds offered for him, half to go to the informer," said the man.

"I claim the half, mind; I gave the information. We'll have them, and——"

"And the man who knowingly harbours them is guilty of a contempt of the High Court of Chancery, and subject to pains and penalties, and imprisonment for life," said the man.

"Is he? then, by all the powers, Mr. Fred Frolic, I've got you at last."

There was a convulsive movement beneath the soldier's coat, and a sound very like a groan.

"What a noise that soldier makes; and, murder! what's he fumbling under his coat for?" said one of the men.

"Oh, nothing at all," replied Fogharty, a trifle alarmed himself. "We'll secure them all to-morrow, the runaways, and the man who has harboured them in the face of the law, which is a serious affair. Leave it all to me."

"Oh, with all my heart; I only wish we had them and safely landed in England, that's all. I am tired of this bog-trotting country."

"And so you shall be before you get out of it," muttered Lanty.

"Ha! ha! it will be all right," said the lawyer, raising his voice; "*we'll have them all*, every man jack of them."

The next moment there was a ringing report of a pistol, and a bullet came crashing through the window.

The consternation that ensued outside the "Frolic Arms" upon the firing of the pistol was intense. The inhabitants of Ballyran rushed from their hovels, armed with such things as just came "handy."

The male population, half dressed, rushed into the place called a street, with the never-failing bit of wood in their fists, while old pokers, griddles, and three-legged stools formed the offensive weapons of the women, who stood bawling and shouting to one another, and asking if the "world had come to an ind, and taken Ballyran wid it."

Then came a rush of persons from the public-house, followed by the soldiers, a few of whom, in order to clear up the mystery, had lighted the torches with which they were provided.

This threw a lurid glare upon the scene, and revealed the wonder-stricken faces of the people who crowded round them.

Lanty, who had rolled over Tim Donovan, was soon upon his legs, and, whipping off the cumbrous great coat of the soldier, was quickly outside where he had left Mike; but no Mike was there, nor was Tim Doolan to be found.

"Where, in the name of the saints, have they wandered to?" he muttered. "Ah, well, they'll be like a bad thirteen, turn up to the fore before long." And so Lanty, tucking his shillelagh under his arm, mixed with the crowd.

It was not long before Fogharty and the runners found their way outside, where they were received with jeers and shouts, especially the lawyer, who, in addition to the fright he had experienced from the shot, had received over his person the contents of the bowl of whisky.

"What's the matter, darlin'?" asked the women, who crowded round him.

"What's the matter, ye born imps!" roared the lawyer. "I have been shot at!"

At this there was a mock cry of sympathy.

"Shot, by the powers," cried Biddy Murphy. "Who is the blaggard?"

Here the eyes of Fogharty fell upon Lanty Shan, who was looking on, and carelessly whistling.

"I believe it's you, Mr. Lanty Shan, who has done me this favour," he said, as he held up his hat. "You missed your mark this time, but when I get hold of you I won't miss mine."

"That's no shot of mine, anyhow," said Lanty, looking at the hole.

"Whose is it, then, you vagabond?"

"You had better ax the hat, you vagabond," replied Lanty.

"Take him up!" roared the lawyer to the soldiers.

"It's nothing to us," replied the sergeant.

"Hurroo, what have the sogers got to do wid it?" shouted the mob, crowding round Lanty.

"About as much as I had me own self," said Lanty. "In the first place, this sort of pistol don't fire off state bullets," and he gave his shillelagh a twirl so near the lawyer and the runners as to make them fall back rather hastily; "and in the next place, you all know Lanty Shan wid the long legs better than to take him for a cowardly snake of an assassin; a fair fight, and Lanty's your man. And, in the next place, if I had fired the shot it would have gone through the head, and not the hat."

"You heard that?" said the lawyer.

"Of course we did; we're not deaf," was the reply.

"I'll have you all up for this. I believe it to be a foul and wicked conspiracy against me, and I offer five pounds to any one who will give me up the offender."

At this a hundred hands were held out.

"Give it to me," shouted the mob; "give it to me, and we'll find him for you to-morrow."

"Ah, you are very clever, ain't you? Find him, and there's the money. Whoever the fellow was," and he glanced again at Lanty, "he shall hang, if I put the rope round his neck myself," and he thrust his hat on his head.

"Do you hear what the lawyer says?— that he'll hang you all," cried Biddy. "By my sowl, he may as well do that as turn us out of our places."

Here a deep groan burst from the mob.

"Which I'll do to-morrow as soon as I have arrested that beggar, Frolic, and——"

What he would have said in addition to the threat, was lost by a blow on his hat, which effectually hid his face from the mob.

There was a roar of exultation at this.

Forcing his hat up, and glaring round him, he ran to the sergeant.

"Did you see who did that, sergeant?" he said.

The man shook his head.

"Out you all go to-morrow," he shouted, foaming at the mouth. "I'll make you pay for this."

And he shook his fist at them.

"There's something by the way of arnest, Master Fogharty."

And a shillelagh fell whack upon his back, which made him spring almost a yard from the ground.

The runners, seeing this state of things, acted well up to their calling, and with a spring they rushed into the house.

"Down with the petty Fogharty," shouted the mob, and the women making a rush at him it would have fared ill for him had he not sprung into the inn like a cat, while the sergeant seeing that matters were becoming serious, caused half-a-dozen of his men to draw up before the door.

"Don't harm the rat," said Lanty; "he'll meet with his desarts some day when he is onawares of it."

He turned quickly round, for he felt the sleeve of his coat pulled, and looking down, saw it was the boy, Phil Leary.

"What's the matter, Phil, avick?" he said.

"There's Mike and Tim awaiting on the Green. They'd spake wid you."

"Whisht! spake aisy. Go and say I'll be wid them."

And, with a sly laugh, the boy glided away.

The mob, seeing the determined bearing of the soldiers, began to make for their cabins, and Lanty walked away with

"THERE'S SOMETHING BY WAY OF ARNEST, MASTER FOGHARTY," CRIED LANTY SHAN.

them, and made his way swiftly towards the Green.

Gradually the crowd drew from around the inn, but all night long outside and inside the wretched mud hovels men and women sat muttering curses and vowing vengeance on those who had sworn that the roof they were under should not cover them long, and often through the night Mr. Fogharty and the runners started up with affright at hearing the loud wail that broke upon the air.

A wail of sorrow and revenge.

CHAPTER XIX.

THE DEATH LIST.

At the same time that the shot had been fired which had so nearly entered up judgment against Mr. Fogharty, and which had such an effect upon the runners as to make them wish they were a thousand miles from Ballyran, a scene was being enacted in a different part of the barony—perhaps the wildest spot that could have been selected for any dark or foul purpose.

On the moor, about a quarter of a mile from the cave of the Devil's Grip, there stood the remains of one of the old Irish churches.

A portion of one the massive stone arches still remained, and in it a large piece of the old stained glass that had once formed its large window, upon which was recorded the representations of saints and other figures.

It had originally been of great dimensions, as could be clearly seen by the old stones still left at the other end, where once stood another arch, but which Time had, in his ruthless course, almost swept away.

No one ever approached these ruins, and for more than one reason; it was more than half a mile from the beaten track of the peasant and the traveller; but another more powerful motive kept the peasants away from it, and that was the legend that the spirit of a murdered priest roamed round the place at night, pointing to the ghastly wound that had deprived him of life.

The superstitious belief had seized strongly upon the minds of the peasantry, that once to see him was to entail ill luck and early death to the beholder, his family and friends.

It is, therefore, needless to say that the place was most religiously shunned by all, and that no one was at all aware that there existed a long underground passage from the vault of the church itself into the cave of the Devil's Grip.

It had been dug and tunnelled ages before, and no doubt had been often used by the fugitives who were flying from religious or any other persecution.

The large vault running the whole length of the church, and which at one time held the remains of nearly all the old parishioners of the four baronies, had not been used for nearly a century for the purpose of burial, and, therefore, the old church became an excellent spot for those who wished to carry on a secret affair of any description.

This spot was the great rendezvous of Black Murtough and his gang, and the only entrance known to them was confided to each man under the most solemn and awful oath.

Upon the night, then, that the commotion took place in Ballyran, there had assembled in this vault some thirty or forty of that body to take into consideration the severe measures that were about to be put in force against them.

Some were standing up against the old grey smouldering walls, conversing in low, deep accents, while others were seated upon kegs and barrels, of which the vault was tolerably full, for this ghostly old place was the chief store-house for the spirits belonging to the gang of Black Murtough.

Perhaps, in no place in Ireland, was the trade of illicit distillation carried on to a greater extent than in the three baronies that belonged to the Stanley family, and not only had it been carried on with the greatest success, but likewise secrecy.

Some of the men had been seized, tried, and sentenced.

Then hopes of pardon were held out to

them if they would divulge the spot where the trade was carried on, but this was met with a laugh of contemptuous defiance.

"I may be a private still-man, and many other things you think bad, but, praised be the saints, I am no dirthy informer!" was the reply of one of them.

The father of Black Murtough was one of them, and he was sent to exile chiefly through the evidence of Fred's father, who was a determined foe to them.

There was not a man of them but carried in his hand a formidable shillelagh, and almost every one of them had a loaded pistol stuck in his belt, and carefully covered over by his frieze coat.

Upon the faces of them all sat a stern and ferocious determination, that plainly showed that no obstacle, however great— nay, even the chance of loss of life itself, should stand in the way of effecting their object.

The half-dozen torches that were fastened to the old stone wall, shed a grim and fitful light upon their faces, and seemed to render the scene more awful in its character.

"I think we're all here, ma bouchals," said Murtough.

"Where is Jan?" asked one.

"Jan? He has made the best of his way to the cutter, which is full of the best cargo that ever went over the water widout paying the king a penny piece."

"And Mickey Doyle," said another, looking round him.

"Mickey? He's gone to Ballyran on a sacret service. He'll be here to the fore," replied Murtough.

"And Paddy Flyn and Ted O'Brien?" said another.

"Lying down in the long grass outside kaping watch. It won't do to be caught napping in these times. Pour out a can of stuff, and pull hard at it before we go to bisness."

A can of the powerful poteen was speedily drawn from a cask, and then handed round.

From this each man took a draught of so powerful a nature as would have rendered those not used to it mad or insensible.

"That's right, my boys; I'm glad to see you like it; it shows the brewing's good and we've got the right hands at the work. Your health, my boys."

In the midst of his draught a noise was heard at the far end of the vault, as though it was three knocks from the hammer of a mallet.

"That's Mickey Doyle," said Murtough. placing the can down; "quick let him in. and when we hear his report we'll know how to act."

Two of the men went to the further end of the vault, and from a secret recess pulled a short, but stout pair of steps; out upon these one of the men mounted, and giving three distinct knocks with his shillelagh, listened for the answering signal with deep anxiety.

It came with four distinct raps; a strong iron bolt was drawn from the inside, the trap pulled up, and the next moment Mickey Doyle was in the vault. The bolt shot back in its socket, the steps were hidden away, and then they all assembled round Black Murtough and Mickey Doyle, anxious to hear the news he had to communicate.

"Well, Mickey, how is the sky?" asked Black Murtough.

"Black, black as—, black and infernal as it well can be," was the answer.

"What's put you out of breath, Mickey?" said another.

"Running to save it. Sure you'd run if the sogers were after you;" and Mickey gulped down a deep draught from the can.

"Sogers; the Lord save us! where?"

"Up at the Castle, in Ballyran; more a coming on purpose to help the gaugers."

At this they all started, and crowded round Mickey.

"I'll bate the lie out of you if I catch you coming the commether over us," said half-a-dozen.

"You'll do what?" said Mickey, springing back; "if you lay a finger upon me, I'll——" and he caught up the heavy tin can.

"Peace, you infernal hounds; what in the fiend's name are you quarrelling about, eh? Am I your captain, or am I not, eh?"

"All the red coats are gone up to the Castle," muttered the man, "and he wants to persuade us that the——"

"Never a bit do I want to 'suade yer either one way or t'other, but I tell you more soldiers are down at the 'Frolic Arms,' and four gaugers, and that more are coming; and that the govermint, bad luck to them, are going to send a magistrate down, and revenue cutters, and a man-o'-war, and sich like things, to stop honest people from getting a living, and, oh, bitther bad luck to them."

"And a pistol bullet that will tell no tales," said Murtough.

"Amen," muttered the rest; "and here are plenty of hands to do it."

"That's right, lads, that's right," said Murtough, taking a roll of paper from his breast. "I've got a list of our foes here," and then taking a small bottle and pen from his pocket, he put it in the hands of a man standing near him; "hould the ink Phelim; it's as red as the blood we mane to have, if forced to it; are you agreed to that, ma bouchals?"

"All, all," was the reply.

"Well, then, here goes. We'll commence with the great man up at the Castle; he's been our bitter enemy since he came into the property. The lady (rest her sowl) was right enough, and never interfered."

"But he'll interfere, and that in a way that won't plase us. I had it all from a soger, who said he was at the bottom of it all, and that he had sworn there shouldn't be a still within twinty miles on him."

"I think we'll put two red marks agin his name, ma bouchals, and when it comes to a third let him send for the priest. Are you agreed?"

"All, all," was the stern, deep reply.

"Well, then, that settles him. Have you put the marks correctly, Phelim?"

"I have done that same thing," was the reply.

"Fred Frolic stands next upon the Death List," said Murtough, and a dark scowl of hate settled on his face.

There was a slight murmur at this.

"What's the matter, do you object, Paddy McGuire?"

"Well," said the man thus addressed, hesitating, "he may be the head of the opposite faction, but he ain't done us any harm."

"Ain't done us any harm!" thundered Murtough, "but his father did afore him, and the young cub will follow in the tracks of the old hound. I say two red crosses agin his name."

"Aye! aye!" shouted a raving McDonnellite, "and all that aid him; they are all alike, Lanty Shan, and——"

"Curse him!" growled Murtough.

"And all the Frolics. Down with them all!"

"Aye, aye, all of them; there ain't a pin to choose among 'em."

And the red cross went down on that death list against them.

"And the red coats every man of them, the officer first," said Murtough.

"Down wid them!" roared the gang.

The repeated application to the poteen was beginning to show itself.

"Didn't ye say there were gaugers, Mickey?"

"Yes, there are five of them; but there's one less by this time."

"How's that?"

"I let fly among 'em in Pat Donovan's parlour this blessed night. I couldn't see who they were, for Pat Donovan had all the winders painted black, in order to save the trouble of claning, so I thought I'd fire among 'em, and then I took to my heels, wid a lot after me; but I gave 'em all the double, thanks to the darkness of the night. I wouldn't have said as much if long-legged Lanty had been after me."

"Well done, Mickey, well done," said they all, while some patted him on the back.

"But, I thought some of you were going to bate the lie out of me, eh?" said Mickey, scowling at them.

"Let that stone sink, Mickey," said Murtough. "Now, look ye, boys, we'll all give up stilling for a week at least, till we see what the weather is like; they can find nothing in the cave if they hunt for a month. We all know the oath we have taken, and the first man that breaks it, or betrays us, dies, though he had a thousand lives."

"Aye, aye. Right, right!" was the reply of all.

"Then listen. In two days comes on the fair of Ballinafad. You'll all of you get round you your friends. The red coats will be there, and we'll trate them as friends and pick a quarrel with them after; and then, mayhap, we'll shorten their number."

"Good, good! and the gaugers, mayhap."

"It will be lucky for us if they're there," said Murtough, with a grin; "bekase we'll send them out to sea."

"To sea. What with?" said Mickey.

"Wid a mighty big stone round their necks," was the reply.

There was a savage laugh at this.

"We'll not be aisily beaten, my friends; we number pretty strong, and there are other little matters stirring among the boys that will help us."

"Where's McDonnell, eh, Murtough?" said a voice.

"Up at Dublin, looking after other matters that consarn us," was the reply.

"And Fogharty the lawyer, why does he hold the money back?" said a dozen voices.

"Ah, well, that's more than I can say; but we'll soon reckon wid him, when we get rid of the red coats, and the gaugers, *ma bouchals.* He sent us a hundred the other night. Come, drink, for we must soon separate; and let each man remember that it is war to the knife to our inimies."

"Aye, aye, war to the knife," was the muttered fierce reply.

"Drink then, a last drop before we say *bannath lath.*"

Then all of them by turns took the can, and drank heartily. Scarcely had they finished when a loud thump was heard upon the trap door.

They all started and listened.

"That's the *danger signal,*" said Murtough; "hold your pace, all of yer, while I see what's the matter, but in case of a surprise, which ain't, however, very likely, see that your weapons are ready."

Then every man flung aside his coat, and took his pistol from his belt, and a dozen of them followed Black Murtough up to the vault, and stood round the place with weapons upraised, ready to fire upon any intruder that might venture to show himself.

Murtough drew the steps from out the recess, and then, pistol in hand, ascended them; and undoing the long massive bolt that secured the trap, cautiously raised it.

"Is that you, Terence Flyn?" he said.

"It's meself and nobody else," was the reply.

"What's the matter?"

"Well, there is a fiery reflection upon the heavens, and over the sky, that I don't like, and other matters I don't like."

"Where's Ted O'Brien?" said Murtough.

"Oh, he's on the look out," was the reply.

"Then come down, your sowl, and take a drop to warm yer."

"I'll do that same thing, and be glad of it;" and he dropped noiselessly into the vault.

Murtough fastened the trap again, and then they all went back to the centre of the place, and Terence took a draught of the poteen.

"That warms a fellow's marrow," he said, smacking his lips, and wiping them with the end of his coat.

"Well, what more, avick?" said Murtough.

"Well, there's been a lot of rockets popping up like signals that something was a going on."

"Ha?" and Murtough's countenance looked as though the darkest shadow of night had fallen upon it, "there's a something wrong," he muttered; and he stood with folded arms for an instant, looking round upon the dark demoniacal faces of the men round him.

"Mickey Doyle," at length he said, "you must go down cautiously to the sea-side just by the cave, and see what's going on, and then make for Ballyran, and see what's doing there; the Philistines are more awake than we thought they were. We've been asleep some of us."

"Ne'er a wink of slape I've had these two nights, anyhow," growled Mickey.

Of this Murtough took no notice.

"Pat McCaul, you make for the house of the Frolics, and see what's doing there. Take care you don't run over Lanty Shan."

"By my sowl I'll give a good account of him if I do," and he grasped his pistol tight.

"Be aisy, you hot-headed fool, it's not for us to draw first blood. Take things quiet until the time comes to rub off some of the names on the list. Be aisy, I say. Now, boys, take a strong drink, go about the work, and do it well."

"Aye, sure, that we will," was the reply of the two, as they took a strong pull at the can.

"You others will stop here till daylight, bekase then if you're met you are going to work, and it will disarm suspicion."

"Right, Murtough! Ah, you have got a head," was the reply of the rest.

Mickey Doyle and Pat McCaul pulled their coats tightly around, and each grasping his shillelagh prepared to set out upon their errand.

"You'll go quietly upon the job, my boys; and don't get popping your pistol again, Mickey."

"But sure there's no harm in it."

"No harm at all, only——"

"Only, what?"

"Only make sure of your man, that's all, Mickey. Away wid you both."

"Never fear," answered the spy, "I'll be bound I hit something."

Then the pair of scouts passed up the steps, through the trap, and emerged into the night air.

There was a bright moon overhead, but the dark, drifting clouds that passed over it at times, obscured it so much as to leave the earth every now and then in darkness and gloom.

Mickey Doyle and Pat McCaul crouched down among the tall, rank grass, that grew thickly through the old church, until they emerged upon the moor.

Then, the rustling of the grass showed that some one had been concealed in it; a head was protruded slowly above it, and that so cautiously, that it seemed to form a portion of the dank weeds itself; then it was raised higher, by degrees, and the unclouded rays of the moon, shining through the ruined columns of the old place, full upon it, showed the pale features and glistening eyes of Little Phil the fairies' child.

There was a bright, quiet smile of joy upon the boy's face; but he remained motionless as marble, until the figures of the two spies had sunk down out of sight upon the moor.

Then he rubbed his hands with gladness.

"They thought I was soft, did they? We shall see—we shall see. I've got your secret, Black Murtough, and I'll pay you out for old scores, that's what I will. Ha! ha! I'll find out more yet. Ha! ha! I'm after you, my friends, and we'll see who gets the best of Little Phil."

And then the boy started off, keeping well in the shade, and carefully stepping over the back of Ted O'Brien, who had, in his long vigil, fallen asleep.

"I'll be close upon you, my boys," said Little Phil, "and soon understand what yer about."

And so quietly did the self-appointed little detective follow the two ruffians, that, with all their cunning, they were not aware that anyone was on their track.

CHAPTER XX.

STILL WATERS RUN DEEP

LITTLE PHIL LEARY, when taken up and fostered by the kindness of Fred Frolic, was thought little more of by the country people than a half-witted child.

Placed by the old huntsman with an aged woman, to look after him, the poor little *gossoon* was suffered to run as wild as one of the shamrocks of the dear old isle, and perhaps, as little cared for.

In the corner of the place where the turf burnt brightly at night, and where the old crones of the place sat round crooning out their old ditties or legends the little fellow, crouched down in a corner, would look up to them with glistening eyes, and take in every word that they uttered.

If the want of education had deadened the sense, the natural sharpness of the boy made up for the deficiency; but, listening, and pleased with all he heard, he kept a strict guard over his tongue; and when by Lanty, who had always looked over him, he was taken up to Frolic House, he at once imbibed a new set of ideas.

With the keen perception of the quick-witted Irish boy, he saw the state of things at Frolic House, and at once shaped his ideas of what was to be done.

Night after night in the old chimney corner he sat crouching over the turf fire, which at times sent up a fitful blaze, in which the boy saw the old huntsman's face peering at him, and then that was quickly overshadowed by the old phantoms of the great, silent hills, in which he had lived so long.

He had heard from the old woman and Lanty Shan the history of the Frolics and the Stanleys; he had laughed over the plot of the whisky being placed in the stable; and then he had formed, in his own quick-witted mind, a plan to make himself a little handy in the matter.

Wherever Lanty Shan went, Little Phil followed as his shadow, with one of those nice little shillelaghs which he had out for himself, and which, with the intuitive love of his darling country for that bit of wood, he could pretty well handle; and so, without anybody knowing what the little neglected boy was doing, he was laying in a large store of strangely useful things, that in case of emergency might become extremely useful.

Unseen, and of little account, he roamed through the baronies, and often heard the Biddies of the place say,

"Ah! the Lord help the boy, what will become of him?"

But night after night, when the old place was hushed in sleep—save where an occasional fight was taking place—Little Phil went roaming away through the dirty streets, and then away into the silent fields, and round by the Devil's Grip, then standing on the mountains, and looking over the glory that in those quiet scenes is the peace of the earth.

Quietly over the mountains and down the gloomy valley did the boy follow the steps of the men he had tracked so well.

For during his lonely watching in the night the old church had been his favourite spot, and, in fact, so fearless was the heart of the last of the old huntsman's race, that he had gone there often to look after the murdered priest, of whom the old traditions had spoken in such mysterious language.

By the seaside, with its wild waves moaning, he left the man Pat McCaul; but with greater fidelity he followed the steps of Mickey Doyle.

"I've got you, my boy," he said; "you wanted to hunt the master, did ye, and kill Lanty Shan; bad luck go with you for that."

And so the boy, Phil, followed the steps of the spy, sometimes crawling through the thick, damp grass, until Mickey Doyle reached the home of the Frolics.

Round and round the place he went, peering and listening, and creeping, and crawling, but all in vain.

Not a sound was heard in the house.

Then he tried the stables.

All was quiet.

"The ould 'un send them luck!" muttered the spy. "There is nothing doing here. They are all aslape. I wonder if there is a turf alight in the kitchen. The Frolies were always good at kaping it up. Bedad, I'll try."

He was about lifting up the latch, when he found himself impelled from behind head first into the place.

"By all the powers, it's meself that's glad to see you, Mickey Doyle!" said Lanty Shan, which was responded to by a loud "hurroo!" from Tim Doolan and Mike, while the sharp keen face of Little Phil peeped in from behind.

"What can we do for you, Mickey Doyle, my darlin'? It's late you're out to-night."

And Lanty winked his eye at Mike and Tim.

"I'd be glad of a light to my dhudeen, Lanty," replied Mickey, in a cringing, fawning tone. "Sure, I knew the Frolics —better luck to them—always kept open house, and so I was just lifting the latch to see if the turf was alight on the flure, when I was sent head-foremost in, and—"

"Say no more, Mickey, say no more. Ye're as welcome as the sun after a storm. Help yourself to the turf, and I'll help you to a glass of poteen. Is your troat dry?"

"As a male-bag. I'd be glad of a sate. The legs that belong to me have been a powerful way to-day."

And with that Mickey Doyle seated himself near the turf, and rubbed his hands together with great glee and satisfaction.

Lanty, Tim and Mike exchanged looks with each other, while Little Phil came sidling up to Lanty, rubbing his eyes as though he had been asleep for a month.

"What's the matter, Phil?" said Lanty. "I'm sure you've had a good long slape."

"That I have," replied the boy, "and so I'll just sit down by Mickey Doyle, and perhaps I may take another."

"By the powers you'll slape your head off!" answered Lanty; "but just as you like, *ma bouchal.*"

Little Phil shambled over to where Mickey Doyle was seated, and, taking the seat in the corner, shut his eyes.

"Didn't I see you down by the 'Frolic Arms' the other night?" said Lanty.

"And what would I be doing down there, Lanty Shan?" was the reply.

"The divil may care for what I do. I only asked the question bekase there's been a mighty fine uproar this very night, and I said wherever there's a row, there will be Mickey Doyle to the fore."

"Much obliged to you, Lanty Shan. I'll be one with you for that; and so there's been a row; and what about, avick?"

"Blarney. You know all about it."

"How could I know all about what was taking place in Ballyrun, when meself haven't been out of Ballinafad these blessed two days."

"Then you've not heard the news?"

"As much news as a turnkey's dog. What is it?"

"You've heard of the rid-coats coming?"

"I've heard that same thing, bad luck to 'em."

"Well, it isn't that. And you've heard they won't let the stills be quiet?"

"I have; bad luck to them again."

"Well, it isn't that. And you've heard that a magistrate is coming over wid a lot more rid-coats and gaugers, and——"

"It's meself that hopes a plague or a faver will break out and take 'em off. Musha, what are we to do for a living?"

"It's a puzzler for a great many to answer that question. I say you've heard of those things?"

"Yes, to my sorra."

"Well, it isn't that, but an old friend of yours was shot dead by mistake."

"The Lord save us! Who was that?" said Mickey, looking dreadfully alarmed. "Shot dead?"

"Yes, and the milintary are after the murderin' assassin, and to-morrow, when the justice arrives, they are going to offer a powerful reward for him. I wouldn't be in his shoes for a goulden guinea."

"Nor I. But who was the man that was shot? Are yer sure he is dead?"

"Am I sure you're living? The bullet went clane through his head, knocking over Pat Donovan, and breaking his leg in two places, for which there'll be damages, which ain't of any consequence, bekase it ain't quite convanient for a man to pay damages after the *skibbeah* has done wid him."

It was a ludicrous sight to see the face of Mickey Doyle during this; he was trying all he knew to keep an unchanged countenance, but the fear that he might have been seen worked so powerfully upon him, that the perspiration ran down his face in streams, and, in order to relieve his face from that annoyance, he kept from time to time raising the tail of his coat to wipe it off, leaving behind it several long black streaks from the mud.

In so doing, he lifted his coat more than once so high that a small, dirty roll of papers fell out on to the floor unperceived by him.

This did not escape the keen, sharp eyes of Little Phil, but, as those of the spy were never kept in one spot, but rolled about, restless as a snake's, Phil saw there was some little danger in it; he, therefore, curbed his impatience to seize it, and pretended to sleep heavily, although his half-opened eyelids were fixed upon the coveted prize.

"What ails the man?" said Lanty. "Why, you sowl, you didn't do it, did you, Mickey?"

"What do you mane?" savagely replied the spy. "Didn't I tell yer I was in Ballinafad? Who is the man that I ——who was shot dead? The saints be wid us, but these are awful times."

"Well, it's a mighty great loss to you and all your party, bad luck to them, for the man shot is—guess who it is, Mickey, *ma bouchal.*"

"How can I guess; was it a gauger? any how, that's no loss."

"No; well, then, I'll tell you, it's your old friend Fogharty."

Up jumped Mickey as though a barrel of powder had been under him, and, at the same moment, Little Phil fell flat off his seat on to his face, and the papers.

"You don't mane to say that Fogharty is shot?" said Mickey, trembling.

"I mane to say that he was shot; and come here, my darlin', don't be alarmed. I'll whisper it—they know the man who shot him."

"The Lord save us!" was the scarce audible reply of Mickey. "What's his name, poor sowl?"

"He's called Mickey Doyle, *ma bouchal,* and he was seen by more than one; you'll take my advice."

"I tell you I was at Ballina——"

"Bally-the-evil-one, you little omadhaun," said Lanty, angrily; "do you think they can be mistaken in such a cunning fox as you are? Take to your heels, Mickey; hide in the hills—anywhere—but kape out of the way of the rid-coats, for there'll be more offered for your head in the morning than ever it's worth."

Mickey Doyle stood abjectly looking from one to the other, as if doubting whether they were in jest or earnest.

"I'll be taking your advice, Lanty Shan," at length he said, "bekase they might be taken me for some other Mickey Doyle, and that wouldn't be pleasant anyhow."

"It ain't any use trying to prove you're the wrong man when you have been hanging an hour or two; Mickey, yer know you're a McDonnellite, and there's no love between us, and it's more than a dozen times that I've whacked you nately, so that your own blessed mother wouldn't have known you; and it's well known that Lanty Shan hates all assassins, vagabonds who use a knife or a pistol instade of natecal fists, or the nate bit of wood, that you know well."

"I do," said Mickey, "and I'll not forget it when the day comes."

"We'll wait till then with resignation; but as it's Fogharty you shot, the rest of society may be thankful, although the judge, when he puts on the black cap, will no doubt be of a different opinion; but take to your legs, man, take to your legs; get off as soon as you can."

"Why?"

"Why, ould Nick burn you, do you want to bring us into trouble and disgrace? Don't you know that when the proclamation comes out it will be transportation to any that harbours you? Phil, *ma bouchal.*"

"Yes, Lanty."

"Run down the road and see that none of the sogers are on the watch."

The boy was off like an arrow from a bow.

"Yer see that we are doing all we can to keep your neck out of the twisted hemp, and it's a great deal more than you'd do by us. But I always like to return good for evil, and so——"

Here Phil returned.

"There's nothing stirring, except widow Mahoney's enjoying the night air."

"Then, your sowl to heaven!" said Lanty. "Off wid your shoes while the leather's good. And, hark ye, Mickey Doyle, if ever I catch you spyin' round this place agin wid your sarpint's eyes, there shan't be a sound bone in your dirty carcass but what will be broken! Be off wid you!"

"I'll do it to oblige you, Lanty," and the next moment Mickey Doyle was rattling along for a shelter in the old vault which he had so recently left.

Then Phil, cautiously putting the roll of papers into the hand of Lanty, whispered to him how he had got them.

"Stir up the turf fire into a blaze and let us see what all this is about!"

Then they drew their seats round the turf fire waiting until, by its light, Lanty could decipher the writing.

"Fasten the door fast, Tim, and then, bedad! I think we'll gain a sacret!"

CHAPTER XXI.

THE COMING STRUGGLE.

By daybreak, the Barony ot Ballyran was up and astir, for more soldiers were marching in.

With them came one of the most vigilant gaugers of the day.

At their head, with the officer, rode Mr. Righton, the worthy solicitor whom Fred had been so anxiously waiting for.

This gentleman being a magistrate, had been appointed by the Government to carry out their full and stern determination to uproot the gigantic evil of illicit distillation throughout the length and breadth of the island.

This was the great bane and curse of a land whose beauties cannot be excelled by any, and whose people, loyal and brave to

the heart's core, may be misled for a moment only to return with tenfold zeal to their glorious patriotism and fidelity; and then, twining the glorious green flag, with its harp of gold, with the folds of the English banner, leave them to mingle while time, glory and honour have existence.

Besides the evil of the private still others existed, such as secret political societies, and these had been gradually increasing to such an extent as to alarm the Government, by their great and powerful ramifications.

Immediately, therefore, it was known that the "illicit distillation" was at once to be destroyed, the secret orders and societies threw themselves into the breach, and took common cause with the still-workers.

Thus the coming struggle bade fair to become one of a very desperate character, as the excited and reckless bravery of its people had upon more than one occasion proved.

Nearly the whole population of the three Baronies sympathised with the still-workers, and would have shown it openly to a great extent, only the inveterate hatred of the different factions prevented it.

For instance, the McDonnell faction were to a man engaged in illicit distillation; on the other hand, the "Fighting Frolics" had scarcely one engaged in the work.

The whole affair had been kept a profound secret, and then, by a simultaneous movement, the military arrived in the different towns, to the surprise of one part of the population and the deep and bitter anger of the other.

Mr. Righton, having alighted for a short time from his horse, and consulted with the officer, was about remounting, when he suddenly found himself accosted by Mr. Fogharty.

"Happy to see you, Mr. Righton," said he. "Come over, I suppose, to settle the Frolic affairs? And under the charge of the military! Very right—very right. Critical times, sir."

"Indeed, Mr. Fogharty. The critical times, Mr. Fogharty," replied the lawyer, bending his keen grey eyes upon the man that addressed him, "are all owing to the *scoundrels* that are the cause of them, and who live and fatten upon the ignorance and gullibility of the misguided."

"Mr. Righton do you mean——"

"Keep your temper," replied the magistrate, holding up his hand. "You will take my meaning in whatever sense you think proper, and with respect to the *Frolic affairs*"—and he smiled—"I am quite ready to enter into them at the proper season, in a way which I am inclined to think will not be much to your satisfaction; and, thirdly, I am not under the *charge* of the military at present, although I am sorry to think they will have their hands full before long."

At this, it was only by a powerful effort that Fogharty kept his naturally violent temper under, but he inwardly felt and knew that he had his master before him.

"I am going up to Frolic House, upon a very serious charge against its master."

"Indeed!"

"Yes. He has been conspiring with a certain Captain Frank Hardy, to inveigle and carry off an heiress, and a ward in Chancery, for which, having them under his roof and harbouring them, he is under——"

Here the pompous, petty Fogharty stopped short for Mr. Righton had ridden off.

"Curse him! I'll beat him yet; but what brings him here, I wonder? Now then, my men," he said, addressing the Bow Street runners, "we have no time to lose. Follow me. There's little doubt but that fellow, Righton, will warn him, and the birds will be flown if we are not in haste. That business settled, I must to Stanley Castle, and—ha! humph! I see!"

Followed by the runners, Fogharty started off amid the groans and execrations of the women and children, who had not forgotten his threat the night before.

He was honoured by more than one stone thrown after him, and an intimation to say his prayers if he took off a door or a bit of thatch in any of the hovels in the town of Ballyran.

When Mr. Righton arrived at Frolic House, he found its master in close consultation respecting the necessity of placing a pair of gates up.

In addition to Lanty Shan and Tim, there stood by them another person, dressed in the long frieze coat of the peasantry; a large flapping hat covered a crop of red hair, and he had a handkerchief tied round his face, as though he was suffering from serious pain in it.

The surprise of all was very great when they saw Mr. Righton ride into the woeful-looking courtyard.

Hastily dismounting, he shook hands heartily with Fred.

"Long looked for, come at last, Fred," he said, grasping his hand. "I've given orders, and in a very short time Frolic House shall be the pride of the country. What do you think of that, eh?"

"But, sir, my father's debts——"

"Will be all wiped off as if by a sponge. A suit in the chancery court, that has been there beyond the memory of man, more shame for it, is all but decided in your favour, and the long arrears, &c, will be——"

Here he was stopped by Lanty and Tim seizing him by the hands, and nearly dislocating the shoulders.

"Say it again, say it again wid your own beautiful mouth, hurroo!" and off went Lanty's coat. "Tim, ye divil, just tread on that by way of compliment."

"Be quiet, you fools," said the lawyer. "What do you want to knock one another about for, eh?"

"Just for the *love* of the thing," replied Lanty.

"Love of the—— What is it I hear about a ward in Chancery? Here's that serpent, Fogharty, to take you all up for something or the other."

Here Fred's eye glanced at the countryman who, quietly taking a dhudeen from his pocket, lighted it, and, seating himself on the large stone by the side of the wall, began smoking with the greatest unconcern.

"Not a movement of this escaped the keen, penetrating eye of Mr. Righton.

"Well, you see, sir," said Fred, laughing, "I was——"

"I neither want to see anything or hear anything that does not concern me. Mum; here comes the scamp."

And Mr. Righton and Fred stood engaged in conversation as Fogharty and the runners bustled into the place.

"Ha, humph, I see," he muttered. "Now, sir, tell that person," and he pointed to Fred, "your business."

At this rude speech Lanty's shillelagh was raised, and, had it fallen, would have spoilt Mr. Fogharty's fun for the day, but a warning from Fred prevented it.

The man then read the warrant directing him to take into custody the person of Captain Frank Hardy for contempt of the High Court of Chancery, and then went on about pains and penalties.

"I know the person so described well; he is an old and dear friend of mine. You are welcome to search the house, but mind you don't pay a visit out of one room down into another through the ceiling."

The men, at this, laughed.

"A mere subterfuge," said Fogharty; "follow me."

"Stop, Mr. Fogharty," and Fred placed his hand gently on his collar; "what have you to do with this, eh?"

"No assault, sir, no assault! To do with it? everything, sir; ask the officers."

Fred did so.

The chief officer saw at once that Mr. Fogharty was not exactly a favourite, and that he was calculated to bring them into trouble.

"I know nothing of him, sir; he offered his services to bring us here, and he has done so, that's all."

"Just as I thought. Lanty, show those persons over the house, and let them satisfy themselves that I have no persons concealed there; and, Mr. Fogharty, you will be kind enough to move your body off these premises."

"Not yet, sir, not yet. I have business with you; you don't escape me—if you do, you have only another to beat."

"I shall have *another* to bate when I come back," said Lanty to him, and he disappeared with the men into the house.

"Now, then, Mr. Frolic."

"Be quiet, sir; do you not see I am engaged with a *gentleman?*" said Fred.

Tim Doolan, who was holding Mr. Righton's horse, thought it a pity that Mr. Fogharty should have all the court-yard to himself, for the little rascal was pacing about all parts of it.

Tim, therefore, walked the horse about, and hemming Mr. Fogharty more than once in a corner, backed the horse so close upon him, that the learned gentleman rushed out of the place, vowing vengeance; but, not seeing in his haste that the countryman sitting at the gate had stretched out his leg, he went rolling over it head first into the road, to the infinite delight and fun of the crowd assembled.

By this time the Bow Street runners had completed their search, and returned into the court-yard.

"Well, gentlemen," said Fred, "have you found the runaways?"

"No, sir," said the chief officer; "there is no one answering the description, and we shall get back to England as fast as we can."

"I should advise you to do so," was Fred's reply. "Lanty, take them into the kitchen, and put the best you have before them, at least, if they have not found the English fugitives; but they must not go without tasting Irish hospitality."

"I'll do that same thing, sir," replied Lanty, with a knowing wink at Tim. "Come along wid me, gentlemen, and if you don't ate out of a gould dish, you'll get what is far better, a hearty welcome, so come along."

"THE RED WARNING WAS ON THE GATES."

"And, Lanty, take good care of the house. I shall be going up to the town."

"Sartainly, sir," and then he muttered to himself, "The house is big enough to take care of itself; you don't go alone anywhere in these peaceable times anyhow."

And he led the way round by the kitchen, followed by the men.

Fred proceeded into the house to fetch his hat, when Mr. Fogharty rushed forward to speak to him.

"Mr. Frolic," he roared, "I must speak with you."

"If it is legal business, Mr. Fogharty, you had best speak to me, his legal adviser," said Mr. Righton.

At that moment Fred returned.

"Legal business! What other business can it be sir, eh?"

"Well, sir, go on."

"Well, sir, when are the bills accepted by his father—I wish my neck had been broken before I had seen him—and——"

"I wish it had, Mr. Fogharty, most devoutly," replied Fred. "It will be, *some* day if you bide your time."

"I want none of your sarcasm, Mr. Frolic; you are more handy at that than paying your debts. I am speaking to Mr. Righton."

"Well, sir, go on," said that gentleman.

"Well, sir about the bills. There is a large sum upon them, and I shall enter up judgment upon them."

"I have stopped all that, Mr. Fogharty," said Mr. Righton, coolly.

"Stopped what, sir? Do I hear aright?"

"Perfectly; I have by an order from the court stayed all further proceedings."

"Indade! that's news to me. And upon what ground?"

And the lawyer seemed to be monstrously nervous.

"Upon more than one ground; and, although my time is very precious, I'll try and satisfy you."

"If you please, sir."

"Well, then, in the first place, the bills are all of them informally drawn."

"Ha! ha! You'll be clever to prove *that*," and he snapped his fingers.

"It is already proved; in the next place they were obtained by fraud, and——"

"What! holy mother," roared Fogharty, "do you impute fraud to me? I'll make you pay for that. Fraud! he——, fellow," he said to the countryman, who still sat on the stone, "come here; I'll call you as a witness. Say that again, Mr. Righton;" and he pulled out a dirty memorandum book. "Here, you fellow, listen."

"It's not of much use; the man's as deaf as a post," said Fred, laughing.

"I think you said fraud, sir—eh?"

"I did, and I repeat it; not only fraud, but one of no common nature, for the poor gentleman was, at the time, incapable of understanding what was said to him; besides, he never received the smallest consideration."

"A subterfuge, sir—a mere subterfuge, sir. I'll bring a respectable witness to prove that every farthing was paid him, and that he received it in notes, and that if ever there was a fair and honourable transaction that was the one. Pray is there any other little matter that you'd try and frighten me with?"

"Well, yes, there is another, and that is the most serious of them all. A matter that will involve your life."

"Ha, ha! by the powers, you do it well, Mr. Righton. My life! Go on."

"I said your life, Mr. Fogharty, and I mean it. You are still determined to go on with the suit against Mr. Frolic?"

"Determined! By my soul, there is nothing can hinder; I'll have every farthing, or I'll——"

"You shall never have one farthing of it," said Fred, breaking in warmly. "I have heard all, and am prepared to resist to the last."

"Are you? Then you'll rush further into ruin than you are already. Upon what ground,"—and the little rascal cringed—"may I humbly ask, am I to be cheated out of my own?"

"Upon the grounds of forgery, Mr. Fogharty," was Fred's stern reply.

At this the face of the rascal became perfectly livid.

"Forgery!" he gasped out. "Ha, ha! you're joking."

"You'll not find it any joke," replied Fred, sternly.

"And who is the forger?"

"You! I denounce you as the forger of certain bills said to be signed by my father, and for which crime most assuredly you shall be punished."

At this denunciation the poor wretch for the moment appeared completely paralysed, and Fred and Mr. Righton gazed somewhat pityingly on him.

But the next instant he seemed to recover all the ferocity of his nature, and, raising his bent body up, he glared wildly upon them.

"Liar!" he bawled forth, at last. "I'll have your blood for this!" And he seemed as if, like a wild cat, he was about to spring at Fred's throat.

But Fred, taking the thick hunting-whip from Mr. Righton's hand, held it up.

"Hark ye, you little pettifogging rascal, if you dare to raise a finger against me, I'll thrash you so that the hangman will be spared his office; leave this place immediately—on the instant!" and he pointed with his whip to the road.

By this time Lanty had returned with the men, and, overhearing all this, he quietly approached Fogharty from behind, and, grasping him by the collar, almost lifted him off his legs.

"Do you hear what the masther says, yer lump of dirt? and so you and your tricks are bowled out, are they?"

Fogharty wriggled and struggled under the hands of Lanty, muttering curses in a most awful manner.

"Ah, it's no use your cursing and spluttering in that way; come away wid yer," and he dragged him towards the entrance.

"I'll have your lives—your blood!" he gasped.

"If you don't be off, I'll have some of yours first," and Lanty raised the shillelagh; then, with a powerful twist of his arm, he pulled him outside the court-yard, and applying his foot most vigorously to the lawyer's back, sent him flying off the premises.

He raised his hand with a menacing gesture at them all, and as well as his rage would let him be understood, he muttered an oath of deadly vengeance, and, buttoning up his coat, disappeared.

"Lanty — quick!" said his master. "Out with the horse, I am going with Mr. Righton into the town.

It was soon done.

"Now, my man, you will perceive that no persons whatever, resembling those you have been in search of, have been here."

"You're quite right, sir," said the chief officer, "and I shall disturb you no more; and, without meaning any offence, sir, I

shall be delighted when I have turned my back upon this."

"Whisht! Not a word. It's not our fault if the finest praties and buttermilk don't agree wid yer stomachs. They must be quarely made."

"Look ye, my men, myself and this gentleman are going back to the town, and shortly there will be a conveyance that will take you back to Dublin."

"Once there, sir," said the man, "and you'll never catch me again in Ballyran."

And he muttered something not very complimentary.

"And don't make any mistake, my friend," replied Lanty, "Ballyran don't want to see your swate faces any more, bekase you spoil the look of the place altogither."

With that, Fred and Mr. Righton rode out of the, place, followed by the men.

Directly they were out of hearing. Lanty took a couple of leaps up in the air.

"You're safe, sir, you're safe. They are all gone, and the ould un may have the rest. Go into the house wid you, and get into yer proper habillyments, I think they calls them."

The captain, for it was he who had quietly been smoking a dhudeen, sprang up, laughing.

"Right, Lanty, and now all fear is over from those fellows, I must make myself active among ye. I don't like that Mr. Fogharty."

"You're not sing'lar in that, sir; the man that likes that contemptible cur ain't fit to look at."

"He means mischief."

"No doubt; but we'll stop his maning afore long. I put Mike on his footsteps, and Tim I lave in the house wid your honour," and Lanty began buttoning his coat.

"Why, where are you off to now, Lanty?" said the captain.

"Where am I off to, did you say?"

"Yes."

"Can't you guess?"

"No."

"I thought not. Well, then, I'm after the masther. There's serious times a coming on, fearful times, and when a man has got a host of inimies, as the masther has, why, then——"

"He doesn't deserve them, Lanty."

"Ah, that's the very reason he's got them; the McDonnell's will have his life if we don't kape on the look-out. But I'm off."

"I'll go with you, Lanty; he shall have more than *one* friend at his side in the moment of danger."

To rush into the house, assure his darling wife that all the danger was over, and then to join Lanty, was but the work of a moment; and in a few minutes Captain Hardy and Lanty Shan were hurrying after Fred, in the direction of "Swate Ballyran."

During this, the town had been cast into a state of great excitement.

The gaugers who had accompanied the magistrate, Mr. Righton, had been busily employed putting up large proclamations upon the "Frolic Arms" and other houses.

They set forth the determination of the government to do away with all "illicit stills," and warned the people of the punishment that would be inflicted upon them in all cases where the law was disobeyed. There was likewise a reward offered to any person giving information.

In many cases no sooner were the officers' backs turned, than the bills were torn down, or plastered with mud, so that not a sowl could read them.

The angry passions of the people against the gaugers were so excited, in fact, that the men had to take refuge in the "Frolic Arms," and place themselves under the care of the military.

The public-house was at once laid under a complete state of siege.

Stones and mud came flying in it, matters were becoming serious, and the officers had already told the men to make ready to drive the mob back.

A tall, raw-boned fellow, a McDonnellite, was upon the point of heaving a stone at one of them which must have killed him, when he found himself sprawling on his back, and Fred Frolic, with upraised whip, standing over him!"

At this the McDonnellites uttered yells of rage and defiance, and were rushing upon Fred and the small band of "Fighting Frolics" who had rallied behind him, and a conflict of a deadly nature was imminent, when Mr. Righton spurred his horse between them.

"Mr. Frolic," he said, "you will spare him the punishment his dastardly conduct deserves, and I thank you for your courageous behaviour, which at least has saved life."

By this time the fellow had crawled back to his party.

"And hark ye, my men, I give you a word or two of advice. Do not attempt, in any way, to molest the military or civil force in the performance of a very painful duty; any person who is caught defacing in any way the proclamation affixed on any of the buildings will be sent to the assizes and severely punished. I should advise you now to disperse to your several abodes, and not in any way attempt to interfere with the due course of justice."

"We don't want any rid coats or you here at all; and you'll find you made a great mishtake in coming," shouted a McDonnellite.

"I again advise you to conform to the law," was the reply.

"What has *he* got to do with it?" said the man, pointing to Fred.

"Everything, fellow," said Frolic, "I am here, and will do everything in my power to see the laws respected and obeyed."

"We'll sarve you out for it, *ma bouchal;* your tumble-down place is bad enough, but it shall be worse before long. You'll only repint this job once and that will be as long as you live," roared the McDonnells.

"I treat your threats with the contempt they deserve," said Fred, turning to Mr. Righton. The McDonnells, furious at the contemptuous coolness with which Fred treated them, groaned and hooted at him; and the fellow whom Fred had hurled to the ground flung a heavy stone at him.

"That for you," shouted he.

"And that for *you,*" shouted Lanty, as he sprang at him and with a crushing blow levelled him with the earth.

That was quite enough; the next moment the two factions were again at it, and if possible with more powerful and bitter feelings of hatred and animosity.

Mr. Righton spoke to the officer in command of the troops to assist him in quelling the riot; but Fred knowing the parties better, advised him not to interfere.

"Let them fight it out," he said, "themselves; if the soldiers interfere with the fight of the factions, they will join against them, and the carnage will be awful."

"You are right, Fred," said the magistrate, grasping his hand.

And so he was, for the McDonnells were no match for the Frolics, and in a very short time they were routed and dispersed, flying from the scene with loud yells of revenge, while the blood ran streaming down their faces.

Lanty and his party did not pursue them; they were satisfied that they had avenged the insult offered to their leader, whom they found, to their great satisfaction, uninjured, the stone having missed his head, though it sent his hat flying some distance.

The row being over, the magistrate ordered fresh placards to be pasted up amid the deep anathemas of the women and the children, who looked upon the suppression of the stills as taking the bread out of their children's mouths, whereas it was intended to assist, with their own industry, to put more into them.

The town having, in a great measure, resumed it quietude, Mr. Righton and Fred, with the officer, were about entering the "Frolic Arms," when the former felt his sleeve pulled.

"Well, Lanty, what is it?" said that gentleman, turning round. "That's an ugly crack you've got on your head."

"Well, yes; but, you see, it's at the *back*. I never got one in the *front* yet. You see, I was just polishing off Pat Ryan and Tim Doyley, when some blaggard gave me a dacent *polthough** behind, the murtherin' coward!"

"I shall be glad to see the time when all this fighting is abolished," said Mr. Righton.

"You will, will you? Well, when that comes to pass, Ireland's ruined back and edge. What would we be widout the two S's—the shamrock, heaven bless it, and the shillelagh? Botheration! to doing away wid either the one or the other; but that ain't what I've got to say."

"Well, then, what is it, Lanty?" asked Fred.

"It's a mighty sacret, and was found out by Little Phil, who has more cunning in his head, pluck in his heart, and speed in his feet than most men, and then, och! murder! the twist of his wrist in his twirl of the shillelagh, and——"

"Never mind the shillelagh now, Lanty, what's the secret?"

And Mr. Righton smiled.

"It's nothing to laugh at; but you don't think I'm going to tell a sacret in the open air, do you? What do you take me for?"

"A clever fellow," replied the magistrate."

"Many thanks for a compliment at the expense of truth, your honour; but I forgive you, bekase you're the friend of my master. So, if you plase, I'll just go wid you into the iligant parlour that Pat Donovan keeps for the convanience of his friends."

Laughing heartily at this, Mr. Righton, Fred, and the officer, led the way into the house.

"Now, Lanty," said Mr. Righton, as they seated, "take a seat, and let us know this important secret."

"In the first place, it wouldn't become me to be sated in the prisence of gintlemen, and seeing that," here he glanced at the window; "och! murder! that won't do!" and he sprang to the door. "Pat— Pat Donovan!" he shouted, "come here, you *commether*, you're a muddle of a landlord!"

"What the divil is the matter now?" said Pat, popping in his great shock head of hair. "You'll make sich rows that you'll frighten the hens out of the nest, and Ballyran will run short of eggs."

"Come here, avick. Do you see that winder, or rader where a winder ought to be, only the murdering bullet that smashed it missed Fogharty—bad luck to it."

"More's the pity, I say," replied Pat.

"Well, then, have you got a whisp of straw?"

"More than that," was the reply.

"Then fetch it, and stuff up that winder, bekase we don't want any listeners."

"I'll do that same thing, Lanty," and away ran Pat, and in a very short time the wind and the listeners were blocked out.

"Now, Lanty, make haste, for we have a great deal to do," said Mr. Righton.

"And so have I, for the matter of that. Well, you see, the last night that ever was, Mickey Doyle, *bad scran** to him, paid us a visit, and in the course of conversation he dropped from his pocket an iligant roll of paper, which Little Phil secured with great dexterity. Well, we read them over, that is, I did, for the

---

* Blow.

* Bad food.

divil a bit can Mike or Tom rade, and Little Phil himself has stuck fast at letter P, and——"

"Well, what does it say?"

"Blood, murder, and burning, and a few other trifling things," said Lanty.

"Ha, ha, ha!" laughed Fred.

"Don't laugh, master," said Lanty, "until you're assured it's a joke. I'll give you the papers, and then, I think, you'll say seeing is believing."

Then Lanty put his hand in his pocket, but drew it out empty, then he tried his other pockets with the like success.

"The divil burn the papers, where have they got to?" he muttered; "sure I ain't been robbed of them," and the perspiration began to roll down his face. "If I thought anybody had been playing larks, his thick skull should ache for a month," and then, in his perplexity, down went his *caubeen* on to the floor, and for a moment he kept smoothing down the fox crop.

"Whoo, hurroo! I have it! It's that ugly blow that's done it, bad luck to it!" and then, after taking a spring or two up in the air, he seized the *caubeen*. "I thought, if my head forgot it, the old hat would remember it. What a *gommach** I've been," and with that he took out his knife, and, cutting round the lining, took out the papers. "There they are, your honours," he said, and he laid them down upon the table before them.

Mr. Righton took them up, and glanced at first slightly at them, but the next instant, those who were watching him, saw that the coolness had changed to deep excitement.

"This has been a lucky find for you, Lanty," he at length said, "and, at any rate, will serve as a warning. Does any one besides yourself know of these papers?"

"Only those I told you of," replied Lanty.

"I mean the contents?"

"No. I kept the contints to myself; I thought it more prudent, like."

"You ought to be made Lord Chancellor," said Mr. Righton.

"I'd rather not, if it's all the same to you, sir," said Lanty. "I've no taste that way."

"Well, then, we will excuse you; but

how did you satisfy the curiosity of your friends?"

"Oh, aisy enough; I told them they were Mickey Doyle's scores, and upon that score they were satisfied; lave me alone for putting them on the wrong scent; but what are those crosses for, eh?"

"Why, they mean mischief, Lanty, and diabolical mischief. This is a list of the proscribed persons, against whom the lawless band of smugglers and still-workers are determined to wreak their vengeance. It is necessary for us all to be on the alert to check it, for which purpose I shall order a few of the troops to be quartered upon you, Mr. Frolic."

"With all my heart, sir," was the reply.

"How will we fade them?" whispered Lanty.

"Oh, we'll look after that, Lanty. In the meantime, I will take charge of these papers; there is a slip here purporting to be a receipt, the hand-writing of which appears to be very familiar to me."

He appeared to reflect a moment, when suddenly there rose a wail upon the air, followed by fierce yells of rage and defiance.

The next moment they all hurried from the house into the open air.

There they found Mr. Fogharty with some dirty, ill-favoured man, about to visit those who were the tenants of the Stanley property.

"What is all this, Mr. Fogharty?" said Mr. Righton.

"I apprehend, sir, that it is a matter with which you have nothing to do," replied Fogharty, with a diabolical grin upon his face. "I am empowered by Sir Edward Stanley, of Stanley Castle, to demand certain arrears of rent, and if they are not paid, to pull off the roofs and turn the tenants out."

Here again a wail arose from the poor squalid women and children, while the men stood sullen and scowling, looking on as if indifferent about the matter, but yet in their hearts brooding over a deep revenge.

"What will we do, sir?" said Biddy Murphy, "if they turn us out into the open air, and take the roofs off; they'll not have much trouble in doing that, by reason that there is scarcely one on."

"No matter," said Fogharty, "roof or no roof, can you pay the rent, it's a matter of——"

---

* A simpleton.

"Oh, hould your talk now; if it was a matter of farthings, you couldn't have it—bitter bad luck to the man who sent you."

"He'll suffer for it," said the deep stern voices of the men.

"This is a most cruel, as well as ill-advised proceeding on the part of Sir Edward, and how he can employ a scoundrel like that, puzzles me" said Righton to Fred.

"Mr. Fogharty," he added, "I am not in the habit of asking favours of you, or any man, but as I consider this is most likely to lead to a breach of the peace, I must beg of you to desist until I ride over and see Sir Edward respecting this."

"My orders are to proceed at once, and not wait for anybody or anything," was the reply.

"Indeed!"

"Do you hear the scoundrel?" shouted one of the men. "Are we to stand by and see our wives and children turned out into the open air because we can't pay the rint? and for what?"

And he raised his gaunt arm, and pointed with a finger of scorn and derision at the half-roofed mud hovels, which would have been a disgrace to the wilds of Africa.

"Stand by me, men and fathers, and shed the last drop of your blood rather than see those you love cast into the street to rot and starve! you're not men and fathers if you do."

At this appeal to the wild passions of the poor half-starved wretches, the men seemed to start from their apathy, and rushing in a body to their hovels, stood before them with their formidable shillelaghs raised to resist any attempt that might be made upon them.

The women, headed by Biddy Murphy, armed themselves with the "stone in the stocking," a blow from which would be instantaneous death.

This formidable battle-array somewhat dismayed Mr. Fogharty and his men.

"I call upon the military to aid and assist me," shouted Fogharty."

"The military shall do no such thing, sir," said Mr. Righton, warmly; "they come here to preserve peace and order, not to assist those who are anxious to break it."

Here a loud shout arose from the mob, mingled with the cries of "God bless your honour, God bless you!"

"I call upon you all," said Fogharty, who was resolved not to yield an inch, "to bear witness that the magistrate himself refuses to aid the law."

At this, Mr. Righton took out his watch suddenly, and looked at it.

"Indeed, Mr. Fogharty," he replied, with a smile, "you seem to have *forgotten* your laws; and it's lucky I'm here to prevent *your* breaking it."

"I'd be glad to know how that is," said Fogharty, looking up with a cunning leer. "I think I have studied the law as well as you have."

"The dirty part of it," said Fred.

"Hurroo, your honour! you'll stick up for us," shouted the mob.

"Keep the law, my friends, and it will always protect you," was Fred's reply.

"Well, what about the law? I'd be glad to be instructed by my betters," and Fogharty chuckled heartily.

"Well, then, you shall be, Fogharty," said the magistrate. "The *law* says that all cases of eviction shall take place within *certain hours*; the hour is just past ten minutes, and so, Mr. Fogharty, you will have to wait until to-morrow morning's sunrise, and by that time I'll take care that no eviction shall take place."

The shouts of the men, and the wild screams of the women, satisfied Mr. Righton that he soothed for the moment the wild passions of the mob, as they rushed up to him and Fred, shaking hands and dancing wildly.

Fogharty's face turned to a mixture of white and yellow, and he shook with the rage of a baffled tyrant; but he was aroused from all that by fears for his life.

The women began dancing and yelling round him, while they whirled the fatal stones in the stocking about with as much ferocity and ease as the men did the bit of wood.

Dismayed at this, Fogharty and his men made a rush at the door of the "Frolic Arms;" but there they found themselves opposed by Lanty Shan and Pat Donovan.

"There ain't a bit of room for the tail of a mouse, let alone the body of a rat," said Lanty.

"But I insist!" roared Fogharty.

"To ould Nick I pitch your insisting!" said Pat Donovan. "You'll not come in. D'ye think, bad luck to you, I want the house pulled down about my ears?"

"Would you see me beaten to a jelly?" he said.

"Wid all my heart," said Lanty; "and it's meself that wouldn't mind helping."

"Look ye, Mr. Fogharty, this place is rather dangerous for you. Make the best of your way back to the castle, I shall be there myself shortly," said Righton.

Fogharty took this sensible advice, and he and his men made a quick exit, while Fred and Mr. Righton kept the mob back.

Then they mounted their horses.

"You will ride with me to the castle, Fred?" said he.

"I think I had better not. The reasons I'll tell you as I go along," was the reply.

The magistrate looked at him for a moment, but said nothing.

"You will let half-a-dozen of your men take up their quarters at Frolic House," he said to the officer. "I shall not be long before I return from Stanley Castle."

And then, giving Lanty some silver, to which Fred added more, they rode off amidst the prayers and blessings of the half-famished crowd.

Lanty soon had his portion of the work done, and shouldering his shillelagh, he marched off with the soldiers to Frolic House, accompanied by the host of women and children shouting, screaming, and dancing for joy.

CHAPTER XXII.

THE RED WARNING.

DURING this time, the band of which Black Murtough was the head had not been idle.

Scouts and spies had been sent round for miles to summon all their confederates; and the "secret societies," who were planning and plotting for other purposes, gave them all their aid and assistance.

Secret meetings were held, and measures resolved upon, and spies posted in every barony, and in the shebeen shops and the public-houses.

The *Red Oath of Vengeance* was administered to all, and secret signs and ominous passwords were made known to them all.

Mickey Doyle, when he had got some distance from Fred Frolic's place, slackened his speed, and then, looking round him, began to reflect upon what Lanty Shan had told him.

"I've made a mighty pretty blunder, 'pon my sowl, in shooting Fogharty, instead of a gauger. Who would have thought now that a bullet would ever have gone through his thick skull, especially when it warn't aimed at him? Murder! murder!" he said. "Fogharty of all men, too! why, he owed no ind of money to the firm, and if he's dead they'll never get a rap of it, and it's meself they'll murder if they find out I did it."

Here he came to a fix; his thoughts were completely confused.

"What will I do if I go to Murtough, and tell him I am a dead man? and if I kape from them, they'll think I've turned traitor, and I'll be shot like a dog."

He took off his *caubeen* and wiped the perspiration from his face.

"Bedad, I wonder if Lanty Shan is coming the *commether* over me. If he is, if I don't put a bullet through him, I'm not Mickey Doyle. I'll go and hide until it's dark, and then I'll creep into Bally-ran, and see a little into the matter myself."

And then he started off again, making for a lone sheeling that stood upon the road to the mountains, where he hid himself snugly for the rest of the day.

At Stanley Castle matters had been rather stormy between the baronet and Bell; and the morning after the affair at Ballyran he desired her presence in the library.

When the message was communicated to her, she was just about departing for her usual gallop.

"Sir Edward wanting to see me in the library!" she said, "how provoking. What can it mean? Say I will be with him directly."

Accordingly, a few minutes after, Bell,

attired in her riding habit, and whip in hand, entered the library.

"Well, pa, what is it?" she said.

The baronet looked up with a frown.

"Sit down," he said, coldly; "our conversation may, perhaps, be a lengthy one."

"Well, now, that is the very thing I detest; long conversations, long faces, long tongues, and long sermons."

"I perceive you are going out for a ride?"

"Yes; now, that I do like—a long ride over the mountains or down the valleys, or sometimes a gallop round the sea beach, with the waves dashing their white spray over me. I had a narrow escape though once at that."

The baronet had a difficult task to perform, and he was pondering over the best means to begin it.

"Indeed," he said abstractedly.

"Yes; I never told you, but as I know you like anything bold and daring, I'll—"

"Not always in females," he said, dryly.

"And why not in them? I have read of some deeds performed by them, that many of your gallant sex would have shrunk from."

"I dare say. I'll hear the adventure another time. I sent for you——"

"Yes, that I know."

"To have a little earnest talk with you."

"Of course I didn't expect you had sent for me to *look* at——"

"Will you be serious, Miss Stanley?"

"Well, it's rather a hard task, but I'll try."

"For the future will you confine your rides to the park?"

"Why?" she asked, looking up at him.

"The country is in rather a disturbed state, and I am fearful of——"

"Oh, nothing for me, my dear father; there is not a soul for miles round would hurt the daughter of Bell O'Riley."

"But you are *my* daughter," he said.

"Well; and so I was my *mother's*, and you won't mind if I say that I love that dear mother's Irish name better than I do anything else in the wide world. But tell me, sir, how far am I to ride?"

"Well, as I said before, the country is in a disturbed state, and——"

"Well; and who disturbs it? I am sure I do not. Well, then, I'd keep to the park. but 'Sprightly Frolic'—isn't it a darling name for a barb, eh?—he won't let me; do all I can, over the rails, just by the little stream, he will go, and there's no help for it."

"But there must be," replied the baronet, sternly. "I am determined that all acquaintance with that beggar shall cease."

"And I am determined it shall not!"

"How?"

"At least, as far as *I* am concerned."

"Do you dare disobey me?"

"Yes, in any cause that is *unjust*; if you have any reason for your hatred against Mr. Fred Frolic, why not say so at once?"

The baronet, at this, sat looking at his daughter, as though he was about to confide to her the reason of his bitter, bad feeling against the Frolic family; but he paused.

"Come, my dear father, what is it, eh?"

"I don't like the young man."

"What! Why, all the country are in love with him. What a noble, generous fellow he is! Why, there is scarcely a want that comes under his notice but it is instantly relieved;" and then, heaving a sigh, she said, "and the dear fellow is so poor!"

"Bell Stanley," said her father, "do you know what you are talking about?"

"Yes, perfectly well. Ah! it's no use frowning. I love the Irish as the Irish love me; and, as long as I have health, I will always cling to them. They may be at times warm; but there is nothing on the earth to surpass them in their strong courage and love to their country."

It was delightful to see the proud form of the "Irish girl," as she stood up defending the dear land of her birth.

Sir Edward looked at her for a moment, and felt that he was somewhat dismayed at the courageous deportment of the girl; but the secret rankling in his breast forbade him to act with anything like an open feeling.

"I desire you to give up entirely the acquaintance of that man, Frolic."

"Give me your reason?" asked Bell.

"I shall not," was the reply.

"Then I shall not give up the acquaintance," was the reply.

"Then you shall not ride beyond the confines of the park, and I will at once give orders to that effect."

He rose to ring the bell, when the door

was thrown open, and a servant ushered in Mr. Righton.

"Ah, my dear Miss Stanley, I am *more* than delighted to see you! Sir Edward, your servant."

Sir Edward bowed stiffly.

"I hope I don't interrupt any pleasant interview between you and your daughter, Sir Edward?"

"As far as *I* am concerned you do not, Mr. Righton," said Bell, extending her hand.

"Why this visit, Mr. Righton?" said the baronet.

"One of a very urgent nature, Sir Edward. Of course, you are aware of the present disturbed state of the country, especially in the baronies partly belonging to you?"

"Yes; and every measure that it is possible to take in repressing it is now being done," was the reply.

"Yes, but pardon me. The one you have commissioned that respectable gentleman, Mr. Fogharty, to undertake, was not one calculated to do good."

"Do you mean the eviction of those persons in the barony of Ballyran?"

"Yes; I hope you don't mean to persist in it?"

"Certainly. Why not?"

"Why not?" said Bell, who had been listening. "Because it is unjust."

"My dear child," said the baronet, "this is really no business of yours."

"But it is business of mine, *mon pere.* *You* don't mind my speaking French, Mr. Righton? It's a downright shame! What are these people to be turned out for?"

"They don't pay their rent," was the reply.

"Rent for what, sir?"

"The houses they live in."

"The what? Houses? Ha, ha!"

And the girl's laugh rang through the room.

"Ah, well, it's no laughing matter."

"It is not, indeed, Miss Stanley," said Righton; "and if the warrant for the eviction is not rescinded, it will light a conflagration of which none of us will be able to see the end."

"I will not give way, Mr. Righton," said the haughty man.

"Then I must enforce it, Sir Edward. I am appointed magistrate over all the baronies, and have discretionary power to act. This one act of yours, Sir Edward, will only irritate the feeling that the

government have the greatest anxiety in soothing."

"I was insulted in the place, and even stoned. I'll drive them out, and level the accursed hovels with the earth."

"Well, there will not be much trouble in doing that, for they are nearly on the ground already," said Bell. "I am off. I'll gallop over and see into this myself."

"Be careful, my dear young lady," said the lawyer.

"Careful of what? Well, you call yourselves men, and tell me to be careful. Why, I'd walk through the most turbulent mob you have; and the only finger they would raise against me would be to the head, out of respect."

And she was leaving the room.

"Stop my dear young lady," said Mr. Righton, "I will ride with you."

And the lawyer bustled up.

"Your order to restrain that rascal Fogharty, Sir Edward?"

"I don't see *why* I should yield."

"There is every reason why you should. If your act and deed is the cause of any riot, why then the lord lieutenant must be informed."

"Well to prevent any riot, Mr. Righton, I will."

"Accede to my wish; give it to me in writing, Sir Edward."

Sir Edward sat down, and wrote out the required order.

"Thank you. I will again ride over in the evening to consult you in other matters. In the meantime, you will keep the troops you have well on the alert. Certain papers have fallen into my hands, which throw some insight into matters."

"I shall be happy to see you in the evening," replied the baronet. "In the meantime, I am going to be busy, and put the castle in order in case of a siege."

"A proceeding I very highly commend, Sir Edward."

And so saying, the lawyer hurried out of the room, and mounting his horse rode off.

Once through the park gates, and into the high road, he saw, afar off, Bell cantering quietly along, and by her side Fred Frolic.

"I shall live to draw up the marriage settlements yet," he muttered, and spurring his horse, he galloped hard in the direction of Ballyran.

In the dead of the night, when all the tumult and din of the day were hushed;

when the moon, unclouded in its glorious majesty, rode high in the heavens, suddenly, on the top of the mountain, by the Devil's Grip, there shot up a blaze of light that threw its reflection over the surrounding scenery and the waves of the ocean far beyond.

Then the figures of men were seen rising from the earth, and crawling through the long grass that grew round the old church.

Cautiously they trod down the road, and then, emerging in scattered groups, each took a different route.

The party who took their way towards Stanley Castle and the barony of Ballyran, halted not on their way only for a moment at the gates of the former.

Two of the parties stood at the gates, while the rest kept a good look-out.

Then again they sped on to Frolic House, acting with the same care, and then they cautiously dispersed.

The next morning, when the sun rose high in all its glory, upon the gates leading to Stanley Castle there was marked a large red cross, and when Lanty Shan went out to look around him, he stood looking upon the old wall with wonder and amazement, for there was also marked the ominous red cross.

"Well, that's coming it mighty strong, anyhow," said Lanty, as he stood with his shillelagh tucked under his arm.

CHAPTER XXIII.

PHIL AND THE FAIRIES.

LANTY SHAN stood looking at the warning so vividly marked upon the old wall of Frolic House with rather more anxiety than at any other time would have possessed him.

While doing so he felt assured that some dangerous deed was at hand, and he made up his mind that he would assemble all the boys of the faction round him, and so defend the master to the last gasp of life.

"We shall have a tough murderin' fight for this, anyhow," he muttered, "but we'll win, as we have done before."

And grasping his shillelagh, and cocking his caubeen jauntily on the one side of his head, and twisting the tails of his long frieze coat under his left arm, he looked round him with an air of defiance, as though the foe was now before him.

At that moment Fred, accompanied by Frank Hardy, who had now resumed his usual garb, entered the yard.

"Well, Lanty," said Fred, "what's in the wind now?"

"A mighty purty blow up before long, anyhow," was the reply. "It doesn't require any ghost to tell us that."

And he pointed to the red mark against the wall.

Fred and Frank gazed at it with looks of undisguised astonishment, and while doing so, were joined by Mr. Righton.

"Good morning, gentlemen; what is this?" he asked, as he dismounted. "Humph! this red mark against the place, in a measure explains the papers found by that sharp boy, Phil Leary."

"By my sowl!" muttered Lanty, giving his shillelagh a twirl, "the rale explanation will only be found at the end of this. Well, Phil, what is it now, avick?"

The boy had crept noiselessly to the side of Lanty, unperceived either by him or any one else.

"There is a great dale of mischief brewing. They've put the same mark against the wall of the great place, the Castle, only it's a dale larger. I saw them do it."

And he pointed with outstretched hand towards the place.

"You saw them do it, Phil!" said Fred. "When was that?"

"It was when the red light shot up over the Devil's Grip ayont there," was the reply.

"A light?" said Mr. Righton.

"Yes; they're cunning men those. They wait till you're all aslape, and then they commence their work." Here he laughed quietly, while his eyes glistened with delight. "But they've got one as handy as themselves."

"And that's yourself, Phil," said Lanty, patting the boy's head.

"You may say dat wid your own handsome mouth, Lanty," replied Phil, with a

"WITH A LOUD SHRIEK THE GAUGER FELL DEAD TO THE GROUND!"

knowing wink. "You see when I try and get a wink at night the *little people** come dancing about me, and ax me to go out upon the hills, and join them in their vagaries, and they won't let a wink o'slape touch the eyelids till I do."

The three gentlemen looked at each other with surprise and wonder.

"Ah, you may stare sir"—and the boy took Fred's hand—"but it's as true as the Book. Didn't old Phil, the huntsman tell ye that, masther. Oh, he knew all about it. He knew I was a *shingaunt* he did."

And Little Phil drew himself up with such an air of conceit, as made Lanty laugh, and spring up like a cork, while the gentlemen smiled involuntarily at it.

"You may laugh, but it's lucky that I don't slape of nights."

"I think it is," said Fred, kindly, and anxious to gain more information from the boy.

"I have found out the mystery," said Phil, with a knowing, mysterious smile.

"Have you?" said Mr. Righton. "Well, then, come tell it to me, and I'll give you that to spend at the fair of Ballinafad, to-morrow."

And he placed a bright, shining piece of silver in the boy's hand.

The effect of this upon Phil Leary was electrical.

"He drew himself up to his tallest height, and threw his head back with an air of proud defiance, while his eyes seemed as though they were stars of fire, and the breath came heavily through his nostrils.

"I don't mean any offence by this," he said, "bekase you are a friend of his," and with his left hand he pointed to Fred; "but I'll send this on to Ballinafad before me."

And with his arm uplifted, he hurled the coin in that direction.

And then he was springing off, when Lanty caught him by the arm.

"What the divil are you about, Phil, eh?" he said.

"What is *he* about," and he pointed to Mr. Righton, "that he offers me the bribe of a dirthy informer!"

And he tried to get loose from Lanty.

"Phil," said Fred, taking the boy by the hand, "Mr. Righton did not for one moment mean to reward you as an in-

former, but because he admires the skill and dexterity with which you have acted; and Phil, you know I like the grandchild of my poor old huntsman too much to allow him to be insulted."

And he warmly pressed his hand.

The boy's eyes glanced from the one to the other with cold looks of indifference, but when he felt the warm pressure of his master's hand, it seemed as though his whole nature instantaneously changed, and he held down his head.

That one touch of nature had subdued his pride.

"I beg your pardon, sir," he said, approaching Mr. Righton, and holding out his hand. "I have no doubt it was meant kindly, but what I am doing is to save the masther, and—and—I don't want any reward for doing that."

"I know you don't," said Mr. Righton, warmly, "and I honour you, my boy, for your noble sentiments; but I did not intend that little present as a *bribe*."

"Ne'er a bit," said Lanty. "The boy is right again, but you see he's got some blood in him. Lave him to me, sir," and he winked at Fred. "And so, ma bouchal, you were out all night. It's well to be the likes o' you."

"What was I to do, Lanty? Sure, and I was tired enough to have slept for a month, but then *they* came and roused me up, bekase, you know, they are always looking after the good, and circumventing the blaggards, when they are trying to do harm."

"Sure you are right, Phil," said Lanty, signing to Fred and the others not to interrupt; "there's not your equal to be found anyhow or anywhere; and so *they* came to you, eh, Phil?"

"Sure they did said the boy, earnestly, and with glistening eyes, "and I never saw them so grand afore; there was the little queen came and took me by the hand as though she wanted me out for a dance; but it warn't that; she meant that I was to go out, for she pointed up to a dark cloud that was sailing over the house, and I knew what that meant, and I said, 'My beautiful darling, *cushla ma chree** there ain't any fairer on the earth, or in the heavens, or in the say, than you are,' and then she smiled and whispered, 'No Blarney, Phil; you're not one of us if you let mischief walk abroad widout looking after it,' and with that she held out her beautiful fingers, and then the whole of the people came in dressed in green, sparkling all over with gould, and——" here Phil stopped, and gave forth a heavy sigh.

"What, ma bouchal?" asked Lanty.

"They got hould of my arms and legs, and some got behind my head, and I was lifted up as aisy and as tinderly as a mother lifts her babe, and then they all danced to the door, and that I knew was a signal for me to follow."

"And you did, Phil, you did? Your sowl to glory! You didn't hang back?" said Lanty, excitedly.

"How could I hang back when they led the way? was it likely? Could I stop behind when they told me to go forward? Why, they were dancing all over the place, and it blazed as if a million lights were in the room, and the door flew open, and away over the fields and the place we ran and danced, until we came to the Castle gates, and then, oh, *murther sheery!** they disappeared."

"That was mighty onpleasant," said Lanty, "bekase you were all in the dark."

"No, the moon was shining, and there, against the gate—whisht, spake it quiet—I saw who put the red ban agin the wall."

"You did?" said Mr. Righton. "I'd give a hundred pounds to know them; I'd——"

"Whisht! you'll spoil all," whispered Lanty.

"I saw the blaggards," said Phil.

"Ah, they were the *little people*; it was all moonshine, Phil."

"Was it? Your brains are woolgathering, Lanty; it was Paddy O'Flyn, Ted O'Riley, and a particular friend of mine, and yours, and——"

"The divil a bit a friend of mine," muttered Lanty.

"Who was it, avick?"

"Mickey Doyle, ha, ha! the man who tried to shoot Fogharty; pity he missed."

During this, Mr. Righton had quietly booked the names of the men Phil had named.

"Well, and what next?" said Lanty."

"Then they came here, and did the same, and went their ways, but not before I paid Mickey Doyle with a sartain mark."

"What was that, Phil?"

"I let fly a large stone at his head, which knocked him over clane into the mud, and the other two ran as though a fortune was waiting for them at the other end of the journey."

"Did the blaggard see you, Phil?" said Lanty.

"Not a bit," was the reply.

"Then we're safe," and Lanty sprang up in the air.

At that moment Captain Brabazon, with a couple of mounted troopers, rode into the courtyard, and, speedily dismounting, saluted the gentlemen.

"Happy to see you, gentlemen," he said; "everything seems quiet."

"Very," replied Mr. Righton; "the slumbers of the volcano ere it belches forth destruction. Have you seen a mark similar to this on the gates of the lodge leading to the castle?"

"Oh, yes. One of the servants mentioned it at the breakfast table; Sir Edward laughed at it, but Miss Stanley thought it meant something serious; for my part, I laugh at it and despise it."

"Miss Stanley, captain—you will pardon me—has the only sensible head among you. We happen to know what those things mean. The pride of Sir Edward won't let him see it."

"Some joke, I suppose, sir?"

"A joke that sometimes ends in death," said Mr. Righton, gravely. "However, there is no time for talk. There is something meant in the placing that red cross there, and upon this house. The men we know well who have done it, and I shall issue warrants immediately for their apprehension, and place them in your hands for execution, Captain Brabazon. Here, Lanty," he looked round, but no Lanty or Phil was to be seen. "Where the deuce have they got to? No matter at present. I should wish you to leave in this house some half dozen of your men for the security of the place. I have reason to think that its safety is endangered."

"And you go by that red mark, I suppose?" said the captain.

"And other information, which plainly tells me that we have got a dangerous enemy before us; and our force is but small to cope with them. Knowing this, I have already sent for more troops, but in the meantime we must not show any fear."

---

* Murder everlasting

"Fear, sir," replied the captain, warmly, "what before an undisciplined mob, men acting against the laws! I should think the very sight of my men will be sufficient to——"

"Rouse them into rebellion, captain," said Fred; "and I should advise that not a soldier should be seen until——"

"What, sir, do you imagine that my men are going to hide like rats in holes and corners? No, sir, they are here to carry out the laws, and they shall do it," replied the captain, with warmth.

"Well, sir, and who said they could not, or should not, carry out the law? I know the disposition of my countrymen well, and I always advise a pacific tone with them up to the last moment, and I think I am right, sir," said Fred, warmly, appealing to Mr. Righton.

"Quite so, and so is the captain; had we only to put down the 'illicit stills,' all would be well; but we have other more powerful enemies behind all that to contend with."

"And may I know, sir," asked Captain Brabazon, "who they are?"

"Well," replied Mr. Righton, with a smile, "you see my instructions are *private*, captain, and must remain so."

"But, sir, as captain, I am——"

"Entirely under my command; nay, start not;" he placed his hand in his breast pocket, and drew forth a paper; "you will perceive that it has the royal seal, and that it says that the whole civil and military force are to act entirely under my orders."

"It is so," said the captain, "and I shall most cheerfully assist you in any operation you may wish to carry out. I have for the moment been misled."

"No doubt; our friend, Sir Edward, has not always the coolest judgment; but come, let us enter the house, and talk over such matters as are meant only for ourselves."

And with that they went into the house, and sat some time in deliberation, the two mounted troopers keeping watch at the door, much to the astonishment of the passers by.

An hour elapsed, when Mr. Righton, Fred, and Captain Brabazon came out, and rode swiftly into the barony of Ballyran. There things had quieted down considerably. The paper Mr. Righton had obtained from Sir Edward had completely stopped all Mr. Fogharty's charitable proceedings against the roofs and the doors of the wretched hovels, and as the three rode into the place, the whole population turned out to greet them with blessings and thanks. Then they heard that a number of men, strangers, had halted on their way to Ballinafad at Pat Donovan's, and tried to make the soldiers drunk, but the men, having been forewarned, had nobly resisted the temptation, and the others, finding their object was seen through, had departed the back way across the fields.

During the night numbers of men kept passing through the barony, few of them stopping to rest, but anxiously making the best of their way to the great fair.

Lanty, Mike, and Tim Doolan, the heads of the "Fighting Frolics," were busily engaged all night long collecting the boys, and subjecting the bits of wood to rather severe tests, in case of any "accidents" the next day.

Little Phil tried hard to gain a place near the old church, but almost at every point was warned back by a sentry, who threatened to warm his brains with a pistol-bullet. So he climbed the hill of the Devil's Grip, and there watched until the darkness of the night fled before the rising beams of the morning sun.

CHAPTER XXIV.

THE FAIR AT BALLINAFAD.

THE great fair of Ballinafad was the largest one for miles round the country, and was the means of supplying the smaller baronies round it with articles of consumption for months to come.

Small flocks of sheep, with herds of heifers, and knots of little, rough, hardy ponies, were there for sale, and here and there a flock of goats, while butter and eggs, and many other things, both useful and ornamental, were there to be found.

There were plenty of canvas tents erected, and others of a less fashionable appearance, and among them more than one where the "rale stuff," that had never paid a copper for duty, could be had—not by the noggin, but by the keg or the cask—and round these tents prowled tall, gaunt figures of men, with their coats buttoned tightly round them, and the usual powerful weapon in their hands.

There was a fearful look of defiance in their faces, as they paced round and about the tents that held the illicit stuff, at once the bane and the ruin of the land.

The barony, itself, was of no great extent, and, strange to say, had not a mud hovel in or near it.

The buildings upon it were of a very superior character, compared with that of Ballyran, and the reason was that the whole barony belonged to the Stanley family, whereas in the other case a very small portion of Ballyran paid rent to them.

In the high street of Ballinafad, there were respectable shops, and more than one respectable inn, with good entertainment for both man and beast, and even post-horses could be had at a short notice, the *short* notice depending upon how soon the lame ostler caught the beasts that were feeding in the fields, a feat that generally took a couple of hours in performing.

The fair itself was held upon the outskirts of the town, but so close upon it, that it seemed to be a part and parcel of it.

The amusement fair was beyond that one, and was, therefore, but scantily attended, until the other had concluded its business.

Never in the memory of the oldest inhabitants was the fair ever known to be so densely crowded.

The people seemed to come from all parts, and a great many of them boasted they had walked full twenty miles to see the fun, and so, all through the night they came toiling in, finding their way into the inns and the low shebeen shops, while the greater portion made their way into the fair field, and there passed the night either in the tents drinking heavily, or outside on the grass, sometimes singing and dancing, or telling old tales and legends until, tired out, they fell asleep.

So, about two hours after midnight, the whole barony and the fair beyond was almost as still as the mountains and valleys afar off.

The principal inn, the "Stanley Arms," had, by a private arrangement entered into by Mr. Righton, been reserved for himself as the chief magistrate, and for the officer and the soldiers; the principal gauger and his four assistants, also taking up their quarters there.

A small body of soldiers had entered the place at the same time as the others entered Ballyran; but, if any of the inhabitants had been up and stirring shortly after midnight, their wonder would have been very much increased at seeing another body march in, headed by Captain Brabazon, Mr. Righton, the gauger and his assistants. The gates and doors of the inn were then closed for the night against all comers.

Below the other end of the barony, and close against the fair field, stood another inn defined by the title of the "Four-leaved Shamrock;" from floor to ceiling this place was crowded, and that nearly entirely by men—reckless, daring, desperate men—who kept up the whole night in one round of hard drinking and swearing, oftentimes declaring, with bitter exclamations, "they'd be glad when the morrow came."

Down stairs on the ground floor, there

ran at the back of the house a long narrow place that might have been once a skittle alley. In this room sat Black Murtough with four others of the gang.

They were all heavily armed, and had been drinking freely.

"I don't care that," said Murtough, snapping his fingers, "for the red-coats that are up at the place yonder. We are ten to one of them. I thought they would have brought up all the others, but all I have got to say and stick to is this, that if they molest us let them look out, that's all."

"Aye, aye; we are all agreed to that," was the reply.

At that moment hurried steps were heard along the passage, then the door was heavily kicked at, a word shouted out, the heavy bolt was forced back, and in rushed Mickey Doyle, his face bathed in perspiration and blanched with fear, followed by Fogharty, pretty well covered with mud, and his hat crushed into a shapeless mass.

Mickey Doyle had no sooner entered the room, than he fell on his knees and then on his face on the floor.

"The Lord save us!" he groaned. "Don't follow me; if I did kill you, it wasn't done on purpose. And if you are dead, why don't you slape in pace and quietness?"

"What's the fool mane?" roared Fogharty. "I'll soon tell you whether I am dead or not."

And with that, snatching a shillelagh that lay upon the table, he gave Mr. Mickey Doyle such a whack that he sprang up as if a galvanic battery had charged him.

"Murder! murder!" he shouted.

"Silence, you cursed idiot!" said Murtough, seizing him by the throat and shaking him. "Would you bring the whole town down upon us?"

"Take away Fogharty's ghost," he cried, piteously.

"I'll shake you into one," said Murtough.

"So you are the villain that shot at me, are you? What did you take me for, you blundering scoundrel?"

"I—I took you for a gauger," was the trembling reply. "They said you had got four of them with you."

"What," said Murtough, "seated with four gaugers? Are you selling us, Fogharty? If I thought so I'd send a bullet at you that shouldn't miss its mark."

And he levelled a pistol at him.

"What are you about, eh, Murtough? Would you kill the staunchest man among you? They were *not* gaugers I was with. Yon trembling idiot has misled you."

Fogharty then explained the affair to Murtough and the rest of the gang, which so overjoyed Mickey Doyle, that he sprang forward, and would have embraced Fogharty, mud and all, but the lawyer warned him back by a twist of the shillelagh.

"Keep off," he said; "it's more by my own luck than your judgment that I am here. There, I forgive you; be seated, all of you, for I have much to say, and give me a hot tumbler of the craythur, for I am wet through to the marrow of my bones," and the lawyer shook as though he had the ague strong on him.

"How did you get that stumble, eh, Fogharty?" asked Murtough.

"I owe that, with a long list of other pleasant trifles, to Mr. Lanty Shan," said he, taking up the tumbler of hot punch, and having a good pull at it, "and may what I've swallowed turn to arsenic if I don't pay him. I met him and others this night, and, with no more ado, he lifted me up and threw me into a ditch, without as much as saying, with your leave, or by your leave. I'll give the man ten pounds that beats him into a jelly to-morrow, and I'll give the same sum to the man that does the same to his master."

"We'll look after him, rest aisy; but what's the news? how will things go off to-morrow, eh?" asked Murtough.

"Bad. I've heard the gauger and his men are going to search all the tents after what he calls illicit stuff, and he's to be backed by the red-coats."

"The man that forces his way into my tent, I'll shoot him, though I die on the gallows for it," and Murtough uttered a fearful oath, the rest joining him. "Why, it would be utter ruin to us. How came they to know anything about it, eh?" and he scowled round at the men seated near him. "Have we any traitors among us?"

"No. Traitors! Stuff and nonsense, they only *guess* it," said Fogharty; "but, you see, I gathered here and there a good deal respecting what is going on, and it's as well to be on the guard. Can't you move the stuff right clean away?"

"What, and lose the sale at the fair? What the divil is to become of us if we don't sell the craythur after it's made? I tell you I won't move a drop of it; if they saze the stuff I'll have their blood for it, and that I swear by the blood of my father!"

"You remimber the red-coats, friend Murtough."

"Oh, yes, I'll remimber them at the proper time," he replied, with a grim smile. "You don't think for a moment I'd forget them?"

"There is a precious lot of them around and about the place," and Fogharty shifted about on his seat very nervously.

"Stuff! Nothing to be compared to us. If the worst comes to the worst, we have got 'em from all parts. The rale boys will be up to all manes to defend what is their own."

"Aye, that is all very well, but the sogers are——"

"The sogers are only men, and man opposed to man hasn't much to fear," and then he fell into a deep study for a moment.

"I thought McDonnell would have been here to-day," he said, after awhile, and his brow grew as black as midnight. "What keeps him so long in Dublin?"

"Settling his business with the agent he went to see. He must be treated tenderly," was the reply.

"What for? Curse him! Don't he owe us the money, eh?"

"Of course he does; but he don't seem inclined to pay just now, and he must be temporised with," said Fogharty, in a wheedling tone.

"Do you mean to say that he refuses?"

And, with a fierce oath, he sprang upon his feet.

"Well, no, I don't say that he refuses distinctly, but he hangs back, and, you see——"

"Oh, yes, I see; stop till this affair is over, which ever way it may go, and I'll take a trip into the city myself, and I'll see if I can't bring him to reason, or I'll hammer it into his brains with this."

And he lifted a heavy stick.

"Let us get over this affair *first*," said the lawyer, "and the rest will follow aisy."

At that moment there came a peculiar knock at the door.

"Who is there?" said Murtough, with a pistol ready in his hand.

A password was given, and then the door was cautiously flung back, and Pat

Ryan, one of the scouts, entered, then the door was securely fastened again.

"What now, Pat — anything fresh? Take a pull at this."

And Murtough handed him a jug of punch.

"It's meself that wants it," said Pat, taking off his caubeen and wiping his head, that seemed wet with perspiration.

Then, after a good draught of the steaming punch, he set the can down, and took a long breath.

"Anything else stirring?" asked Murtough.

"Plenty. The ould one himself is stirring, and so must we be," was the reply. "The whole place is filled with red-coats."

"What!" and the gang started to their feet. "More sogers?"

"More! There don't seem to be any ind of them. I was watching down by the ind of the street, and there was a pretty fog stirring up, so that you couldn't see the ind of your nose, when I hears a tramp! tramp! 'What the divil is that?' says I, and I listens again, when I heard the word of command given. 'Red-coats,' says I, and the fog lifting at that moment, as if on purpose, I could see them all in a body come marching down from the hills."

"Where did *they* come from?" said Black Murtough.

"Oh, they are the men that have been up at the Castle, and joined by most of the others from Ballyran. We'll have some hot work out of all this."

"We shall, and it will be work upon which the mark of blood will be seen. Upstairs, Mickey, and tell the men that they are all to move down to the tints where the stuff is lying. Let them see that their arms are ready."

The door was unfastened, and then Mickey stole quietly out, to carry out the orders given to him.

"You have yet time to do as I tell you, Murtough," said Fogharty. "The carts are there still, no doubt. Get them away, man, before the gaugers come out and stop them."

"You're not a bad man to give advice, Fogharty, but I'm one of those that never could take it," said Murtough, flinging open the shutters. "You see the morning light is fast peeping over the mountains; there is no stopping that, is there?"

"Not by any act of parliament that I am aware of," said Fogharty.

"Well, then there is no act of parliament that shall stop me in the determination I have entered into; now, then, are you ready, my men?"

"Aye, aye, we'll teach the gaugers and the sogers a lesson," was the reply.

"Aye, that we will," said Murtough; "so let us to our place, and they shall find they have neither fools nor children to dale with."

Grasping his formidable blackthorn, and pulling his coat tightly around him, Murtough threw open the door, and emerged into the passage, followed by the rest, except Fogharty, who had told them he should follow. What he told them was one thing, what he meant quite another; he meant to stop where he was.

As Murtough and his men went out from the house they separated, some making for one part of the fair, and some for another, for the gang had three tents for the sale of their spirits, and one which served as a sort of place where the business could be carried on, sales effected, and money paid.

Into this tent Murtough and some of his men passed, while all intruders were kept out by a rough looking man, who kept parading backwards and forwards.

The morning had fairly broken, and the fair for the sale of cattle, &c., was filling fast, when Mr. Hawkseye the principal gauger, with his men, walked quickly from it, and made his way to the tent where Black Murtough had just entered.

In his attempt to enter he was stopped by the man.

"Yer can't pass; I tell you the tint ain't open for customers yet," was the rough reply, as the shillelagh was raised.

Hearing the noise, Murtough sprang out, pistol in hand, which he levelled at Hawkseye.

"What do you want here?" he said in a loud tone. "Attempt to enter, and you are a dead man."

The gauger, not at all alarmed at this, was about to spring upon him.

But a moment's thought made him pause.

His followers stood well and firmly by him, while three or four of his gang clustered round Murtough.

For a moment they stood surveying each other.

"Look ye, my man," said Hawkseye, "you don't know me."

"No; and I don't want to make your acquaintance," was the reply.

"Well, that is candid, but I must make yours. I must search that tent."

"What for?" was the stern reply.

"You have read the proclamations that are stuck up?" said the gauger.

"Yes. What have they to do with me?"

"Nothing at all, if you have no illicit spirits there."

"Illicit what!" and the smuggler sent forth a hoarse laugh. "Somebody has been playing the *commether* nicely with you."

"I hope they have," said the gauger, with a smile, "and so, if that be the case, you'll have no objection to my entering and judging for myself, eh?"

"Not in the least. I did not know what to think when I heard you spake at first. You see we Irishmen are not the quickest men in the world. Enter, sir. I am sorry the *refreshment* I'd like to give you ain't quite ready."

The blanket that hung down in the front of the tent was pulled aside, and, following Murtough with two of his men, the gauger fearlessly entered.

Hawkseye was somewhat surprised at finding the tent comparatively empty, with the exception of some old tables and benches, and in one corner of it a large heap of straw.

"You see, sir," said Black Murtough, with a great deal of mock politeness, "we were just going to get ready for the customers—getting them some tay and coffee."

"And a very good thing, too," said Hawkseye, with a quiet smile.

Then approaching the heap of straw, he stooped down, and pulled it up.

"Up rose the shock head of a woman.

"Arrah! bad luck to you, what are you about?" she called out, at the same time catching up a large stone that lay by the side of her. "Can't you let a lone woman get a slape? What do you want here?"

And she sat up, clutching the stone.

Black Murtough and his men burst into a hoarse, brutal laugh at this, while the gaugers could not resist a smile.

"She don't look like illicit stuff, does she?" said Murtough, with a sly grin.

"Well no, my friend," was the reply.

"You see, we have all of us a duty to perform, and I am only performing mine."

And so saying he left the tent, followed by his men.

"I hope you'll have better luck next time, sir," said Murtough.

"I am *sure* I shall, my friend," said Hawkseye.

And with that he made the best of his way back to the town to consult with the magistrate and Captain Brabazon.

"The fellows have been in this instance too cunning for me," he said, "but I shall have them yet. But it will be useless for me to make any seizure without the aid of the military.

"And that aid you will cheerfully and willingly have," was the magistrate's reply.

"In the midst of the fair they will be thrown off their guard, and then I'll show them that they are not so cunning as they pride themselves upon being."

In the meantime the fair began to fill with comers from all parts.

Car upon car, laden with laughing, smiling, happy Irish lasses; then the farmer, on horseback, with his wife behind him, their whole mind bent upon what the half-dozen heifers would bring, while Pandeen kept up a loving conversation with the darling hope of his heart.

Great was the surprise of all the people who came from a long distance to see the large placards posted up, prohibiting the sale of any whisky but that which had paid duty.

And mingled with this was a deep muttering about the hardship of not letting people make what they like and drink what they like.

"What'll they do next?" said one of Murtough's gang, to a small knot of persons who stood listening to one who was reading the proclamation. "By my sowl! we'll have to ask them when the sun is to shine, or the moon go to bed. That for the placard, or whatever they call it!" snapping his fingers. "They'll not catch me paying much attention to that, anyhow."

"Or any of us," was the reply of the rest.

"They'll put the red-coats upon us, Darby," replied another.

"If they put the red-coats upon me, or they lay their fingers upon what don't belong to them, they'll get the end of this upon their top-knots," and he sent his blackthorn twirling round his head. "Who's the man to say no to that?"

"Not a man when the time comes," replied the others, fiercely.

"They shall have my blood first," said another.

"And mine—and mine;" and then they grasped each other's hands, and muttered the "secret oath" that bound them together.

Separating from each other and mixing with the crowd, they kept stirring up the bad and evil passions of the disaffected, and occasionally taking a noggin of that powerful poteen that acted almost as fire upon their blood and excitable dispositions.

On the night previous to this, there had been a great muster of the "Frolic Faction" in Ballyran.

The meeting was held outside the "Frolic Arms," with Lanty Shan at the head.

It was a wild and strange scene.

The men must have numbered, at least, one hundred, and as they stood, surrounded by the women and children, half clothed, and with their fierce inquiring eyes and faces, there was a something strange and unearthly in the assembly.

"You have all agreed to act under my direction, *ma bouchals*," said Lanty, as, perched upon an empty barrel, he addressed them; "and if you do that, everything will go right."

"Good luck to you, Lanty Shan," said the crowd, "you're not the worst of your sort."

"I hope not. Well, then, in the first place, it's the masther's wish that we shouldn't march to Ballinafad in a body."

"And why not, Lanty?" called out a man.

"Why not; because if we did, and we met any of those murthering McDonnells, it's not long before we should be in the midst of an iligant scrimmage, and that's what we want to avoid."

"Do you mane to say, that we are to run away from them?" said Mike, "I'll niver do that as long as I am Mike Murphy, and a tailor by trade."

"Hurroo, we'll stand by Mike," shouted some of them.

"I'll ask you, Lanty Shan, if the fair will be a fair, if there ain't a fight? By my sowl, if that's to be the case, it's meself that will stop away."

"Why, you great *omadhaun*, who wants

you to give up your trate of a fight? I am only asking you to go to the fair in ones and twos and threes. There's sure to be a row, good luck to it, but the masther don't want us to begin it. Now do you understand?"

"Oh, bedad. I see my way clearer," said Mike.

"And a good whack on your head would open your eyes a little wider, Masther Mike," said Lanty.

"There's not a man but yourself dare say twice to that, Lanty Shan," and off went Mike's coat.

"Twice," said a voice in the thick of the crowd.

"Who said that?" and Mike jumped round with a fierce look and a twist of the blackthorn.

"I did," said Biddy, twisting her great fist on Mike's bit of a neckcloth; "if you've got the fighting on you, come home and we'll have it out there."

And with that, spite of his struggles, the little tailor was dragged to his cabin amid the laughter of the rest.

Then Lanty, calling for a loud cheer for the "Frolics," jumped down from the barrel, and ran home to prepare for the next day's amusement at the great fair of Ballinafad.

CHAPTER XXV.

THE FATAL SHOT.

MR. FOGHARTY still kept himself in seclusion at the "Shamrock," deeply revolving in his own mind a variety of matters.

In the first place, he was not extremely delighted at the prospect of affairs.

He was more than alarmed at the threat held out to him by Fred Frolic of denouncing him as a forger, and inwardly felt that in that case the ground would crumble from under his feet.

Then, again, he stood in a very precarious position with Black Murtough and his gang.

He was their cashier, and received all payments for the great quantities of the illicit poteen that had been from time to time forwarded to the capital and other places by Jan and his lugger.

He held now in his hand a large sum of money belonging to them, and he felt that if things went wrong with them at the fair, that they would very soon bring him to a reckoning.

"I think I had better keep myself quiet within doors until I know how things are going on without; if Black Murtough gets the best of the matter, which I don't think he will, I can easily join them, and if——"

Here his cogitations were interrupted by the entrance of Mickey Doyle.

"I thought you was in the fair, Mr. Fogharty," said Mickey. "The business for the cattle and the sheep and the pigs is nearly over, and, then, by the piper that played before Saint Patrick, we'll have a little bit of fun. Arn't you well?"

"No, Mickey. I have a palpitation of the heart, and——"

"The what?"

"The heart, you fool."

"And where's that, Lawyer Fogharty? I've heard talk of such a thing very often. I'd like to see a lawyer's heart!"

Fogharty caught up the poker and certainly Mickey Doyle would have had his head well battered with it if he had not beat a precipitate retreat, for the iron weapon went flying down the passage after him.

Then came loud shouts from the outside, and Fogharty, impelled by a sudden curiosity, buttoned up his coat and walked forth.

The business of the one fair was almost concluded; those anxious for the fun and frolic of the other were rather rudely driving away the cattle, while a number of pigs, which had failed to captivate a purchaser, were sent wandering about, to the great perplexity and dismay of their owners.

In the other part of the fair, all was bustle and excitement; the business part of the day having been concluded, all parties gave themselves up to the wild fun, so characteristic of the national character.

There was everything that could be required, and a trifle over, while round the tents there was a most powerful odour of poteen.

All was stir, bustle, and fun; kind speeches and welcome words went round, while among others there was a deeply-knitted brow, and a powerful twitching of the fingers round the blackthorn.

Round and about the tents opposite to where Black Murtough and his men seemed most to congregate, was Lanty Shan, Mike, and Tim, with all the women and children of the "Frolic Faction,"

The McDonnell faction, headed by Murtough, seemed to be gathering also in great numbers.

It was drawing towards evening, the sun sinking with a red glare behind the distant mountains.

At that moment Fred, and his friend, the captain, walked into the fair, while from the opposite side came Mr. Righton and Captain Brabazon.

Mixing among the group might be seen Hawkseye, the gauger, attended by his men.

More than a hundred invitations had been sent forth by the McDonnellites to the Frolics to come out like men, but they had only been answered by a quiet shrug of the shoulders.

"Wait a bit, ma bouchals; we'll be with you by-and-bye!" shouted Lanty. "We're just enjoying ourselves, and then you'll see what the time o' day is."

Then the McDonnells sent forth loud shouts and groans against them, coupled with more than a dozen coarse threats uttered against Fred and his friend.

This was received with a good-humoured smile and a laugh, which only irritated them the more.

While all this was going on, it was observable that the tent of Black Murtough was completely hemmed in by his men, so that there was no approaching behind the canvas covering.

Hawkseye and his men had several times essayed it, but in vain.

Still the wary gauger kept his eye upon their movements, and, leaving them for a moment, made his way to the opposite tents.

While conversing with Fred, a cry was raised to make room for a car that was leaving the fair.

The top was carefully covered over with straw, and on the top of that an un-fortunate pig was tied down, which raised a number of piteous squeaks and squeals.

The horse was lean to starvation, and the driver very little better.

"What the deuce Paddy Blake," shouted Murtough. "are you bringing your pigs and your cart through the fair this time o' day, eh?"

"Sure, what's a fellow to do wid his pigs, when he can't sell them, or give them away, for the matter of that, for it is a giving-away price they offer a poor man."

"Well, yes, better be jogging, Paddy, or if the fun begins, you'll not get very aisy out of the crowd; there's a noggin for you, and God speed you on your way home."

Paddy took the noggin with many thanks, and was about putting his car and horse in motion, when he found standing at the head of the horse one of the gaugers, while on the other side of the vehicle stood Hawkseye.

"And so you could not sell the pigs, eh, Mr. Blake?" said Hawkseye. "How many have you, and what's the price?" and he thrust his hand down among the straw.

"Oh, the likes of you don't want to buy pigs," growled Black Murtough, trying to thrust himself in between the car and the gauger.

"Indeed," said the other resisting him, "I should rather think that is my business," and looking up to Mr. Righton and the captain, he nodded his head very significantly.

"I'd be glad to get on my road, sir, if you plase," said Paddy Blake, "I have a long way to go, and the nights are not safe, and I'll try another market for the pigs."

"Well, but I want to look at the pig," said Hawkseye, and he proceeded to untie the cord that confined it, and kept it fast.

"Leave the man alone," shouted the gang. "What has a gauger to do with pigs?"

And they gathered round the car with raised shillelaghs, and brows frowning with anger.

"There is something more than pigs in here, and I warn you all not to interfere with me in the execution of my duty. Off with that pig and the straw," he said, to one of his men.

The man was about to spring up in the

"AWAY LEAPED FRED, DOWN INTO THE DEEP LAKE"

No. 11.

car, when Murtough, who stood partly back by the wheel, drew forth a pistol, and, aiming it at the unfortunate man, fired.

The bullet went true to its mark, and the poor fellow, uttering a loud shriek, fell dead to the ground, shot through the heart.

At this daring act, Hawkseye and his party drew back; the next moment a stone came whizzing through the air, and catching Captain Brabazon on the temple, he fell as though dead from his horse.

"Down with the gaugers, bad luck to 'em!" roared the McDonnells, and with that they commenced a furious onslaught upon them.

Up to this time Fred and his party had remained quietly looking on, but when the shot was fired that hurried the poor man into eternity, they rushed forward.

Fred was about raising Captain Brabazon from the ground, when a stone came rushing through the air, and glancing by the head of Fred inflicted a severe wound.

Starting up to see who the assailant was, Lanty saw the blood trickling down his master's face.

With a loud shout, and calling to the "Fighting Frolics," he dashed into the thick of the opposite faction.

The shouts, the cries, and the sound of the blows became appalling, and the hurling of the fatal stones in the stockings by the women caused many a one to bite the dust.

Murtough's numbers more than doubled those of the opposite side, and the Frolics, contesting every inch, were fast losing ground.

At that moment Mr. Righton rode up with the soldiers.

At the sight of them both paused for an instant.

"I call upon you all," he said, addressing the people, "instantly to disperse. I give you five minutes to do so, and then, if not obeyed, I shall call upon the soldiers to do their duty."

"And who cares for you or the sogers?" said Murtough, a stream of blood running down his face from a fearful gash in his forehead.

"I have nothing to say to you," returned Mr. Righton; "you are a murderer, and, as such, the law will take cognisance of you."

He took out his watch.

"Captain Brabazon, I am glad to find that you are not seriously hurt."

Still the gang, headed by Murtough, yielded not, but stood looking upon the other side with a contemptuous grin, and a dark scowl of deep determination.

"I shall perform my last act of duty, and then I leave the rest to you, Captain Brabazon."

He took from his pocket a roll of paper, and began slowly to read just as the last gleam of light was fading away.

During this stones and other missiles came flying through the air.

Still the intrepid magistrate stopped not until he had finished every word.

"There are many innocent people mixed up with this lawless mob, and I should be sorry if innocent blood were shed. Let your front rank fire over their heads, and see what effect that will have," said the humane man.

The captain shook his head, but putting his hand to his cap, gave the requisite orders.

The volley was received with a hoarse laugh.

"Ha, ha, ha!" roared Murtough, "they are only pop-guns; let us have them for the gossoons to play with. Follow me."

And he sprang forward, followed by the mob.

But he had made a slight mistake respecting the pop-guns, for they were received with a volley that sent some half dozen rolling on the ground.

But this did not daunt Black Murtough.

He threw himself into the thick of the men, and then a fearful struggle for the mastery commenced.

Lanty Shan and his men saw all this, and, with a wild hurroo, attacked the band of Murtough in the rear.

This effected a diversion in favour of the troops for the moment, and before the McDonnells had recovered from their panic, the soldiers had re-loaded, and stood ready.

Still the fight raged, and that with all the bitter enmity that deadly hate could supply them with.

But both soldiers and mob had got so mixed together that it would have been madness to have fired.

During this the car, with its contents, which had given rise to this scene of blood and ruin, had been standing perfectly still, except that the driver, not liking the appearance, had decamped.

But when the rush of both parties came against it, over went the car, the pig, and the rest of its contents.

The pig, finding himself at liberty, set off at full gallop, to the discomfiture of more than one person in its flight.

But the rest of the car's contents came down with a crash, and immediately the odour of strong poteen rose upon the air, while the "craythur" rolled down in streams.

Hawkseye was right.

While Murtough was keeping all of them engaged in the front of the tent, others were loading the car at the back, in the hopes of getting it off.

It had now become quite dark, and, therefore, friends and foes were alike undistinguishable.

This just suited Murtough, for he found that his followers had become pretty well worn out, and so, therefore, passing the word among them to give in, they delivered a few parting blows, and sullenly withdrew from the scene, but not before they had raised up the dead body of one of their number, and borne him from the field.

The others were mere flesh and blood wounds, and shillelagh cuts, which counted for nothing.

"This has been a sharp affair, sir," said Hawkseye, to the magistrate; "but it is only the beginning of a good many others."

"I think, Captain Brabazon, you had better get your men together, and we'll be moving back to the town," said Mr. Righton.

Having issued directions as to the carrying of the wounded man to the inn, Hawkseye walked boldly into the tent, and placing his hand down by the side of the straw, pulled out four large links.

Then procuring a light, he, followed by his assistants, proceeded into the other.

"Ha, ha! I thought so; a goodly number—twenty kegs—which I seize in the name of the sovereign."

"And couldn't you spare one of them just to drink the health of the sovereign in? I'm sure we should be very glad, and so would that person, for paying him such a compliment,"

And Lanty gave the gauger such a wink, that that functionary burst into a loud laugh.

"We'll see about that when it's safe under lock and key."

"Ah, if it once gets under lock and key there's an end of it," replied Lanty.

With the assistance of the soldiers and the Frolic boys, the car was soon placed again on its wheels, and they commenced loading it with the kegs of the condemned poteen.

Then Hawkseye, with a pistol in one hand, and guarded by the military, began his march back to the "Stanley Arms."

The affray that had taken place had entirely put a stop to the fair, for once the fight begun it extended to all parts, and each person had to look out for himself.

In a very short time there was not a tent left standing.

The very demon of discord seemed to have broken loose, and was exercising its most baleful passions.

Through crowds of sullen faces, and followed by many a muttered oath of vengeance, the party took their way with their spoil.

It was late at night when they entered the gates of the inn, and then they were immediately closed, and fastened in the securest way they could be, a sentry being placed outside, who was soon, however, withdrawn, as the sight of him only served to irritate the already highly excited mob, who had assembled before the place in great numbers, hooting and howling.

Meanwhile, the whisky had been conveyed into a large stable at the back of the inn, under the care of Hawkseye and two of his men. One of them was missing, and it was feared had met his death, in addition to the poor fellow whose corpse lay in the large room of the inn.

In the stable, there stood Hawkseye and his two men, with Lanty Shan, Mike and Tim.

"Sure, we'll be after assisting you, sir," said Mike.

"Thanks, my friends; we'll get the poor beast out of the cart, and stow away the kegs and lock the place up, and then you shall have what refreshment you want."

"Ah, you're the gintleman to serve, after all; that is after the masther," replied Mike.

Now, Mike had, during this, been holding up the torch, and busying himself in a mighty bustling manner, when, all at once, over went Mike, light and all, and the place was in total darkness.

"The divil have the wheelbarrow, it's me leg that's smashed, anyhow. I'll be a limping tailor all the rest of my born days. Ochone, Biddy, where are you?"

"Get another light!" shouted Hawks-eye.

"I am all right, your honour," cried Mike, "it was only the leg of the barrow that was smashed."

"That's lucky," said Hawkseye. "What an infernal time those fellows are getting a light."

And he ran into the inn himself for one.

The moment after Mike disappeared, but in an instant returned, just as the light appeared.

Then the kegs were removed from the cart and carefully counted.

"Nineteen!" said Hawkseye. "I am certain I counted *twenty!*"

"Perhaps one dropped off in the road," said Lanty, looking hard at Mike.

"Are you sure there was twenty?" said Mike, with an innocent look. "I am a bad hand at figgers myself. Och, murder! I have it!"

"Have you—where?"

"No doubt you left it in the tint."

"That's not very likely," replied the officer, dryly.

Then he proceeded to fix the *broad arrow* upon the kegs; then fastening up the doors, he fixed the same mark upon them, and then the whole party went into the house.

"Here, Lanty, avick, and Tim, I'd spake a word with you. Whisper!" said Mike, lingering behind with them.

"What is it, you divil? You've been at some of your tricks, Mike."

"What do you mane? What a *com-mether* you must take me for. Will you make one of the party?"

"At what?" said Lanty.

"Tasting a drop of the craythur out of the keg that hasn't got the *mark upon it?*"

During this the discomfited smugglers had made good their retreat to the "Shamrock," and when the house was as full as it could hold, the doors were closed.

They all looked the worse for the fearful affray, and the curses of Black Murtough were loud and bitter.

"Bring us plenty to drink, and let it be strong," he shouted, "we're baten for a time, but by all that's holy, we'll pay the debt off, and that with a swinging interest; eh, lads."

"Aye, aye, we'll do that," was the reply.

The landlord entered, bringing with him a can of the strongest poteen that could be brewed, and followed by Lawyer Fogharty.

The wise fellow had kept at a respectful distance, during the affray, watching with feverish interest upon which side the victory would fall, so that he might trim his sails accordingly.

He saw the defeat of his party, and would have made the best of his way back to his dirty dingy office in Dublin, but he saw some of the "Fighting Frolics" were on the look-out for him, and so he abandoned the idea, and made the best of his way to the "Shamrock" inn.

"Listen to me, lads," shouted Murtough, as he raised a horn of liquor, "listen to me, I say. Will you pledge me in a toast?"

"Aye, aye," and every man sprang to his feet.

"Ah! Fogharty, are you there? Fill him up a cup."

"Here's a speedy death to those who have this day ruined us."

It was drank with an oath too fearful to repeat, and then down went the horns with a clang upon the table.

"Now, then, what's to be done?" he said; "of course you have heard what has occurred, Fogharty?"

"I have both *seen* and heard the whole affair," was the reply.

"Well, and what do you think of it?" said the dark leader with an oath.

"That it is bad, very bad, and great caution must be observed to make it come square again."

"Caution! What for?" said Murtough, fiercely.

"What for? for your own safety and that of the rest of us," was the reply.

"We'll have revenge for the death of the poor fellow they shot down. There shan't be a brick or a stone standing either in that castle or the ruined house of the Frolics if I die in the flames myself. They shall blaze with a fierce, damning blaze that shall teach them a bitter lesson. Do you hang back?" and he clutched the barrel of his unloaded pistol as though he would hurl it at him.

"Not I," said the lawyer, slightly shrinking back at the action ; "but they'll have you to-morrow unless you take care of yourself. You shot the infernal gauger, and to-morrow's light will see a reward posted up for your apprehension, and, if once they get you, they'll hang you, though you had a thousand lives."

"The lawyer's right," muttered the others. "Make the best of your way to the retreat. You know we can't afford to lose you."

"Fogharty is right," said they all, crowding round Murtough.

"Put on an old slouched hat, pull up the collar of your coat, and get out, you and three or four others," said the lawyer, eagerly ; "leave the rest of us to look out here."

"By all that's good, you're right, Fogharty," said the smuggler ; then he sprang to his feet, and in a few minutes was ready. "You'll let me know in the day, arly," he added.

"We'll fix the time for the grand meeting. Who'll go with me ?"

Instantly four men sprang up, and, without any further delay, they left the room, and were soon out in the street.

It was still crowded with persons, but they were soon over the fields, and in the ruins of the old church.

Then the usual signs were given, and in a few minutes they had disappeared from sight.

The cave was dimly lighted up, and as the men, headed by Murtough, strode up towards the centre of the place, the head of a man raised itself up from a heap of straw.

It was tied round with an old black handkerchief, and the face was black, although clots of blood hung upon it, which the matted hair could not conceal.

It was Jan, the Captain of the Black Lugger.

CHAPTER XXVI.

THE CONFLAGRATION.

BLACK MURTOUGH and the desperadoes who had accompanied him to his place of concealment, started back with looks of wild affright, when they beheld the death-stricken face of the smuggler.

"In the name of all that is good," said Black Murtough "is that you, Jan ?"

"Yaw, all that is left of Jan. Give me some drink. There is a raging fire in mine throat that shall burn like der deyvil."

The drink was speedily found, and handed to him.

"Raise me up, Murtough. I am as faint as though I was going to slip mine wind."

He raised the drink to his ashy lips, though his hand shook terribly.

He swallowed the draught of liquid fire as though it had been water from the spring.

"Ah, dat is goot, and brings the blood, the *old* blood back again to my heart ?"

"Why, Jan, what is all this, ma bouchal ?" cried Murtough. "Fiends of darkness, you are badly hurt !"

"Ha, ha ! Hurt ! I have been more than half-way to the man they call 'Davy Jones ;' but you have not seen all, my friend. Bring the light closer. This place is as dark as—as——"

Here the daring, bold smuggler gave a groan, and sank back, gasping for breath.

He lay for a time perfectly still and motionless, so much so, that the twinkle of his heavy eyelids was discernible, while his breathing was so heavy, as to convince them that a desperate struggle was going on for life.

Suddenly Murtough seized a large vessel of water, and dashed the contents over him.

It seemed to have the wished-for effect, for he flung his arms wildly about, and then, by a powerful effort, he raised himself up,

Then passing his hand over his face, he pushed back the wild, matted, clotted hair, and stared around him.

"Where are you hurt, eh, *ma bouchal?* and what can we do ?" said Murtough.

"Yaw, I am hurt everywhere. Hold the light, and you shall see."

He raised his hand to his breast, and,

with a violent effort, tore aside the old guernsey shirt, stained with his blood.

A thrill of horror ran through their frames, used as they were to the sight of blood, for there across the broad chest ran a deep gash, from which the blood still slowly oozed.

He then tore off the handkerchief, and there, across his forehead, there was another wound, that seemed as though it had partly healed.

Still it was fearful to behold, for the cut had gone downwards, inflicting a terrible scar upon the cheek.

"Yaw, that is not all," he said, in hoarse tones. "There is anoder at the back of the skull that has nearly cut it in half."

"Where is the lugger, Jan—and the cargo—and the crew?" asked Murtough.

"Gone to the bottom, to the deyvil!" was the hoarse reply. "Ha, ha, ha! we fought like raging demons to the last. Not a keg did they get. No, no, der deyvil! *not one!*"

And he sank back again, as though exhausted with his efforts.

At this appalling news, Black Murtough sprang to his feet, and, with a deep, bitter groan of despair, struck his forehead with his fist.

"May a curse light upon all them that are persecuting us, and may a swift and terrible revenge fall upon their accursed heads! But I must know more of this. This is no time to slape, but to be up and at the work."

With that he knelt down, and raised the wounded smuggler up, and wiped away the blood from his face and eyes.

Then he bandaged, in a rough but safe way, the wounds, and putting a large stone against Jan's back, he placed another horn of poteen against his lips.

He drank it eagerly, and, after a pause, opened his eyes.

"Thanks, thanks, Murty; dat is goot, and Jan will weather the gale yet."

"Of course you will. Ah, you are getting round, and you have been dreaming and joking."

"Sapperment and blitzen! what shall I joke about, eh? Is this a joke?" and he placed his hand on his chest. "Or this?" and he raised his hand to his bandaged head. "I think all this is a long way ahead of a joke."

"But about the black lugger and the cargo?"

"Have I not told you? Gone to the deyvil! Hark ye, Murtough, we have got some dark traitor in the camp."

"What do you mane?" said the other, fiercely.

"Yaw! what I say—a traitor, a deep, accursed traitor, who has sold us."

"Who is the villain? I'll brain him though he was kneeling to the priest. Do you know him?"

"Nein, or he would not live long. Listen! the cargo was on board, the money paid, and we were thinking of having a clear run again for more, when I was boarded on both quarters by the infernal custom-house sharks, who want to see mine papers. Den I could see—thousand deyvils!—that there was villany on foot."

"'We have been long on the look-out for you, Captain Jan,' said the head officer.

"'Yaw! and now you see me I hope your eyesight is very mosh better. Yaw! I will show you my papers wid pleasure,' I said.

"'My men, search well the lugger,' cried the officer.

"And they went below. I gave my mate the office, and while they are below he shall make more sail on board the lugger, cutting adrift the two boats with the men in them.

"There was a loud cry, and then all rushed upon deck. But the lugger was well under weigh.

"'Ah, ah! mynheer, I've got you at last!' I shouted.

"His answer was a blow at me with his hanger, which caught me just on the head side-ways, and then we closed, donder and blitzen. I have never had such a tough fight before.

"They all fought like fiends when I got hold of his throat, and the next moment we were in the water. I let go with my one hand, and the next my dirk was buried in his heart, and there was blood around me. Give me some drink! my throat is parched."

He drank deeply.

"But the lugger—the cargo—and——"

"Donder, wait a moment till I can get my breath. I cleared away the hair, and —ugh!—looked out for the lugger.

"She was not far off, and I was making for her, when I could see a light spring up the hatchway; there was a roar like that of a hundred canon, and away went lugger, cargo and crew, to the deyvil head-long.

"I was picked up and put ashore, and made the best of my way here. Donder, I hope all is well."

"All is bad. The gaugers and the sogers are down here, bad-luck to them; they've got the best of us for the present, but that luck won't last. I made short work of one to-day. Come round me, boys, and I'll tell you how we'll proceed in future."

At the "Stanley Arms," meanwhile, the consultation was of the most anxious nature. Neither the magistrate, Mr. Righton, Fred, or Hawkseye, had the slightest idea that the plot was so deep or so complicated.

"I shall cause a bill to be posted to-morrow, offering a reward of one hundred guineas for the apprehension of the murderer, Black Murtough, for shooting that poor man. I have already sent an express over to Dublin for more troops, and I shall swear you and your friend, Captain Hardy, in to aid and assist me in carrying out and enforcing the law."

"We are quite willing, sir," was Fred's reply, "and you cannot give us anything more consonant to our feelings than an opportunity of defending the law, a duty that all right-minded men at all times cheerfully obey."

And with this, they sat down to partake of some refreshment, a thing they very much needed.

In an out-house at the further end of the yard, and close against a low wall that was fast tumbling to pieces for the want of a little handy repair, sat another party.

Lanty Shan and Tim Doolan had accepted Mike Murphy's invitation to taste a drop of the "craythur" out of a keg that hadn't *got a mark* upon it, and round the keg the trio were assembled doing full justice.

"How did you manage this piece of bisness, eh, Mike?"

"Well, you see, when the light went out I fell for'ard, and the darlin' rowled into my arms, and it ain't in human natur to let out of our arms what we love in our hearts." And Mike gave them a most expressive wink of his eye. "The divil, Black Murtough, little thinks where his craythur is going. What will be the end of this?" said Mike, with a knowing look.

"I hope you'll not have the heartache until it's finished; there's more in the pot than will well bile, Mike; we have hot work yet."

Here there came a loud thump against the door, as though a brick had been hurled against it.

They all started up.

"The Lord save us! What was that?" said Lanty.

"The murtherin' McDonnells about to storm the place," said Mike, grasping his shillelagh. "*Bathershin!* they won't show their faces agin to-night. Who's there, knocking in that unsamely fashion, and disturbing gentlemen out of their first slape?"

The answer came in the shape of another thump.

"Are you going to thump the door down, you good-for-nothing *gommach?* None of your *kimmeens;* by the *piper of war* you'll get it if I come out to you."

Thump again, and louder.

Lanty flung the door open, and there stood Little Phil.

Lanty started back.

"What brought you here, Phil?" he said. "Your sowl, come in."

And he pulled him in by the collar.

"What's up now?"

"A great dale," was the reply. "I'd see the magistrate or the masther."

"What about, *ma bouchal?*"

"On a matter of private business."

"Come away, then."

And Lanty and the boy were leaving the out-house.

"It will be just as well that somebody will stop to watch over the keg, here," said Mike.

"Quite right, Mike; it can't be in better hands," replied Lanty.

They were not long in crossing the yard and gaining the room in which the gentlemen were still deliberating upon the plans to be carried out the next day.

In the midst of it the door opened, and Lanty and Phil entered.

"Well, Lanty, what is it?" said Fred.

"Well, it's nothing at all to do wid me; it's Little Phil got a something to say to the magistrate."

"I have got something to say to both," was the boy's reply.

"Well, then, out with it, my lad," said Righton.

"Which will I begin with first?"

"Ha, ha! whichever you like."

"Well, then, there's a note for the masther, and when he has done with it you can read it."

The gentlemen laughed at this odd way of delivering a message.

Fred recognised the handwriting immediately, and hastily broke the seal.

The note contained but a few words:—

"In consequence of the anxiety Sir Edward has been in, the last few days, he has been suddenly stricken with an attack of paralysis, and is quite speechless. Come to me.   BELL."

"What is to be done?" said Fred, hurriedly. "This is a severe trial for Miss Stanley, especially at the present moment."

"Yes, and I am sorry to say that it has not been the first attack. I cannot leave here," and he paused a moment. "In spite of what has occurred, Fred, you must go over at once. You know the *red cross* has been placed there as well as on your own place, and therefore it becomes us all to look out. I suppose you will not disobey the commands of your superior officer?" and the magistrate smiled.

"Not in any case," replied Fred, rising, "and certainly not in this."

"I shall go with you, Frolic," said Hardy, "and afterwards make the best of my way home to protect my wife."

"For whom, to-morrow, I advise you to accept the invitation Miss Stanley sent. In the troublesome times coming on, the Castle will be the safest place."

"I agree with you, sir," said Fred; "and to-morrow we will try and arrange it."

Both Fred and his friend, the captain, had come well armed to the fair, so that they were fully prepared, in case of any attack.

"Shall I give you a couple of my men?" said Captain Brabazon.

"We don't want rid-coats," muttered Lanty.

"No, thank ye. They would only be a mark for any gentleman anxious to accommodate us with a bullet. No, Lanty will do, and——"

"Phil Leary, if you plase, sir," said the boy.

"I am afraid of——"

"What, sir?" asked Phil.

"Of danger to you, Phil," said Fred, kindly.

"Then, why ain't you afraid of it to *yourself*, eh, masther? I said I'd bring your answer back, and Phil Leary will keep his word."

"Be it so, Phil. They'll never be cowardly enough to injure a boy like you."

"I don't know that. Mickey Doyle is on the look-out for me, and so am I for him. We don't love each other *intirely*."

"We'll lave by the back way and go over the fields," said Lanty, "for the mob are gathering more than ever in front."

"Your advice is good, Lanty Shan," said Mr. Righton.

At this moment, a fierce yell was heard in the front of the inn, and a shower of stones, that speedily cleared the windows of all their panes; another heavier volley, and the shutters, crazy and creaking as they were, upon their old, rusty hinges, came crashing into the room.

In a moment the whole scene in front of the house was visible.

The daring band of "still-workers," aided by numbers of others, equally disaffected, had assembled there.

Their strong and evil passions had been still further inflamed by the quantities of spirit which they had imbibed, and which rendered them mad and reckless as to any consequences.

There, by the light of a few torches, they stood yelling forth their cries.

"Throw out the gaugers. Hand out the stuff you've robbed us of, you thieves!"

"We'll mark you all for this!" shouted a brawny giant of a fellow, waving his shillelagh in one hand, and a torch in the other.

"You're a broth of a boy to turn against your own countrymen. Mister Frolic, we'll give your house a warning, bad luck to it," roared another, and whiz came a lighted torch among them.

"Will you disperse? You shall neither have gaugers or spirits. Disperse, I say, or it will be the worse for you;" and Mr. Righton was advancing to the window, when a heavy stone catching him on the shoulder, sent him reeling back into the room.

"Clear the street with the bayonet, Captain Brabazon. Where is Hawkseye?"

"Guarding the seized stuff," said a voice, "and he swears he'll destroy it before they shall have a single keg,"

By this time Captain Brabazon had formed his men, and the gates of the inn being opened, the men, headed by him, came out with a rush.

There was a volley of stones, and then a flight, for few have ever stood long before the charge of the bayonet.

While this was going on in front, a party of the gang had made their way round to the back, in order to get hold of the stuff, and the gauger.

Hawkseye, however, was quite equal to the occasion, and had so securely fastened the place up as to resist all their efforts to open it.

"Run down to the 'Shamrock,' Jerry Riley, and borrow a crowbar; there's an iligant one there, that will do the bisness in a pig's whisper," cried one.

And away ran Jerry.

It had been part and parcel of the tactics of the mob to draw all the force they could from the inn, so that they should get back the stuff they had sworn with bitter oaths they would have.

On the other hand, Hawkseye had sworn that not a drop should ever again fall into their clutches.

Seeing, therefore, that the soldiers had been drawn away from the place, he at once determined upon the course to be pursued.

He, therefore, told the remainder of his men to keep inside the house, and, while the lawless mob were deliberating in front, he removed quietly a couple of boards from the back, and crept in.

Then, taking a phosphorous box from his pocket (for the expert gaugers of those days were pretty well prepared for emergencies), he at once procured a light.

The place itself was full of old dry straw and wood, and the kegs themselves were covered with it.

He was a bold man, and had been all his life engaged in the Revenue Service.

"What do you want there?" he said, loudly.

"By the powers, that's the voice of the gauger!" the mob cried. "Give up the stuff, you murdering thafe, that you have robbed us of, or we'll have your life!" was the fierce reply.

"You'll not be so hard, will you?" he said, in a bantering tone; "the stuff don't belong to me."

"Bad luck to you, will you give it up peaceably?" they roared out.

"I can't. I haven't got the key, but if you'll only wait a few moments, you shall have some of it, as hot as you like it."

And so saying, he thrust a light into the dry straw that covered the kegs.

It blazed up fiercely; then throwing himself down on the earth, he crept again through the aperture he made, and standing for a moment to witness the effect of his daring conduct, he made the best of his way into the inn.

The fire was not long in taking effect upon the place, the kegs themselves were pretty well saturated with the stuff outside, and soon caught with fearful rapidity, and clouds of dense smoke rolled through the place and the crevices of the building, blinding those who stood without, and driving them back.

Loud shouts of execration and deep bitter growls, broke from the mob, when they saw this, and, so frantic were they in their rage, that they tried with their hands to tear down the boards.

It was all in vain; the fiery monster had gained the ascendancy; the spirit had caught, for the fierce heat having burst one of the oldest and most worthless kegs, the contents ran out, saturating the straw so that, in a short space of time the whole place was like a raging furnace of molten flame.

At that moment Jerry Riley rushed up bearing the crow-bar; but there was little occasion for it, for the whole place was wrapped in one bright mass of glowing fire.

"I'll have some out," roared a fellow who was already mad and infuriated with what he had drank, and with an awful oath he rushed in.

He was seen no more, for the fumes of the burning stuff in one instant seized him, and he fell suffocated into the flame that seethed and roared around.

In doing this daring act, Hawkseye had only calculated upon destroying the out buildings and the contents; he had forgotten its proximity to the old inn, to which the leaping flames were fast approaching.

At seeing this, the mob roared and shouted in their savage rage.

"We'll give you a roasting and a warming now, ma bouchals!" they shouted, and they jumped and danced about like exulting demons.

In the midst of this, Mike and Tim, who had been indulging in the "craythur comforts," and had comfortably fallen asleep over the affair, were roused up from the heavy slumber they had fallen into, and with a wild cry of "Hurrah for the Frolics!" rushed out of the place they had been so comfortably placed in.

Then the others, fancying the whole body of the fighting faction were bearing down upon them, rushed pell-mell out of the place, which was now lighted up with a bright vivid flame, for it had extended to the old inn, from which the parties who had been deliberating inside found it necessary to beat a retreat.

It was a scene of wild and fearful confusion.

In the distance the soldiers were still engaged driving the mob back, which they did amidst a shower of stones and whatever missiles they could find, while round the building the band of Frolics, who had gathered together to defend the master, were headed by Lanty, having a "scrimmage" with a lot of the McDonnell faction.

The whole inn was by this time wrapped in one fierce sheet of fire, spreading its wild, weird-like reflection far over the country.

Hawkseye, upon this matter, had wisely kept his own counsel, and the whole was attributed to the rage of the men who had been deprived of their illicit material.

Outside the inn, were now assembled Mr. Righton, Fred, and Frank Hardy, while a few minutes after they were joined by Captain Brabazon and his men.

Tired and wearied out, all parties seemed inclined to a cessation of hostilities.

The McDonnells, disappointed of their day's profit and pleasure, sullenly withdrew into the field where the fair had been held, there to nurse their vengeance and their wrath.

The Frolics gave their blackthorns a rest, for they were too tired to follow up their victory, and so they stood looking on the fire that was fast consuming the old inn.

The first streak of morning was seen flickering over the far-distant mountains, as the flames, having worn themselves out, fell into darkness.

At times a wild shout was heard in the distance, as though some of the revellers were determined to have the last of it.

At length the rising sun began to shed its beams of glory upon the wild scene of desolation and ruin.

Its rays fell upon the smoking, blackened building, and slanted across the fair field, showing the hundreds of men, women, and miserable children, huddled together, endeavouring to sleep, the broken, half down tents here and there giving a shelter to many of those who, with gashed face, and swollen, darkened eyes, gave fearful evidence of the affray.

Just as the light broke upon this wild scene, Mr. Righton gave the word, and then, headed by Fred, Frank, and the captain, the troops slowly began their march back to the castle.

In the rear came Mr. Hawkseye and his men, protected by the remnant of the Frolic boys, while Lanty and Little Phil marched alongside of them.

"Well, Phil, how did you like the fair, eh?" said Lanty. "It's been a mighty hot one while it lasted, and, by my sowl, it's my belief that the *fire is only just lighted.*"

And tucking the blackthorn under his arm, and his hands into his pockets, Lanty marched gaily on, with Phil by his side.

CHAPTER XXVII.

THE DARING LEAP.

WHEN the party arrived at the castle, they found Sir Edward Stanley had relapsed into such a state of unconsciousness as to render him quite insensible to everything that was going on; the whole management of the castle, therefore, devolved upon his high-spirited and noble-hearted daughter, Bell.

Being well informed by Fred of all that had taken place, she sent four trusty servants over to Frolic House, and, in a very short time, the runaway ward in chancery was warmly welcomed and quite at home in the castle.

During the whole of that day, reports were brought in by Little Phil of how "matthers were going on in the fair."

The lithe, active boy flew over the mountains, into the barony, and, gliding about, formed his own conclusions, and was back again with his report, to the castle.

The last he brought determined Bell Stanley to write the note she did, and it was with great anxiety she waited the return of her trusty little Mercury.

However, neither he, nor the persons she most anxiously wished, came, and so the two girls sat at the highest window in the castle, talking and watching all through the night.

Then, suddenly came the red glare over the mountain tops, causing the alarmed girls to cling closer to each other.

"What fearful scene is that?" cried Mrs. Hardy.

"One that is a warning to us to be well on the alert," was the reply.

And with that, Bell descended the stairs, and calling up the servants, and the half-dozen soldiers that had been left in the place, they proceeded to well secure all parts of the castle.

Great was their joy when Fred and his party arrived at the place; and when somewhat recruited from the fatigue they had all of them undergone, a consultation was held as to the best means to fortify the castle against the attack they knew would be made against it.

In the baronies, in the course of the day, large placards were posted up, offering the large reward of one hundred pounds for the apprehension of Black Murtough, for the wilful murder of the gauger's man.

This, instead of striking consternation into the breasts of the "still workers" and smugglers, roused their rage to the highest pitch, and at several meetings the *Red Oath of Vengeance* was again entered into, and the red cross, that had been marked against the walls of the castle, and Frolic House, had an additional *two* placed against them.

Fred Frolic saw that no effectual resistance could be offered to the ruffians who had sworn to level it with the ground, and so, gathering the few articles of value left him, and placing them for safety in the castle, he turned his attention to devising every means in his power for the preservation of Bell Stanley.

Lanty, therefore, had full charge of the house of the Frolics, and well and truly did he and his two friends, Mike and Tim, keep watch and ward over it.

Little Phil was the active little messenger between the two points; at the same time he kept a close eye upon the doings in the cave.

Crossing the fields one morning, when just by the cross roads by the castle gates, he was suddenly pounced upon by his bitter enemy, Mickey Doyle, the spy.

"Ha, the top of the morning to you, Phil Leary," said the ruffian, who bore about his person evident marks of the fray he had been engaged in.

"The same to you, Mickey, and many of them before the rope crosses the neck of you," was the reply.

"That's well," said Mickey. "I'd be shaking hands wid you."

"I'd rather be excused, Mickey."

And he edged away from him.

"Well, I'm not aware that I've done anything to desarve this; but, I am glad to see you all, the same. Bedad, I'd like to know what you are always wandering about the old church for?"

"Would you. It's looking for the ghoust or the *spirits*, perhaps, and that's all you'll know."

"I'll know more, and so shall others."

And he advanced threateningly towards him.

"Keep back, Mickey, or I'll make a hole in the skin of ye."

And he drew from his breast a long-bladed knife.

"The divil a bit do I care about that."

And he made a spring at him; but the boy, agile as a leaping fawn, sprang aside, and the next moment the knife was buried deeply in the shoulder of the spy.

"You've got more than you will ate for a month to come," and the boy rushed off in the direction of the castle.

With a deep and bitter curse, Mickey pulled the knife out of his flesh, and was after him.

Over the wall sprang the boy, with the baffled ruffian after him, and across the park, towards the broad and almost bottomless lake he rushed.

At the same moment, Fred, mounted on his gallant old hunter, was riding to the castle in another direction.

Looking up, he saw the boy racing for his life, followed by Mickey, armed with a knife.

There was a bridge that crossed the road here, with a low wall and arch crossing the lake. Upon this Bell Stanley and her friend stood waiting the arrival of Fred, when they were aroused by loud shouts and a wave of his hand to stand aside.

"TAKE A FOOL'S ADVICE," CRIED LANTY, "AND KAPE QUIET."

As he came thundering over the grass, Phil, seeing no other way to escape his enemy, who was rapidly nearing him, sprang boldly into the lake.

The horror and consternation of the girls were fearful, but Fred heeded them not, and giving Rocket free reins, leaped over the wall, away into the deep lake.

"Keep up, Phil, for the love of Heaven! and I'll save you."

But the difficulties were very great. There, just in that very spot, was a thick, tangled mass of weeds.

"Keep out of the weeds, Phil, or you are lost," he shouted.

"I can't kape up long, masther; I'm not much of a swimmer," gasped the bold-hearted boy, for the current was fast carrying him into the gulf of death.

Fred urged his gallant old horse round the weeds, but to his horror he felt the horse's strength was failing.

"Another trial, brave old Rocket," he shouted "and we have him. God bless you! old horse," he added, as the animal, as if answering the appeal, made a desperate plunge forward.

At the same moment Fred seized Phil by the hair, and flung him across his saddle.

Then came a wild scream of joy from the old bridge, as the highly excited girls sank on their knees with a prayer of joy to Heaven for the safety of both horse and rider.

The bold rider and the fearless boy were not quite out of danger, for the currents of the lake were rapid and whirling, and the old hunter felt, as all will feel, the effect of age and hard work telling upon it.

Fred saw all this, and so, bidding Little Phil cling closely to the saddle, he slipped out of it himself, and taking the bridle of the old horse in his hand, he cheered him on, and kept his head well up.

This had the desired effect, for Rocket, lightened of his load, appeared to gain renewed strength, and breasting the current boldly, they at last gained a shelving part of the lake, and then Fred, springing on the grass, soon had the good old horse up alongside of him, and, with him, the "little boy of the fairies."

The next moment Phil was dancing on the grass, to the great amusement of all.

Bell Stanley rushed towards them the moment she saw them touch the land.

"Thank God, Fred, you are safe!" said the warm-hearted girl, her head sinking on his shoulder. "Oh! how my heart sank when I saw you dash over the wall!"

"Ha, ha! no doubt, Bell. But how mine throbbed with wild exultation as Rocket cleared the wall, and dashed into the lake. Well, Phil, *ma bouchal*, and how do you feel after your bath, eh?"

"Cool and comfortable, masther. What a coward that Mickey Doyle was not to follow. But I gave him a mark on his shoulder he won't get rid of aisily."

By this time they were joined by Mr. Righton and the captains, who had been concerting upon the means of defending the castle.

They had gone over it and found out the weak parts, and set the soldiers to work to strengthen them as much as possible and as well as their means would allow.

"We shall hold out pretty well against the fellows, if they try it on," said Mr. Righton.

"And try it on they will," replied Fred. "They are a desperate set, and, foiled as they have been, they are only lying quiet for a time, that they may make their spring the more certain and deadly. I wish that some of us were away."

And he half glanced at Bell and her companion.

"Well, upon my word, Mr. Frolic, that is very complimentary. I suppose you wish us out of the way, that you may have all the sport to yourselves? Now sir, speak the truth, is it not so?"

"Well, then, Miss Stanley——"

"Stop, sir, my name is *Bell* Stanley, and so was my mother's before me, and I am not ashamed of it."

And she drew herself proudly erect.

Fred at this sent forth one of his merry, frolicsome laughs.

"Well, my dear Miss Stanley," said Mr. Righton, "although I do not wish to lose your society, yet I wish both you and Sir Edward, and this dear young lady, were safely lodged in Dublin town."

During this they had been gradually nearing the castle.

"Many thanks for your kind wish; perhaps you'd feel easier if you were there yourselves," and she smiled.

"I'll answer for myself, that I am very well content where I am," said Fred, pressing Bell's hand to his lips.

"And I," said Bell, standing under the arch that led to the castle, "would not leave this dear old spot, although all the 'poteen workers' were against it. Here," she said proudly, looking up, "here my dear mother was born, here I first saw the light of heaven, and now it is in its hour of danger, I am with it, and with it will perish rather than desert it; and so those that like Dublin better, can make the best of their way to it."

So saying, she entered the castle, with a proud smile, and a heart that knew neither fear nor cowardice.

"She has a noble nature," said Captain Brabazon.

"And the *real Irish blood*," replied Fred.

CHAPTER XXVIII.

MR. FOGHARTY AGAIN AT FROLIC HOUSE.

ALTHOUGH Fred Frolic had removed the few relics of his dear parents from the old mansion, it was not to be thought that he abandoned the old spot in which he was born.

"May I take the liberty of axing you a simple question?" said Lanty, to him.

"As many as you like, Lanty," was the reply.

"Well, then, sir, is it up at the castle that you're going to live intirely?" and Lanty's eyes twinkled as though the water was gathering in them.

"What the deuce makes you ask such a stupid question, eh, Lanty?" said Fred, staring at him.

"Bekase you are moving the things that made the ould place look like the ould place; that's the likeness of the masther, and the one of the mistress, and many little things that were as valuable as the light in Lanty's eyes; but come what may, the ould walls and Lanty go together."

"And who says you would not go together? and who says they would ever be forsaken! Why, Lanty, man, what's ailing you?" and Fred placed his hand on his shoulder.

"Well, just nothing at all, but do all you can, you can't help ould thoughts getting into your head, can you, masther?"

"No; but you see, Lanty, what those men have done," and Fred pointed with his whip to the *three red marks* upon the wall, "and you know if they come here, which most assuredly they will, they are six to one of us, and that is rather long odds."

"That for the long odds, or the short ones either," said Lanty, snapping his fingers. "We've bate the dirthy *spalpeens*

before, and by the piper of war, we'll bate them agin, aisy—aisy—aisy——"

"We'll do all that men of courage can, or dare do, Lanty, you may take my word for that," said Fred, warmly.

"And you may take my word for as much again, and more, if you can find it, and Tim's word, and Mike of the slave-board, and Pat Donovan, of the hotel, and Dan Riley, and Patsy Kelly, and——"

"All the rest, Lanty, all good men, and true; and when everything is settled I'll not forget to reward you and them for what you have done."

Down went Lanty's *caubeen* in the mud.

"What do you mane by reward, eh, masther?" replied Lanty.

"Don't be in a passion, Lanty."

"I'm as cool as a melting snowball, but I want to know what you mane by reward? the divil burn it."

"Well, you shall know some day; in the meantime look well after the old house; every moment I can spare I shall be with you, and as soon as the place is quiet, the new one shall be commenced. How do you stand for money, Lanty?"

"Mighty powerful, seeing that we have got more than we can spend," was the reply.

"That's handy," said Fred. Keep a sharp look-out. I can trust you old fellow," and, so saying, Fred rode off.

"There is no doubt about that," muttered Lanty; "and, as far as trusting goes, you can trust me," and he looked up at the old house; "and I'll go bail that as long as I have a fut to stand, and fingers to hould you, my darlin," and he gave his faithful blackthorn a twirl round his head, "and you may take your oath you'll niver be desarted. And now I'll go and have a bit of convarse with Mike and the other boys," and Lanty made the best of his way into the kitchen, where Tim and Mike were indulging in the pleasure of a comfortable dhudeen.

Mr. Fogharty, when giving his best advice to Black Murtough to conceal himself until the affair had "blown over," had two very powerful motives; one of them was that by getting Murtough out of the way, he could manage to do the same for himself, and the other was that by so doing, he could still keep his clutch upon the money (no small sum) belonging to him and the band of still workers, not only in the barony of Ballinafad, but in others as well. So, all that night and best part of the next day, he kept himself carefully secluded in the "Shamrock inn," comforting himself with the best that the landlord (one of themselves) could place before him.

"It was the worst day's work I ever did when I put my legs in Ballyran after that accursed debt of old Frolic. I should have fought the battle in the city; and only let me get back to that place, and may I walk upon hot cinders in silk stockings if ever you get me out agin."

He took a good pull at his punch.

"I niver saw the sky so dark afore," he muttered; "they've found out about the Frolic bills. May the old 'un toast that accursed fellow Righton for that; and if they were to find out that I am principal cashier and general attorney to the Murtough gang, I wouldn't give much for my chance of the woolsack. I must get out of this widout its being known. I must get a disguise, and——"

The door opened, and he started up as Mickey Doyle, the spy, looked in. His face had such a deathly pallor upon it, and his eyes such a stony glare in them, that Fogharty started up as though a ghost stood before him.

"The lord save us, who is that, and what do you want?" and he grasped the old iron poker that stood handy.

"Don't you know me?" said Mickey, staggering in, and falling in a seat.

"Why, it's hard to tell in these days who's who; but the powers be good to us, but I think it's Mickey Doyle. Why, man alive, what is the matter?"

Mickey, before he answered the lawyer, finished a tumbler of punch belonging to Fogharty, which seemed to put new life into him, and send a little more colour into his face.

He then related his meeting with Little Phil, and the result of it.

"I lost a great dale of blood, Mr. Fogharty; that has made my face the colour of a flour sack—a sort of whitey-brown. But I'll have his life for it, the imp of Satan."

And he uttered a tremendous oath.

"Well, I would; and I wouldn't be long about it; and if you can give his master an inch of lead or steel, you'll count upon Fogharty as your friend."

"One at a time," growled the spy. "I swore an oath that I won't break very aisily as I lay in the long grass, bleeding, as I thought, to death, but I'll catch him, and then——"

"Settle the account, and give a receipt in full; but I tell you to be quick, or they'll *have you first.*"

And the lawyer grinned.

"What do you mane?" said Mickey, in great alarm.

"Mean? the meaning is plain enough. There will be a reward offered for you, the same as there is for Black Murtough, whom I should at once advise you to join. Haven't you seen the proclamation?"

"Not I," replied Mickey, surlily.

"Ah, well, you should use your eyesight. There is one hundred pounds reward offered for him, and if they get him, he'll lose the race by a neck, and you'll do the same; the boy will swear that you were one of them, and——"

This was enough for Mickey; he rose up, although every limb in his body shook.

"Shall I go at *once?*" he asked.

"Certainly; the soldiers are gone, and that accursed magistrate, and the others; to-morrow they will be hunting all over the country after you. Away with you, and tell Murtough I'll come myself when it is quite dark and see him in the old vault."

"You know the password?" said Mickey.

"Yes, I should think so; I shall keep myself snug until dark, and then make the best of my way; be off, and if ever you wanted your legs to serve you, let them do it now."

With this wish, Mickey stole from the room, while the cunning lawyer indulged in a quiet chuckle at the clever manner in which he was playing his cards.

"I shall get rid of them *all,*" he said,

rubbing his hands; "pah! all, there are only *three* I care anything about, the brutes Murtough, and Jan, and McDonnell; and now to get ready for my disguise as a countryman, because I must get out of the town unobserved."

And with that he called the landlord in.

"Did you get what I told you?"

"I did. A capital coat reaching down to your heals, and a *caubeen* that will concale your face from every mortal soul. Oh! you'll look iligant in another man's rags."

And the man left the room, returning quickly with the articles he had named.

"They belonged to Tim Guffin, who was kilt yesterday, and so you'll never be asked for payment."

Fogharty shuddered as he put the coat on.

"What is the matter?" said the man.

"Was the man killed in this coat?" he asked, somewhat nervously.

"Sure he was; he was shot by one of the sogers—bitter bad luck to him—a nater shot I never saw in all my days."

"Can't you get me another? Suppose I am taken for the man."

"How can you be taken for a man that is killed stone dead, eh? Oh, don't be nervous, lawyer; I have heard of people walking into dead men's shoes, and why not into their coats? Where is the difference? There's no other, I tell you."

"Well, then, curse it, I must put up with this."

"It's Pat Malowney's choice—that or none," was the reply.

In a few minutes he was so transmogrified that very few persons would have known him; then, sitting down, he called for another tumbler, just to settle his nerves before he started on his journey.

It was dark when he started, and no one who met him would ever have taken him for Lawyer Fogharty.

He had fastened the coat round him with an old belt, and pulled the hat well over his face; and so he passed the inn, whose ruins were still smouldering.

Round it was a group of persons of both sexes engaged in deep converse, occasionally pointing to a large bill that was pasted up.

He stood still and listened.

"It's meself," said one, "who wouldn't mind getting that one hundred pounds, eh, Tim? It's a powerful sum of money, and you could have *lashins* of ating and drinking for it, *ma bouchal.*"

"It will be no two or three men that will ever take Black Murtough; I'm no coward, but I wouldn't care to stand before him single handed," replied another.

"Bathershin! he is but a man. But there is another man I'd like to see advertised for."

"Who is that, *ma cushla?*"

"Lawyer Fogharty," was the reply. "What say you, avick?" placing his hand upon that individual's shoulder.

"What's Fogharty done?" asked another.

"What's he done? More mischief than a dozen Black Murtoughs. He has ground down the poor as well as robbing them, and would think no more of taking the roof off the heads of widders and orphans than I would drinking a glass of the craythur to the health of a friend. I'd have a pull at the rope with all the pleasure in life if Fogharty were at the end of it; he is at the bottom of all the mischief, there's little doubt of that."

At that moment Fogharty saw an opening in the crowd, and so, sauntering slowly past them, he got clear, and made his way quickly out of the street of Ballinafad.

He was soon out into the open road.

"It was lucky I had this disguise on. They say listeners seldom hear any good of themselves, and in my case it comes very near the truth," he muttered. "I'd give a trifle to be in my own office, in the swate City of Dublin, and——"

At that moment, he was passing within sight of the old church, when suddenly a man stood before him, armed with a powerful bit of blackthorn.

"What's the time, *ma bouchal?*" said the man.

"Nine," was the prompt reply.

"That's well. What's the word to a friend?" again asked the man.

"*Bannath lath,*" was again Fogharty's prompt reply.

"All right," said the man. "You are one of us. Give us the grip of a friend."

And he held out his left hand, grasping the shillelagh with his right.

The grip was given, which brought *real* tears into the lawyer's eyes, a thing that had not been seen for many a day.

"I'd like to know your name, *ma bouchal,*" said the man who was placed upon

"ATTEMPT TO ENTER, AND YOU ARE A DEAD MAN," SAID BLACK MURTOUGH.

the road as one of Black Murtough's scouts.

"My name?" replied Fogharty, for a moment hesitating.

"Yes, your name, avick?"

"Phil Guffin," was the reply.

"Phil Guffin, the pig driver. Well, sure you are grown mighty tall since I saw you down at the fair."

"The divil a bit. You mane my brother Tim, him that was shot yesterday."

"Well," said the scout, "it matters little. I knew it was *one* or the *other*."

"Well, *bannath lath* again to you," said Fogharty, anxious to cut the matter short. "I must be off. I have got a lot of pigs coming into Ballyran, and I want to get to them."

"Oh, wid all my heart. All I hope is that the bastes will go to a fine market. *Bannath lath* again to you. Stop, Phil. You haven't got a taste of baccy about you?"

"Ne'er a bit, sure!"

"If it's only as much as will fill up the hollow of your tooth, I'd be thankful."

"I haven't a bit, or you'd be as welcome as myself."

"Well, the saints be wid you."

"The same to you and yours," was the reply.

Fogharty sped away up the road, and had scarcely passed the old church, then just in sight, when he was stopped again.

The same questions were put, and the same answers returned, with a like result.

"Black Murtough is determined to keep a good look-out, and for the matter of that Fogharty won't be a day's march behind him. He can swear to that. I think I am all right now."

He was soon over the hill, and across the fields, until he came out by the cross roads by the old sign-post.

He paused, looking at the lodge gate that led up to the castle, and leaning against it, he could just see, by the glancing of the moon's rays, the *three blood red crosses* on the wall.

He took off his hat for a moment.

"There will be some hot work there, shortly," he muttered, "and the sooner Fogharty is a long way off, the better. I'd do no good with Sir Edward; he won't last long, and then—ah, Fogharty, get on wid you."

He walked off at a quick shambling pace. While he was talking to himself, at the old finger post, he was not aware

that a pair of keen, sharp eyes were fixed upon him from over the wall; and when he had started off, he knew not that, following at a short distance, was Phil Leary.

"What's that Fogharty about? I know him," said the boy, to himself. "No good, I'll be sworn. I must see into this, instead of going to the old ruins; they are safe enough, but that ould rascal must not get out of the clutches of Phil."

Mr. Fogharty could not make his way to Ballyran without going past Frolic House, unless he went a long way round by the fields.

"There's no one about, and I am safe enough," he said, as he neared the house, "and by the powers, there'll not be much of it left before long," and, so saying, he stopped, and looked up at the place.

"And so you won't pay me my bills," he muttered, savagely; "and I'm a forger, am I?" and he shook his fist at the place. "There shan't be a stone of you left standing, before long. Black Murtough will be down upon you, right soon, but I'll be in Dublin long afore that."

The next moment he felt a tremendous whack across the shoulders, and then he was seized by the collar and shaken, as though he was a rat in the jaws of a dog.

"The divil a bit will you see Dublin this many a day, you ould thafe," said Lanty Shan, twirling his shillelagh before his eyes, while round him stood Tim and Mike, and one or two more; Little Phil dancing about with delight.

"What's the meaning of this, eh?" said Fogharty, "are you going to murder me?"

"Not yet," replied Lanty, with a grin, "but we'll tache you a lesson how to behave yourself for the future."

"You'll let me depart on my journey; I'll have you punished for this, as well as other matters."

"All in good time, Fogharty; but you see, first you must get us; now, you see, we have got you."

"And what are you going to do with me?" he said, in a cringing, whining tone.

"Try you by court martial. So come along aisy," was the reply.

"I'll not go. I'll give you a——"

"No, I'll give you a——" and whack went the shillelagh upon his shoulders. "A friendly welcome; how do you like it, eh?"

"I'll, I'll—have—Murder!" he shouted.

"Call away my darlin', you haven't got

any of your friends, McDonnell or Murtough, to help you. Bring him along, Tim and Mike, to the court of justice."

"I'll not go, I'll be tried in Dublin," he roared, and kicked.

"That you will, soon enough, make up your mind to that; aisy with him," said Lanty.

The next moment, in spite of his struggles, he found himself lifted from the ground, and in the strong arms of Tim and Mike, while in the front danced Phil, Lanty marching behind and trying to keep him quiet with sundry pokes from the faithful shillelagh, the others following with many capers and twistings of the fingers.

In this way Fogharty was carried to the stables, and having been placed upon an old barrel, and well held up by the collar, he glanced around him with looks of terror and alarm.

The place was pretty well filled with the "faction," and a few whom Mr. Fogharty had done his best to evict from their homes.

At this sight he felt as though his last hour had come, but thought the best plan was to put (no difficult thing for him) a face of brass upon the matter.

"I demand to know——" he began.

"Silence in the court," said Mike, accompanying the request with a slight touch of the famous sleeve-board.

"Lanty Shan shall be judge," shouted the others.

"Wid all my heart," said Lanty, "and you shall *all* be the jury, and then you can't but say you've had a fair and impartial trial, any how."

"You'll be kind enough to respect the dignity of the court, prisoner."

"What's your name?" and Lanty grinned at him.

"I shan't tell," replied Fogharty, sulkily, "you know it."

"Bad luck to you, we do," was the response of the others.

"You say true, we do know it; you are placed before us as a noted vagabond and perjurer, and a forger, and if that's giving you a character, I don't know what is. Are you guilty or not, you vagabond?"

Fogharty made no answer.

"Rouse him up, Mike, avick; what do you let the prisoner fall aslape for, bad luck to you?"

A magical touch from the sleeve-board made Fogharty jump up.

"Am I guilty, you bitther bad lot? What am I charged with?" he said.

"Hark to that now, what is he charged with," said Lanty, "why, bad luck to you, with everything that is mane, dirty, and disgraceful; haven't I told you what you are, ain't that enough?"

"No, you can't prove anything; not one of you would be believed on your own oaths."

At this a yell arose from the rest that made Fogharty regret that he had opened his mouth so wide.

"You hear what he says, that you are a set of blaggards. After that, what do you say to him?"

"Guilty, guilty, the vagabond," was the cry.

"Guilty of what?"

"Trayson! Murder! and the likes of all that," was the reply.

"You say that upon your consciences?" said Lanty. "Put your hands upon your consciences and say it fairly."

In an instant their hands grasped the blackthorns, which they raised in the air.

"By our consciences!" they cried.

"You hear that, Fogharty," said Lanty. "You've been found guilty by a jury of your countrymen—more's the pity, for it's a disgrace you are to them—of the most haynus crimes, and it now only remains for me to pass the sentence of the court upon you."

Here Fogharty made a desperate effort to escape, but the next moment found himself sprawling on his back.

"Your trying to escape from the hands of justice aggravates your many crimes, and we must endeavour to bring you to a proper sinse of mind by giving you time for repintance. Mike, bind his arms tight to his dirthy carcase."

Here Mike produced a stout piece of rope, of a decent length.

"Will that bear his weight Mike, avick?"

"I'll go bail it will, and a dozen pigs like him," was the reply.

"Pass it dacently under his arms and see that it is tight, bekase I shouldn't like it to slip and fasten round his dirthy neck."

Mike, with a glorious grin on his face, passed the rope under the arm-pits of Fogharty, whose face was blanched with fear and terror.

"Are you going to murder me?" he yelled. "To hang me?"

"No, my darlin'. We are only going to hang you up *to dry*. Fasten his arms, Mike."

Then the tailor passed a cord round his arms, binding them tightly to his sides.

"Listen to me," he said. "I'll give fifty—nay, a hundred pounds, to give over this nonsense, and I'll swear never to proceed against any of you for——"

"Hould your tongue, you blaggard. For offering a bribe to me, the judge, the rope ought to be tied round your neck; *but we* will be merciful *for the present.* Bring him away."

The moon was shining brightly when they led the trembling Fogharty into the open air, followed by all who had assembled in the stables.

Crossing along the front of the house, they came to a large pool of dirty water, over which hung the powerful branch of a tree.

"Take him round to the back of the tree, and tie him up to the branch. We'll give him an hour to make up his mind if he is guilty or not, and then when he is brought to a proper sinse of what is right, we'll consider what the *rest* of the sentence should be."

Spite of his struggles and his cries for mercy, in a very short time Fogharty hung suspended from the branch of the tree, which shook and swayed under the burden.

"Look ye, Fogharty," cried Lanty, who stood on the opposite side of the pond, "you had better take a fool's advice, and be quiet, for by the powers, if you kick about much down will come the branch, and you'll fall into the iligant place beneath, clane and dacent."

And acting upon this sensible advice, Fogharty kept his limbs quiet, though he uttered deep and bitter curses against those who stood opposite, laughing and reviling him, until even the gossoons and pigs came out to have a look at the lawyer hanging with his dirty trunk upon the branch of the tree.

CHAPTER XXIX.

THE BATTLE OF THE DEVIL'S GRIP.

THERE is death in the castle; the proud, unbending possessor has passed away, while the toil and tumult of life was busily moving around him.

Without, upon the green sward, are assembled Mr. Righton, Fred, Frank Hardy, Captain Brabazon, Hawkseye, and the soldiers.

The former is in deep conversation with Little Phil, who is now bent upon wreaking his revenge upon Black Murtough and his gang.

Then the word is given, and they march forward quietly, and in a few moments the whole party are in the road, and, guided by the boy, are on their way to the old church, for it was there that Phil had seen some of the band emerge in the dead hour of the night, when they thought no eye beheld them.

As they neared the ruins, Phil whispered to Fred.

"They had better let me go first," he said.

"Do as you like, boy, we can trust you," was the reply.

Phil glided away like a serpent among the long grass; outside the old church he stopped and listened, but not a sound met his ear; then he gained the inside of the building upon which the moon shone in all its splendour.

No one was there.

In the rays of the moon he held up his hand, and then the whole party marched silently up, and concealed themselves effectually.

A short time only elapsed when the head of a man appeared, as though emerging from the earth.

He looked round.

"All's right," he said, "the divil a soul is here;" and he sprang upon his feet.

The next moment a gag was passed over his mouth.

He struggled hard, but it was all in vain. He was secured, bound, arms and legs, and thrown down among the long grass.

The next instant, Hawkseye sprang down, and was instantly followed by Fred, Frank, Righton, and the soldiers.

Scarcely had they entered the place, when Murtough caught the light upon the red coats of the soldiers, and springing upon his feet,—

"We are betrayed!" he shouted, with a fierce oath; "be ready, men!"

"Surrender in the name of the law," shouted Hawkseye, rushing forward.

"There is my answer," yelled Black Murtough, and he fired, with deadly aim, at the gauger.

With a fearful cry, he sprang up, and fell dead at the feet of Fred.

The next moment, all were engaged in the fierce conflict of life or death.

In the fierce struggle that was going on, Fred had seized upon Black Murtough, and, aiming a fearful blow at him with the butt end of his pistol, he felt the grasp upon him relax.

At that instant the few dim lights that had been burning in the cave were completely extinguished, and the vast vault was suddenly cast into total darkness and gloom.

All was still save the groans of the dying.

The soldiers had ceased firing, and those in command of them were at a loss for a moment what course to pursue, when suddenly, at a long distance off, there was seen a gleam of light.

"By Heavens! there is a subterranean passage leading to the sea shore," shouted Fred.

Then the light became more vivid and distinct, and the forms of the smugglers could be seen rushing through the aperture.

"Forward, men!" shouted Fred, "and secure the villains."

At this they advanced, but were compelled to go slowly, for the obstacles in the way rendered the passage perilous in the extreme.

Murtough, although partially stunned by the blow from Fred, had still sufficient strength to exert himself in saving his followers.

He seized Jan, therefore, and, with the desperate strength of despair, dragged him towards the entrance of the cave by the sea, which was rushing against the entrance.

"Your sowl to Heaven, Jan! rouse up. I'll niver desart you," said Murtough.

"Ah, sapperment it is all of no use; the last grain in the glass is all—all, blitzen; look to yourself, it is all over with me."

Murtough saw that this was but too true, for just through the hole in the cave he could see the invading force approaching.

"Hell's curse upon them! they are coming. What is to be done?" he said to Jan.

"Done, blitzen, and——ah! there is ten tousand deaths tearing at my chest; sapperment, will you do as your dying friend wishes?"

"Yes, yes. May the foul fiend——"

"No time for words. Make the best use of your legs, and live to revenge us all," said Jan.

"I will, I will," said Murtough.

"Give me your hand. There is the grasp—one of a dying man who never shrunk from his foe or betrayed his friend. Now fly, Murtough."

"I will; but it is only to avenge you, Jan," and, rough and daring as the nature of the man was, a tear stood in his eye.

He wrung the hand of his dying comrade with the last grasp of friendship, and disappeared.

The fast expiring Jan dragged himself further towards the waves, one of which washing over him, seemed for the moment to revive him.

The old sea foam, that he had ridden over so often—boy and man—seemed to be singing his dirge, as he by an almost supernatural act of strength dragged himself up on a large piece of rock, and throwing one arm round a jagged portion of it, held firmly on.

At that moment Fred and the leaders of the party approached the entrance of the cave.

"Men, present arms!" said the captain, and the men brought their pieces to the level.

"Hold!" said Fred. "He is but one man, and seems dying. Surrender! Resistance is useless."

The scene at that moment was awfully striking, as the tall form of the bold smuggler drew itself up to its greatest height.

The drifting clouds passed rapidly across the face of the moon, so as to

THE DEATH OF BLACK MURTOUGH.

shine fully upon his pale and bleeding face.

He made an effort with one hand, and dashed aside the matted locks, then clutching the rock with it, he raised his clenched right hand in the air, while a hoarse laugh broke from him.

"Ha, ha, ha! Mynheers, you have tracked me to mine lair, and now what is your pleasure?"

"Surrender, or we shall be compelled to fire," said Fred.

"Why parley with the fellow?" said Brabazon.

"A wounded, and an unarmed man, foe as he is, ought not to be shot down like a dog, without giving him a *chance* for life and repentance," replied Fred, indignantly.

"Surrender, is it you ask?" said Jan. "The word never was heard before but it was answered in a way that I cannot answer now. The answer was a bullet— yaw—a bullet. Surrender. Ha, ha! What, Jan Hydel Ren, he who has braved these wild ocean waves, man and boy, forty years! Ha, ha! It has come to something; but as every man is worth his price, what will you give me to surrender, eh, mynheers?"

"Nothing; and so be quick," was the reply.

"And what if I do not surrender, eh?" was the fierce answer.

"We'll fire at you!" shouted Brabazon. "Make ready, men."

"Well, then, may a blighting curse seize upon you and yours for ever! Fire!" he shouted, as he sprang over the rock into the foaming waves.

The sound from half-a-dozen guns rang out, and the balls rattled hard upon the rock, but none touched Jan.

He had with all the strength of despair sprung out into the ocean, and before the men could ground arms, the body of the daring smuggler was floating slowly down into its inmost depths.

The tide, impelled by the wind, had been rapidly rising, so the party of victors were compelled to retrace their steps.

Lights having been procured, they went searching along the cave—one part of which Fred remembered so well— until at last they came into the old vault again.

There lay the body of Hawkseye, cold and rigid, the eyes open with that awful stony glare, the right hand still grasping the pistol.

Black Murtough had taken his aim well, for the bullet had gone through the very centre of the head, causing instant death.

Two of the soldiers had fallen, and it appeared as though they grasped each other in the agonies of parting life, for their hands were partly clenched round each other's throat.

While the soldiers were removing the bodies, they were surprised at hearing a voice proceed down the trap.

"Below there. If yer all dead don't spake. Are you alive, masther? It's Lanty Shan that axes the question."

"Safe and sound, Lanty," was the reply.

"And you ain't got the worst of it. Och, murder; but this is wonderful!"

And down came Lanty into the cave, followed by Tim and Mike, who, losing their legs, came rattling down head first.

By dint of great exertion the bodies of the dead were got out of the vault, and placed in the old church.

It was then arranged that the body of Hawkseye should be conveyed to the castle, while a guard should be kept over the others.

Over those of the smugglers did Little Phil anxiously look.

"There is no Mickey Doyle among them," he muttered. "I must be on the look-out for him, or he'll be on the look-out for me."

And again Phil eagerly scanned the faces of the dead still-workers.

At last they were ready, and leaving a sufficient guard over the corpses, they started off.

"We heard there was a scrimmage going on here, and thought we'd just be at the fore in it, and so we started off widout a moment's thought," said Lanty, to his master.

"And who did you leave in the house, Lanty?" was the reply.

"The divil a sowl; we hadn't time to think of the house when the master of it was in danger. Och! I'm wrong intirely; we left Fogharty."

"Fogharty! what do you mean? Where did you leave him?"

"Well," said Lanty, and he rubbed up his old fox crop, "we left him hanging."

"Hanging! what do you mean, Lanty?"

"I mane hanging; not by the neck, only by the arms; there is no harm in that; he was regularly tried, and con-demned, and exe——"

"I hope you have not committed mur-der, Lanty?"

"The divil a bit of murder is there in it; if the branch of the tree breaks, it can't be laid to my charge; I didn't fix it."

"Directly I get to the castle, I'll ride over and see what all this is about; I am not at all satisfied."

"Some people are never satisfied," muttered Lanty, "and here is a case in p'int; but I think Fogharty must be satis-fied by this time."

They had now gained the old cross road, when they were all startled by the appearance of a fierce red reflection in the sky; and so suddenly did it first burst upon them that it caused them all to stand and look upon each other's faces in wonder and amazement.

"What's that?" cried Fred. "Have they set Ballyran on fire; it's mighty little they will have to burn there."

The flames seemed to shoot up more fierce every moment, illumining the place round for a considerable distance.

Fred stood looking at them with folded arms and a sorrowful countenance.

"The vengeance of the *red crosses* is being carried out," said Fred, with a deep sigh.

"What do you mane, master?" said Lanty, looking up at him with a face of alarm.

"While you have been away, Lanty, they have set the old house on fire."

The horror on the face of Lanty di-rected all attention to him, as he stood with straining eyes looking upon the glowing light in the sky.

Then, with a fierce yell, he seemed to spring again into life, and, muttering a fearful oath of agony and rage, he rushed off, followed by Mike, Tim, and Little Phil.

Fred Frolic was right; the home of his birth was in flames, and so far the in-surgents had satisfied their vengeance upon him.

Mickey Doyle and another of the gang had watched well their opportunity, and, when they had seen Lanty and his fol-lowers rush off they prepared accord-ingly.

They collected all the dry old stuff they could find, and, piling it in the centre of the house, they set fire to it.

The material was of a dry inflammable nature, and the flames speedily flew among the old timbers of the house, and when they saw the deed of vengeance was complete, they made the best of their way out, and struck into a road where they knew they should not meet any one.

Once they paused and listened as though somebody was shouting and call-ing out for help, but, thinking it to be a ruse, they kept on their way.

The cries they heard proceeded from the unfortunate, miserable Fogharty.

He had for a time after he was left alone remained quiet, according to Lanty Shan's directions; he could not well do otherwise, for he was stupefied by the fearful position he was placed in, and so, with his head sunk down upon his breast, he hung up to the old branch as though life had departed.

"Oh! what would I give now for my bitterest foe to come and end this misery. I feel as though I was dying. The Lord have mercy upon me!"

Here his mind wandered.

"We'll keep the money ourselves, McDonnell, and peach upon them, and then we shall be all right."

Here he was still further horrified by the sight of the flames sending their re-flection over him.

This almost paralysed him, for his mind conjured up something else, that the fire would reach him, and he should be burnt to death.

This roused him to exertion, and, as well as his voice would allow him, he shouted out for help.

None came, and then he seemed to shake off all stupefaction, and make a desperate struggle for life, and he writhed his body about as though he would burst his bonds asunder.

In doing so the old branch of the tree began to bend in a way that told him, unless he was quiet, it would break and let him down into the dirty slimy pool head first, where he had no other chance than that of being smothered.

"Curses on them, deep and bitter ones, hang upon their heads for ever—die or not, I'll hang here no longer."

And with that he made a desperate plunge.

The branch gave a fearful crack.

"Lord save us, I am going," he groaned. "I'll be smothered in the pool. The heavens be praised, how the old house is burning. Ha, ha, I've got you at last, Mr. Frolic, have I?"

He sent forth a laugh and a shout of infernal joy, and wriggled his body about at the thought of his revenge, that he forgot his perilous position.

Snap went the old branch, and down went the cowering villain head first into the dark muddy pool.

The force of the fall released his arms from the rope, and so he managed to scramble out through the filthy mass of mud and slime, more dead than alive.

He at last crawled out, reeking from head to foot with the foul stuff that he had fallen into, and bringing upon his person the venemous, crawling things that had not been disturbed for years.

He tottered towards the house, trying to get the mud from out of his eyes, but in vain.

With fear and fright, and the horrors he had undergone, he sank on his knees.

"I am a dying man," he said; "they have killed me." His tones were hollow and gasping. "I'd be thankful even for a cup of water."

He tried to raise himself on his knees, but sank partly down again.

Then he listened, and hearing shouts in the distance, he rose up and tried to run, but only staggered as though he had not the strength of a child in him.

By a desperate effort, however, he rushed up to the house, now roaring with flames.

"Ha, ha!" his laugh was that of a demon. "I am revenged!" He reeled and fell down upon the step.

At that moment, Lanty, Tim, and Mike, and all the population of Ballyran, rushed up.

"What's here?" said Lanty, as he turned over the body.

"The heavens be good to us," said Lanty; "*Fogharty fired the house, and dropped dead in the act!* The Lord save us! He's paid the penalty."

CHAPTER LAST.

AFTER THE STORM COMES THE CALM.

WHILE Lanty and the rest of them were gazing upon the dead body of Fogharty by the light of the fast expiring fire, Fred and Frank Hardy rode into the yard.

Fred cast a hurried glance around, and saw at once that the ruin of the old house, the place he was born in, was complete; and then his eyes fell upon the distorted face of Fogharty.

"He has met his death in compassing my destruction; place his body in the stables, Lanty, and I will see that he is decently buried."

"Dacently buried," muttered Lanty; "a dung-hill would do for the likes of him."

"Lanty, he has injured me and mine deeply," replied Fred, sharply, "but *he is dead*; with that the war between us is over; remove him."

The fire had burnt itself out, and as the stables and domestic offices of the house were separated, they were only partially injured; into the stables, therefore, some of the people removed the body of Fogharty, and covering him over with a few old sacks, they left him.

"Well," said Lanty, standing by the side of Fred, "it's lucky it's no worse; we might have been in our beds, and then —och, murder! what's to be done now, masther?"

"Well, Lanty," replied Fred, his usual good humour having returned, spite of all the trouble that surrounded him, "it has saved a vast amount of trouble, although had the villain lived, I would have punished him severely."

"Well, bedad, I think he was punished purty well; but how has it saved any trouble, eh?"

"Why, you see, it was going to be pulled down, and they have anticipated us by a few weeks," was the good-humoured reply.

"The divil fly away wid them for their —I think you said anticipations, masther; what is to be done now? where will we all go?"

And here the crowd raised a loud wail.

"There are the stables and the kitchen, and, perhaps, a little corner more left, in which you can take shelter—that is, the women and the children; but you, Lanty, and all the Frolic boys, I shall want with me up at the Castle; the danger is not all over yet. Where is Phil Leary?"

"Here I am, sir," answered the boy.

"Come here, Phil."

And Fred, taking him a little apart from the rest, whispered to him.

"I'll do it," said the boy, "I'll do it."

"I know you will, and that well," replied Fred; "but mind you do not run into danger."

"A fig for danger," he said. "I'll put myself in sich a state of disguise, that shall puzzle Mickey Doyle and all his crew; lave the matter to me."

And here Fred whispered him again.

"Of course I will," said the boy; "the castle is the place sure enough; lave it to me."

And he ran towards the kitchen, and disappeared.

Fred explained to Lanty what his object was in dispatching Little Phil upon his errand.

"Look ye, Lanty, it's no use grieving over this," and he pointed with his whip to the smoking ruins; "our object now is to defend the living, the old place can be restored."

"No, it can't," replied Lanty. "If it was ever so beautiful and new it will niver look in the eyes of Lanty Shan like the *ould place*. I'll niver see the room agin in which your dear parents lived and died—rest their sowls—I'll niver see the place agin where ould Phil, the huntsman, gave his last view halloo, and I'll niver see—bathersin! don't talk. If a new place is ever so beautiful and iligant, it ain't nothing to the *ould place*, where boyhood danced and sang, and the ould faces gladdened the place with their smiles and kind words. Oh, Fogharty, Fogharty! When I meet you again, I'll have a long score to sittle. The divil burn you for this. At all events, for the present——"

And poor Lanty gazed ruefully upon the blackened ruins of his birthplace.

Fred was deeply moved, for a host of stirring recollections came pouring upon him, and, grasping the hand of Lanty, he wrung it hard.

"You're right, Lanty, you are right," he said. "The old place is *the* place after all," and a tear stood in his eye.

"Well it can't be helped. What will I do now, eh?"

"Give all the women and gossoons something in the old stables and kitchen. Send for Maguire, and let him put the corpse of that wretched man in a coffin, and collect all the men of the Frolic side, and bring them up to the castle. There will be warm work there before long."

"I am glad of it," said Lanty, grasping his shillelagh. "It's time we had something to do."

"Black Murtough has escaped, and while he is at large his desperate associates will cling round him and do some desperate deed of violence. Lanty, *ma bouchal*, do not forget my instructions, and follow to the castle as soon as you can."

And so saying, Fred and Frank rode off.

The women and children that remained about the place had what refreshment could be got at handy for them, but, before they left, those who had run the risk of being evicted by the cruelty of Fogharty went into the stable, and took a last look, leaving behind them a very equivocal sort of a blessing.

Then Lanty, mustering together some twenty or thirty of the Frolic boys, shouldered their shillelaghs, and made the best of their way to the castle at a rapid pace.

That bold, desperate man, when for his own safety's safe, and at the dying request of his old comrade, plunged into the water, soon gained the shore and ran, with bitter curses on his lips, in the direction of the town of Ballinafad.

"If I can only gather a few of my staunch fellows around me, I'll show them yet what I can do. Ruined, ruined!" and here he paused and tore his hair, stamping on the ground in a fit of frenzy and rage; for, as he stood sheltered by a thick clump of heath, he could see the fires that the guards had lighted, round which a trusty sentinel was pacing.

"They'll seize upon all that is in the place, bitter bad luck to them; but I'll show them that they have not got the best of Black Murtough yet."

And, with that, he dashed along the road, and taking the direction of the fields, came out near the "Shamrock" public-house, into which he rushed like a raging, maddened fiend.

The desperadoes had not yet dispersed, and when he plunged into the room in which they were seated, he was received with a wild hurrah.

"What have you got to shout at?" he said, at length.

"At seeing you again," said one of the men.

"At seeing me again?" and he sent forth a discordant laugh; "seeing me, a ruined man, broken up and dying!"

"Why, what has happened?" and they started hurriedly to their feet.

"We have been betrayed; the old vault has been surprised by the gauger and the soldiers. I shot the gauger—the saints be praised!—but we were overpowered. Jan, my old comrade, is dead, and I am here among you, a broken man, and with only one account to settle."

The long room that this meeting was held in kept continually having an addition of men and boys, until it was full.

"Are you all with me—true to the core as of old, eh?" and Murtough sprang upon the table, brandishing his formidable bludgeon.

"All, all!"

At that moment Mickey Doyle and another man rushed into the place.

"Well, Mickey, your news?"

"Good. I've paid off one old score," was the reply.

"What is that?"

"I fired Frolic House. The divil a bit of it is standing now; it was a fine blaze!"

"Hurroo! bravo Mickey! more power to your elbow, *ma bouchal!*" and the wild mob crowded round him, shaking hands, and offering tin horns of steaming poteen.

"You are one of us, Mickey," and Murtough grasped his hand.

"Sure I am, and have always been. I'll just do the same thing up at the Castle, and find out that Phil Leary, settle him, and die happy."

Again the shouts rang through the room.

"Listen, ma bouchals. We have but little time to settle this work in, and so, what we do, must be done quickly; there'll be more soldiers down upon us, so let us send everybody out of the room that we don't want, and then we can consult upon what can best be done."

"Aye, aye, let us to it," said the rest, in deep tones.

"Get out of this," said Mickey, giving a boy, with scarcely a rag to cover him,

a kick; "what are you slaping there for, eh?"

The poor boy, so served, rose up slowly, shrugging himself together, as though annoyed at being disturbed, and, with a whining cry and a deep moan, shambled from the room.

He crawled down the passage, and out at the door, just escaping a buffet from the landlord.

And slowly he went along, rubbing his leg, where the savage Mickey had kicked him, until he had gained the fields; then he cast his eyes slowly round him.

There was not a soul far or near.

Then he raised himself up from the crouching attitude he had assumed, and, with a laugh, raised his finger, pointing it in scorn at the house he had just been expelled from.

"Ye little thought Phil Leary was so near you, you black-hearted villain! Fire the Castle and kill Phil Leary, will you? We'll see!"

And with this, Phil bounded away over the fields, making the best of his way to the Castle. Over the wall he bounded, and, in a few minutes, he was with Fred Frolic and the rest.

The news he had to tell surprised them, but, that over, they bent their minds to the important task of giving their enemies a warm reception.

"Bell, dearest," said Fred, "this will be a sorry sight for you, and will need all your woman's courage."

"Well, sir," replied the high-spirited girl, "and in the hour of need that will not be wanting. Courage and hope, Fred, will carry us through many a stormy day."

"I shall be near thee, dearest, to protect you."

"You will be where the point of duty calls, Fred, and I will be there, too; it may be the wounded may need assistance. I don't expect that we shall escape unscathed."

At that moment a message arrived from Mr. Righton, requesting their presence in the library.

They found him perusing a paper, which, upon their entering, he placed in Fred's hands.

"You will find there," he said "an account of the quarrel that occurred at the University, between your father and Sir Edward, which appears never to have been forgotten or forgiven. It is aston-

ishing how the quarrels of youth sometimes cling to the man; but so it is."

Bell took the paper from Fred's hand,
and, without glancing at it, went to the
fire, and threw it in.

"So perish the dark feud of the past;
let us hope that the brilliant future will
atone for all. Let the memory of the
dead rest without a dark cloud upon it."

And she extended her hand to Fred.

"Come," she said, "let us see that
there is nothing wanting to render us safe."

And so, like a commander of a little
army, attended by her staff, Bell Stanley
went among the soldiers and the Frolic
boys, with a cheery smile and a kind
pressure of the hand for all.

So the day passed.

The night, as it fell upon the earth, became intense in its darkness, and, in addition to that, a thick mist gathered so as
to render the darkness more appalling.

The few soldiers were posted in various
parts of the grounds in ambuscade, and
ready to act upon the word of command
being given.

Within the castle the Frolic boys were
ready at a moment's notice to rush in,
and repel the ruffians should they gain an
entrance.

Fred had been anxious to place Bell
and Mrs. Hardy in the vaults, out of
harm's way; but to this Bell and her
friend gave an indignant refusal.

The mist that had come down suddenly
began to disappear, and the moon appeared struggling for mastery with the
dense masses of clouds.

Little Phil Leary had engaged to act
as scout, and, as such, had taken up his
station at the old finger-post; but the
wily Murtough knew that a look-out
would be kept, and so leading his band,
in number nearly two hundred, to a more
secluded part of the park, they climbed
over unobserved, and were rushing upon
the castle, with loud yells and cries, before
any one was aware of it.

A sharp volley from the troops dropped
some dozen of them; but still, at the cry
of Black Murtough, they pressed on, and
rushing up the steps, and throwing themselves against the door, they burst in with
a crash, and Murtough bounded in with
the spring of a tiger.

Flying upstairs, he was met by Fred
and Frank Hardy.

"Frolic—villain! I've got you at last,
you informing scoundrel!"

"Liar! you only fight with the rope
round your neck!"

And Fred fired, but, in the confusion,
missed.

The next moment he was hurled back.

Over him sprung Murtough, thinking
he was dead, and rushing upstairs, with a
shout for the baronet, met Bell, who was
rushing down to Fred's assistance.

Before he could seize her, she had, with
a wonderful coolness and precision, fired
the pistol she carried.

The ball shattered the right arm of the
ruffian, and it fell powerless by his side.

With an awful imprecation on his lips,
he staggered back, and at the same time
Fred and his party, and the brave Frolic
boys dashed after him.

"Five hundred pounds for the murderer!" shouted Righton.

"There is no one will get that money,"
he shouted, as he rushed on to the battlements of the castle.

Here he was hemmed in.

He looked down, and below him was a
thicket of trees.

"I can reach them."

And he hung by the left arm.

"I'll bate you yet, my bitter curse on
you all."

There was a shot, an awful yell of rage,
a wild scream of agony, and the body of
the smuggler and still-worker went top-
pling over, crash through the trees, a
sheer hundred feet down, while Fred and
Bell and the others gazed upon his awful
descent with horror.

Outside the conflict had ceased, and
the smugglers fled before the soldiers.

Among the first to fly was Mickey
Doyle. He had been found out by Phil;
flying with all the speed he could, he
neared the lake, when Phil sprung upon
him.

There were sudden sharp blows from a
blackthorn, and with a deep groan the
detested spy fell back in the waters.

The rapid current carried him speedily
out, and his hands were seen clutching
the empty air, then into the thick mass of
the weeds he was hurried, and lost to
sight for ever.

In half an hour from that time the conflict had ended, with a fearful loss on the
side of the smugglers; and in one short
month later the lawless trade was over.

On the body of Fogharty certain papers
were discovered which strongly implicated
McDonnell; and Mr. Righton, determined

to crush out the illicit trade and bring to justice all connected with it, communicated with the authorities in Dublin.

But McDonnell was warned of the fate of his friends, and decamped.

"Curses on them all, and Fred Frolic in particular. I'll never rest till I have brought him down."

He disguised himself as a peasant, and set out for his own home.

"They won't think to look for me in this guise," he said. "Bitter bad luck to them."

The sun was sinking behind the mountains, and the shades of night were gathering over the earth, when McDonnell, his face hidden by the broad brim of his hat, stood at the cross roads, with his arms folded over the breast of the old frieze coat, looking towards the Castle.

"It's there he is," he said, in a bitter tone. "He is there with *her*. But I'll turn their love to sorrow, and then make my way to England. He has hunted me down, and there shall be blood shed before I'll rest. Whisht! By the powers it's himself that comes this way, and alone. Now or never!"

He pulled his hat lower down over his brows, thrust his hand into the bosom of his coat, and laid it upon the butt of a pistol he had there concealed.

Then casting a quick anxious glance around, he slunk back into the shadow of a hedge and watched the advancing Fred.

Fred Frolic came on humming a merry tune and smiling in the happiness of his heart, entirely unconscious of his danger.

Lanty, ever anxious for his master's safety, had expressed a desire to walk with him, but Fred laughed at his faithful follower's fears.

"Why Lanty, there's little to fear, now that our enemies are destroyed. Besides, I shall not go far from the Castle."

"Sure and it's not the distance ye may go but the danger you may meet, master," said Lanty.

"That is all over now," said Fred.

"Maybe not," said Lanty. "There's many a McDonnellite as would like to bate the life out of you, if he got a chance."

"I won't give him a chance, Lanty, so rest easy, my good fellow, and look after Bell Stanley till I return."

"It's meself that would die for her, master," returned Lanty, "and so would Mike, and Tim, and all the boys."

"I'm sure of that," said Fred.

And he turned to go.

"Stop, master," said Lanty, "you'll not be going widout taking a stick wid you."

And Lanty took his blackthorn from a corner, and placed it in the hands of Fred.

"Sure an' it's an iligant weapon. It's laid out more McDonnellites, bad luck to them, than there is knotches upon it. Take it, master, for sure ye may want it, who knows."

Fred, willing to humour him, took Lanty's shillelagh and went forth.

Tucking it under his left arm he went on humming a tune and dreaming of Bell, till he stood opposite the spot where McDonnell crouched in the shadow of the hedge.

At this moment McDonnell sprang out before him, and, dashing his hat from off his head, revealed his features to the surprised Fred.

"Fred Frolic," cried McDonnell, "you have come to your doom. Take it, and with it the everlasting curse of the man who hates you, alive and dead."

As he spoke he levelled a pistol at the head of Fred, and pulled the triger.

Had Fred Frolic hesitated but an instant, that moment had been his last.

As McDonnell confronted him, he had grasped the shillelagh, and the instant he caught the gleam of the pistol barrel he struck it up with a powerful blow.

There was a bright flash, and a loud report, a terrible shriek of agony, and the body of McDonnell rolled over at his feet.

The bullet intended for Fred Frolic had entered the throat of his would-be murderer.

For a few moments Fred stood looking upon the writhing wretch, thankful for his own escape, and horrified at the fate of his foe.

Then he knelt down, and raised the head of the dying man on to his knee, eager to assist the man who would have slain him.

As he looked into the convulsed face of McDonnell, with hurried footsteps Lanty and Phil sprang to his side.

"Master, master, are you safe?" cried Lanty.

"Yes, thank heaven. But he—McDonnell—I fear is dying. He would have slain me, but the ball that was meant for me has been turned upon himself. What can we do for him, Lanty?"

Lanty shook his head.

"Nothing," he said.

"He is dying," said Fred.

"Sure and it's glad I am. I could not rest, master dear, and followed you along with Phil."

And he wrung Fred's hand as he spoke.

Phil stooped down and looked into the face of the wounded man.

"It's McDonnell sure enough," he said.

"Sure and I'd know the dirthy spalpeen if I didn't look at him at all," said Lanty. "Bad luck to him."

McDonnell uttered a groan.

"It's your desarts you've got, you murdering villain," said Phil.

"He was crouching under the hedge, lying in wait for me, and but for your shillelagh, Lanty, I had now been dead," said Fred.

"And I'd have been—och, the divil, but I'd bate the life out of him."

And Lanty picked up the blackthorn, which Fred had dropped on the ground.

But a look from Fred, and he tucked the stick under his arm.

"It's not Lanty Shan that will hit a wounded man," said Lanty. "It's justice he's got, and he desarves it."

"And it's revenge I'll have yet before I die," shrieked McDonnell.

He seized Fred by the throat with both hands.

"I swore to destroy you, and——ah! curses, my strength fails me—my sight is going—I—devils, he will escape me—my bitterest cur——!"

As Lanty tore his fingers from his master's throat, the mouth of McDonnell filled with blood, his head rolled from side to side, a gurgling sound came from his throat, and he was no

Fred laid him gently back on the earth and rose slowly to his feet.

"Lanty," he said, "carry him to the Castle, and see that none offer insult to his remains. Remember, death ends all our quarrels and all our enmities."

So saying he turned sadly away, and retraced his steps to the Castle.

Five years have elapsed since these stirring events occurred, and on the battlements of the castle, which is indeed a castle, stand a couple in the very prime of life. At their feet are playing with an Irish deerhound two children, while standing by the side of the gentleman is one whose foxy head of hair points him out as our old friend Lanty Shan.

"Well, Lanty, foster brother," said Fred, grasping his hand, "this is better than the old times; there's a new barony, and the smoke curling up from the row of white cottages, almost hides the chapel, in memorian of those I loved so much, and the old house I was born in."

"We," whispered Lanty.

"Right. There is not a discontented heart, or a sorrowing eye around us; and see, Little Phil's leading the hounds out; and the roads are good, and the hedges rich with the perfumes of May. Great and glorious! Oh! my country, remain true to thyself. With the rose and the thistle, then we'll twine the bright green shamrock, and dare faction to separate them. What say you, Bell?"

Bell flung her arms round the neck of her husband, and, with a low voice, her eyes melting with excess of happiness, whispered, "Courage and hope, dear Fred, and——"

"What, dearest, what?"

"What! 'Erin go Bragh.'"

www.ingramcontent.com/pod-product-compliance
Lightning Source LLC
Chambersburg PA
CBHW080830250626

47160CB00008B/2891